"This is Bear's first collection of short stories, and one hopes it isn't her last….These stories are widely varied in both structure and theme, but there are a few unifying factors: integrity, loyalty and identity… nearly all are worthwhile, and there are a handful that are heartbreakingly perfect in form, execution and content…"
— *The Romantic Times*

"A glorious hybrid: hard science, dystopian geopolitics, and wide-eyed sense-of-wonder…. I hate this woman. She makes the rest of us look like amateurs."
— Peter Watts, author of *Starfish* and *Maelstrom*

"Elizabeth Bear has carved herself out a fantastic little world."
— *SF Crowsnest*

"This is a superior piece of work by a writer of enviable talents. I look forward to reading more!"
— Paul Witcover, author of *Waking Beauty*

"An enthralling roller-coaster ride through a dark and possible near future."
— *Starlog*

"I can… assure readers that here there be nifty Ideas about natural and artificial intelligences; satisfyingly convoluted conspiracies; interestingly loose-limbed and unconventional interpersonal relationships; and some pretty good jokes."
— Russell Letson, *Locus*

"Bear's greatest talent… is writing about violence in a way that George Pelecanos, Robert Crais and… Parker would envy."
— *The Huntsville Times*

"Gritty, insightful, and daring—Elizabeth Bear is a talent to watch."
— David Brin, author of *Kiln People*

the chains that you refuse

Other books by Elizabeth Bear include:

Hammered
Scardown
Worldwired
Blood and Iron: A Novel of the Promethean Age
Carnival (forthcoming)

the chains that you refuse

ELIZABETH BEAR

night shade books
SAN FRANCISCO & PORTLAND

First Edition

ISBN-10   1-59780-048-1
ISBN-13   978-1-59780-048-8

Night Shade Books
Please visit us on the web at
http://www.nightshadebooks.com

CONTENTS

L'ESPRIT D'ESCALIER:

NOT A PLAY IN ONE ACT

SCENE 1

Time: 1962

Place: Delancey Street, Lower East Side, New York City

They cashiered him when he failed to kill the dragon. He'd expected no less; a warrior of the General's tenure learned that honor and acknowledgement seldom went hand in hand.

He had refused the option of a dignified withdrawal, a quiet resignation. He'd made his enemies earn his absence, forced them to cast the unearned blame: a kangaroo court, a dishonorable discharge, imprisonment. Fire and water didn't mix, and the General understood that. He hadn't broken. He had made his enemies crush his pearl, tear his fins, take him to the wall.

He took a perverse sort of pride in it, as the water in the broken fountain in the atrium of the Delancey Street brownstone where he now resided stirred his ragged fins. The tiles he swam over were cracked, their cobalt-blue glaze split, revealing plain, fired red clay beneath. The lotuses that shimmered under the skylight were browned at the edges. There was no frog in his pond, no splish and no splash, no minnows and no mud and no dragonfly nymphs to make tasty afternoon snacks when the sunlight painted his scored scales mottled red and black and gold, revealing the cicatrix of an old scar on his flank, near the tail half-gnawed away. It all looked flat, plain, through his one remaining eye.

Bondage. A cell for a forgotten hero.

It didn't matter. The *General* knew his honor was intact, even in ignominy. His opinion was the one that mattered.

His, and his god's.

SCENE 2

Time: Eternity

Place: a fern bar in the Afterlife. There is a pool table, a black pay telephone in a silver carapace, and a painting of dogs playing poker on the wall. A stair with a brass banister dominates stage right, ascending to mezzanine level with a door at the top through which all entrances and exits will occur.

The lights fade up on Ginsberg, Marlowe, Eliot, Shakespeare, Keats, and Shelley clumped chattering around the brass-railed, dark-wood bar. A ponytailed blond bartender in a black turtleneck polishes cobalt-blue glasses with a stained cotton cloth.

The pay telephone rings shrilly, and continues to ring. No one answers.

Marlowe *(to Ginsberg)*: Forsooth, thou'rt an ugly man, Allen—

Ginsberg: I'm an *angry* man. *(Beat, as he winces in pain.)* You ought to know the symptoms. *(They exchange a long look, wrathful or smoldering. Marlowe turns away first, and steals Shakespeare's beer. Shakespeare, deep in conversation, does not appear to notice.)*

Eliot *(at large)*: I don't belong here. I don't belong here—

Keats *(coughing into a handkerchief spotted with strawberries, or perhaps blood)*: Oh, stop it, Tom. You don't belong anywhere, to listen to you. England, America, it doesn't matter. You might as well be adrift on a raft in the middle of the ocean, one wave away from drowning, the way you carry on.

Shelley: Can we *not* talk of drowning, Jack?

Keats: Sorry. I didn't think. *(He coughs.)* Ruddy cough. Doesn't it know I'm dead? *I* know I'm dead. You'd think a cough could follow the clues as well. Kit's not got a bleeding, sodding hole in his skull and Will's not rotten with the French pox. Why am *I* bound to this damned cough?

Marlowe: It's all about priorities.

Ginsberg: We ought to have a poetry reading.

Shakespeare *(doubtful)*: Poetry?

Keats: Of the wide world I stand alone, and think / Till love and fame to nothingness do sink.

Ginsberg: And that's why you can't stop coughing, Jack. You write lousy poetry.

Keats: As I know you to be in pain with your cancer, Allen, I'll forgive the insult.

The door opens. A wild-haired man in denim picks his way down the stairs, clinging to the brass railing as if he might blow—or stagger—away, otherwise. It is the poet Richard Brautigan, bleeding from a self-inflicted gunshot wound to the head.

Shakespeare folds into himself at this new arrival. His shoulders slump. He glances down at his hands, and turns back to the bar. Marlowe nudges him good-naturedly with a shoulder, and Shakespeare returns a glare.

Shakespeare: He's not one of us, Kit.

Marlowe: *(Draping his arm congenially around Shakespeare's shoulders; Shakespeare doesn't seem to mind. Brautigan reacts with dismay.)* Pshaw. The lad worships thee, Will. Least thou can'st do is tend thy hand in welcome. Beside that, he's but newly dead, and miserable.

Shakespeare: The *lad* has some years on you, Kit. And Allen's more newly dead than he—

Marlowe: Living, perchance some years. But I am senior here. Even to you, sweet William, though only John's my junior. And *Allen* didn't die by his own hand—

Ginsberg *(overhearing)*: Shocking everyone, I'm sure. Which reminds me, has anyone seen Oscar lately? Or Byron?

Shelley: George doesn't get enough adulation here to suit him.

Marlowe: —go. Talk to the lad.

Shakespeare looks up and back down quickly, but apparently he's accidentally caught Brautigan's eye. Shakespeare heaves a sigh as Brautigan smiles broadly and staggers forward, while his quarry pretends to be engrossed in a conversation with Marlowe.

Marlowe: Ah, Will. You only look at me when you wish to evade another.

Shakespeare: *You're* not going to treat me as your muse, now, are you, Kit?

Brautigan *(insinuating himself between Marlowe and Shakespeare, his shoulder to the former as Marlowe gives Shakespeare an utterly deadpan look)*: Will? What are you drinking? *(He raises a hand to the bartender, while Shakespeare and Marlowe exchange a glance behind his shoulders.)* Terry, get my friend here another. And one for me as well, please. Have you written anything new, Will? A sonnet?

Shakespeare: No, Dickon. I've told thee before; I write not, now that I am dead.

Ginsberg: I don't see why being dead should stop you. Nothing else apparently did.

Brautigan: A little respect, Allen.

Ginsberg *(pressing a fist into his side and wincing)*: Why start now? Shit, Terry, don't you have any morphine in this place?

Bartender: If this were the old days, I'd tell you to check behind the bricks. Somebody would have left some heroin lying around.

SCENE 3

Time: the Millennium

Place: Delancey Street, Lower East Side, New York City

Terry Mashiter's alarm goes off at 11:43 a.m., but the clock is fast, so it looks like noon. He gropes for the snooze button halfheartedly and slaps it twice to make it work, then settles back into the nicotine-scented embrace of his comforter, dragging his pillow over his head. It is a cold, icy Thursday in March.

It is time to go to work.

The snooze delay expires; the alarm clock sounds again. Terry slaps it off, but this time he doesn't snake his hand back into the warmth of his swaybacked pressboard bed. Instead, he flips up the lid of a plywood cigar box with a pen-and-ink drawing of a girl in a feathered Robin Hood cap and the words *As You Like It* on the lid, and strokes his talismans. The butt of an unfiltered Camel cigarette, a magic bean, a page torn from an issue of *Vogue*. A subway token, a silver 1962 quarter that rings when you drop it, a Moleskine notebook, illegible from having been dropped in a mud puddle or something worse. Other things, more or less at random.

He pulls out the magazine page, pressed flat, the text and images slightly blurred between two scratched layers of glass, and the fibers of the torn edge visible, preserved forever in their anaerobic prison. Staring at an exaggerated sketch of a redheaded girl in a black beret, he slides his other hand inside his sweatpants and idly begins to masturbate.

He's not thinking about the girl in the picture. He's thinking about the girl who drew it.

It's laundry day.

That nuisance accomplished, he returns the pressed page to the cigar box, climbs out of the sag in the middle of the mattress, sheds his sticky sweatpants into a pile on the floor, and staggers toward the shower, scratching his belly. Later, clean, he slicks his thinning, greying blond hair back into a ponytail and fixes it with an orange-wrapped elastic, then skins on jeans, Chucks, and a green T-shirt that reads *Sunflower* in flaked white print across the chest.

He sits down for two hours before work to write on a five-year-old, off-brand personal computer. Five pages of playscript is a better than average day. He reads it over, and thinks it's pretty goddamned funny. Nobody else does, but such is life.

The telephone jangles as he walks out the door. He doesn't answer, just walks downstairs, not trusting the elevator. He stops in the lobby to glance up at the skylight, and then hunkers beside the old unworking fountain to feed the fish.

There's only a single fish, a gargantuan one-eyed koi whose back breaks the surface of the water every time he moves. Terry thinks the koi's probably eaten any other fish that might have shared the fountain with him.

Terry feeds him anyway.

SCENE 4

Time: 1962

Place: Delancey Street, Lower East Side, New York City

The General was wise among fish. Though he dined on pellets of moldy Wonder Bread and not on hazelnuts (like the legendary salmon of learning), he had a great deal of time for contemplation. The young human with the hair as bright as the General's own golden scales had left when the sun was high and the slant of light through water left-to-right and slipping to the side. He would return when the electric lights glowed overhead, and if all had gone well, he would fete the General with crumbs of rice crackers and broken bits of pretzels, and perhaps even pause to converse a little before heading up the stairs to his own dinner.

Someday, the General would like to find a way to make life easier for the young man, although he was *gaijin*, foreign, although he was the enemy.

That didn't mean what it would have, once, before the General became the enemy as well.

The General grew hungry. The General drifted softly, floating, in anticipation.

SCENE 5

Time: Eternity

Place: A fern bar in the Afterlife.

Marlowe, Keats, and Ginsberg nurse their beers around the free lunch at the corner of the bar. The bartender is still polishing glasses.

Ginsberg: You just make the Devil too damned attractive, Kit. That's the problem with Mephistopheles.

Marlowe: And I argue, 'tis precisely what he needs to be. Attractive, or who would fall in love with him? Your demon Moloch just isn't *pretty* enough to work as a seducer. Who would fall for him?

Keats coughs.

Ginsberg: But they do. They *do* fall for him. Consumerism. Demons. Moloch. Read your Milton.

Marlowe: Milton! That pompous ass. Call Moloch the Beast, but devils and dragons are supposed to be lovely to look upon. Seduction is part of what makes them terrible, terrible and fair. "And he defiled Topheth, which is in the valley of the children of Hinnom, that no man might make his son or his daughter to pass through the fire to Moloch."

Ginsberg: You're so full of *shit*, Christopher. That's the thing, man, it's all plastic paint and, and… waxed turds covered in S&H Green Stamps. It's not real. It's got a shiny surface, brazen idol, you bet, and then you poke it and it kind of caves in around the hole you made and it's like a little *asshole*, you know, oozing shit—

Keats: Could the two of you *be* more pretentious?

Ginsberg: We could be Tom. He'd be ranting about how the Japanese say the dragon is three-toed, and he grows extra toes when he leaves Japan, but the Chinese say the dragon is five-toed, and his toes and his morals atrophy when he leaves China. And Kit here would quote the Bible at him like the cawing divinity student he is, and we'd be off—

Keats *(coughing):* Tom's not so bad.

Marlowe leans back on his barstool out of the line of fire between Keats and Ginsberg. He catches the bartender's eye; the bartender smirks at him, but doesn't comment.

Ginsberg: Eliot, Eliot, they teach him in colleges. Who cares about that? It's… staid, it's not the future, it's the past.

Bartender: Allen, can I get you another one?

Ginsberg: No, Terry. I don't need a beer. I need to get laid, that's what I need. How come this place isn't like it was in the old days? I remember when it was broadsides pasted to the walls and a stage in the corner built of cinderblocks and it didn't have a liquor license, but you could hide your pot in the storeroom if you liked. Where the fuck did the fucking *ferns* come from, man?

Bartender: *(quietly)* Same place the name did, man. Moloch. Where else?

The pay telephone rings shrilly, and continues to ring. No one answers.

Bartender: Fuck. I have *got* to get to 1962.

SCENE 6

Time: the Millennium

Place: a pretentious Greenwich Village bar

Terry arrives at Moloch's at 3:30 on the dot and lets himself in with his key. He ties on his apron and gets to work, daydreaming. It doesn't take much presence of mind to set up the speed rack, set out the free lunch, prepare the garnish trays; he's tended this same bar since 1955, when the place was still called Sunflower, although they served coffee and soup when he first got the job, and not beer.

There was a girl who used to work here too, who used to paint murals on the wall, until the new owner got her an illustrating job with a fashion magazine. She stopped coming by after that; Terry doesn't see her anymore.

Terry has a cache of the old shirts. He took all the leftovers home after the name change. He has only fifty left, but he figures if he washes them inside-out in cold water they'll see him through to retirement.

A little before four, Terry waters the ferns and philodendrons and brushes the felt on the pool table. He checks the coin return on the black rotary-dial pay telephone—the only thing in the bar other than the scarred wood floor that's been there longer than Terry has—and makes sure the photographs and clippings and caricatures of Ginsberg, of Kerouac, of Burroughs and Kesey and Cassady and Corso and Snyder and Brautigan and McClure and di Prima and Whalen and Ferlinghetti and Waldman and Orlovsky and people whose names even *Terry* doesn't recognize, they're that obscure, hang straight.

None of them would recognize what had become of Sunflower, anyway.

Terry polishes the brass railing on the stair ascending to street level against one wall, and at 4:00 promptly, he unlocks the door. Moloch's is a tourist trap.

It doesn't get afternoon trade.

Terry smoothes his green T-shirt down over his skinny chest and his middle-aged pot belly, makes sure it's tucked into his apron strings and the top of his pants and that his ponytail's tidy, and heads back to polish the bar. The customers will be along eventually, and Jackie and Maura come on at six when things start to pick up.

There's plenty to keep him busy until then.

The first customers wander in around five, which is the beginning of happy hour, as advertised on the placard in the window of the door at the top of the stairs. The cocktail waitresses follow an hour later—Jackie five minutes late and Maura ten minutes early, predictably—and by nine it's a steady stream of customers playing Bob Dylan and Thelonious Monk on the CD jukebox in the corner, and Terry's even started to hope the owner won't show up tonight.

He hopes too soon.

Mr. Ryusaki always pauses at the top of the stairs and scans Moloch's with a slow oscillation of his head that reminds Terry of Conan Doyle's description of Moriarty. He always wears a belted, black velvet jacket with a brocade collar that looks like something Hugh Hefner would order in red, and he always spiders his weird gnarled hands down the brass banister as he descends, the old wooden stairs silent under his slight weight, in a manner that gives Terry a bright green, creeping wiggins as bad as watching a cockroach crawl up his leg.

Terry wishes it was busier, so that Mr. Ryusaki would leave him alone, but it isn't, so he keeps polishing a glass he's already polished once. He leans against the back bar, waiting for Mr. Ryusaki to come on over and say whatever pain-in-the-ass thing he plans on saying tonight. Mr. Ryusaki owns the brownstone Terry lives in as well as the bar where he works. Terry feels as if he should probably be polite, for the koi's sake, if not his own. If it weren't for Terry, after all, who would feed the fish?

Tatsu Ryusaki is tall, for a Japanese man of his generation, and he wears his fingernails filed into long ovals, like a woman's. It makes his hands look inhuman, like the talons of a predatory bird. He leans across the bar on his elbows, fingers twisted together, the knotted joints making them look as if they were meant to interlock. Terry wonders how he got the pearl ring onto his finger, past those knuckles.

"Mister Ryusaki," Terry says. He pours the boss a glass of the house red, sets it on a napkin, and slides it across the bar with his fingertips without being asked.

Mr. Ryusaki picks it up and frowns over the top. "I need you to stay tonight, Terry. Johnny got hit by a taxicab; you and Maura are going to have to close and clean up."

"Johnny all right?"

"Torn ligaments," Mr. Ryusaki says. "He'll heal. He called from the ER. I can get somebody to cover his shift tomorrow, but I need you and Maura to cover tonight."

"Yeah," Terry says, wiping the dry, polished bar in thoughtful circles as the pay phone begins to ring. "You said."

Mr. Ryusaki leans back, his wine glass in his left hand, and frowns. He's a narrow man, with a ferret face that pinches around the eyes when he's irritated with Terry, which he usually is. "Get a haircut, Terry," he says, turning toward his office as the phone jangles again. It's an old phone, with a real hammer and a metal bell. The sound it makes is not a hesitant sound. Customers are craning their necks curiously now, as the damned thing rings again. Terry ignores it, breathing his sigh of relief a moment too soon.

Mr. Ryusaki doesn't pause, but he snaps back over his shoulder as he's leaving, "And answer the goddamned phone."

Terry pauses with one hand on the bar gate, his towel tossed over his shoulder. "If I'd killed that son of a bitch when I met him," he mutters, "I'd be out of jail by now."

There's nobody on the line, of course. There never is, when he answers, "Moloch's."

But he can almost hear the ghosts sighing on the other side.

SCENE 7

Time: the Millennium

Place: Delancey Street, Lower East Side, New York City

By the time Terry makes it home, the sky is grey. There's no such thing as dawn on Manhattan, or sunset either, but they haven't quite figured out how to roof the whole island in—yet—and the light still seeps through the cracks. It's a rare night when he still feels the urge for company after his shift in a bar crowded with pretentious twits who come because Kerouac kept his stash behind a brick in the back wall when it used to be a coffeehouse and impromptu soup kitchen.

It's a rare night when Terry feels the urge to do anything but scrub, after twelve to fifteen hours in a miniature Disneyland dedicated to capitalizing on a plasticized memory of revolution. *Caricatures,* for Christ's sake.

The whole fucking place is a caricature.

Terry stops by the broken fountain, in the grey light falling through the skylight, and digs in his pocket for a baggie full of crumbs. He remembers another era, when the baggie wouldn't have had a zip closure, and it wouldn't have been crumbs of bread that it held—and he wouldn't have been shaking it onto the stagnant surface of a make-believe lily pond.

Still, he casts the bread on the water and watches the nested *Vs* of the big koi's hungry approach. The damned thing is almost a carp; its round mouth breaking the surface looks big enough to swallow a mouse.

"I wish I'd had the sense to kill that son of a bitch thirty-eight years ago," Terry says conversationally, rubbing the last few bits of pretzel from the bag. "Fucking fern bar's an abomination before the Lord, and naming it for a character in 'Howl,' that's just adding insult to injury. Man, I wish you could have seen the place back in the old days, fish. I wish it was still like that now."

The koi churns back and forth, back and forth. Terry figures a cat or some sort of big predatory bird must have been what got him; there are three parallel scars across the side of the fish's head with the ruined eye, the proud flesh high and bare between the scales.

"That was some shit," Terry continues, before he turns away to climb the stairs. "Hippies and beatniks and queers, oh my, hippies and beatniks and queers."

SCENE 8

Time: 1962

Place: Delancey Street, Lower East Side, New York City

The golden carp, gobbling crumbs from the surface of his prison, heard someone make—

—a wish.

SCENE 9

Time: Eternity

Place: a fern bar in the Afterlife.

Marlowe and Ginsberg are still arguing, although now they're standing beside the pool table. Keats leans over the bar, his chin on the back of his hand, coughing into his spotted handkerchief occasionally. Shakespeare sits beside him; the blond bartender is pouring.

The door at the top of the stairs opens.

Enter Brautigan. He stops to take in the scene, and seems drawn particularly to Ginsberg and Marlowe, who are insulting one another genially and shooting pool.

The two poets hesitate. Their eyes lock. They stare at one another for a moment, and then move toward each other violently. It's hard to tell who kisses whom; their mouths meet roughly and they seem to struggle as much as embrace, pushing, dragging one another down atop the pool table.

Brautigan witnesses the entire thing. His eyes bug out of his face, his head whirls around on his neck, and his impressive mantle of hair stands straight out around his head as if electrified.

Stuffing both hands against his mouth, Brautigan runs up the stairs.

The pay telephone rings shrilly, and continues to ring. No one answers. The bartender glances over at the writhings atop the pool table and sighs tiredly.

Enter Moloch, painted in tongues: a slender man, ferret-faced, in a black velvet smoking jacket with red and gold three-toed dragons embroidered at the collar. He pauses at the top of the stairs, one knotty hand splayed upon the brazen banister. *A forked tongue flickers between his lips. Brautigan leads him by the arm, pauses, and points at Marlowe and Ginsberg fucking on the pool table.*

Moloch watches for a moment, then lifts his chin and stares at the bartender. The bartender looks up, looks over at the poets on the pool table, and shrugs. He never stops polishing the glass in his hands.

Trailing Brautigan, Moloch descends the stairs and crosses to the bar. He lifts the gate and ducks through it; the bartender and Keats don't seem to notice his presence—they are, in fact, frozen as if they are stuck in time. As Shakespeare begins to figure this out, waving a hand in front of Keats' face, Moloch ducks under the bar and comes up with a shotgun, which he raises in both hands.

Shakespeare: It won't work, you know. Kit's already let go. Your bullets can't hurt him.

Moloch: I've got no interest in Master Marlowe, Master Shakespeare. He's long lost any power to harm me. *(He presses the shotgun on Brautigan.)* Do you remember how to use one of these, Richard?

Brautigan touches his bloody scalp and then reaches out with red-stained fingers to take the shotgun.

Brautigan: I think I can figure it out.

Moloch: Ginsberg. Do it, Richard.

Brautigan looks from Moloch to the gun to Ginsberg and Marlowe, and slowly reaches out and hefts the thing, taking it out of Moloch's hands.

Moloch: Are you too much of a sissy to get this right either?

Brautigan raises the gun to his eye as Moloch steps back, vaults the bar casually, and walks toward the stair. As the demon ascends, the poet studies his quarry like a hunter watching a tiger from a blind.

The door closes behind Moloch. The others present in the bar seem to snap back to themselves, and Shakespeare and the bartender shout and lunge, reaching for the gun in Brautigan's hand. The bartender yanks Keats to the floor as Marlowe's head comes up; he and Ginsberg break apart, Marlowe pushing Ginsberg under the pool table right-handed and reaching with his left for his rapier.

Too late.

The shotgun roars, and the reek of sulfur fills the bar as Shakespeare wrests it from Brautigan's hands.

Marlowe, his face fixed in an attitude of surprise, pitches over slowly, backward, and falls to the scarred floorboards. Brautigan's head droops between sagging shoulders as Shakespeare tosses the shotgun away. Shakespeare crosses the few steps between them and embraces him. Shakespeare's hands come away from Brautigan's hair, dripping red.

Shakespeare (*patting Brautigan's shoulders*): What, lamb, still bleeding? There, there. There, there. If you let go of the poetry, your wounds will heal. The dead can't change the world, poor Dickon.

Brautigan: Turtles. I just wanted to say… something about turtles. I don't know. Maybe pancakes. Goldfish, you know, those big fucking goldfish, the ones like underwater Panzers. Something important. Something about why you didn't love me, Will. Why you loved him more….

Shakespeare (*still soothing*): I know. I know.

Marlowe's corpse stands up and examines himself, dusting his doublet off daintily, with fingertip flicks. He watches Shakespeare and Brautigan for a moment, and then shrugs, smiles at the audience, and turns his back, heading toward the bar, where the bartender is already drawing him a beer.

Bartender: You're taking that well.

Marlowe: It's not the first time I've been killed in a bar. Good thing it wasn't Allen, though.

They're joined by an obviously rattled Ginsberg, who hands the bartender the shotgun, which he has retrieved. The bartender takes it, breaks it, and reloads it thoughtfully while Ginsberg reaches over the bar to draw himself a pint.

Brautigan: Allen, I couldn't—

Ginsberg: Kerouac was an anti-Semitic, homophobic little asshole, Dick, and I still put up with him. Don't think anything of it. Terry, where are you going with that gun?

Bartender (*on his way to the stairs up*): To change the name of my fucking bar, Allen. It just sank in. *I'm* not dead.

Ginsberg: That'll never work, man. C'mere and kiss me.

Bartender: *What?*

Ginsberg: Kiss me. That's the only way to get to 1962 from here.

The bartender looks at Ginsberg, and looks at the gun, and looks at Ginsberg again.

Bartender: Don't worry about it, man. (*Beat*) I've got a magazine.

SCENE 10

Time: the Millennium

Place: Delancey Street, Lower East Side, New York City

Terry doesn't stop at the top of the stairs. He unlocks his apartment—two deadbolts and a regular lock—and goes straight to his bedroom.

He finds a shotgun he never owned before in the middle of his bed, checks to make sure it's loaded, and retrieves the preserved page of *Vogue* from the box on the nightstand. He lays it down in the center of his tightly made bed and stares, for a moment, at a picture sketched for money by a girl who used to paint the bare plaster walls of basements in vivid psychedelic colors, a girl who should have grown up to be an artist, not an advertising executive.

"Break glass in case of emergency," he says, and—applying pressure with the shotgun barrel—suits actions to words.

When he kisses the drawing this time, static-stuck needles of glass cut his lips. "It's time I admitted it was over between us, sweetheart," he says, and then he crumples the blood-marked paper left-handed and stuffs it into his mouth. His tongue bleeds; his gums bleed. Something hard and brittle crunches between his molars. He swallows, and then he cocks the gun.

In the mirror on the way through the living room, he sees himself. His clothing is bright and unfaded; his hair is sunlight blond, and down all over his shoulders. His lover is not home; he hopes she's not at Sunflower painting the walls. Not today.

"Look out, Moloch," he says. "Here I come."

He wraps a jacket around the shotgun, and descends the stairs into 1962, where he walks past the tinkling fountain and outside, on his way to catch a train.

Tatsu Ryusaki is at Sunflower; he looks not a day younger than he will thirty-eight years later. He walks around the basement coffeehouse with the building's owner, poking into corners, peeling back broadsides shellacked to the walls, and scratching his thumbnail across the garish murals. He discusses with the owner how much Ryusaki will pay for the old building and how soon he will be able to end the leases of the current tenants, including Sunflower.

Terry waits until the current owner is poking around behind the bar, and Mr. Ryusaki is by the storeroom door. "Mister Ryusaki," Terry says, from the top of the steps. As the businessman turns, Terry drops the jacket, lifts the gun to his eye, and fires both barrels without saying another word.

Ryusaki does not burst into flames when he dies, but a single white pearl rolls from his hand across the floor, and disappears under the bar. Terry scrabbles after it, leaving the shotgun where it fell, while the horrified owner grabs the black pay phone out of its carapace and screams for the police.

Terry leaves him there.

Terry is dropping the pearl in the fountain when the pigs come to arrest him.

The koi swims after it as it shimmers through the water, his mouth wide enough to swallow a mouse.

Terry doesn't fight. As they lead him away, he cranes his neck, to see if there are any ripples in the fountain except the ones from falling water.

He doesn't think so.

They call him Terry the Dragonslayer in prison, although nobody can remember who came up with it. He serves seventeen years. He writes a fictionalized account of his time in prison; it's well-received, although the judge rules he can't make any money off it because it's directly related to his crime. When he gets out, he takes his old job in that coffeehouse down in the Village, and impresses the Boho wannabe poetry-slam crowd with his prison tattoos and his stories about Allen Ginsberg, and he answers the phone on the first ring, every god-damned time.

"Sunflower."

Even Ginsberg shows up once in a while. He still lives in the neighborhood, and he still writes, and the murals on the peeling plaster bring back memories, even after all this time.

GONE TO FLOWERS

I close my eyes and try to feel my left hand.

I'd swear to God it still dangles on the end of my arm just as it did for the first twenty-four years of my life: taut sensation like a strand of razor-wire looped from elbow to fingertip tells me so, cutting the numb absence of flesh. I want to slap my right hand over the pain, expecting the hot trickle of blood between my fingers. Instead, they curl on the cold metal examining table I'm sitting on, my skinny body stripped to the waist and shrouded in a paper sheet for decency's sake—not that I have all that much to cover up.

"It itches."

"I'm almost finished with the bandages," the doctor, Captain Valens, answers. "Not much to do for the itch, I'm afraid."

"I've lived with worse." My scowl tugs at scar tissue when I glance down. Captain Valens has laid his warm human hand on the gleaming steel of the prosthesis. He might as well touch the hand of a statue. From a point seven centimeters below the proximal end of my humerus, I will never feel anything but phantom pain again.

It must be antiseptic fumes making my eyes sting. The doctor grins at me. "So, what do you think of my masterpiece, Corporal? Not exactly sexy, but it works…"

He's wrong. Dull gleams ricochet off the curved surface as I rotate the wrist, close precise fingers into a fist. It has a sensual air, despite—or because of—its look of pure, seamless evil. The months I've spent with the prototypes and simulations, the days in surgery and the weeks of recovery, the puckered red scars ridging my spine: this is the payoff.

It's sexy. Far sexier than the rest of my fire-scarred body, and I hate it with the sort of ideological loathing that used to be reserved for nuclear weapons and enemy politicians. Which is hypocritical, given the money and metallurgy the Army has spent into my scrawny carcass: after nine years in service and that last bad one, I'm less meat than metal.

I examine a stained pulmonary chart on the wall, but Valens picks up my distress. "The prostheses will get better over the years," he says like a mom who desperately wants her kid to like a dubious present. "That's the next step from a prototype. We'll get a polymer skin on it to match the other one. Hell, someday you'll have sensitivity, heat, cold, you name it."

I force a scorched jack-o'-lantern grin and give him the finger. "Well, whaddaya know? It works."

And then the door to the treatment room bangs open and I grab for my shirt as Gabe Castaign barges in, a young Yankee nurse caught up in his wake. He's still in uniform, still wearing his baby-blue beret. "Sir!" she tries again, reaching for his sleeve without quite daring to grab him. "You simply *cannot* just walk in here…"

"Maker!" The nurse falls back a pace. Gabe has that effect on people. "You got the bandages off already? How does it feel?"

A shirt button cracks in thirds between machine fingers: the one between my breasts. Of course. I curse in French and try to be more careful. "It feels like a goddamn train wreck strapped to my shoulder. But I'll get used to it." Then I realize what his presence in Toronto must mean. My face goes slack in hope and the fear that that hope is in vain. "Gabe—it's over? Tell me it's over." I'm pleading, even knowing it doesn't have to mean ceasefire. He could have been recalled for security detail. They don't let tourists up the CN tower since the last round of bombings. Bloody shame. Bloody isolationists.

He glances at his boots, shrugs broad shoulders. Castaign looks the role his great-great-grandfather lived, brawny bear of a fur-trapping northerner with eyes like bay water and hair that would be tousled if it weren't clipped high and tight. Even kept short for a helmet, it curls some. "Papers signed within the week. Nothing official yet, but peace has broken out."

I hit him at chest level and he wraps his arms around me. A moment later he gasps. "Ease off, Jenny!" He rubs his ribs as I back away. "Remind me not to arm-wrestle you."

I can't meet his eyes. "Sorry."

I'm sure they're looking at one another, Valens and Castaign, and I almost feel them reach the decision to go easy on me. Gabe drops a hand on my good shoulder, drawing my eye. "Hey, it's just a bruise, eh? No sweat."

I grin to show I'm trying, turning the damaged side of my face away, exquisitely aware of his touch. Stepping back is damn hard. I manage. "No sweat, Gabe." His eyes are very blue. I look down to button another button, glad of the excuse. "Let me get some clothes on, will ya?" To Valens: "Can I go?"

"Off-campus? Sure, why not? Sign out." Valens wads gauze into the biohazard bag and peels off his gloves.

"I'll meet you outside in ten minutes." Gabe reverses his headlong charge with a flourish, bootsteps ringing on the speckled tile floor, still trailing that flustered nurse. And *that* is Captain Gabriel Castaign, CA.

I take a deep breath and finish buttoning my shirt.

It's more like seven minutes, but Gabe is already surrounded by his usual court: two second lieutenants and another noncom today, standing under bare trees and streetlights. A smaller population has been a mixed blessing: Canada's stayed more civilized than most of the world, but my generation went almost entirely to the military to keep it that way. Especially since the troubles down south closed the border: even the less-radical isolationists admit Detroit and Boston are uncomfortably close to home.

I'd lay odds that Gabe and I are the only ones here who've seen combat yet. Old joke: the difference between a second lieutenant and a private is the private has been promoted.

They'll learn.

Gabriel's friends regard me with blended awe and diffidence as I limp over, feeling the cold in every bone I've ever broken. Just after Christmas, the weather is already bitter.

Gabe hails me as if I hadn't seen him first. "Hey, Casey! This is Bruce and Kate and Peter, but you can call him Horse."

I clasp the hand Peter extends so tentatively. "A man called Horse?" I ask him. He smiles in confusion, but Gabe laughs out loud. He's a fan of old movies too.

"Ladies, this is Jen Casey, but you can call *her* Maker."

"Maker?" the female lieutenant asks. Gabe has been trying to hang a nickname on me, and it seems to be taking.

"A very bad joke," I reply. She raises an eyebrow and nods, familiar with Gabe's brand of bilingual puns. She's military intelligence, petite and shapely, with a pert nose and neatly cropped hair, on the right side of the yawning gulf between officer and noncom. I want to hate her for all of those things, but she doesn't flinch when—crisp, smiling—she takes my hand.

"Casey," she says. "You must be here for the research project. Did you have much spinal damage?"

Damn. I shake my head. "It's less interesting than it sounds." Damn. I stuff the prosthesis into my pocket to get the weight of their sidelong glances off it.

I haven't been off the National Defence Medical Center—the old Toronto General Hospital—campus in two months: I don't drive anymore and I've been too self-conscious to walk through Toronto's narrow, grey, neon-painted streets. I make them stop by my room on the way out so I can change into a better shirt and a warmer jacket. The boys turn their backs like gentlemen while I do it, even though I duck into the private bathroom—my room's only real luxury. Kate calls through the crack in the door when she lights on something that interests her.

"Is that an eagle feather, Maker?"

Nosey bitch. I pause a moment to ungrit my teeth. "A gift from my sister when I enlisted," I say, unwilling to give her so much but even more unwilling to look ungracious in front of Gabe. "Nell did the beading herself." I come out of the bathroom to see Kate's hand hovering over the shelf beside my bed where the terracotta-colored feather lies in a nest of chamois, bright beads winding the shaft. Warrior colors, violet and red.

"You have a sister?" Gabe asks, surprised. Kate drops her hand, but can't resist brushing her fingertips along the gorgeously mottled vane.

I flinch. "She died." And drag a leather coat out of the cabinet and zip it. "Let's go."

Gabe knows where to find every seedy dive and piece of rough trade in three provinces. The place he chooses features modern music and retro decor, with a striped carpet that makes my eyes ache. Kate leans forward, listening intently while Gabriel tells war stories, and then my arm aches too. Fortunately, the story where he pulls me out of the burning APC at the risk of his own life and the price of my left arm is not featured tonight.

The other three are off on a restroom errand when he reaches across the table and pushes raggedly fringed hair out of my eyes, tracing burn scars with one thick, nibbled finger. "When's this getting fixed?"

"Sweet virgin, no!"

He frowns and leans back, finishing his drink. "You're not a victim, Jen. Why you wanna wear your wounds like a badge?"

Chewing on my lip, I search for the answer that will make sense. "Over a hundred hours of surgery. I can't do anymore." And then I hate myself for the look of pity that crosses his face, so I laugh and shrug it off. "Besides, why bother? The service owns my ass for another eleven years, Gabe. Or until the state of emergency is rescinded and the Mil-Powers Act revoked. You holding your breath for that?" Besides, it's not like my good looks ever got me anything but grief. And Chrétien.

Gabe dials two more beers and doesn't answer until they're on the table. "They're not going to send you back out, Maker."

I know. I'm an ideal test subject: healthy enough to survive the ordeal and make a good adaptation to the tech, desperate enough to sign the waivers—and too badly traumatized to ever safely put in a fight again. You'd have to be crazy to allow your spine sliced open and electroconductive cones implanted in your brain to operate a pile of used-car parts. The long flexible box cuddling my spinal column might continue to work for years yet—unless it triggers a total failure. You'd have to be crazy to let somebody do that. Crazy. Or crippled.

The others return before I can answer, and after Kate leans over and kisses Gabe on the side of the neck I plead invalidity and exhaustion and creep away. I don't want to be around to watch… but I don't want to go back to NDMC, either.

Kate's eyes follow me as I head for the door.

I wander in and out of the PATH when it gets too cold on the street, and I spend a long time just standing on a corner of Yonge, watching the traffic go by, stippled by the lights of a garlic-noodle shop and a fetish store. That cold chews through my leather jacket until I find another dive in self-defense. I get my drink and sit with my back to the bar, trying to ignore the anchor on the monitor telling me the eighteen-hour-old ceasefire in South Africa has been broken with shots fired near Port Elizabeth. I learn about an engineering lab bombing at the University of Guelph, and receive the reassuring news that a group of extremists are rumored to have stolen a shipment of high-level nuclear waste somewhere in the U.S. Midwest. I concentrate on the crowd to distract myself from the closed-captioning crawl. Inevitably, someone catches my eye.

He might be nineteen. Then again, he might not. Anyway, he's staring at me. Hair half-cropped and half-ragged in Christmas shades of red and green, a studded leather jacket, rings and studs through his soft golden skin: probably the child of one of the families that immigrated from Hong Kong in the '90's. He's got guts, coming here alone. Plenty of people can't tell Beijing from Kyoto, and the Japanese are not… popular since our little altercation over the Malaysian trade issue.

My plastic cup cracks in the metal hand. I set the remains on the bar, shaking amber droplets of beer onto the floor before I swagger over to him, three-quarters drunk. I have to yell to be heard. "You got a problem?"

"You look pretty fucking razor, you know that? Where did you fight?"

Disarmed, I half-step away. "South Africa. New England, before." He gestures me to sit. I hook a stool over with my boot. "What's your name?"

"Xu. Everybody calls me Peacock." He gestures to his hair by way of explanation. He looks more like a parrot to me.

"I'm Casey. You can call me Maker."

He nods, stands. "So, Maker. You wanna dance?"

I've never been beautiful, but even crippled I've kept some grace. If you can fight and you can screw, you can dance. I think I shock him. He moves with a wiry finality I like, and he doesn't flinch from my scars or from the grip of the machine. He pays for my next drink and we both know what he's buying. We bang our glasses together dizzily; the room spins in hellish Technicolor, a whirl of noise and clientele. He shouts in my ear. "You said you were in Africa!"

I nod hard. He leans closer. "You know a Benson Xu?"

I shake my head and shout back. "Your brother? What is he?"

He puts his mouth against my ear, which makes sense—except he's come to stand between my knees and his hands brush my thighs. "Armor," he shouts.

"He died near Cape Town."

I gulp my whisky and set the glass on the bar. "When?"

"Six months."

I wave my good hand at the prosthesis. "I was out of it by then. I was heavy infantry. A driver." I wonder why he's not in service. Exemption, or something else? I push the thought away: if I don't ask, I can say I didn't know about it, later.

He grins, reaches up, touches a bit of metal at my collar. I'd forgotten I was wearing a unit pin. "I noticed." He shrugs. The moment is… intimate.

Over the reek of the crowd I smell leather, liquor, sweat, and the harsh chemical scent of dye as he moves in for the kill. That's okay, because he's not even pretending to want me. Nobody wants a tall, hook-nosed girl with a war-torn body. He wants a symbol. He wants to honor his dead.

I can be a symbol. Hell. I could use a symbol of my own.

I close my eyes as his hands clench on my thighs, thumbs pressing into muscle as his mouth comes down on mine like a blow struck in anger. I reach up and make a fist in his hair, but I have to open my eyes to do it because I have no sense of where the damned hand is. He groans into my mouth, catching my lip between his teeth, pressing me hard against the railing. The pain is welcome, a counterpoint. It's been a long, long time, but it all feels even better than I remembered.

Our teeth grate together until I taste blood. The crowd jostles us; my stool tilts dangerously under me as I close my eyes again and cling to him for support. I barely have the wit to open the steel hand when I feel him spin away.

There's three of them, but only two move well. The other one is a clumsy giant and all three seem oddly off-balance and slow. Someone shouts something: I can only guess at the words. The big one reaches for me, slut kissing a yellow-skinned boy in public. The other two square off with Peacock.

I put my hand into the big guy's chest, feeling no resistance. His flesh jumps away from my touch: it's the familiar time dilation of combat, seeming even more exaggerated tonight. Green twigs snapping; he rocks backward, mouth open in a perfect, silent "O" as he tries and fails to breathe. He sags to his knees with a certain stately grandeur.

I move toward the next one, bringing my knee up into his crotch as he turns away from my new boyfriend. *Yeah, the girl can fight.* The son of a bitch is wearing some sort of protection and he grins as he swipes at me. Slow, clumsy, slow… a hand moves toward me at three-quarters speed. I step around him and elbow his face into the bar. Bone crushes. He falls.

Peacock bleeds from the inside of his right arm, but has a knife in his other hand. Another customer rises behind the last thug, raising a chair, and someone else beans *him* with a bottle, knocking him into the bad guy. Well, that's a riot, then….

I grab Peacock's arm. Eyes wild, he's ready to strike until he sees it's me. He catches my sleeve; we break for the door and scamper into the alley, a couple of kids with stolen apples in our pockets and the market in an uproar behind. The air burns cold. I fall against the wall, sick with adrenaline and alcohol. Peacock slumps beside me, breathing labored. "Shit, my jacket!"

"Shit, your *arm*!" Remembering blood, I yank his coat off. "You should have stitches." His blood clots my fingers, flesh and steel alike, in sticky strings.

"No hospitals. No cops."

I meet his eyes for a breathless second before I nod. *I'm glad I didn't ask.* It's a nasty slice, but the bleeding is slowing, so I improvise a sort of field dressing with a bandanna and make plans to do more about it later.

He bounces on the balls of his feet. "You were fucking fantastic! I've never seen anybody move that fast!"

"I've always been quick." *Seem a little quicker this time, Jenny?* Another thought I don't have time to deal with. Now. Ever. Tailored drugs have become de rigueur on the combat lines. There are rumors of other things. Permanent things.

Smoke. Military legendry, like the recruit who lines his sleeping bag with plastic wrap for a winter hike and freezes to death in his own sweat.

I knot the bandanna and drop his arm. His coat falls aside unnoticed as he thrusts me back against the grimy stones, our breath tattering in clouds strobelit by the city. He doesn't seem to care that he's shivering as he reaches under my jacket and grabs my shirt collar, bruising my mouth with his, ripping the shirt open with a brutal efficiency that rends cloth and pops buttons. His hands clutch my breasts; his knee presses hard between my legs. Teeth rake my throat, his breath hot in my ear; my wet skin stings with cold.

It wouldn't be the first time I've gone down on a stranger in an alley, and I'm tempted to see if I can make him forget just how cold it is. But my pants are too tight for anything else, and I hear sirens. "Peacock, where can we go?"

He groans. Urgent, insistent: "Right here. Right now."

I start to push him away but he catches my hands. I panic and freeze, convinced if I struggle I'll hurt him bad... until he bends quickly and slurps my nipple into his mouth, and each thump of my heart cracks distant and ponderously slow. A wet, rough tongue, the pressure of his thigh against my sex, his fingernails marking my right wrist become my physical reality. The dangerous cold, the heat of his body, the roughness of the stones—

—narrow to a tunnel and vanish.

The blackout must last only seconds because he still holds me against the wall, but now it's with concern. Red lights flash across his face. Voices bullhorn-distorted into the pronouncements of monsters bang my ears. "Are you hurt?" He sounds like a sergeant I used to know. "Are you hurt?"

The words make no sense the first time. The second time I manage to shake my head. "Come on!" He yanks my arm. I stagger after, dizzy drunk, catching my shoulder against stones. I fall, skinning both knees through my jeans; he drags me up. We run.

His squat is on the second floor. A stained mattress smells of sweat and fear, but it's warmer inside and he has a little kerosene stove and a first aid kit. I get his shirt off, listen to his breath slow and steady through his nose while I stitch his wound. He grunts when needle pierces skin.

My shirt is a ruin, so I toss it aside. After I treat my knees I can't face fighting bloody jeans over the wounds, so I lie back on his pillow in my jacket and underwear and try to relax while I wait for the shakes to end… until he comes to me and kneels down and puts his mouth over mine.

I return the caress. Softer, this time. Less like something to prove. We're both human now, human and wounded, and we've seen each other weak. He opens my jacket and admonishes me. "You're too skinny. I can count your ribs." I flush, reaching to kiss him so I won't think, residual heat flooding old burns. He touches the place where my prosthesis joins my body, his eyes huge and dark in the inconstant light. "Fuck. Does it hurt?"

I don't like him touching me there. "It hurts." He smells of antiseptic, of blood and leather, and I'm what he wants me to be, wounded and war-weary, which is not what he wanted before.

Peacock pushes me down, hand sliding from my biceps to my collarbone. He spreads my legs insistently, shoving the leather jacket aside to press his teeth into my shoulder. Shocking pain immobilizes me for a long, seeking moment, until I hear the indrawn snuff of air through his nose and my own breath hisses out between clenched teeth in a long and shameless groan. He wraps his arms around me, coat and all, and my skin grows wet under scratchy blankets as we move.

But I'm not there. I'm across town, feeling nothing as I watch the body I've lived in for years kill two men without appreciable effort. I hear green branches breaking like rotten ice. A chill without relation to the cold settles into my bowels. I've killed. Special Forces, heavy infantry.

I've never killed without orders before. Never done it without the cold, conscious decision to close my finger on the trigger, my hand on the hilt. Peacock's hands brush tender, livid weals along my spine, trace unshapely outlines of nanoprocessors, knead deep onto slick, ropy burn scars. The pleasure's like a twisting blade, more intense than anything but fire. I barely feel it. His sweltering body presses my chill skin; I wonder if I will ever be warm again.

He blows out the stove to save kerosene and we lie in the urban half-dark and let the city paint our skins in warrior colors, red and gold and violet. I light a cigarette, let the match burn until flame sputters against steel. He trails a casual touch down my side. "You're Native, aren't you?"

I grin at the friendly, dancing coal of my cigarette. The little, red light leaves time-lapse trails across my retina. "I'm part Mohawk and part Canuck. Metis. A mongrel." I feel—not good, but amiable, detached from the pain. It's enough. For now. "I come from a long line of iron workers and electricians."

"So of course you went for a soldier. You're a girl. You could have got out of it." It's a funny, anachronistic turn of phrase. I stare at him speculatively until I remember where I've heard it before. There's a song my mother used to sing, before she died. Pretty song. "Where have all the husbands gone? Gone for soldiers, every one…"

"Three meals a day and a warm place to sleep without having to steal or whore for it? Sign me up." I gesture expansively with the cigarette. "I wasn't drafted, Peacock. I enlisted." I don't mention the other things. I never talk about the other things. The tracks went away with my arm, and I can even enjoy being touched, these days. Nine years in the service. Nine years after Chrétien. The Army saved more than my life.

I earned Nell's feather, dammit. The same way warriors always have. I don't feel Peacock touch the arm, but he taps on it with questioning fingers. "Was this a part of the bargain too? How about the combat enhancements?"

I pretend I didn't hear the question.

Harsh chuckles. "Don't play dumb. I know it's not supposed to exist, but I saw you fight." There's a little hitch in his voice that turns the next line into a joke at his own expense. God bless his black little heart. "And—I mean, I've never had any complaints, but I've never made a woman faint before, either."

I open my mouth to deny it and choke. The cigarette tastes like old socks. I pinch it out as he sits up and wraps his arms around his knees. "Don't you hate them even a little? For turning you into—" he hesitates, as if the drama of his words troubles him "—turning you into a killing machine?"

"Why aren't you in service? Why do you live in a squat?"

His lips quirk up. "I'm an objector."

"You're a deserter."

He rolls over, fits himself against my side. I both crave the touch and am repulsed by it, and so I lie there, rigid, while he curls his fingers into my hair and tugs hard enough to make me gasp. "I got fired." And then he slides his body over mine once more, and even my slight resistance fails.

For all the city is bright, the darkness feels profound. Peacock speaks. "You didn't know."

I swim back into reality. He's robbed me of my armor, my control. The son of a bitch made me cry. I won't forget that. Won't forget, either, how every touch resonated wildly under my skin. If the fight didn't convince me of something wrong, sick, strange inside me… the last hour would have. My voice is the voice of a stranger, pressed shaking through my teeth. "You ever miss your brother,

Peacock? You ever think if you turn over your shoulder real quick, you might catch him standing there?" That shuts him up for a good long time. He slides away in the darkness. "Maker. I've got a friend you should talk to."

I laugh. There's nothing funny left in the world. I'm a hole even the darkness could fall into. "A shrink?"

He runs his hand the length of my body, leaving behind a bruised feeling that's nothing to the ache inside. "No." The silence is agony, but I'm not asking. Eventually, he tells me anyway. "A reporter."

I look around Gabe's quarters for something to throw, but nothing seems fragile enough to interest me. I slam the door instead. Twice, because it feels good. "Jesus Christ, Gabe! They fucking raped me. They put something in my body that I don't want there! And all you can tell me is, 'You're not thinking clearly'? Merde!" I clench my right hand into a fist. Servos creak as the left one matches it.

He sets his cup aside and leans forward on the blue tweed modular, uncrossing long legs. "Apparently not."

Tired carpet fibers twist under my feet. I launch into another rant, sunlight glittering on dust motes stirred by my restlessness. "Corporal," he interrupts. "Sit the fuck down."

I drop onto institutional tweed, hating myself for it but unable to disobey a command. I was a goddamn good soldier once upon a time.

"Now talk. Calmly, and one problem at a time."

"It's not just the arm. It's... other things." I fight the urge to claw at crawling skin, as if I can still feel Peacock's handprints. "Jesus. They did something to me. To my nervous system, to my brain."

"Maker, you don't really believe that shit."

Something about his dismissal crystallizes my rage into a cold, intelligent fury. My voice drops into its normal register, steadies. "Tell that to the guys I wasted last night."

His eyes get a little wide. "Pardon?"

"I killed two people last night. By accident. It was self-defense, but I tell you I did not mean to kill them. They started a fight. And then I had no control."

He searches my face for signs that I can hear the craziness in the things coming out of my mouth. I hold up the prosthesis. "I punched a man's chest in with this, Gabe."

His face goes blank with unbelief. Gesturing him to his feet, I stand. "I am *not* crazy." Focusing everything on not responding, on letting myself take the punch. "Hit me, Gabriel."

He looms, blue eyes worried, wrinkled brow. "Maker...."

"Do it!" He hesitates. I swing, aiming to miss, and he moves faster than anybody that big has a right to, fluid and sharp on the balls of his feet. Left hand across his body for a grapple, grab the metal wrist and twist me to the ground, twice my mass and all that weight to carry me down. Except:

I slip away from his grab, block high, turn to the side as his other hand goes past me. The prosthesis moves like a hammer: teeth grit as I pull the shot, turn it from a vicious cross into a staggering block, feel the dumped momentum of all that metal twist my shoulder and neck, tug of the weave through scarred muscle. Then Gabe's wrist is in my hand and I bend double, put him over my shoulder. Put him on the floor. It costs me something not to slam that fist through the bridge of his nose between startled-wide eyes. He blinks at gleaming steel, hands coming up too slowly ever to stop me.

Elapsed time: three tenths of a second.

I stand up, reconstructed hip creaking audibly, and turn my back on Gabriel Castaign. He doesn't speak as he gets off the floor and pads to the kitchenette.

It's raining ice outside. My missing arm hurts like dipped in fire, and that's not a metaphor. I could have killed him. If he'd been half a step faster, I might not have been able to stop myself. "Is it broken?"

"Just sprained, I think." Disarrayed half-curls bounce as he presses a coldpack tight to his wrist. "All right. I buy it. They screwed you." His gaze turns level and considering. "Now I think you'd better start to look at this rationally."

"Rationally! *Merde!*" Gabe holds up one finger, and I hate myself worse for wanting him more. Ashamed, I fall silent.

"*Oui.* Rationally. There's nothing you can do to fix what's happened. So decide—now—if you're mad enough to destroy your career, pick up a dishonorable discharge, and maybe go to jail."

I never thought of the Army as my career before. "Jail?"

"Look. I'm telling you this because I'm your friend, but you never heard it from me. I was invited to answer a few questions at four o'clock this morning. Questions about you. Where we had gone, what we had done, when you had left the rest of us and what your excuse had been. I wasn't—at home, and they knew exactly where to find me. Mil-Int, I mean.

"I didn't know you'd killed anybody. But you're in trouble, and it's Army trouble, not civilian." He flips the icepack to the floor. "The evidence is under your skin, and it doesn't look like anybody intends to bring charges. It can wait."

"Wait. I see." Trembling with defused adrenaline, I turn toward the door. He watches me go, and something unsaid drags at the air.

Valens smiles as he opens his office door. Over his shoulder, I see metal-topped desk, institutional yellow block wall. "Casey! I wasn't expecting you until this afternoon. Problem with the arm?"

"Captain Valens." I step past him into his office, still shaking, thinking the cold in my bones is from more than the ice in my hair. He turns to face me and all my good intentions fail. "You son of a bitch. Jesus Christ, Valens. Or are you going to try to tell me that you didn't know?"

He examines me and nods once. "No. I knew." The corner of his mouth lifts. "I must say, you're taking it rather well."

My face should make him pale. I can't understand his calm. *I'm* scared of me. Why isn't he?

I only hit him once, but not for lack of trying. Fast as I am, I only manage the one swing before the door bursts open and someone starts yelling orders and my name. I spin and freeze like a bunny in the shadow of a hawk. Two MPs, one high and one low, weapons drawn.

One of them orders me up against the wall. Stupid, Jenny. Would *you* have let you out of your sight, if you were them?

The MP sidles forward, his partner centering her weapon meticulously. There's a kind of Marx Brothers moment as he tries to cuff me, but the other cop has one of those trash-tie things that riot cops use. That goes over the metal wrist okay. It isn't worth getting shot to find out if I could break it.

Valens' arm dangles. I hope I broke it. "Captain." The male MP moves to silence me. Valens stops him with a gesture.

"Casey."

"What you did to me was wrong, sir."

Valens grins. "What I did was make you whole, Corporal. Or would you prefer to spend your life in a wheelchair?"

I stare at the MP's shiny boots. He's ready to lead me out when Valens speaks once more, softer still. "And Casey?"

I look him in the eye. He smiles.

"It's, 'You son of a bitch, *sir*.'"

Not exactly bright lights and hoses, but a stark room with a stark table and a chair as hard as the face of the man who questions me. Another chair for him. Coffee for us both. The cop's name is Major MacInnes. I'm in deep shit.

"It would be best for you if you cooperated, Corporal."

"If you would ask me a direct question, sir, I would be glad to." I twist my fingers together with the steel ones and stare down at them.

"Treason is a capital crime, soldier. Canada is at war."

I meet his gaze. "And I am a soldier who fought in that war, sir, to the best of my ability. Until I could not fight any longer." I'm wallowing. I know it, and he knows it too.

I close my eyes and sag back in my chair, holding myself tight to keep the chill outside. The sound of paper scuffing wood makes me crack them open again. MacInnes—who, of course, with a name like that, is black—stands and drops a slender folder before me. "Open it," he orders. "Tell me what you see."

"A photograph. Young soldier, Blue Beret. Canadian flag." The soldier is an oriental male, about seventeen. He seems familiar, but all young soldiers look alike: severe and attractive in a baby-blue peacekeeper's hat. I used to look like that too. *We were supposed to be the good guys.*

"Now this one."

I understand. "It's Peacock." It's the same photo, image-shopped to add two years, a dye job, and a dozen piercings.

"You know him?"

"I met him in a bar, sir."

"And what was your interaction, Corporal?"

I meet his gaze squarely. I really want to smile, but can't make it happen. "Sir. We got into a fight, sir."

He waits.

Damn me to hell, I look away. "We had an encounter, sir."

"Sexual?"

"Sir?"

"You *fucked*, Corporal?"

"Sir. Yes, sir." Heat paints my face, not banishing the chill. Questions tell you a lot. They had me surveilled. I wonder if they lost me in the brawl, or…. I hope they had fun.

He stands back, head rocking side to side. "I admire your goddamn taste, Casey."

I feel so cold. I cradle my coffee mug closer in the metal hand. Absently, I rub the prosthesis. It's killing me. There's something alien in me, and I can't get it out.

MacInnes turns a wry look at me. "His name is Bernard Xu." The corners of his mouth dip, carving furrows beside his nose. "We believe he was involved, among other things, in a car-bombing in Quebec two months ago; you might recall it."

Mary Mother of God. Oh yes I do.

"We can run him in on minor charges, and under the Mil-Powers Act, we have a lot of latitude. But that bombing… will be a high-profile case. And we have no probable cause. We have no proof." He pauses. "You might be up on some serious charges, Casey. Not just assault.

"If he tried to recruit you… if he told you anything… you could come out of this a hero, Corporal."

War hero. Wounded veteran. Could they just tattoo 'charismatic witness' on my forehead? And of course it has to be a clean, shiny, highly public trial.

We don't need to give them any more martyrs.

He knows I'm crazy when I start to laugh.

I walk into the night alone and no more damaged than when I came in.

They'll give me time to think about it. I'm not under arrest yet, but soon, soon, I imagine. I make a game of examining the passing cars, deciding which ones might be watching me before I realize there could be a tracer wrapped around my spinal cord.

I find a quiet bar to hide in. Inevitably, Xu finds me.

"Peacock." He lets his hand trail down my arm, feels me stiffen, pulls it back slowly. "Or should I say, Bernard?"

He grins, but I think it's forced. "The Army got to you, then?" I just look at him, and he nods once, satisfied.

"How much of a setup was it?"

"What, the other night? I didn't expect to get grabbed. But I saw you, and that—" he gestures to my arm "—and that—" touches the pin I'm still wearing "—and you decided to pick a fight with me and I figured, what the hell." He grins again, more honestly. "I *like* you, Maker. I want you on my side."

"There's a name for that. Treason."

"War. A war against imperialism and greed. What they're doing in South Africa is evil. What they did to you is evil."

I scowl. He takes my silence as encouragement. "It's really simple. I've already tainted you. This life—" and he touches my pin again, fingers brushing my throat, smiling when I shiver and jerk back "—is over for you."

Unless I hand MacInnes this kid's head.

"We can take this to the soft-hearted public. They won't like what the Army's done to you." He pauses. "This could be the biggest thing since Somalia. You might even stay out of jail."

His triumph makes my skin itch. Everybody wants to use you, Jenny. Yeah, well, Jenny may hang, but she won't be used.

"Maker. We can end this war."

I close my eyes. I'm back in Cape Town, Durban, Pretoria. It's not our war, is it? It's never been our war. But then—then whose war is it? "I've gotta go." I turn away, walk away; he hurries after me, reaches for my elbow, flinches when I spin. He's afraid of me. That hurts worse than I expected.

"Think about it. What's left for you there?"

I think about Gabe. I think about an oath I took. I think about the metal under my skin, while that skin creeps off my flesh. I think about Valens' smug face, and I clench my fists, already hating myself and all my choices.

I owe the service something. Something for giving me a way to not die in a gutter, to get clean, to get rid of Chrétien. I snuck out of his apartment, filled out the paperwork, enlisted at sixteen: two years before they could have drafted me. Emancipated youth, no living guardian to sign. It's not my body, it's theirs. Except.

I still want Valens' polished brass ass in a sling. And I like this kid. Dammit.

Homicidal idiot kid. But a kid, a human kid, and one with the guts to do something, anything, even if it's wrong. I tilt my head, study Peacock's gold-studded face. "Did you really try to blow up the Prime Minister's car?"

He grins, steps back. "Do I look like a mad bomber?" Silence like a hangman's rope until he nods. "We *did* blow up the Prime Minister's car. We missed the Prime Minister, though."

"I'll be in touch." He calls after me and I walk faster, until I lose him in the crowd.

Hell could be freezing over beneath my feet. A skin-peeling wind wails off the lake and the sidewalk is cold as iron, but the freezing rain has stopped. And at least these shivers feel normal. The service owns my body, my loyalty, but not my soul. It's cost me something, this Army, these wars. And I don't mind the price. I don't mind fighting to keep my home safe. I don't mind the cold, and I don't mind the pain. Oh, Canada.

I mind it when they take without asking, though. But then, they gave me something, too, didn't they? And I was happy to sell myself to them when it was the price for not being sold. I know well enough what you'll do when you're tasting gun oil, when the edge of the knife is on your throat, steel so cold it's hot. Whether you're a scared runaway on a Montreal back street, or a nation eyed by hungry neighbors.

It's not about Canada. Dammit. It's about Valens. Peacock. Me. I lean against the ice-sheathed trunk of an unhappy tree and watch the headlights roll by. Peacock kills for what he believes in. So do I. The difference is… what's the difference again? Peacock thinks he's a patriot. And I bet Valens thinks he's a good soldier too. Hell, we're all good soldiers. We're just fighting different wars.

My steel hand scars the bark when I pull it away, and I wince. "Sorry."

Peacock is a patriot. And whatever I owe Canada is paid in full by the startled look on Gabe's face as he watched the machine I wear weave like a snake in front of his nose. Except.

Except.

Gabe finds me on a bench by the parking lot on the NDMC campus. "Happy New Year, Jenny. Aren't you cold?"

I barely look up. "Is it?"

"It's New Year's Eve and cold. I don't know if it's happy."

His voice worries me. "Gabe. What's wrong?"

"I've got a goddamned Mil-Int Major assuring me that if I cooperate, I'll be protected, and they won't take 'I don't know' for an answer. Jesus, Jenny! What the hell did you do?"

"I got laid, Gabe. Fucking A." I cough with laughing, my face down in my hands—the left one cold enough to hurt. He slides an arm around my shoulder and I haven't got the strength to shake it off. I want to lay my head against his chest and cry. I wish he weren't an officer. I wish I didn't owe him my life. I wish I were five-foot-two and pretty.

I sit up straighter and his hand drops. He shakes his head, stares away. "I don't like the way this country's going."

"What've they got on you?"

His laugh is as dry as mine. He stretches his legs, spine creaking as he arches against the bench, and he stares upward. "I told Kate some of what happened to you. She went to her commander. I didn't stop to think—it's all classified, of course. The technology they're testing on you doesn't officially exist. I've never heard of some of the regulations they quoted at me." His voice is so level he could be delivering a field report, and I know if I looked at his face I wouldn't see a thing but professional cool.

I understand as clearly as if it were spelled out on a blackboard. Scratchy smell of chalk-dust, scratchy voice of a nun, scratchy skirt on my legs, and scratchy knowledge in my head. I reach out at first with the prosthesis, stop, touch his arm with my own hand. "Gabe, I'm sorry. This isn't about you. Protect yourself. Give them whatever they ask for." *Lie.*

"The *hell* you say!"

My head jerks up. He stares at me. "Jesus Christ, Jenny, do you have any idea what you mean to me?"

My heart stops in my chest.

The words come out of him slowly, forced through taut emotion. "Jen, I…" He tries again. "Look, Maker, you're a regular guy, right? I mean… you're my best friend."

I force a smile, certain the pain in my chest means I am going to die. "You're my best friend too." The lie is easy. A lie of omission. A lie of protection. So what's his need to know? "Look—I'll see you later, okay?"

And leave him gaping after me as I walk away, pain like the socket of a lost tooth that I can't stop probing with my tongue.

I'm so cold I'm not even shivering, and it has nothing to do with the winter outside. The door of my institutional little room clicks locked behind me. My clothes strew the floor like a shed skin as I stumble toward the bathroom. I tear the cloth unbuttoning my cuff. Clumsy.

Jenny Casey, cyborg. Sweet Mary, Mother of God.

Kneeling by the tub, I turn the water on as hot as it will go and pour shampoo under the stream, watching the bubbles rise snowy and ephemeral as dreams. I lay my cheek against cool porcelain and wait for the tub to fill.

By the time I slide into the scalding water I'm shaking again. I crouch in the bath and hug my little-girl scabbed skinned knees. Gabriel. Oh my God, Gabriel.

I lie back, letting the water take the weight of the metal arm, easing the strain in my neck. Constant pain is easy to forget. Like chronic loneliness, you don't notice it until it ends, and then the relief is suddenly immense.

I run metal fingers through my soapy hair. Warm from the water, they almost feel like flesh. Almost. I can't feel my own hair between my fingers. It could be anyone's hand. It could be his hand. *Stop it, Jenny.*

Think. Hot water sears old burns, works into aching joints. Relief and pain are all the same. I want to take that metal hand and claw my own skin back, rip nanoprocessors off my spine and yank until thread-fine wires a yard long hang dripping from the alien fist. I could make a pretty good start on it before I did enough damage that the system quit. I don't mind dying, and I don't mind going to jail. I don't owe Valens anything. Or Bernard Xu. They're good soldiers and so am I.

And Gabe Castaign crawled through fire into an upside-down APC *twice* to save a girl he'd never met from a bad, a very bad death. He had skin grafts on both hands; we were in the burn ward for weeks together. And the only reason he's in trouble now is because he's like a handle on the back of my head. Jerk him around, and Jenny will do whatever you want to protect him. Flip a switch and watch her dance.

And what am I? Machine? Woman? I'm not even sure anymore.

But I'm valuable. Like an old laying chicken back on the farm, not for myself but for what I can produce. Experimental data, and Peacock. The water in the tub cools while I think about how easy it would be to let the metal arm pull me under, to take a deep breath, to drown. Drowning hurts too, but I'm not scared of pain. *So what are you scared of, Jenny?* Green twigs snapping. Gabe's eyes cold and wide.

It seems supremely natural to let that hand slide across my breast and belly, stroking my own flesh as I might the flesh of a lover. The machine doesn't feel like a part of me: it's alien—*other*. The servos click faintly as it moves, sound amplified by the water. I watch as shining fingers wander in slow circles, toy with one of the nipples Peacock called pretty, tangle in the dark hair between my thighs.

When I don't fight it, the hand is sensitive, clever—not graceless and rough. I'm surprised by delicate variations in pressure and movement, caress and hesitation. Fingers trace patterns on my skin, metal hotter than flesh. I shiver, slide down in the water and let it creep between my thighs.

In the end, it is my own tongue that betrays me, and not the machine. In the end, under the touch of my own steel hand, with the taste of soapy water in my mouth, I hear myself say Gabriel's name. And the water's cold as the rain outside before I'm done with crying.

I stand and hook a towel off the rack beside the door. The gesture, when I don't stop to think about it, is almost automatic. *You've lived with worse things than that, Jenny Casey.* And will do again.

I don't have to like it to endure.

I finish my toilet and dress slowly, carefully, taking the time to adjust each button and cufflink. No makeup, but my hair is tidy and my fingernails are trimmed. My left hand gleams. I check the mirror one last time before I leave my room, noting the taut expression of the professional soldier.

Jenny Casey, cyborg. What the hell.

It's not a long walk. Major MacInnes looks unsurprised to see me when I tap on the open frame of his door, not marking the wood. He glances up from his work and gestures me inside. I let the door swing shut and he waves me into a chair.

"Good afternoon, Corporal. At ease."

"Good afternoon, Major. I need to talk to you."

He reaches for his coffee, makes a face when he finds it cold. "I imagined you would. What can I do for you?"

I swallow, hesitate, forge ahead. MacInnes is a good cop too. We're all patriots here. "It's more what I can do for you. Major… sir. Leave Captain Castaign out of this, and I will give you Bernard Xu."

He chews his cheek while he looks at me, considering before nodding once. "We'll need his confederates."

I close my eyes and think about Valens' face plastered all over the evening news. I open them and meet MacInnes'. "That can be arranged. But first, sir, please, your word."

Good Cop gives me half a smile. "Castaign is home free. As long as you come through." He gestures me to rise and continues. "I'll be in touch regarding the details." He glances down at his papers, but I have to make sure.

"Sir?"

He doesn't look up. "Dismissed. Happy New Year."

"Happy New Year, sir."

I don't feel the cold on the long walk back to my room, or rather, it doesn't feel any different than the cold under my skin. I unlock the door like the machine I will pretend to be and I stand, back pressed against it, shaking, not deserving the release of the tears gorging my eyes. We do what we have to do for the people we have to do it for. Every one of us. We choose the living, or we choose the dead.

I will not cry for you.

My flesh hand and my metal one are fastidious and gentle as I wrap Nell's feather in the chamois and stow it deliberately in the belly of my trunk. Feathers are given to warriors. Warriors do what's right, no matter what the cost.

The monitor in the corner of Gabe's living room opaques; the announcer's voice drones over images of a Peacock looking curiously naked in black, combed hair. "In other national news, the trial of Bernard Xu ended today with Xu's conviction as the ringleader of the terrorist group responsible for last summer's assassination attempt on Prime Minister Severin. The prosecutor credits the testimony of Master Corporal Genevieve M. Casey, a decorated veteran of the South African Conflict, as instrumental in the case." The image shifts: a thin, intense woman in dress green perches on the witness stand like a crow in a naked tree. She's terribly scarred, but seems comfortable in her damage.

I lean forward on the blue tweed modular and pick the remote off the coffee table. It's suddenly hard to swallow.

"Xu and Casey declined comment, but reliable sources…"

I change the channel before they get to the part about the sentencing. Or any more news about Africa, where the fighting has worsened again.

Gabe gulps a forkful of narrow noodles, scooped from a tinfoil container. "Master Corporal?"

"Came through three days ago." I shrug. "Fools are going to turn me loose on the kids."

"You're going to be an instructor?"

I nod. I'm sure that he can see how scared I am. I'm taking those lives in both hands. Maybe I can teach one of them something that will keep him alive. Maybe. "They can't send me to fight. And I can serve as an object lesson on why you duck."

Gabe slaps me on the shoulder, his hand lingering a second longer than it has to. "You are going to be great."

I wonder. I hear again MacInnes' voice, from this afternoon, warmly congratulatory as he invited me to join the rest of the prosecution witnesses for dinner. I feel again the pressure of his hand on mine, and flinch. "You did the right thing, Casey," he'd said. "You did right by your country."

I smiled at MacInnes, cursed hypocrite that I am, and told him I had a dinner date. Yeah.

I look over at Gabe, who never needs to know, and I look back down at my beer. I did the right thing. I did not choose my country. I did not choose revenge. I chose my friend.

Noble words, but the beer tastes like hell.

THE COMPANY OF FOUR

Many are the days and the nights. Many are the things that must be, that have been, that never should be. Much is the time that passes. Much is the time that remains. Few are the memories which are more than a handful of dust, to be let run through the fingers. Such are the dangers: "Am I not powerful? Am I not fair? Do you not love me, Niamh, Daman, Daithi?" Such are the words, of a black spell cast.

This is the Company of Four, as they ride through the shadows between *here* and *there*. This is the Company of Four, and the barred light moves across them as they ride beneath the branches of strange trees.

Here is a dark-magicker, mage of little power, or, perhaps, who is denied his power. Here is a jester decked in bells and black and silver motley, a jester sad as snow. Here is a bard with a curse hung on his shoulders like the mantle of his trade. And here is the fourth…

What Faeric touches cannot be trusted, and yet. And yet, the very air about the tall, fey man whispers, "Believe me." There is a look of honor in his carriage and on his curl-crowned brow, and below that beautiful brow gleam eyes as blue as shadowed snow. His charger and his mail are as white as any good king's, and the sword at his knee is straight and swift. He is as fair as his companions are dark.

The magicker is slight and sleek as the rapier he bears, and his supple grace reveals a cool, feline charm. His dark hair is simply parted, and falls to his collar, as straight and smooth as a young boy's. With the bard, he shares a fierce love, a brotherhood that might only be ended by steel through both hearts—steel like the steel in his ten bright rings.

That bard's heart beats in a chest massive as a bull's, and his face is lined by weather where the magicker's is strangely smooth. He is almost silent, usually somber, except for when he weaves his tales out of music and firelight and wine. His matted hair is a dark cloak on his shoulders, his full beard hides the lips that rarely smile.

The jester — she is different. There is something inhuman in her night-colored skin and her star-tinted eyes. Her costume is quartered silver and black, and on the seams of the silver side bright bells are hung, thousands and thousands of infinitesimal, sweetly chiming spheres. They are woven on chains into the moon river of her braid, and each one sings a different note.

She rides close to the magicker and the bard, as if drawn to their bond even as she is not quite included in it. She loves them well, in her secret way, and they know and return this, but she is cautious. Friendship can snap like ice, just as you trust it with your weight.

The jester and the magicker tease and fence with words, and she juggles her steel and copper balls and rings in fanciful bridges and arches. The bard watches, and sometimes a faint smile might curve his moustache, and sometimes he slides a word or a phrase into the dialogue as tight as a carpenter planking a ship. He is humming softly to himself the while, and the music is sad and deep. The white lord rides ahead and slightly to the side, and seems lost in his own thoughts, his own travel.

The magicker pays little attention to the reins, rather playing with his rings. They are of faceted steel, and there is one on every finger, and each thumb as well. They are lovely things, each one different and cunning and graceful. They have left on his skin, beneath, a rash of long wear like the scar of an ancient blister or burn.

The jester catches her balls and rings and slips them into a pouch that hangs from her saddle. She lifts up her reins, which she had hung about the neck of her grey mare, in her black left glove, and she urges her mount up beside the lord. "Where are we bound now, Master?" she asks him, and he is jerked up from the depths of his thoughts like a startled fish upon a hook.

"To the castle of Fearghall," he replies. He glances over at her, and there is a questioning expression on his face. She hears his voice over the pleasing jangle of her bells. "Lately of Niamh."

But though he watches her eyes closely, he sees no recognition of the name. His gaze is disconcerting, however, and her mare shies a pace away from the pale stallion before the jester can bring her under control. Her eyes, guileless, return to his. "You say that name as if I should know it, Master." She glances down at the path below her horse's feet, then up again, perhaps more bold than wise. "Yet I do not."

"I have heard nothing of this king, Fearghall," the bard interjects, his thoughtful baritone puzzled. "Is he a new King?"

The lord smiles, and white teeth flash between rose-petal lips. For a second, the sun tangles her fingers in his golden hair, like a lover, and he is crowned in light. "A new King." His eyes crinkle in amusement. "Aye." And he turns away, and lifts up the reins of his milk-white steed, and breaks into a canter and away, ahead of the rest. The bard blinks slowly after him, but says no more.

And so they ride, until their eyes strain against the edges of the strangling dusk. And then the four dismount, and the magicker sees to the horses, and the jester builds the fire. The white lord watches, until they bring him his dinner, and the bard paces and grumbles and refuses to eat. It is the night of the full moon, and food, for him, has no savor.

As the white lord rolls himself in his blankets on the other side of the fire, the magicker and the jester build it higher. The bard continues his pacing, restless, irritation and rage in every line of his body, every movement of his flesh. When he tugs ineffectually at his clothing, the magicker stops him, and begins to unfasten his laces, undressing him as one might a child. As he removes each item of clothing, he gives it to the jester, who folds it piece by piece as it is handed her. When the bard at last stands naked except for the impressive pelt that nature gave him, the jester turns away, and places his clothing in his pack, and his boots beside his saddle.

The bard sits down on the ground, and, lost under some tremendous pressure, buries his face in his hands. The magicker pats his shoulders ineffectually. Full night has fallen. The moon parts the branches of the trees with long fingers and smiles down at them, beside their pathetic campfire. It is a cruel and a terrible smile.

The bard begins to scream.

He rises to his feet, his neck corded in agony, his chest seeming to swell with the power of each indrawn breath. The magicker croons affectionate nonsense, but he does not touch the bard. The scream continues forever and then longer, wailing out into the pitiless night as the bard jerks convulsively, his body wracked by brutal seizures. His flesh melts — he expands — he wrenches apart and seamlessly knits together as bones crack and muscles twist and the bottomless scream deepens and deepens into a final, shattering roar, and in his place there stands a giant bear, a bear so black that only its eyes and teeth and its red, red maw are visible in the firelight.

The bear snarls, and soft, heavy paws begin to pad toward the blanket-wrapped figure beyond the fire. The magicker runs to meet him, steps into his path, spreads his beringed fingers on hands held wide. "No," he says, softly, his own eyes finding the small, piggy eyes of the bear.

The bear rears up, menacing, showing fangs and claws that could destroy him with one casual blow. The magicker holds his ground. "No," he whispers again, his voice calm and serene. He is trusting of the bard's love. The jester, standing behind him, hearing the tinkle of her bells, is less so. The jester does not believe in love.

In the bear's dim mind lives hatred, lives passionate fury and rage. It wants to rend the soft, pale thing wrapped in the blankets. It wants to smash it to earth until there is nothing left. But the ones who guard it — they are to be protected. They are adored.

It is too much for such simple understanding. It tries to shoulder them aside, and they will not move, and it will not push hard enough to risk harming them. The bear presses its broad chest against the magicker, and the jester, with her heart between her teeth, runs up and throws her arms about its hairy neck. She clings to it like a burr, lost in the dark fur, hearing the low rumble of its growl over the frantic clamor of her bells. She does not know why it needs to destroy their guardian, but she knows it must be stopped, even should it cost her life.

With a final snarl, the bear tears free of the encircling arms, and shuffles into the night. Magicker and jester sit side by side by the fire, awaiting its return.

The bear pads into the camp before sunrise, and lays its heavy head down on its paws, and when he raises his head he is a naked man once more. "If I had known, if I had known, Tam Lin," the bard murmurs, and then the magicker brings him a steaming cup and the sun glances around the corner to be sure that it's safe to come out and the night, at last, is done.

Midday brings them to a castle under a hill with thorn trees growing at the crown, where they are made welcome and given to eat, and to bathe. It is the seventh anniversary of Fearghall's ascension to the throne, and nothing will do but for there to be a masque. And at that masque will mage and bard and jester all perform.

The jester lingers in a curtained doorway, gazing into the mirrored hall, and she listens to the strains that the bard pulls forth from his harp strung with golden wire. She watches him upon the stage, and thinks, *That is not his harp*, and does not know why, because it is the harp that he has strummed by the fire, every night when he is not a bear. He has no other. She watches the bright skirts of the ladies and the gay coats of the lords, and does not venture forth into the hall. There is an ache across the bridge of her nose, like unshed tears, and she feels, all at once, both forlorn and at home.

"Finnegan," says the King, as his and the white lord's footsteps carry them past the curtained doorway, "Hiding them in this way is clever enough by half. But are you quite sure that it was safe to bring them back here, on this night of all nights?"

"It is seven years since the spell was cast, Fearghall," the white lord replies. "Tonight is the night that is must be renewed, and this is the place where the spell may be cast." He sighs.

The King, tall and fair and golden and costumed as the rising sun, tugs at the lobe of one pointed ear, raises a pointed eyebrow. "Would that we could simply slay them."

But the white lord's answer is lost to the jester's ears as they sweep by, and are gone into the crowd. The implications of the speech, however, are not.

Under a spell, she thinks. We are under a spell. The bard's curse — is that my Master's doing? She leans back against the arch of the door, feels the cold roughness of the stone snag at her motley, and listens to the rustle of her bells, in time with the rhythm of her heart. If only I could think, she muses, mind already drifting onto something else. Just for a moment, clearly think…

The hand at her elbow all but startles her into a scream. She jumps and stiffens, and her bells clash, and whatever erring thought she chased is gone. She whirls, and the magicker stands behind her. In his hand that does not rest on her sleeve is a cage of doves, with which he will later conjure. "Jester," he says, softly, insistently, raising his hand to her cheek. "Jester. This is important."

"Mage?"

He turns away, sets his doves down by the wall, where they coo and rustle within their cage. He straightens again, and takes her by the shoulders. Behind her, in the mirrored hall, she can hear the patter of dancing feet, the strains of the harp, the bard's sweet baritone voice raised in song. *Iron's hard, and gold is cold. Steel is bright, and silver bold. Emeralds for a lady, and diamonds for a queen, and jeweled masks for thy features, never to be seen…*

"What is your name?"

It is all drowned out in the chiming of the bells. "I…" Her expression shifts to shock and terror. "I do not know. I do not…" She stands, braced as though expecting a blow, and looks up at him with her wild eyes wide in her child's soft face. "I must have a *name!*"

But the bard's song is ending, and the magicker is picking up his doves. It is his turn to perform.

Still he pauses, one hand on the curtain, drawn back to permit him to pass, and he turns back to the jester, who stands, still stunned. The light glitters in the facets of the steel rings on that hand. "Yes," he says, and his voice is level and conversational, as if enquiring after the butter. "I suppose we all must, after all." And then he walks into the mirrored ballroom, and the curtains fall shut behind him, and the jester is alone.

The masque would persist till sunrise, as is the nature of such revels, but the King retires when the clock strikes three, and the white lord some few moments before him. The jester and the magicker have already made their way up the servant's stair to their own small room, and there, warmed by a brazier, they wait for the bard. The jester sits perfectly, awesomely still, willing her breath to stop, willing her heart to beat more softly. At last, at last, there is silence: her bells swing, perhaps, but they do not jangle or rustle or tinkle. She sits with her head cocked slightly, as if listening for something. Earlier, she had told the magicker what she had overheard.

And then the chamber door opens, and the bard comes in, and sets his cloth-wrapped harp against the wall. The jester turns her head, and a dozen bells chime sweetly. "Jester," the bard says, "Is something wrong?"

She shakes her head to an astounding, silvery dissonance. "For a moment," she says, "just for a moment, I thought I heard someone calling my name." She sighs, and tugs her braid. "I felt that I knew something that I ought to know. But the feeling has passed, now."

"There is a harp," the bard says, "Hanging in the throne room." He settles back, against the wall. "And a sword hanging beside it, among all the trophies and banners."

The magicker looks up for the first time. "And?"

"And I feel I ought to know them, from somewhere."

The jester starts, eyes wide as if shocked. "What does it look like?"

"Which? The harp or the sword?"

"The harp!"

The bard sighs, takes a piece of bread with cheese from off a tray. "It is red wood, strung with silver wire." He shrugs. "It is silver. I cannot touch it, after all."

She leaps to her feet. "I must see it! I must!"

The bard chews and swallows, but is not slow in getting to his feet. The jester reaches her hand out to the magicker, who declines it and stands on his own, brushing crumbs from his lap as he does. He slides his sword in its scabbard into his belt, and the three exit the door in a single, silent file. The mage watches the back of the jester's head as she follows the bard down the stairs, and something nags at him, stirred by the sight of her braids. Beneath his skin he feels the shift of power, of magic being cast, but dimly, muffled and distant. Better born with no talent at all, he thinks, than with such a small one. Like the minor poet who knows the meanness of his gift, I am doomed to a lifetime of frustration: to be able to comprehend beauty, but not create it. His fingers itch at the thought, feeling swollen and engorged.

The throne room is still torchlit, although there are no revelers here. Strains of music still drift across the courtyard from the great hall, though, and the bard's feet shuffle a bit in an ursine dance as he crosses the hall. "There."

He gestures up at the harp, which is hung just at eye level, just across from the throne. It is a lovely thing, the wood red as holly berries, the wire of true silver. The jester looks at it in delight. "Oh, it is yours, it is yours!" she cries, not knowing how she knows this, knowing it is true.

"How can it be?" the magicker asks. "It is silver…"

The jester shakes her head, and the bells clash, and she looks crestfallen. "I do not know. And I do not know my name."

"You have only to name a thing," says the bard, "To comprehend it."

The magicker smiles. "Of course. That is the nature of…" His voice trails off, and he stares away, as if after his beloved. "…the nature of magic…"

His head snaps around, and he grasps the jester hard by the arm. "Sit there, on the steps of the dais," he commands her. "No, better, on the throne."

She steps back from him, tugging against his grip. "I cannot sit on the throne."

"Do it," he orders, and she follows his pull to perch, reluctantly, on the edge of the giant chair. The magicker reaches into his pocket, and draws forth a knife, small and sharp. It is the one he shaves with.

Carefully, quickly, he cuts the bells from her costume, and breaks them one by one under his heel. And then, from the same pocket, he brings forth a comb of bright silver, and he touches it to the end of her plait.

She starts up. "Do not!"

He shows her the comb. "I have never seen you with your hair unbound, lady," he tells her. "Humor me."

Trembling, she takes the seat again. Something almost soul-deep in her rebels at the thought. Something deeper, however, welcomes it. "Do," she whispers, and clenches her fingers on the gilded wood.

It is a tedious task, freeing the intricate plaits from the strands of chains and bells. Somehow, they have not matted in, but they are tightly and complexly woven. He is surprised by the color, the texture of the unleashed mass of her hair.

It is like water as it rolls down her shoulders and over her thighs to pool on the floor. It is soft and thick, wavy from being bound, of a thousand shades of grey and white and argent and alabaster. It is a river, a thunderstorm, a sea, running, quick and silver, in rivulets and brooks and breakers over everything.

For the jester, it is as if each chain he slides from her tresses is a chain off her heart and her mind. "I feel," she declares, "as if I am just about to remember something terribly important."

As the magicker slips the last chain out of her moon-colored hair, his rings become caught in the strands. He tugs them loose, but not before the jester catches and holds his hands. "Why do you always wear those?"

He frowns. "I must."

She is insistent. "Why? Who told you?"

He steps back, drops the chain to the floor with a rattle of metal. "I do not know," he confesses. He pulls his hands from hers, leaving the silver comb in her grasp. "Someone."

"Some strange taste of magics on this." It is the bard's voice. He has turned, at last, from the harp on the wall.

"Aye," says the magicker. "A compulsion. But to help or to harm?"

She nods, and bites her lip to taste the blood. "If you do not know, can it be for good? All the more reason, I think, to be rid of them."

He wants to explain that magic does not always work that way, that sometimes the recipient of a spell must know nothing of it for the spell to be truly effective. "There is a great sorcery being wrought within these walls tonight," he offers. The bard looks over at him and nods.

"I feel it, aye."

The magicker looks back at the jester, and silently holds out his hands, fingers spread wide. He looks away. "Take them," he tells her.

One by one, she wrestles them free. They are tight, and have worn grooves in the flesh of his fingers. One by one, she drops them to the cold stone floor.

The magicker feels a sudden easing, as though the rings had bound his chest, and not his fingers. He looks into the jester's eyes, and feels something there, some flicker of recognition. "Name?" she asks him, and he shakes his head.

"You?"

"Not yet," she answers. As one, they look to the bard. "If we were bound…"

The magicker presses his lips together. "He must be too. And the white lord?"

She shakes her head, and no bells ring. "Remember what he said to the King?" She looks down at the backs of her hands, the shine of the silver comb in the right one. "Is there a way to tell what binds him?"

"Not without his name," the magicker answers. The jester casts about the throne room, as if looking for a solution. Then she looks up, startled, into the eyes of the mage. "Daithi," she tells him, and the bard turns suddenly toward her.

"What did your say?"

"Daithi," she says again, this time looking at the bard. "Can't you both hear it? *'Am I not powerful? Am I not fair? Do you not love me, Niamh, Daman, Daithi?'* It's perfectly clear. It's the white lord's voice — Finnegan's voice…"

The magicker shakes his head slowly. "That's the binding. They are repeating it… you first, lady, that's why you hear it now."

Her head is bowed, suddenly. "Aye. I feel it. The pressure…" But the magicker has turned away, murmuring under his voice, "I am Daman…"

A flush of power colors his skin, and he raises his eyes to those of the bard. "And you are Daithi, and I will know how you are bound…"

Daman the magicker holds out his hands, and lets the power run into them, unfettered by intricate steel. And then he lays those hands upon the brow of the bard Daithi, and then, unhesitating, plunges them into his matted hair. "There!" he cries out, as Daithi winces in sudden pain. "This!" And in his hand is a tuft of hair that is coarser and blacker even than that of the bard, and reeking of sharp animal musk.

"Bear fur?"

"It's all matted in with his own." Daman turns back to Daithi, who glances from one to the other. The jester holds out the silver comb, and Daithi blanches.

"Silver…"

"Will work all the better. Come, bard, sit on the throne and let me comb out your hair."

Daithi crosses the room, sits as the jester sat before him, and looks down at the litter of chains and bells upon the floor.

Daman comes up before him, and holds out both hands. "Hold tight to me," he instructs, and Daithi reaches out with his long musician's fingers and wraps those of his friend within them. He closes his eyes, then, and grits his teeth, and groans between them as the silver comb brushes his hair.

Slowly, meticulously, the jester combs out the mats. Bit by bit, the scatter of hair upon the floor grows into a pile, and then a heap. Daithi bites through his lip and weeps silently as the blood flows into his beard, but he does not cry out and he does not flinch away, and at last, the jester is done.

He looks up at her with new eyes, then, and releases Daman's hand to wipe the blood from off his face. "Your Majesty," he calls her, and kneels at her feet, and she gestures him rise, the bard of her court. And Daman fetches his sword and Daithi's harp from off the wall, and the two brothers, so alike and yet so different, smile at one another and then turn to their queen.

"The spell," she whispers, sagging back against the throne. "Daman, attend me…"

And then guardsmen are running into the torchlit room, and behind them two tall, golden-haired figures in white, and Daithi blows the dust from the Red Harp of Coinleach and strikes, once, hard, the lowest string. There is a trembling, and a shattering, and a note that rolls on and on and on as the drawn swords in the guardsmen's hands shiver into splinters, and the guardsmen themselves raise hands to ears and cry out in pain.

Finnegan pushes them aside, and comes forward, reeking of foul herbs and with his hands spread wide. He takes another step toward Niamh, and Daman's drawn blade gathers the light as it flashes toward him. He dives aside, and then Fearghall has a blade in his hand as well, and the battle is joined.

Niamh levers herself to her feet, her hair falling about her like a rich garment and one hand clenched on each arm of her throne, and raises her burning eyes in a black face to Finnegan's blue ones. "Am I not powerful?" he whispers, as her eyes meet his. "Am I not fair? Do you not love me, Niamh….?" He says her name as a caress, and there is no question in his voice — only acceptance of allegiance duly offered.

"Aye, you are powerful," she whispers. "And aye, you are fair." Her hand extended, she steps toward him, and smiles a sweet, sad smile. And slaps him once across the cheek, hard enough to leave an ivory handprint that flushes slowly scarlet on the fairness of his skin. He rocks backward, and she strikes him again, and he falls before her fury, to lie amid the broken chains and bells.

He tries to stand, and Daithi is on him, one powerful hand pressing down until he kneels, head bowed, before the fury of the queen. "And I do not love thee, Finnegan Fey, for I know thee, and thy soul is black as thy face is fair. Be silent, or we will have thy tongue cut out, slaver, usurper, sorcerer." There is a clatter across the hall, and Niamh looks up to see that Daman has disarmed Fearghall. Daman gestures Fearghall, as well, to his knees.

Niamh leaves the throne, strides across the room to stand before him. "Who?" she asks him. "Fearghall, you fooled us once. Tell us, Fearghall, who are we?"

"You are Niamh," he answers, eyes downcast. There is a bleeding cut across his cheek. It is already healing. "You are Faerie." His tongue seems to choke him. "And they are Daman and Daithi, your mage-champion and your bard."

"And what are we, Fearghall?" She touches his head. "Tell us, and we may be merciful."

"You are the queen of the Seelie Fey," he answers, and she smiles and turns away. "Daman," she says, and her mage looks up from his prisoner's form.

"Majesty?"

"They are immortal. We cannot have them executed, any more than they could us. And I have promised this one, at least, some mercy. What shall we do with them, Daman?"

He appears thoughtful, and Daithi's voice speaks from across the chamber's width. "Majesty?"

"Daithi?"

"I have — an idea…"

In the court of the Queen of the Seelie Fey, there stands a red rowan and an ash tree. The limbs of the one are hung with chains and bells that tinkle and chime in the wind, except for those that are strangely crushed and broken. The branches of the other are decked with ten steel rings of strange and lovely design, forced onto the twigs as if onto the fingers of a hand.

ICE

The stallion was gnawed and bloody, but he was not dead.

Snow fell between us, gentling the contours of the battlefield where my brethren had died with their backs to a raging ocean, but I could see him sprawled in the gathering drifts among the gaunt bodies of a half-dozen of Loki's vile-wolves. A final abomination still panted nearby, a tar-colored monster struggling to rise as I approached. It had the strength neither to attack nor flee.

I took a deep breath of the crystalline air, and with it came a realization: *So the vile-wolves* **can** *be killed.* And then I wondered, *Why didn't the valraven just fly up and escape them?*

An old wound, garnered fleeing, stung my thigh, and a hesitant step carried me toward him. I had lost my helmet somewhere; I shoved dirty-blonde braids long as my arms out of the way. Far below us, the ocean foamed against boulders and ice at the foot of the seacliffs. The stallion raised one of his twin heads, and thrashed his shattered wings. His brown eyes shone white-rimmed and wide with fear beneath the horns. His other head, the antlered one, flopped on a broken neck, tongue lolling between fanged teeth. Under the tattered velvet of his hide, his lungs heaved; the blood that frothed from his nostrils was painfully bright. His wings—which should have been improbably white as unicorns—were streaked and daubed with blood and filth, while his struggles had churned earth and snow and gore into a horrible mire. I am ashamed to say I hesitated.

Oh, Muire, I thought, *woman, for pity's sake.* So I went to him, kneeling down beside him in the ice and the mud and the blood. I reached out an uncertain hand for his porcelain muzzle, and I let what Light remained shine out of my eyes, feeling as if it faded already. I had never touched one of the valraven before: the angelic destriers were for better warriors than I.

He grew quiet at my touch, and I almost wept at the terrible extent of his wounds. He sighed and pushed his face against me, as a horse might with a friend. That act, somehow, struck me with more pity and horror than any other thing that I had seen on all that cruel and terrible day. How many fallen? How many failures? And not the least of them mine. I struck the tear from my eye: I was not deserving of pity, even my own.

The day had gone poorly for Othinn's children. Far greater of my brethren than I fell that day. I had seen Strifbjorn dragged down by the trickster's hungry wolves; seen Menglad Brightwing die on a kiss, her will and being snuffed out like a candle flame; seen Arngeir thrown down and savaged by the tarnished.

To my eternal shame and sorrow, I fled the field and lived, while my brethren fell like tears.

Æðorian's weight across my back felt like a silent accusation. Only respect for the blade kept me from hurling her away. I was no longer fit to bear her.

Instead, I spoke softly to the stallion. "The Aesir have failed," I told him. "The enemy have the day, and the war, and you are dying, Bright one. Can I give you mercy?"

He squealed in fury, knocking me onto my back as he surged upright, bracing himself spraddle-legged on broken limbs. LIVE! he demanded in my mind, more the shape of defiance than any sense of a word.

I scrambled to my feet and stood, panting, facing him. Broken, unbowed, he met my gaze until I looked down and stepped away. I spread my hands so that he could see how the Light flickered back from them, rolling slowly up my arms as if being peeled away. Soon, the aura that shielded me would be gone.

"I abandoned the Light," I whispered, "and without it I can do nothing to heal you."

But then an edgy, grieving howl drifted to my ears from across the ice. I shuddered. The wounded vile-wolf twitched and whined, and I glanced reflexively at the sky. There were no stars to be seen and, not far away, the vile-wolves were hunting.

"I will be quicker than they," I told him. He seemed to shrug his broken wings and turned his face away from me, as if in dismissal. I shrugged as well, turning to leave him to his choice, there on the snow-silenced battlefield.

But I passed too close to the crippled vile-wolf, which lunged and snapped at me with a moment's desperate agility. I skittered back through the snow, tripping, and tumbled wildly into a bloodied drift. My fingers found the object I had fallen over, recognizing armor and cooling flesh. Suddenly, I understood why the valraven had not flown up, why he had stood and permitted himself to be savaged.

I had fallen over the corpse of his rider, whom he would not have left while she yet breathed. The drifting snow had covered her. As I struggled to disentangle myself I saw the sword by her outstretched hand, ice freezing to the lashes of her open eyes, and the blood-spotted banner on which she had fallen. It was dark midnight blue, spangled in silver: starlight on the water.

The stallion regarded me, and shame rose in me in response to the weight of his gaze. I stood and dried my hands carefully on my trousers before I drew Æðorian and stood beside him.

"What is my life worth, now, anyway?" I asked him conversationally. "As well die here with you as later, alone."

He snorted, crimson blood dripping from his nostrils. In pity I reached out and laid my hand against his cheek. *No such courage in all the world*, I thought, and made myself ready to die.

Lean shadows drifting across the white distance, they came. Their ribcages protruded with eternal hunger; their backbones and tails were knobby and spined. Great splayed paws held them lightly on the snow, and their maws dripped slaver as they fell down on us like a breaking storm.

It was a small pack, four of them—not the dozen it had taken to pull down Strifbjorn. Still, I was not Strifbjorn, and the crystal sword was dark in my hand.

The first vile-wolf lunged in low while two others went wide to flank me. The fourth slunk around to the right side, apparently considering itself enough for one wounded valraven. The stallion somehow reared up on his taloned hind feet, striking out with cloven forehooves. The vile-wolf dodged away: the warsteed was too slow, too gravely wounded. When he came down, his hooves barely grazed the beast's flank, and he fell heavily to his knees.

I brought Æðorian up from low guard in a sweeping blow, almost weeping at the darkness in her crystal blade. She connected with the vile-wolf, opening a gash along its ribs and belly. It was thrown back, but quickly rose to its feet and turned to nose the bloodless wound. Its molten, ravenous gaze returned to me, and the tail wagged once, twice, a third time in slow mockery.

In utter silence, it lunged again.

I had turned to deal with the two that were attempting to take my flank. Vile-wolves hunt like wolves; one distracts the prey while the rest make the true attack. I held Æðorian in my hand like a lance, and the closest vile-wolf sheered off from her point.

I spun slowly to keep the three vile-wolves in my sight. The last one skulked up to the downed valraven behind me with a mincing, predatory gait, but I had no attention to spare for it or him. I shook hair and sweat from my eyes, and raised my blade once more, feeling my lips curve back in a vicious smile.

Perhaps a bit late, but I was dying now as I should have died that afternoon. There was some satisfaction to be had in it.

And then, as things will in combat, everything happened at once.

I caught a flurry of motion from the corner of my eye as the stallion suddenly, gracelessly, moved again. At that moment, all three of the vile-wolves stalking me lunged.

Æðorian seemed to move with a will of her own: she sang through the air in a hurtling arc and clove the first vile-wolf in two. It shrieked—a high, thin sound—and fell to the ground, forelimbs still scrabbling toward me. The second one fastened its jaws in my forearm only because I threw that arm up in front of my throat, while the third tried to swing wide and hamstring me.

Half spun about by the force of the vile-wolf's assault, I glimpsed the source of the commotion behind me. The fourth vile-wolf had tried to tear out the stallion's throat, thinking him finished. He was not; as I watched, his teeth clamped in the vile-wolf's shoulder. That great white head snapped up to shake the foul creature the way a spitz shakes a rat, and it screamed, screaming again when the valraven threw it against the ground. Unable to stand, he knelt on it and tore twitching gobs of darkness and bone out of it with his teeth.

I brought Ædorian down desperately, barely getting her blade in between the fangs of the attacking vile-wolf and my thigh. The other one dragged at my arm, still silent. Meanwhile, the front half of the one I had dismembered hauled itself toward me grimly, gold eyes narrow in concentration and hate. Forgetting myself, forgetting our defeat, in fear and in horror I called up on the lost and fallen Light…

And was answered by a flash and a flare in Ædorian's crystal blade—a surge of brilliance crackling from my eyes, streaming from my mouth, and shining madly from the wound in my arm. The valraven had torn the struggling vile-wolf's flesh away from something red beneath its deathless hide; I saw him sink his teeth into that something and rip it free. The vile-wolf gave a horrible shriek.

The circling beast leaped at me, and I swung Ædorian in a flat curve that bisected its chest. The blade flamed and spat, and the vile-wolf came apart like a torn feather-pillow as Ædorian pierced its heart. The one that had my arm released its hold and whirled to run, but I took two steps after it and drove the blade down between its shoulders, feeling the spine part and then the brief resistance of its unholy heart. It gave a despairing cry and expired.

I glanced at the valraven, who had ripped the heart of the no-longer-twitching vile-wolf in two. He cast it aside with something like disgust, and looked up at me.

Ignoring the blood running down my arm, I turned back and dispatched the injured vile-wolf. Then I wiped Ædorian on my trousers and slid her into her sheath. A proper cleaning would have to wait.

I knelt beside the valraven again, and laid my hand on his shoulder. **Kasimir,** I heard inside my heart, and my eyes went wide. I knew the honor he did me. Only a valraven's rider may know his name.

"I am not worthy, Bright one."

He just snorted and let himself slump down in the bloody snow. **Will you wait with me?**

It was not so much words as a desire, a feeling in my heart, and I nodded.

And then I felt the Light singing within me and started to my feet. "Maybe," I said aloud, "Maybe…"

I shook my head, holding out my hands. A lacy cirrus of fire flickered along my skin. "I can try…" I whispered. I already knew his answer. Live.

Miracles happen as they will. I spread my hands open, and I called on the Light.

It was not as it had been in the past: I could not feel the overwhelming presence and comfort of the Light surround me. Rather, what I called came from within, and seemed limited in scope. The quality was different—rather than the certainty of what to do and how to do it, I knew what my options were: the mercy he had already refused… or a gamble on wild magic that might very well destroy us both.

I knew I could not heal him. But perhaps I could turn him into something else. I chose, and called on the Light.

The earth itself quivered and ruptured, deep and deep. The snow at the crevice melted instantly, the torn, brown soil laid bare. The valraven shuddered, trying to surge to his feet, but quieted at my whispered plea. And then, bone edging through his skin, he did scramble up. Molten metal crawled from the earth, stinking of some chthonic forge, and when it touched his flesh he screamed. *Oh, Light,* I prayed, *what are you doing?*

There was no answer.

I smelled scorching meat, heard it sizzle over his piteous cries. He shrieked, but he did not struggle, and I know not how, but he stood. Over the awful crying I heard the nauseating crack of twisted bones healing, of bent limbs straightening. The white-hot metal burned through him, reworked him inside and out, made him more than alive, something alien, something *other*… And yet he endured. He lived on.

I watched in awe and horror, heard my own voice as the voice of another. "Iron horse," I whispered. "Iron angel…" I looked down at my hands.

The Light had left them.

Conscious, impassive now, he straightened slowly. Both heads on their long necks turned to regard me, white rings already fading around living brown eyes in sculptured faces. His new skin cooled, his new bones hardened, and his bright new wings opened and flexed, feather-perfect. I could hear the soft whisper of the tiny interlocking barbs on the pinions as he fanned his wings like a declaration of war. Steam hissed as he took a step and a low, slow whistling breath blew from his nostrils. He shook out his mane, and each hair of it was a single, gleaming, steel-blue wire.

The snow sublimated under his footsteps as he came to me, my clothes smoldering where he touched. I laid my hand flat against his shoulder and jerked it away in a moment, scalded.

I took a step or two back.

"What are you?" I whispered.

Kasimir, he answered, as if in my ear. **Sorcery and steel.**

"What are you?" I asked again, and his eyes were warm and soft.

I am War.

I turned my head, looked away. "Why did you tell me your name?" I knew the answer. "I am not worthy of you."

I would not choose one unworthy.

"I fled." He graced me with the steady regard of four patient eyes. "I fled the vile-wolves, and the tarnished ones, and I hid while our allies died."

Heat rolled from him—the heat of the forge, the heat of a summer's day: a physical pressure. My torn arm ached; it was still bleeding. "I am a coward. I will bring you pain."

What pain could equal the pain of this creation? The antlered head ducked suddenly down, and he folded his wings neatly and began to vaporize the snow about his hooves with short, sharp nudges of his muzzle—shyly, and so like a horse. I turned away again. I was not worthy.

"Kasimir," I said softly, just to taste it once, to taste the wonder of his offer. "The Light has failed."

We are the Light that remains, he replied, and I could make no answer. *He* had not failed. *He* had not broken, and run. *His* honor was intact. How could I remain with him and face him?

"No," I said. "Oh, no…" And while I still could, I took the first step away.

Behind me I heard the rattle and the rustle of his wings. **When you name me, I shall come.** A knowing feeling with his next words. **You will come back to me. You are not so fallen as you think, and I am the coming Age of the World.** With a masterful leap he was airborne and gone, and I was blessedly, terribly, finally alone.

I stood on that battlefield a long time before I returned to myself. The snow fell all that night and into the morning, and the dawn was recognizable chiefly by a lightening of the gloom. The cold did not trouble me, and I did not feel the wind then as I would feel it later.

In the end, the simple passage of time brought me back to my senses.

I had no way to bury the bodies in the frozen ground and not enough fuel to raise a pyre for them. I labored in silence and with bare rest, piling up course upon course of stones there on the killing ground, at the edge of the cliff over the ocean where we had turned at bay. When I could not reach the top I packed snow into a ramp, up which I toiled until I had built a wall eight feet tall and a bowshot long. The wound in my arm healed quickly, although it left a white scar. I did not know cold, then. I did not know hunger, although to my sorrow I had known and quailed at fear.

When I fell into a snowdrift and could not lift myself, I rested. I chewed snow from the battlefield for water—for thirst was beginning to haunt me—and sometimes that snow was frozen solid with the blood of my brethren. I built a wall. When the wall was built I stacked the bodies in its lee, course upon course of them, and by the time I had finished that task I felt the first stirrings of what I would eventually come to identify as hunger.

There was nothing to eat. *I am becoming mortal*, I thought, and welcomed the seeming revelation. Mortals live a little, proscribed time, and then their shells are laid to rest, and their spirits hale off I know not where. Surprising, I know. But my kind and I were always firmly tied to the earth under our feet, the stars overhead, the Light upon the waters in the primeval darkness.

I could do nothing for my hunger so I worked. I laid crystal blades in the hands of dead warriors, and I found ways to move the bodies of the valraven to lie among those of their masters. I buried the tarnished as well as the valkyries and the einherjar: we were brothers again, in death. The vile-wolves... I left them where they had fallen.

It snowed and I was thankful for the snow, because I did not wish to look up and see the sun, or the stars. I found one crystal blade abandoned, washed up among the rocks, and I put her with the rest: Svanvítr, with a knotted brass pommel more elaborate than that of my own blade. I knew to whom she had belonged, although I sorrowed that I did not find his body among those of the tarnished.

Ragnarok. It was prophesied. It was *not* foretold that any of us would survive.

I walled the bodies around, stone upon stone, and then I levered up the slabs for the barrow's roof and laid them in place. I grew thinner and paler as day piled upon day like stone upon stone. My strength waned at first, and then began to grow again, far outstripping that of mortal Men. I did not call upon the aid of miracles: I feared I would be answered, and I feared more that I would not.

In the end it was complete, and the snow stopped falling, and the clouds broke, and I stood over the grave and watched the sunrise paint the grey granite boulders with lichens of blood and time. I hoisted Æðorian to my shoulder. I had thought of leaving her there, to mark the barrow, but it seemed... indecent. So I kept her. Instead, I plunged into a crevice the staff of a tattered standard of midnight blue, decorated with myriad tiny flaring four-pointed stars in glittering silver.

The sun flamed, breathtaking, crimson and incarnadine and vermilion and hellebore and scarlet; I gasped in awe as it rose over the sea. I breathed it in with all my strength, coughing at the unexpected clash of cold air with my lungs. It was new, all new, and I hated every shiver and chilblain and cracked lip and droplet of snot.

I thought of stepping into that sunrise from the top of the barrow. I pictured my fall, tumbling, and the wreck of my body on the sea-ripped boulders below. I imagined the brief sensation of flight, considered it very carefully, and I closed my eyes.

I spread my arms wide, feeling the bitter sea-breeze tug at me, almost lifting me up, and I took a deep and singing breath. This time, I did not choke on it.

I stepped forward, and the echo arrested my movement. **Live.** I struggled, tangled in a spiderweb of doubt, of despair, of self-hatred: *I'm no good to anyone and it will be quicker than waiting fifty mortal years to die and no one will grieve for me and Strifbjorn is dead anyway and who cares, who cares, who cares?*

Silence. Long, still, empty silence. And then his voice, or the memory of his voice: I was too far gone in hunger and grief and exhaustion to know which. **Live**, it said. **One makes what difference one can.**

And the moment passed.

I opened my eyes. The sunrise was over: there were splinters of gold dancing on the dark water far out to sea, and that was all. It looked like a path.

I turned around and headed south, toward the lands of men.

HIGH IRON

There had always been jobs that paid hardworking men well: men of scant social grace, men with histories, men of mahogany or copper or freckled skin unacceptable to their era. Paid well, that is, if you didn't mind losing a few fingers, catching a red-hot rivet in a tin funnel—the way Clardy's great-grandfather did—and didn't mind the risk of dying, a stain like a burst mosquito, on the pavement eighty-six stories down.

Pete Clardy's family were ironworkers from way back. Buildings didn't go up that way anymore, boots on steel. Which is why Clardy found himself hanging in microgravity in a bar called Mike's on an unhappy excuse for a planetesimal.

Clardy drank a beer, which was skunked, but he didn't complain. It was all skunked; it was still beer. He had his spotless boot propped on a spotless bench and his back wedged into the corner where the yellow plastic wall met the grey one. He missed dirt sometimes, dammit.

"Damn Finnegan anyway," he muttered.

Yurcic looked up from her own beer, polishing the sweat off the side onto her cheek before the droplets got big enough to drift. She cocked her head at him, shaved strip of artificially copper hair drifting across her forehead. "What?"

"I said, 'Damn Finnegan.' For not putting up the cash for a wake." Clardy drained his beer, punched another one—also skunked—and sipped more slowly.

Yurcic shook her head. "Had a wife."

"I gotta kid. I still left you guys a little something, if…." Clardy knocked his own narrow, grease-black crest of hair out of his eyes. It was the same way his more-times-great-grandfather might have worn it. Clardy didn't know the source of the tradition, but it was practical enough.

"Yeah. If." Yurcic took her beer a little more slowly. Wise, he thought, given that the compact, stocky, little body under her coverall couldn't have pushed fifty-five kilos, Downside. Like Clardy, she kept one foot on the floor, white-clean magnetic boot holding her down. "You've got a kid?"

"Girl." He smiled, paternal pride wrinkling the corners of sharp, black eyes. "Sixteen. Smart. Mother won't talk to me since I got out of the joint, but takes my money just fine. Katy—she's gonna go to college."

"I've got a kid too," she said. "Wish my old man had thought so highly of me." Yurcic finished her beer. "You're right. This ain't much of a wake. Hel-lo…."

He followed her gaze. "Fresh meat." Spine stiffening just a little as he noticed the attenuated body in the white coveralls.

She nodded. "That was quick."

"Spacer," he said. "Look at the scrawny muscles. He's from Outside, not even Upside."

"Must be off the *Eagle*." The *Bombay Eagle*, a non-Company ship, had made station the day before. "What's he doing in miner whites?"

Clardy sucked his lip. "Floater got kicked off," he said at last, with satisfaction, nipple of the beer clinking against his teeth. "Had to take an honest job. Screwed up aboard ship somehow, and they terminated his contract."

"Huh. How can you tell?"

Clardy motioned with an index finger. A thick wad of synthetic covered the back of the floater's hand. "They ripped his service chip. He can't go home."

The spacer caught the line of his gaze and gave him a hesitant smile. Clardy glanced away.

Yurcic laughed and killed her beer. "So either of us *can* go home, Clardy?"

Clardy grunted. "Hope he's not on my crew, that's all."

He was.

He offered to rope Clardy in, even, though the senior miner mocked him for his caution. "Booster pack," Clardy said. "I drift, I come back."

The spacer—O'Shaughnessy, still wearing a thick head of red hair to go with the freckles—nodded. "Anybody come after me if I Fall?"

"Got your pack on?"

O'Shaughnessy nodded again. Clardy coughed in his hand before he pulled his own helmet on, sealing the zipstrip with a touch. He reached out, slammed and sealed the spacer's faceplate, leaned their heads together. "Keep it on. It's a long way Down. Outsider."

The spacer flinched away from the disdain in his voice. Clardy had reason to think of that later.

"Pocahae," Clardy muttered as he seated the last of ten charges, setting the detcord, and sealing the net around the little rock they'd picked out of the swarm of others. He fired his pack and backed away. It wasn't his tribe, but what the hell: the sentiment applied. *Today is a good day to die.*

The rock read rich in ferrous compounds, a good strike. A lot of them were water and hydrogen ice, useful, but the real money was in the high iron. More in the bank. If he lived long enough to put his kid through school, Clardy was going home with money to retire on not too long after it.

High iron. A whole different meaning now than when his great-great-grandfather had worked the Empire State, his great-grandfather the World Trade Center. His People had been prized in the trades even then.

Clardy's forefathers weren't afraid of heights. Clardy laughed at the thought and turned his head to regard the sprawl and wonder of the great seething sulfurous arch of the planet, ringed in a dirty white wedding band, covering half his horizon. The other way the view was cold and limitless, stars like floating phosphorescence in a bottomless sea.

He looked over at O'Shaughnessy, clumsily tying off his side of the net that would hold the ore fragments together after the blast. The tow line was set. Clardy backed away. He didn't bother to tell the new kid to find cover before they blasted.

He'd learn or he wouldn't last. Not like anybody would notice one less floater, Upside. Goddamned floaters. The old joke: Would you want your sister to marry one?

Hell no. His sister had, and he'd never see her again. She'd signed aboard the *Montreal*, and the *Montreal* almost never came home. She wouldn't be back in-system from her first three legs, to Byhand and out to Yonder, until Clardy was ready to retire for real. Not that he expected to live that long.

When he was being honest.

The net wasn't tight on O'Shaughnessy's side, but Clardy didn't mention that either. O'Shaughnessy'd learn. Or he wouldn't last.

Some old sense of honor might have twinged in Clardy, but he shook it off. Some people just didn't belong up in the iron.

He powered up his pack, and, streaming blue light like a toy model of a spaceman, took cover before the blast.

It was a rock as big as his fist, and it blew through the too-loose net and ricocheted twice before it smacked Clardy square in the middle of his pack. Transferred momentum knocked him tumbling, but the rock chipped off enough velocity on the ricochets so the suit's rigid shielding soaked up most of the impact. It didn't hole him, and it didn't break his back, but it knocked him in all the wrong directions.

Spinning, Clardy fell Down.

He cursed and keyed his pack. Nothing. Twisting his head in the helmet, he saw a thin, nauseating spiral of propellant tracing his somersault.

"Clardy. *Clardy!*" A woman's voice. Yurcic.

"Yeah."

"Any control?"

"Nothing. I'm not holed. Can you come and get me?"

"Hell. Clardy…." Her hesitation was full of white-silver agony. The distant yellow sun was slipping around the curve of the big agate-hued planet, flaring the rings and the atmosphere into incandescent silhouette.

Clardy took the second-coldest breath of his life. The coldest one, he thought, was yet to come. "Fuck it, Yurcic. You've got a kid."

She almost spat in her determination. "Clardy. I'll come. For your girl's sake—"

"You try it, Liz Yurcic, and I'll open my damn faceplate. You've got a *kid*." Nobody came Upside unless they needed the money, unless they had nothing to lose.

A third voice. "I'll go."

O'Shaughnessy.

"Don't you come Down here, floater," Clardy said.

"Hah. I've got a window. Hang tough, Clardy, you're not Falling that fast." Yet. "Kick your beacon on."

That used up power. "Die faster," Clardy answered.

"Freeze or Fall, dirt-foot," the spacer said.

Hell. Clardy keyed his beacon and watched the planet turn.

It was a pretty thing: swirls of sulfur and water ice banding the surface of the atmosphere. The pressure got so intense at the bottom, Clardy had heard, that the gasses took on the qualities of metals. Whatever the hell that meant.

Guess that would be some low iron, then, he thought with detached humor, watching the damn thing come to kill him.

Nah. Floater's right. You'll freeze before you Fall.

He wondered if it was already getting a bit chilly.

Sorry, Katy. Wanted to come to your graduation, when your ma couldn't keep us apart anymore. I've never been a good man. But I did want to come to your graduation.

The big, old planet spun, or maybe it was Clardy spinning; it was so hard to tell. Falling ain't so bad. Wish I could have kept that stupid floater from coming after me, though, Clardy thought, and his radio buzzed.

"I've got a visual on you," O'Shaughnessy said in his ear. "Looks like you've got a little atmosphere leak after all. Just a trace though, I'll patch it."

Clardy mumbled something, feeling sleepy. Something tugged at his suit, and he swatted at it, worsening the tumble. A hard jerk of inertia, and the spinning stopped.

A lungful of fresh air, and his head stopped spinning too. "How the hell did you catch up to me?"

O'Shaughnessy laughed at him, face to face behind the helmet, hooking him under the armpits with both forearms. "Dead reckoning, dirt-foot. I grew up playing tag in this shit." He jerked his head back over his shoulder at the infinitesimally receding planet. "Spacers aren't afraid of Falling. Besides, it was my side of the net that tore. I owed it to you."

Clardy shook his head, swallowed blood from a bitten lip so the blobs wouldn't smear his mask. "Damnfool floater." He stopped. "No, damnfool me. I saw the net was rigged wrong. I figured it would teach you a lesson."

"You were right," O'Shaughnessy said. "Think maybe you learned one too."

And here's the fucking moral of the fucking story, Clardy thought. "Yeah?"

"Yeah. Next time, you'll let me clip your safety line before you try to kill me, you stupid son of a bitch."

"I still don't like you," he said, when they had been silent too long.

O'Shaughnessy laughed and punched him on the shoulder through his suit. "And I still don't give a shit whether you like me or not." He paused. "What's your kid's name? Yurcic said you had a kid."

She had. "Katy," Clardy said, reluctantly. Not wanting to share her. "I've never met her. Her mom keeps me away."

"Pretty name," O'Shaughnessy said. "Figure she deserves to meet her old man some day?"

"Figure if her old man deserves to meet her." The seasick yellow planet spun under the floater's boots, but that wasn't where Clardy's dizziness came from. "Figure if she'll want to when it's time. Her mom's got the right of it, O'Shaughnessy. I ain't no good father. I ain't no good man."

Clardy felt O'Shaughnessy's shoulders rise and fall inside his suit, knew it for a shrug and a dismissal. Moving on. "Figure a man learns something new every day."

EE "DOC" CUMMINGS

ravening cruiserbeams
hurled across an unresisting sky:
grapple slickly withal
(brave men dine on
                pan fried steak)
indomitable. hurling
atomic violence in concentrated quintessence
: blindingly brilliant annihilation

(a
sh
ie
ld

f
a
l
l
s
)

nobody, not even boskone, has such big guns

THE DEVIL YOU DON'T

The stranger's wide-brimmed hat a cast darkness across his face that the slanting sun could not relieve. He forked a dust-dun gelding as if he slept there, his big, spare frame draped in a worn poncho that might once have been black, his shadow spreading ragged black wings over the earth behind him and the flanks of his pale dappled mount. The gelding's trudging feet raised yellow puffs of dust from the hardpan between the sagebrush; perfectly round, they tasted of fear.

No one stepped into the street to meet him. A curious hush descended over our little town, which squatted on the edge of the desert like a sunbaked lizard on a rock.

I didn't go out to *meet* him, either; I was already strolling down Main Street's clapboard sidewalk in my severe rust-and-grey dress, an open parasol shading my head. I wore a blued-steel, ivory-handled eight-shooter strapped to my hip and a derringer tucked into my corset, but my ancient and powerful sword was hidden under the floor of a little three-room house on the outskirts of town. It didn't suit the times.

Following my Sunday evening habit, I was on my way to dinner at the Ivory Dog.

The stranger's gaze swept over me without pausing. His eyes burned turquoise above a dust-streaked red bandanna, his nose gaunt and broken behind it. I didn't think he'd miss much, but I strolled along the right-hand side of the street, and the bustle of my skirt hid the gun hung on my left hip. What passed for women's clothing in this country and century was awkward—worse than the bliauts and surcotes we robed ourselves in, when the world and I were young.

But here, out from under the eye of the fervent new Church that was rising in the Old World, I could be a schoolteacher and a doctor. I was of service, and the restlessness of my shame and failure only chewed my heels a little, in this place, and that only deep in the night.

I turned sideways and slipped into the saloon, as if disconcerted by the stranger's gaze. Something about it, indeed, disturbed me: something about him and his horse the color of desert sand and salt flats. I felt him appraise and dismiss me: small, drab, inconsequential. It did not distress me to be underestimated.

Duncan behind the bar glanced up at me when I entered, smiling across the room. Half-a-dozen customers, including old John Jeremiah Kale, the cattle-man, dotted the big, dim room, but the bartender managed a grin only for me. A big man, Miles Duncan, with flaming red hair, missing two fingers on his left hand and one on his right. He used to be a railwayman, a switcher. When the cars claimed his dexterity, he took to tending bar, and he kept a ten gauge under it and his old fiddle hung up on the wall behind.

"Evening, Miss Maura," he greeted me in his slow, endless drawl. It wasn't my name, but it was close enough, and the one he knew me by, and it would do. I had been living in Pitch Creek for two years. The name I was using, Maura MacAydan—"fire-child"—amused me, and was close enough to the real one that I turned around when I heard it called. And though the islanders are dark, if any commented that "MacAydan" did not go with my dust-fair hair and pale grey eyes, I could always smile and answer, "It doesn't, does it?" People don't ask a lot of questions on frontiers.

Duncan's hand trembled as he slid my whiskey across the bar, betraying ner-vousness, as did a quick flicker of desert-sky eyes toward the door. "Booth in the back?"

"If you please, Duncan." I liked Duncan. He reminded me of one of my long-dead brothers, a Child of the Light named Arngeir whom I'd watched die on a snowy battlefield, over a thousand years before.

As I slipped around the corner of the bar and picked up my drink, I murmured so just he and Kale could hear me, "Trouble brewing?"

Duncan looked puzzled, but Kale shrugged, tipped his bottle and then set it back. "Question of the devil you know and the devil you don't," he answered, just as softly.

"Where's Sheriff Brady?" I asked. Rumor had it Marlowe Brady beat his wife, who was the mayor's daughter, but the mayor didn't seem to care and Brady had a shining star, so there wasn't a hell of a lot to be done about it.

A gnawing unease chased the whisky down my throat. Well, perhaps I could have done something, but in the time since the Light failed, I've learned a few things. One is that Evil persists in the world, and another is that no good deed goes unpunished, and the third... The third thing I've learned is that even my kind can grow tired, in time.

And sometimes the best place for a blazing sword is wrapped in oilcloth, under the parlor floor.

Kale snorted into his liquor. "Passed out under a cot in his jail, no doubt. He was on a two-day bender as of Friday evening, and I didn't see him in church this morning."

"Liz Brady was there," Duncan offered. The sheriff's wife never missed a sermon. I nodded and would have replied, but there was a heavy step on the creaking wood porch and Kale's head hunkered down in front of his shoulders again in the posture of an indifferent drunk. Both hands curled loosely around his squat, blue drinking bowl as though he cradled something precious. I ducked into that dark booth that Duncan had mentioned and watched the stranger's entrance in the bartender's looking glass.

The stranger had pulled the bandanna down off his face, revealing a nose even more broken than it had seemed on the street. White lines of scars bisected it in two places, standing out stark against the sun-leathered brown of his skin. His left cheekbone had also been shattered long ago, and his face was not symmetrical. *Pistol-whipped*, I thought. *Probably left for dead.* They didn't look like the kind of scars you got when somebody just wanted to teach you a lesson.

Grey hair poked out from under his dust-covered black hat, and the blue eyes were framed by grizzled brows. He frowned—no, *sneered* at the world with lips that betrayed a certain sensuality, arrogance, and old pain.

Met by silence, he surveyed the Dog from the doorway, and then his bootnails clicked as he stepped inside. His spurs made a little sound as he walked, reminding me of the sound made by a rattlesnake, or dried leaves blowing across stone. His step was certain, although he walked with the heavy trace of a limp. I stifled a familiar sensation below my breastbone, a rising answer to his purpose as the Light within me sought to flare in response.

This man traveled on the purpose for which I was made, and which I abandoned, so many centuries ago.

He had come in the name of vengeance.

A rush of lavender scent and musk, the rustle of satin and lace. Susie intercepted him five steps into the room. Her locks were gold, her looks were free, and if a superabundance of makeup and care made her look older than her twenty-two years, that was the price of her profession. Her dress was deep scarlet today, and she moved with surprising grace for all its weight and her tottering shoeheels. Duncan was sweet on her, but Susie said she'd rather whore any day than ever rely on another man's kindness again.

"Hey there, stranger," she cooed. "Buy a girl a drink?" She laid one manicured hand on his arm as he glanced down at her. Susie was not a little woman, but this stranger was one long pour of ice. His grimace deepened, and he shook his head.

"You ain't the lady I was looking for," he muttered. His voice ran over me like charged fluid: the voice of my brother. A voice I had last heard raised in wrath and fury, on a battlefield long ago… a battlefield I survived, to my eternal disgrace, because I fled it, while my brethren's blood and vitals stained the snow. It was all I could do to keep my seat, and not rise and spin and cry his name.

It's not Strifbjorn, I calmed myself. *You buried Strifbjorn. And besides, this man doesn't look like him.* I swallowed, studying that ruined old face in the looking glass. *Look under the scars. What do you see?*

His reflected eyes met mine, a puzzled expression clouding them. He must have seen my head jerk up and my body shudder when he spoke. I was grateful for the shadows of the booth, more grateful to see no shadow of recognition in his eyes—which were too blue, anyway, not the Light-filled silver of my long-dead brother's. *Worlds and centuries away. It cannot be him.*

But it felt like him. I wondered if he might somehow have returned, looking for me, to deal out the wrath I so richly deserved. And then I dismissed the thought as his gaze turned away from me, disinterested again.

Duncan's help, Millie, brought over my chicken and biscuits a moment later, and the stranger's eyes skipped from the mirror to Duncan's face. The stranger stepped forward, brushing past Susie as if she wasn't there. "You the proprietor?" he asked Duncan, meeting the bigger man's eyes. Duncan nodded, and men cleared out from between the two of them.

"Miles Duncan," Duncan told him, his thick lips twitching just a bit. "What can I get you?"

The stranger nodded, as if Duncan had asked him his name. "They call me Stagolee. And I'll have what the little lady in the corner is having."

He means me, I realized, feeling the weight of his eyes in the mirror again. *Stagolee.* The name nagged at me until I remembered where I'd heard it before. An old ballad, in another place, in a different time, about a bad man by that name, who gunned down a lady's lover and was slain by the lady in turn.

Four hundred years before, in another part of the world.

He did not, to my relief, sit down beside me. I picked at my meal in silence as he sat at the bar and nursed one whiskey and ate, and ate some more. When I could no longer stomach staring at my trencher, I got up to leave, almost forgetting my parasol. There was no way out but past him, and when I stepped out of the booth he knew about the pistol. His gaze was cool, appraising. I left without looking back.

The night came on with an unusual thunderstorm: almost no rain, savage heat lightning. The misting precipitation dampened the weathered sides of my house, which had been whitewashed once and might someday be again. Thick walls and a sod roof muffled the thunder. But I lay awake in my bed, the image of Strifbjorn's ruined face before my eyes, and I wondered what had come before, and what might happen next.

The knock came before sunrise. I opened the door on it carelessly, inured by years of peaceful living, expecting a frantic mother or husband who would drag me into the night with my little black bag in hand, to the sound of my chestnut mare's grumpy snorts and stamps. Instead, a specter leaned out of the darkness beyond my door, a nothing drizzle splattering off his hat and onto my porch, his gun already in his hand. He pointed it at my midsection and smiled. "Miss MacAydan," Stagolee whispered, "I do hope you won't mind if I come in."

I nodded and backed up a step, feeling my skin itch as it tried to crawl out of the path of a potential bullet. I didn't enjoy having bows pointed at me when I was far more immortal than I had become, and experience and improved technology had not improved the sensation. Stagolee held the weapon with familiar ease, and I did as I was told. "Come on in then, Mister Stagolee."

He grimaced and dripped on my knotted rag rug. "Not Mister," he answered. I turned my back on him, praying that he wouldn't shoot a woman in a nightgown in the back, trying to look small and slack and harmless. "You're the doctor in this pissant town."

I nodded. "And the schoolmistress." I took two steps forward, did not hear him following, glanced back. He was right behind me, and I suppressed a shudder. His spurs hadn't even jangled. "Can I take you into the parlor? Get you a cup of tea or a drink? You must be wet through…"

His laugh was a flat, bitter thing like burned coffee. "Please yourself, Miss MacAydan. I just want a few answers."

I entered the parlor and sat, and he and the gun followed me. I moved fairly quickly, and he never complained, and the barrel of the revolver never wavered. Worse and worse. I tried to keep my own expression pleasant, but felt it sliding toward a frown. *This is not Strifbjorn. Not my brother. Strifbjorn is dead. This is simply someone very much like him, as is bound to be born every once in a very long life.*

"What are the questions, Stagolee?"

I had chosen a hard, straight-backed chair. The one facing it was deeper and softer, difficult to get out of. He defeated my purpose by sitting on the edge of the desk. Damn and damn him.

His lips writhed into something that might be a smile. "I'm looking for a woman named Elizabeth Browning." He hesitated. "At least, that was her name. She married a man named Marlowe Brady." The gun never shivered. I felt its point of aim like a pressure—a slow, unwelcome caress.

"He's the sheriff in this town. What's your interest in Liz?"

That cruel, crooked smile crept an inch wider. "Suppose I tell you? What do you care? You're awful brave, for a lady with a revolver pointed at her belly."

"This is not the first time I've had a gun pointed at me," I mentioned casually. I was searching his eyes for any sign of recognition, finding only that confused familiarity.

He nodded. "I imagine not. No tears or hysterics, and you carry that pistol of yours like you know how to use it. You haven't got it now, though, and no fast draw in the world could save you if you did."

"I know." I sighed, and forced myself to sit back. "What do you want to know about Liz?"

It took five minutes. When it was over, he had me stand and turn to face the wall. I heard the click of the hammer being cocked, and braced myself to drop, spin, and kick. His breathing stopped, and I began to move...

Only to find myself facing an empty room.

I was up before sunrise, and I did not put on a dress. I dressed in canvas pants and flannel shirt like any man, high boots on my small feet. I had my red mare, Rowan, saddled before my bad-tempered brown and gold cock crew. As my housekeeper walked up to my door I bid her good day and rode off toward town.

Rowan was feeling her oats, or perhaps the tension running down the reins made her prance. The earth showed no dampness from the night's drizzle, the early mist burning off without a trace. Another suffocating day, a prickle of anticipation soaking the air, and the restive mare between my legs did nothing to reassure me. I checked my gun twice, and stopped outside of town to chamber an eighth and final round.

Duncan was sweeping the porch of the Dog. He glanced up grimly as I hitched Rowan out front. "You usually walk."

"Today is different. What do you know about this Stagolee?"

He studied me intently for a moment. "Trousers suit you, Miss Maura. But this is no mess for you to be interfering in." He turned back to his broom, though the porch was twice swept already.

"Stagolee showed up on my doorstep last night with a gun, Miles," I said. "I want the story. I don't want to get involved. I'm out of the business of rescuing maidens. But I do want to know what's going on in this town."

I'd never called him by his given name before, and he studied me. He grimaced then, and nodded, and leaned the broom up against the wall. "Come inside then. No sense standing out in the heat."

A hawk called over the desert as I followed him into the Dog. He sat me down and poured us both black coffee settled with eggshell, before sliding into a chair across from me. "What did he want?"

I drank the coffee, all but boiling, bitter and good. "Liz Brady. If I've ever treated her for anything."

"And?"

"I haven't. So he left."

Miles Duncan picked up a spoon and turned it over. Fluid light caught in the bowl, and he held it there like a magician might. For a moment, my breath ached painfully homesick in my throat. "It's an old scandal, Miss Maura. It doesn't bear much repeating. Mayor Browning doesn't like to hear it told."

James Browning was a great tall bear of a man, with hair that had been gold before it burned to ash, and muttonchop sideburns. A widower in his late fifties, and if he wasn't any better than he should be he didn't seem a lot worse, either. I cupped my mug in both hands and nodded encouragingly, but Duncan just sat for a long moment and stared up at the dust-covered old violin that hung on the wall above the looking glass behind the bar.

"I had the story from Bart Cashman," he said finally, "who had the Dog before I did. It's a local legend, but it's not told much these days…

"It was about thirty years ago, the first time Stagolee came into Pitch Creek. Mayor Browning was Sheriff Browning in those days, and he had a pretty young wife, and… Well, he had a pretty young wife, and that Stagolee was a handsome man, they say. About a year after Stagolee came into town looking for work, he and Celia Browning slipped out again together, she leaving behind her house and husband, he all his clothes in John Kale's bunkhouse, except what he had on his back.

"Browning was wild, and lit out after him—after them—like a madman. He came back two weeks later with a bullet hole in his knee, a baby girl swaddled in a rabbit's skin, and his wife's body sewn into a canvas sack. He put it about that Stagolee abandoned Celia when labor took her, and she bled to death birthing the child."

Duncan paused to finish his coffee. "So I'd say the son of a bitch has balls, walking back in here. I can't for the life of me imagine what he wants."

I remembered what Kale said to me, soft and low, and I found myself nodding. "I think I understand."

Duncan raised an eyebrow, but I shook my head. "I'm not involved."

"Uh huh," he answered, pouring more coffee into the bowls. "Me neither."

I sipped my coffee. "Miles, did I ever tell you I used to play the fiddle?"

"Really?" He fussed with the spoon some more, balancing it across his mutilated hand. He looked up at last and met my eyes. "So did I."

Things learned before the Light failed can deceive, now. I knew Strifbjorn. I knew him to be stronger, faster, wiser, more skillful, and more honorable than I. I also knew that I had been tougher and smarter and a damn sight meaner, once upon a time. Now all I had to do was remember that Stagolee was not, could not be Strifbjorn. Because otherwise I would expect him to react as Strifbjorn would react, and that could be fatal. Strifbjorn might have pointed a revolver at me—if revolvers had been invented—but Strifbjorn was dead. Unless I had been somehow deceived into believing I had buried his half-eaten corpse. But that is another story entirely.

Yes, Strifbjorn might have pointed a revolver at me. *Stagolee* might have pulled the trigger.

Pausing in the street, I realized I could still smell him, in my mind: damp leather, horse sweat, and gun oil. Fear cramped my tongue like a mouthful of dust. I shook my hair back out of my eyes and turned toward the railing where my mare was hitched, put one boot into her near-side stirrup.

I can't say why or how I found myself walking into the jailhouse.

Marlowe Brady sat with his feet propped up on his battered flat top desk, a half-penny Lone Rider serial with a lurid cover open on top of the shotgun propped across his knees. His lips moved as he read, but at least he was trying.

His dark hair was greasy and unwashed, but his clothes were spotless and his silver star shone more like a moon, it was so brightly polished. He glanced up as I came in: he had the jowls of a bullfighting dog and the shoulders to match.

"Afternoon, Miss Maura." There was a faint sneer in his voice, but he swung his feet down off the desk. My spine locked: I might be shamed and exiled, but I had once been accustomed to a certain amount of respect.

"Afternoon, Sheriff."

I could feel his gaze traveling the length of my body, lingering at my crotch. I simply stared back at him, knowing how cold my grey eyes got when the Light wasn't in them. "And what brings you here, little lady?"

I drew up a chair, because he had not asked me to sit. "I have a question for you, Sheriff. What was your wife's mother like?"

He began to start upright, and then forced himself to lean back into the chair. Deliberately, he turned his head and spat. His dark eyes swiveled back to me, and he grimaced. "She was a whore. Maybe I shouldn't say that in front of a lady…" …*but you ain't dressed like no lady, Ma'am.* "…and maybe I shouldn't speak ill of the dead, but she was a thief and a liar and a loose woman and she deserved what she got. Why the hell should I be telling you this?"

I smiled and stood, and turned back from the threshold to regard him. He knew already, of course. But it felt good to say it, anyway. "Because Stagolee is back in town."

I left him sputtering. By the time he reached the doorway to stop me, I had slipped around the corner and was gone.

Stagolee might be better than I was. But Brady was a bully and a fool.

I walked and thought for a little while before heading back to the Dog. Too long, it turned out: a big, big man with very little swagger, leaning only slightly on the walking stick he used to counter a left knee that would not bend, Mayor Browning sauntered up to me as I was climbing the stairs to the otherwise de-serted porch of the saloon. He laid a heavy, paternal hand on my shoulder and smiled. "Aren't you all gussied up?"

He stepped back a pace as I raised my eyes to his, letting a little of the Light show in them. "Evening, Mayor. What can I do for you tonight?"

"Evening, Ma'am." He paused. "My son-in-law tells me you know something about this… Stagolee." His mouth twisted as though the name tasted bad on his tongue.

"I've seen him around," I offered. I could feel him searching my face for the lie.

Browning shook his head at last. "Liz isn't safe with him here," he told me. "That murdering son of a bitch is going to swing."

"He scares me," I said, quite honestly. "I worry about what he's going to do." The threat in his voice might have been more than he had intended me to hear; his next words confirmed it.

"You just be careful, little girl." He smiled, patted my shoulder once more. "And keep away from that Stagolee. He's been the death of women before."

And he turned and stumped away, leaning on his came, and I fought the urge to let my left hand fall to my gun. He tried to look fatherly and safe and stolid and slow. But the porch didn't creak under his footsteps, and he was two hundred fifty if he was a stone, and not more than twenty of that was where it should not be.

Light and shadows. And damn it to Hel.

The next dawn was just coiling across the sere landscape when I saw Marlowe Brady shutting the door of his house behind him and swinging into the saddle of his horse before heading into town. Rowan, hidden by half-light and a stand of creosote, wanted to stamp and snort when the rangy bay went by, but I quieted her with a hand on her nose and left her tied behind the brush as I walked up to the door.

Muire, you really ought to know well enough to stay the Hel out of other people's marriages by now.

I knocked anyway.

The knees of Liz Brady's calico dress were dirty and she held a scrub brush in her right hand: she had been waxing the kitchen floor. The dress was too hot for the weather, and though she'd splashed her face at the kitchen pump when she heard my knock, she could not hide the redness of her eyes. She moved stiffly, as if her bones ached.

"Hi, Missus Brady. May I come in for a minute?" My voice and face were as open and honest as I could make them. She hesitated, glanced over her shoulder. I stepped forward.

"I don't know, Miss MacAydan. I'm awful busy…"

I lowered my voice. "Liz, let me in. Your husband's gone to town. It will be safe for a moment."

My candor shocked her, and she stepped back the quarter-inch necessary for me to bustle past. She trailed me into her own kitchen, forlorn as a shadow, and I looked from her to the half-waxed floor and found myself thinking about the oddity in the way she moved. Then I sat myself firmly down at the kitchen table while she hovered over me, wringing her hands on the handle of her brush. "Miss MacAydan..."

"Liz, call me Maura," I interrupted. "And listen. You have to get out of this house, and do it now, before he kills you."

"He'd never hurt me," she began, and then she dropped the brush in terror as I surged across the floor toward her and caught her wrists in both hands. She screamed—in agony, not in fear— tears starring her eyes. She glanced down then, the pain in her face replaced by awe and then terror as I stripped the long sleeves back from her arms with casual, inhuman strength and a horrid rending of cloth.

Black, cracked scabs encircled her wrists almost completely, thicker and worse by the knobs of the slender, birdlike bones. The marks were laid over other, older scars, and I had seen enough prisoners in my long life to recognize the like.

She was not much bigger than I, and infinitely less strong. I thought of Brady's bulldog shoulders, and felt the blinding white current of my rage rise up in me.

"Not Stagolee," I told her. "I'm not worried about Stagolee hurting you. Brady, Liz. And Browning too."

A short ride and a pot of tea later, I got her settled at the Ivory Dog. Then I got back on my red mare, rode home, and got the crowbar from the tool room in the little barn. I paced up and down the length of my house, swinging that short length of iron in my hand. The sun was moving faster than I wanted it to, and I had no way to control too many of the players in this little game.

I kicked the wall, cursed hard when an oil lamp tumbled and broke against the raw pine wallboards. Then I hefted the wrecking bar in my hands and started ripping up the parlor floor.

The sun ached on my head, despite the welcome shade of my hat. Liz lay hiding in the cool back room where Duncan kept his bed, three floors below, bandages seemingly all over her body. Duncan was with her, and the Dog was shuttered and closed, just like the rest of Main Street.

I lay on my belly on the roof, a carbine and my revolver by my side, and waited for the short shadows to appear on the street below. Sweat prickled out across my neck; lank strands of hair clung to my forehead. A familiar-unfamiliar weight rested between my shoulder blades—the sheath of a sword I had not touched in years. I stole a pull from my water bottle without raising my head, tasted leather and warm spit.

A horse stamped in the corral down the street, followed by the jingle of chains. The reek of my own sweat, oil and powder, horse manure, the midden out back of the Dog clogged my nose. A hawk called, far off, answered by another. Lovers or enemies: no way to tell from the sound of their cries. The tar on the roof under my hands was melting. I thought of the texture of things with no place on this world, in this time. Sealing wax, ski resin, rosin for a fiddle's bow.

No, rosin belongs here.

Stagolee stepped into the street first, and my thumb moved with practiced strength on the safety of the carbine. He glanced around, but from where he stood he never could have seen something that was not a breeze ruffle the white eyelet curtains in the half-open window of the upstairs bedroom of Miss Pamela's boarding house, across the street. I did, however, and I saw as well the gleam of steel and a flash of ash-colored hair.

My carbine roared and choked simultaneously with the tigerlike cough of the rifle. The gun slammed into my shoulder, and a pane of glass starred and shattered. In the street, I heard Stagolee grunt and then curse.

Another gunshot rang out of the first floor of the Ivory Dog. I was already moving when the shotgun roared its answer.

I abandoned the carbine on the roof: it would only have impeded me. Perhaps the leap was superhuman: had I not been what I am, I would not have cared to try it. As it was, the three-story drop to the ground was jarring, but my knees took most of the shock of landing. Crouched, I rolled with the landing, letting gravity take me to one side with a wind-breaking thud. I needed to keep moving, suspecting that I hadn't done more than wing Browning. The sword across my back bruised my spine.

Blood lay like a banner in the street, but no body. I gasped painfully as I dragged myself to my feet, pulling my sword over my shoulder and into my right hand.

She flared suddenly at my touch, singing with a lost and abandoned Light that might have brought tears to my eyes another day. I had more immediate concerns. Raising the sword-bearing arm to protect my face from the shards of broken glass, I threw myself in through the tavern window.

The big window at the front of the Dog had been broken before, but usually as a result of the forceful expulsion of a brawler. It exploded inward quite satisfactorily, and I caught Marlowe Brady with most of my meager weight across the back of his neck. The eight-shooter skated out of his hand and across Duncan's polished pine floor, fetching up against the base of the upright piano with a musical thump, which was echoed by the sound of the pommel of my blazing sword striking the back of Brady's head and Brady's forehead striking the floor. He fell quiet, and I rolled off him and around behind the bar.

The bullet had gone through Miles Duncan and broken the looking glass.

The blood had already slowed to a trickle, still pulsing weakly from the ragged wound in his side. I knelt in the puddles and spatters of it, remembering other pools of red, another time. As I reached for him he shook his head and might have coughed, but he had no air in his lungs to do it with. His maimed right hand lay inches from where the shotgun had fallen after discharging its useless burden into the bar-room ceiling. It made an interesting tattoo, and would make a better story, one day.

"Miles…"

"Doesn't hurt," he mouthed, and then paused as if to gather breath and strength. He braved a painful smile. "Miss Maura…"

"My fault, Miles…"

"No blame… Miss…"

I shook my head. "My name is Muire, Miles. Long story."

His hand clutched mine weakly. "Always knew… on the lam…" His face contorted as he struggled to breathe. "Last request, Muire?"

"Name it." My words had the force of a vow.

"Bar goes to Liz…" I nodded, and he shook his head to say he wasn't finished. "And Susie. You take my fiddle."

"A treasure." I squeezed his hand, not caring now if he knew my strength, and let the Light come into my eyes—perhaps to comfort him. His eyes widened, though whether he saw me or Death I will never know.

"Scared." A long pause. "See you in Hel…"

"You're going to Halla, Miles." I felt myself smile. "I know it for a fact."

"Never was a… churchgoing man…"

"Churchgoing's got nothing to do with it. They'll take you in or they'll have me to answer to."

Surely I was not lying. Surely, though the Light has failed, souls like his are not lost forever? Surely, somewhere, I have some authority still.

He drew it in, what I knew would be his final breath, and expelled it with a silent tumble of words. I heard them anyway. "…angel? On the lam?"

There was blood on my hands as I closed his eyes, blood on my hands as I picked up his shotgun and stood, just in time to hear the click behind me of a hammer being pulled back. I tensed, and heard that soft, sharp voice cut through the smoke of death and gunpowder. "Don't worry, Miss MacAydan. I know whose side you're on now."

I turned around slowly. Stagolee stood over Marlowe Brady, one booted foot on the unconscious man's back, a revolver in his right hand. He looked directly at me and smiled a crooked smile, showing three missing teeth on the ruined side of his face. Then he glanced back down at Brady and shot him once, fastidiously, in the back of the head.

My shock must have shown, because he grinned at me again and stepped around the sudden runnel of blood and brains that dribbled across the floor to mingle with Duncan's. Stagolee's left arm hung stupidly useless, and his own blood dripped from the fingers of that hand. "Browning," I said to him, and he nodded.

"Missed him," he answered. "Son of a whore."

"Browning killed her. Liz's mom, I mean."

Stagolee pulled Duncan's apron from a hook behind the bar, laid his gun on the counter, and began to improvise a sling. After half a useless, one-handed minute, he looked at me with something that might have been pleading in another man. "What do you say, Doc?"

I bound his arm up while he remained silent, pouring himself a shot into an unbloodied wooden bowl and downing it with his other hand. Then he turned his head and spat, while I stared at him expectantly.

"Yeah, I guess he did." He looked at me straight, then, as I tested my knots. I felt his brutality in that sea-blue gaze, and I remembered how he had smiled as he killed the helpless sheriff. "And another thing."

I nodded. I already knew. "She's your little girl, isn't she? Liz." I felt desolation in the look he shot me like ice in my heart.

"She is not to know," he answered, pouring himself another drink. "Her momma deserved better men, and so does she."

I took the little bowl out of his hand and downed the whiskey myself. "She knows. She figured it all out herself."

He looked at me, and his lip twitched. "Knew I was going to like you."

The last piece of the puzzle fell into place then, with a satisfying click. "Kale knew too. He called you in, didn't he? For Liz's sake."

Stagolee just stared at me, eyes like chips of glass as he picked up the bottle and took three hard swallows. I watched the air bubble up in the bottle. He set it down with a click, wiped his mouth on his sleeve.

I set down the bowl. "Browning's still out there. I think I tagged him."

Stagolee looked at his gun, lying on the bar. He fumbled it open, replaced the empty, clicked it shut. It made a satisfying sound, like a closing door. He nodded his shaggy, gaunt grey head. "Believe you did. Hard man to kill, though."

The back of his hand rubbed across his cheekbone as he said it, and as it concealed the ruined half of his face I looked into the face of my brother: weary, fallen, lost, and broken, but once far more worthy than I. I wondered if it would not have been better to lose immortality and memory both, rather than to continue on as I have, as I will. I smiled at him, and laid a hand on his arm. "Come on, Strifbjorn. We've got a man to kill."

He reacted as if I'd poured whiskey down his throat when he was expecting iced tea. "Where did you hear that name?"

I picked up the eight-shooter and held it out to him, butt first. He gawked at it for a moment as if it had grown eyes and was staring back, but he took it. "I have the second sight," I told him. "Come on. Time's wasting."

But Browning was gone. There was some blood upstairs at Pamela's and his best horse was gone from the ranch house, and his track led out into the desert. It made me damned uncomfortable to know he was still out there, but it wasn't my vengeance to follow.

Stagolee never came back into town. The last I saw of him, he was slumped in the saddle of his good-looking dappled dun horse, riding into the west with his shadow stretched out before him, looking for vengeance still.

I kept that fiddle.

TIGER! TIGER!

What of the hunting, hunter bold?
Brother, the watch was long and cold.
What of the quarry ye went to kill?
Brother, he crops in the jungle still.
Where is the power that made your pride?
Brother, it ebbs from my flank and side.
Where is the haste that ye hurry by?
Brother, I go to my lair—to die!
                              —Rudyard Kipling

It was in India, on the high Malwa plateau in July of 1880, that I chanced to make the acquaintance of an American woman whom I have never forgotten and undertake an adventure which I have long waited to recount. The monsoon was much delayed that hot and arid summer, and war raged between the British and the Russians in nearby Afghanistan—another move on the chessboard of the "Great Game." No end was yet in sight to either problem when I, Magnus Larssen, *shikari*, was summoned to the village of Kanha to guide a party in search of tiger.

My gunbearer (who was then about fifteen) and I arrived some ten days before the shooters, and arranged to hire a cook, beaters, and *mahouts*, and prepare a base of operations. On the first full day of our tenancy, I was sitting at my makeshift desk when "Rodney" came into my tent, ferment glistening in his brown eyes. "The villagers are very excited, *sahib*," he said.

"Unhappy?" I felt myself frown.

"No, *sahib*. They are relieved. There is a man-eater." He danced an impatient jig in the doorway.

I raised an eyebrow and stretched in my canvas chair. "Driven to it by the drought?"

"The last month only," he answered. "Three dead so far, and some bullocks. It is a female, they think, and she is missing two toes from her right front foot."

I sipped my tea as I thought about it, and at last I nodded. "Good. Perhaps we can do them a favor while we're here."

After some days of preparation, we took transportation into Jabalpur to meet the train from Bhopal. The party was to be seven: six wealthy British and European men and the woman, an American adventuress and singer traveling in the company of a certain Count Kolinzcki, an obese Lithuanian nobleman.

The others comprised a middle-aged, muttonchopped English gentleman, Mr. Northrop Waterhouse, with adolescent sons James and Conrad; Graf Baltasar von Hammerstein, a very Prussian fellow of my long acquaintance, stout in every sense of the word; and Dr. Albert Montleroy, a fair-haired Englishman, young around the eyes.

As they disembarked from the train, however, it was the lady who caught my attention. Fair-haired, with a clean line of jaw and clear eyes, she was aged perhaps twenty-two, but her beauty was not the sort that required youth to recommend it. She wore a very practical walking-dress in sage green, fashionably tailored, and her gloves and hat matched her boots very well. I noticed that she carried her own gun case as well as her reticule.

"Ah, Magnus!" von Hammerstein charged down the iron steps from the rail-coach and clasped my hand heavily, in the European style. "Allow me to present your charges." Remembering himself, he turned to the American, and I saw that she was traveled enough to recognize his courtesy. "*Fraulein*, this gentleman is the noted author and hunter of heavy game, Mr. Magnus Larssen. Magnus, may I present the talented contralto, Miss Irene Adler."

"So what is this I hear about a man-killer, *shikari*?" The older Waterhouse boy, James, was talking. "On the train, we heard a rumour that a dozen men had been found mauled and disemboweled!"

"Lad," his father warned, with a glance to the woman. She looked up from her scarcely touched sherry.

I think Miss Adler winked. "Pray, sir, do not limit the conversation on my behalf. I am here to hunt, just as the rest of you, and I have visited rougher surroundings than this."

Montleroy nodded in the flicker of lanternlight. The boys had collected the supper dishes, and we were each relaxing with a glass. "Yes, if we're to have a go at this man-eater, let's by all means hear the details. It's safest and best."

"Very well," I allowed, after a moment. "There have been three victims so far, and a number of cattle. It seems that the tigress responsible is wounded, and taking easy prey. All of the bodies have been mauled and eaten, that much is true. The details are rather horrible."

Horrible indeed. The eyes had been eaten out of their heads, and the flesh off the faces. The bodies had been dismembered and gnawed. If it had not been for the fact that the only prints close to the bodies were those of the wounded tiger, I might have been tempted to think of some more sinister agency: perhaps agents of a Thuggee cult. I was not, however, about to reveal those facts in mixed company, Miss Adler's high opinion of her own constitution notwithstanding.

Across the room, I saw the younger Waterhouse boy, Conrad, shudder. I shook my head. Too young.

Thick leaves and fronds brushed the flanks of our elephants as they stepped out of the cool of the jungle and into more dappled shade. The groundcover cracked under their feet as we emerged from the sal trees into a small meadow. From there, we could catch a glimpse of the grasslands sweeping down a great, horseshoe-shaped valley to the banks of the Banjar River.

"This heat is beastly, Mr. Larssen!" the Count complained.

I glanced across the red-and-gold-knotted carpets spanning the broad back of the elephant we shared with Miss Adler. I sweated even in my shaded perch, and I did not envy the *mahouts* perched astride the beasts' necks in the brutal light of the sun, but I presumed they must be more accustomed by blood and habituation to this barbarous calescence. "It is India, Count," I replied—perhaps more dryly than necessary.

"And the insects are intolerable." Kolinzcki's humour did not seem to extend to irony. I raised an eyebrow, and returned my attention to the trail, keeping my pot gun to hand and an eye out for edible game, as the beaters took a large portion of their pay in meat.

My mind drifted as I sought any spoor or scat of our quarry. There was a strange, oppressive silence hung on the air, and no trace of moisture upon the breeze. I felt a chill of unease upon my neck—or perhaps it was only the shade of the trees as our mounts carried us back down the jungle trail.

I felt the need to break the uncanny quietude. "The tiger," I said to Miss Adler and her companion, "is the true King of the Jungle. No mere lion can compare to him for ferocity, intelligence, or courage. He fears nothing, and will easily turn the tables on a hunter."

"That is why we ride elephants?" The Lithuanian's accent could have been better, but his speech was comprehensible.

I nodded. "Tigers respect elephants, and the reverse is true as well. One will not trouble the oth—"

A great outcry among the monkeys and the birds in the jungle on our left ended my lecture. I heard an intermittent crashing in the bamboo as an antelope sprinted away. Our tiger was on the move.

Our beaters fanned toward the jungle, several of them disappearing from sight among the trees. One or two glanced back at us before vanishing into the brush, understandably apprehensive: there was at least one tiger in that cover who had learned the taste of man.

I directed the *mahouts* back to the clearing, where we could intercept the line of beaters. The good doctor and von Hammerstein were mounted on the second beast, and Mr. Waterhouse with his two sons rode the final one. Rodney walked alongside with a cargo of rifles. Count Kolinzcki fumbled with his gun, and I made a note to myself to keep an eye on the Lithuanian, in case he should require assistance. Miss Adler quietly and efficiently broke her under/over Winchester and made it ready on her own.

We reached the clearing in good order and took a moment to array ourselves. The cries of the beaters rang out—"*bAgha! bAgha!*"—"Tiger! Tiger!".

She was within their net, and moving toward us. Miss Adler drew a deep breath to steady herself, and I restrained myself from laying a hand on her shoulder to calm her. A glance at her lovely face, however, showed only quiet resolve.

Von Hammerstein also readied his gun, as did the Waterhouses and the doctor. Not intending to shoot, I foolishly failed to exchange the bolt-action .303 Martini-Lee for my double rifle.

The moment stretched into silence. I found myself counting my breaths, gaze fixed on the wall of brush. "*Mir Shikar,*" von Hammerstein began—luckily, for as I turned toward my stout and stalwart old friend, I saw the tigress lunge.

The tricky old killer had somehow doubled back and come up upon our flank. She was too close, perhaps a stride away. She made one gigantic bound out of the brush and was airborne even as I whipped my rifle around.

In that instant, my eye photographed her—the twisted forefoot, the sad traces of mange and hunger, the frantic golden eye—and my finger tightened on the trigger.

To no avail. With a hollow click, the rifle failed to discharge. It seemed an aeon as I worked the bolt—jammed—and tossed it aside, extending my hand down to Rodney for the .534 Egyptian. In the instant before my fingers closed on the warm Turkish walnut of the stock, I heard two weapons roar and sudden plumes of acrid white smoke tattered in the hot breeze. The shots caught the tigress in side and breast, tumbling her over and backwards.

She dragged herself upright, and Mr. Waterhouse fired as well, squinting along the barrel like a professional as he put a third and final bullet into the defiant cat. She made a little coughing sound and expired, her body going fluid in each joint.

I glanced around before sliding off my elephant. Miss Adler had broken her Winchester and was calmly replacing the cartridge she had expended into the creature's breast. Von Hammerstein was also dismounting his beast, keeping his weapon at the ready in case he was forced to fire again.

I bent over to examine the kill, and found myself straightening abruptly, scanning the jungle for any sign of movement. I saw only our returning beaters.

Von Hammerstein saw it, and laid a questioning eye on me.

"Her teeth," I said thickly. "There must be a second cat. This one might bring down a man, but she could never manage a bullock. Not with that crippled foot, and the ruined teeth."

It was then that I heard a sound like a throbbing drumbeat, distant but distinct. I did not know what made it, and my curiosity was piqued.

I would give anything to have remained so ignorant.

Three of the beaters did not come out of the woods, nor were their bodies found.

A search until nightfall failed to turn up the men—or, in fact, any trace of a second tiger. Reluctantly, we reunited and turned for the camp, our beaters muttering in dissatisfaction. We resolved to resume the hunt in the morning, and hopefully find traces of the victims and whatever cat had taken them. Dr. Montleroy did get a lucky shot at a leopard, and brought it down, so we had two trophies: the elderly tigress, and a beautiful spotted cat perhaps seven feet in length.

Dinner that night was a somber affair, despite the excellent food: bread of a flat sort stuffed with potato, vegetables curried with tomato and onion, mutton spiced and baked in a clay pot. It was a great relief when the Lithuanian Count pressed Miss Adler to entertain us by singing, and she obliged. Even without accompaniment her contralto was superb and much relieved our heavy hearts.

My sleep, when it came, was troubled by the sounds of a quiet argument nearby—the voice of Miss Adler demanding, "But you must give it back to me!" And a male rumble—stubborn, I thought—replying. A lover's quarrel, perhaps.

I am not sure what brought me from my cot, other than the sort of prurience that a man does not like to admit. I wondered what he had of hers, of course, and a gentleman does not leave a lady alone in a tight spot, even when that lady is an adventuress.

It was Kolinzcki whom she argued with, for I recognized his voice as I moved closer to the wall of my tent, feeling my way barefoot in the unrelieved darkness. He switched languages, and she followed. I was surprised to be able to understand them somewhat, for I speak no Lithuanian. But the disagreement they conducted in low tones was in Russian, and that language I have a fair command of.

"It was not yours to take," Miss Adler whispered, urgency resonating in her trained voice. "Do you know what you'll be unleashing?"

"It is unleashed already," Kolinzcki replied. "I merely bring our noble friends the means to control it."

She sighed, the harsh Russian tongue taking on a certain fluidity when she spoke it. "It is not so simple as that, and you know it. It will be a great embarrassment for my friends in Prague if I cannot return their property. If it seems they are cooperating with the Tsar, it will go hard for them."

He was silent, and she continued in a voice I barely heard under the sawing of insects. "Have I not done everything you asked?"

It was obvious to me that the Count was blackmailing the lovely singer, and I made up my mind to intervene. But as my hand was on the tent flap, I heard again the low, resonant throbbing that had so startled us in the afternoon. Outside, Miss Adler gave a little cry of surprise, and as I came around the corner to confront them, I heard him say in English, "And that is the reason why I cannot oblige you, my dear, as well you know. Perhaps when we are back in civilized lands, we can discuss this again."

She stepped close to him and laid her hand on his arm. "Of course, darling."

Then perhaps a lover's quarrel after all, and already made up for. Silent in bare feet, I returned to my sleepless bed, unaccountably disappointed, and harboring suspicions I did not care to address. Who was I, a Norwegian, to care what alliances and wars the Tsar and the British Queen make against and upon one another? They seemed determined to tear Afghanistan in two between them, in their so-called Great Game: an endless series of Imperialist intrigues and battles. A game, to my eye, whose chiefest victims were simple folk like my Rodney. The best the rest of us—I thought then—could manage was a sort of detached distaste for the whole proceedings.

The morning found us all awake early and unsettled. It was bold young James Waterhouse who sought me out before we mounted our elephants. "*Shikari,*" he said—they had picked up the usage from von Hammerstein, and thought it delightfully quaint—"Did you hear that noise again last night?"

I hesitated. "The drumming? I did indeed." I said no more, but he must have noted my frown.

He pressed me. "That wasn't an animal noise, was it? I heard it when we killed the tiger."

It had absorbed my thoughts through the night, when I wasn't distracted by the implications of the argument between the Lithuanian—or perhaps not Lithuanian—Count and the fair Miss Adler. It wasn't quite exactly a drumming: it was more a… heartbeat. It was true; it didn't sound like an animal noise. But it didn't sound precisely like a human noise either.

"I don't know," I answered uncomfortably. "I haven't heard it before." I turned to aid Miss Adler in climbing the rope ladder to our elephant. Truthfully, the Count required more assistance, and as I helped him up his waistcoat gaped and I noticed the golden hilt of a dagger secreted within it. Great-grandfather's hunting knife, no doubt: too showy, but not a bad precaution. He rose a bare notch in my estimation.

There were some clouds on the horizon, and I thought the wind might carry a taint of moisture. I was eager to find the second cat and travel deeper into the jungle, perhaps to seek a third. We were past due for weather, and monsoon would mean the end of our hunt.

My party were on edge, made nervy no doubt both by the loss of the beaters the day before and by the close call with the tiger. Still no sign had been found of the missing men—even of a scuffle—and I found myself tending toward the explanation that they had deserted. Conrad seemed spooked, and I permitted the brothers to ride my elephant while Miss Adler and her escort traveled with Mr. Waterhouse.

Instead of skirting the forest, we resolved to plunge into it, and search among the bamboo and the sal trees for the second man-eater. I found myself eager as a young man, and by the time we broke for luncheon we had covered some miles into the thicker part of the forest. We found a little clearing in which to enjoy our cold curry and venison with the native bread. I sat beside von Hammerstein, while noting that Miss Adler had taken a place some distance from her Count. I wondered.

I kept the Egyptian close to hand, in case our man-eater should be drawn out by the scent of food or prey, but lunch passed uneventfully. We resolved to take a short *siesta* on the grass in the appalling heat of the afternoon with some of the beaters standing guard.

I again caught a glimpse of clouds massed on the horizon, but they seemed no closer than the morning, so I determined that we should press on after resting, but I must have dozed. I was awakened with a start by the sound of crashing in the brush—something sprinting straight for us. I scrambled to my feet, clutching my rifle. I noticed that the rest had dozed as well—except Miss Adler, who was on her feet, straightening from adjusting the Count's jacket, and loyal Rodney, who was chatting with one of the beaters in their native Hindi.

I brought my weapon to bear on the sound. The beaters moved rapidly out of the line of fire, and I did not spare a glance for the others.

It was no tiger that broke the screen of trees, but a man, ragged and hungry-looking, on the verge of exhaustion, bare feet bloodied as if from some long journey. He did not look Indian but rather Arab—Afghani, perhaps? I cautiously lowered my rifle, and he collapsed at my feet with a cry.

He babbled a few words in a tongue I did not understand. Again shifting my estimation of him, it was Count Kolinzcki who first came to the man's side, bending over him. I watched warily for a moment. The Arab seemed no threat, however, and I gestured Rodney to bring water as I crouched beside him as well. My bearer had just begun to cross the clearing, leaving his post at my shoulder, when the eldest elephant threw up her trunk and trumpeted in alarm.

A stray breeze brought a whiff of scent to my nostrils: char, and hot metal. I cast about for any sign of smoke and noticed the elephants rocking nervously. It seemed obvious to me at that time that they had scented fire, for I knew then of no beast that could so disturb them.

I was both right and wrong.

"Mount!" I cried. The Waterhouses began immediately to move toward the elephants while Dr. Montleroy and von Hammerstein helped the beaters grab up our possessions. I reached down with some thought of assisting the prostrate Arab, but Kolinzcki was already dragging him to his feet.

The Arab grabbed Kolinzcki by the collar, and the fat Count knocked his grubby hand aside. And then, looking startled and sick, the Count pressed his right hand to his breast, with the expression of a man who realizes that his watch has gone missing from his waistcoat.

I remembered the argument of the night before, and Miss Adler bent over his supine form as he slept, but the rush of events did not permit me to inquire.

I barely caught a glimpse of it before it was among us: it came silent as a wisp of smoke, disturbing the vines and brush not at all. It glowed, even in the incandescence of the afternoon, with a light like a coal, and across the back it bore stripes like char. It possessed the rough form of a tiger, but it stank like a forest fire and its maw was a lick of flame.

It sprang to the back of the smallest elephant with an easy leap, transfixing Conrad Waterhouse with its burning gaze. Even as the elephant panicked, he froze like a bird charmed by a snake. The Creature's blazing claws scorched down her sides, leaving rents in her thick hide that I wouldn't have credited to an axe. She screamed and reared up, ponderously reaching over her shoulder in an attempt to dislodge the predator. Her panic knocked Conrad from his feet, and I did not see him move again. His brother lunged across the path of the Creature to shield the fallen boy with his body: a brave and futile gesture.

The Creature avoided the elephant's wild blows contemptuously, plunging to the soft earth like a cannonball as all three of our mounts stampeded and the injured elephant's foot struck James.

The beaters and *mahouts* scattered. The Creature casually disemboweled the closest man: it never even turned its head, already gathering itself for another pounce. Even as I leveled my weapon I knew it was hopeless. I squeezed the trigger and the rifle hammered my shoulder once, and again. Rodney sprinted back to me, my Purdey clutched in his hand. He had two cartridges between his fingers, drawn from the loops on his vest, and he had the rifle broken, loading both barrels simultaneously as he ran.

The good doctor stood rooted in shock. I heard the report of von Hammerstein's gun and a second later, that of Miss Adler. I released my empty weapon as Rodney, spitting fragments of words in his excitement, smoothly handed me the replacement. Mr. Waterhouse was turning to cover the beast with shaking hands, unable to fire as long as we stood behind it, craning his neck in an attempt to see both the quarry and his two sons.

The animal stalked forward, opening its flame-rimmed maw, and I heard again the sound I had compared to the pounding of drums or the throb of a mighty heart. The roar went on and on, and my heart quailed and my hands shook as it slunk one pad-footed step forward.

I readied my useless weapon, determined to die fighting, and Miss Adler loosed her second shot. The bullet ruptured the hide of the beast and a ripple shuddered across its surface as if she had tossed a rock into water. A few spattering droplets of fire shot up, falling to the grass, where they smoked and vanished.

Count Kolinzcki staggered back, down on one knee in fright and despair, his hand dropping from his breast to fumble with his weapon. Von Hammerstein held his fire. I knew he would be waiting for a shot at the eye—a forlorn hope, but the one I clung to as well.

The thunder of hooves spoiled my aim. I raised my gaze from my gunsight to witness the arrival of the proverbial cavalry. A lathered bay gelding—of Arab stock, to guess by its small stature and luxurious mane—charged out of the bamboo in full flight. Its flanks heaved and blood-flecked foam flew from its bit. On its back was a mustachioed officer, who hauled up short on the reins and virtually lifted his mount into the air.

It was a prodigious leap: the little horse's hindquarters bunched and released, and it sailed up and over the back of the Creature. The tigerlike thing twisted in a fruitless attempt to score the horse with its claws, and then recoiled as the rider hurled some sort of pouch at its face. Whatever it was, it hurt! The Creature throbbed again, searing the depths of my ears, and turned and bounded away.

The officer hauled his horse to a stop and whirled it about on its haunches—an unequalled display of horsemanship. The little bay half-reared in protest of the hard handling, and then settled down, pawing and snorting.

The officer gentling it with a hand on its neck was a man of middle years, his hair iron grey as was his copious moustache. He had a high forehead and a sensual twist to his mouth, and his eyes glittered still with the excitement of the hunt.

At the appearance of the officer, the Arab turned as if to flee, and almost ran directly into me. He still wove on his feet, and I detained him easily enough.

"Sir," Miss Adler said, first in command of her wits, "we are indebted to you beyond any repayment."

"Miss," he replied, "it is my privilege to serve. And now we must be away, before it returns."

I identified the British insignia upon his uniform. "Colonel, I thank you as well. I am Magnus Larssen, these good people's guide. We have wounded." The beater who had been disemboweled by the Creature was dead or dying quickly, but I could see James picking himself up painfully, his father crouching beside him with an expression of terrible grief. Dr. Montleroy was already trotting to their side.

"Colonel Sebastian Moran, Her Majesty's First Bengalore Pioneers," he said. I noticed that in addition to a sidearm and saber, there was an elephant gun sheathed on his saddle in much the fashion that the Americans carry their buffalo rifles.

Von Hammerstein and Rodney were crouched where the Creature had been. Rodney held up a burst leathern water-bottle: the object that the colonel had thrown in its face.

"There's no spoor, *sahib*," Rodney said. "It leaves no marks in the grass. Like smoke. There are—" a silence "—specks of molten lead." *Bullets*, he did not say.

I felt a cold, thickening sensation in my belly: fear.

"*Shikari*," began the colonel, but then he hesitated with a glance to the grief-stricken father, and began to dismount and unlimber his gun. "The young man looks well enough to ride. Have him sling the boy over my saddle. We must make it to the river by nightfall."

He spared a glance for the Arab, and another caress for the exhausted horse. "This man is my prisoner. I pursued him from the border, and I will be bringing him back with me."

Kolinzcki, rising to his feet, seemed about to protest, but something in the glitter of the colonel's eyes silenced him. For myself, I merely nodded, and went with von Hammerstein to collect the casualties.

The events of that afternoon return to me now only as a heat-soaked blur. We walked only when we could run no longer. Waterhouse clung to the stirrup of the colonel's horse, trotting alongside it as he steadied his sons. Conrad still breathed, but he had not regained consciousness, and I believed James was suffering an internal injury: he grew ever whiter and more silent, and most of our water went to him.

I knew the Creature stalked us, as wounded cats will, for every so often I caught a taste of its red scent upon the breeze, and the gelding was hot-eyed and terrified. I feared the poor beast's wind was broken: it wheezed through every breath and staggered under its double burden, but it kept up gamely.

The colonel had bound the Arab's hands before him with a leather strap. Through this means, Moran contrived to keep the prisoner upright and moving, although he was staggering from exhaustion.

I came up beside him when we had not been moving long and leaned into his ear. "The Arab is a Tsarist agent?"

"Of a sort," he said, one wary eye on the individual in question. "A tribal shaman. A Personage. And an Afghani, not an Arab." He raked me with a sidelong glance and I nodded to encourage his discourse. "He was travelling to India with an entourage. We stopped the rest at the border, but this one got through.

Fortunately, I've apprehended him before…." His voice trailed off. "What are your politics, Larssen?"

"I haven't any."

He grunted. "Get some." And walked away.

My especial burden was the fat Count, who staggered along in our wake and complained. Miss Adler kept along nicely, bearing her own distress very well, despite suspicious looks from the Count. Almost, I thought he was about to break into open argument with her, but he directed a hard look at Moran and kept his comments to the heat.

Finally, in the haze of heat and despair, Moran turned on the Count. "If you don't stop whining, I'll send you back in pieces!" he snapped, shaking his gun for emphasis.

The Count halted. "A common Englishman does not call me a fool!" he replied sharply. "I am accustomed to a dignified pace, and if this Norwegian idiot had not led us into the lair of monsters," a rude gesture in my direction, "we'd all be bathed and fed by now!"

The colonel's prisoner chose this moment to break in, gesticulating and seeming to berate the Count, shrieking in anger. The Count listened for a moment, and shook his head. He glanced around in appeal. "Do any of you understand this barbarian?" he asked, glancing from one to another.

None answered, but Moran's eyebrow rose in silent speculation.

Night came on more quickly than I could have imagined. My feet were bloody in my boots, and sun blisters rose along the length of my nose where my helmet did not shade it. I grew deaf to the hum of insects, the chatter of monkeys and birds. The sole promise of relief was the black stormfront piling up on the horizon: the long-overdue monsoon, racing northward to greet us. Whenever I found the strength to raise my head, I glanced at those bulging clouds, prayerful, but they never seemed closer. As if some invisible army held them besieged, they roiled and tore, but could not advance.

Dr. Montleroy sought me out as the afternoon waned into evening. "I'm going to lose James unless I can get him to help, and quickly. I may anyway, but there's still time to try."

"What does his father say?" I croaked.

"He knows," Montleroy answered, with a glance over his shoulder to the white-faced man. "It is one son or neither."

I nodded once. "Take all the water. Go."

We pulled Conrad down off the exhausted gelding over James' feeble protests, and the good doctor swung up behind. Moran poured water for the horse into his hat, and the animal sucked it up in a single desperate draught. "Go like the wind," he said to it, and slapped it hard across the flank. It startled and bolted,

Montleroy and James bent low over its neck.

"Godspeed," said Miss Adler from beside me. I glanced around in surprise. It was then that I noticed that the Count was missing.

No one had seen him fall behind, and we could not turn back. Mr. Waterhouse, von Hammerstein, and I took turns carrying Conrad, who drifted in a fever. He mumbled strange phrases in a language I had never heard, but which seemed to discomfit Moran's prisoner greatly.

The prisoner attempted to speak to me, but I could only shake my head at his foreign tongue. He tried von Hammerstein as well, to equally little avail, and Moran did not interfere. I had the distinct impression that the colonel watched out of the corner of his eye, as if observing our faces for any sign of comprehension, but the chattering of the monkeys meant more, at least, to me.

With her paramour gone, Miss Adler stalked up to the front of the group. It was she who first identified the clearing where we had killed the tigress. We paused for breath, and the prisoner threw himself down in the long grass and panted.

"Two more miles to the river," she said, in a flat and hopeless tone, resting the Winchester's stock on the ground. Moran glanced from her to the rapidly darkening sky and grunted. Waterhouse's face clenched in terror and I knew it was not for himself that he feared.

"We could try to run it," offered von Hammerstein. He shifted the still form of Conrad Waterhouse on his shoulder and stared out toward the grasslands, a calculating look on his face. "Could you keep up, Miss?"

The woman frowned. "I dare say." She bent down to unlace her boots while Rodney held the Winchester. She stepped out of them and knotted them over her shoulder.

The monkeys fell silent. The prisoner started up, eyes staring, and he cried aloud—"*Ia! Ia hastur cf'ayak 'vugtlagln hastur!*"—and then, in mangled Hindi, "The burning one comes!" His eyes shimmered insanely. His voice was exultant. I wondered why he had not spoken Hindi before, at least to myself or Rodney.

"Run," Moran shouted, yanking on the leather strap, and we ran.

The six of us, Moran dragging his captive, pelted out of the sal and down the slope of the land toward the riverbank. Around us the grass burned from gold to bloody in the light of the sunset. An enormous orb, already half-concealed by the horizon, lit the scene like the Plains of Hell.

I ran with my hand clenched on my rifle, heedless of clutching grasses. Rodney darted ahead with one hand on von Hammerstein's arm, nearly dragging the laden man. Conrad bounced on his back, voice raised in a peculiar shriek, raving a string of words that pained my ears.

The ground blurred under my feet, and as I passed Miss Adler I caught her elbow and dragged her along—she was running well, but my legs were longer. Ahead of me, I saw Moran give an assisting shove to Waterhouse and turn around to yank the leather strap again. His prisoner simply piled into him, swinging his hands like a club, teeth bared to bite.

"The dagger!" he shrieked in broken Hindi, foam flying from his teeth. "You fool, or it will have us all!"

Moran moved with the speed of a man half his age. "Go on," he yelled at me as I moved to help him. He ducked under the prisoner's swing and brought his gun-butt up under the man's jaw. As I pelted past, the Arab tumbled boneless to the ground, and Moran raised his weapon.

I flinched, expecting a shot, but Moran snarled as he hauled the prisoner to his feet.

I caught my breath in my teeth. It hurt. "Not… going to make it," Miss Adler groaned between breaths.

A lone tree rose before us as I stole a glance over my shoulder. We were less than halfway to the river, and I could see the red glow of the sunset matched by an answering inferno only yards behind.

Von Hammerstein and Waterhouse had reached the same conclusion, for as we drew up we saw them crouched in the grass. Rodney stood just behind them, his eyes very white and wide in his mahogany face. He clapped my shoulder as I passed him, and I realized that he was younger than Conrad Waterhouse, over whose raving self he stood guard.

"Good lad," I said to him, which seemed wholly inadequate, and I came and stood beside him. I remembered that we had given all our water to James, and nevertheless I found my fear lifting. I was resigned.

Moran came up to us and took in the situation with a nod. We turned at bay, the devil before us and the sunset at out backs.

It let us see it coming—a glowing spectre in the darkness, a demon of flame and fear. It leaped through the tall grass toward me—a bound of perhaps forty feet. I caught a very clear view of it as it gathered itself. Flaming eyes glittered at me with unholy intelligence in the moment before it leaped.

I felt something rise in my heart under that regard, an antique horror such as I had never known, and I heard Waterhouse whimper—or perhaps I myself moaned aloud in fear. Words seemed to form in my mind, words of invocation that I both knew and did not know, powerful and ancient and evil as maggots in my soul: "Ia! Ia Hastur…"

I emptied the .534 at it, to no effect. Beside me, I heard von Hammerstein's gun choke and roar twice. He reached for a second one. The reek of powder hung thick upon the air.

The beast was midair—it was among us—Conrad had risen to his feet with madness on his face and thrown himself at Rodney. Waterhouse caught the blow, staggered, and bore the boy over onto the ground, kneeling on his chest and bearing his hands down only with great difficulty. Rodney never flinched.

I dropped the empty weapon. "Boy. *Gun!*"

Rodney snapped the Purdey into my hand, and I aimed along the barrel with a prayer to Almighty God on my lips. Moran was distracted from his prisoner, shaking his weapon loose and raising it in a futile and beautiful gesture. His luxurious moustache draped across the scrollwork on the gun as he sighted, and he placed two shots directly into the beast's eye as it lunged.

The flaming paw hurt not at all. It struck me high on the thigh, and I felt a distinct shattering sensation, but there was no pain. I lost the Purdey, and I saw poor Rodney hurled aside by a second thunderous blow. He fell like a broken doll, and he did not rise. Mr. Waterhouse started up to defend his boy, and was knocked backward fifteen feet into the tree before its next blow crushed von Hammerstein against the earth. I felt the impact from where I lay.

Moran turned with his gun, coolly tracking the Creature. He did not see his prisoner rise up from the ground clutching a rock in his bound hands, and my shout came too late. Even as he spun, the villain laid him out.

Then, suddenly, Miss Irene Adler was standing behind the prisoner, something glittering in her hand. She drew her arm back, and with a Valkyrie shout she plunged the Count's dagger deep into the Arab's back. The man stiffened, shuddered, and clawed, tied hands thrust into the air as if to drag Miss Adler off his back. I was eerily reminded of the poor, wounded elephant.

He sagged to his knees as the Creature snarled its throbbing snarl and spun about on its haunches. It took a step toward Miss Adler and screamed as only a cat can scream.

The prisoner fell to the ground dead, and Miss Adler stood defiant and braced behind the corpse, ready for whatever death might find her. Seeming unaffected by the death of the Arab, the Creature crouched to leap. Pain grinding in my broken leg, I started to drag myself upright with some futile idea of hurling myself on the thing.

At that moment, the rain came.

The monsoon was upon us like a wall of glass, and the Creature screamed again—this time, in agony. It turned this way and that, frantic to escape the raindrops, like a dog that seeks to elude a beating. Each drop sizzled and steamed as it struck, and with each drop the devil's light flickered, spots appearing on its hide like the speckles on a coal sprinkled with water.

It twisted about itself, shrieking, and finally seemed to collapse. A sickening scent of char rose from the wet ashes that were all that remained.

My leg flared at last into agony, and a black tunnel closed upon my sight.

I groaned and opened my eyes on a vision of bedraggled and ineffable beauty tucking a jeweled dagger into her reticule. There was a tarpaulin under me—wet, but dryer than the ground—and another one hung over the branches of the tree to shield me from the worst of the rain. I recognized it as gear Rodney had carried. Moran lay beside me, under a blanket, quite still.

She laid a damp cloth on my forehead and smoothed back my hair before she stood. "Your leg is broken. I beg you to forgive me for leaving you in such straits, Mr. Larssen. I assure you I will send help, but I must leave at once: it is a delicate matter, and vital to the security of a certain Baltic nobleman that the theft of this dagger from his household never be proven—either by the English or the Russians."

"Wait," I cried. "Miss Adler—Irene—"

"You may certainly call me Irene," she replied, something like amusement in her voice. I saw that her gloves were burned through, and the palms of her hands were blistered.

I tried for a moment to formulate a question, but words failed me. "What has happened here?" I finally asked her, trusting that she would understand.

"I am afraid you have been rather overtaken by events, my dear Mr. Larssen... Magnus. As have we all. I came here to retrieve this dagger, which was stolen from a friend of mine. The rather vile Mr. Kolinzcki, whom I fear is neither a Count nor a Lithuanian but an agent of the Tsar, stole it and brought it here with the intention of providing it to this Afghani sorcerer."

She spurned the corpse with her toe.

"For all I know, he intended some foul ritual of human sacrifice, which may have greatly discomfited the British Army. At the very least, it seems to have had the power to control that." She gestured expressively to the pile of ashes. "A pity I had to kill him. I imagine he would have befuddled British intelligence greatly, if they had the chance to interrogate him. But once I understood that he was somehow holding back the storm—"

"Monsoon. If I may be so bold as to correct a lady."

"Monsoon." She smiled.

"But how? You cannot tell me how?" I wished I could grit my teeth against the pain in my leg, but they chattered so that I could not manage it. I did not look to where Rodney lay, out in the cold rain.

"It seems that there are things in heaven and earth that lie beyond our ken as Western minds of scientific bent."

I nodded and a wave of pain and nausea threatened to overwhelm me. "The Count?" I asked.

She lifted her strong shoulders and let them drop, her expression dark. "Left behind and eaten, I presume. I assure you that your assistance has been invaluable, and that the war in Afghanistan may now come to a close."

She set a pan of rainwater and a loaded pistol close by my hand. "The colonel is alive but unconscious—it seems the blow rendered him insensate." A final hesitation, before she turned to go.

She turned back, and seemed to study my face for a moment. I hoped I saw something like affection there. "I am also very sorry about Rodney."

It was a very long, cold night then, but the villagers and Dr. Montleroy came for me in the morning. We did not speak, then or ever, of the thing we had seen.

James survived, although Conrad never regained himself. I had occasional dealings after with Colonel Moran, until he left the region for cooler climes. I understand he has come to a very bad end.

As for Miss Adler—her, I never saw again. But my dreams are haunted to this day by her face and, less pleasantly, by those eerie words—*Ia! Ia hastur cf'ayak 'vugtlagln hastur!*—and I have never since been able to take up a gun for sport.

THE DYING OF THE LIGHT
(WITH AMBER VAN DYK)

When John Keats was my age, he had been dead for
seven years.

                             The necrophilia makes it seem dirtier than it
                                           really is.
Cold comfort, muttered over the phone by 3 a.m.
friends with obviously something better to do.
                         But it's not the love, not really. It's more my
                   distraction, a ringing bell calling my name. When
               she calls I salivate. Her voice sounds like static,
               like electricity. Sparks fly when we're motionless,
                         in stasis. When she's cold.
Like sleeping or whatever else happens under
covers on shiny frostbitten autumn nights. John
Keats, dead and so tragically young.

Like each of them, it's what he did before *dead*
that matters.

                  Now ice forms on her skin, and I remember her
                    fingers were slim, slender, like knitting needles
             or pins. With her arms out wide like that she was
             easy to keep still. But when she said my name, it
             had too many syllables. So I leave her hanging,
                she's left me, and I walk, and all the doors are
                                    open.
I'm not here for him—or Shelley either, another
one, sucking great agonizing gasps of cold
seawater into faltering lungs. All the palely
loitering I need hangs in Boston Goth bars.
                  They're all the places I used to know. Between

drinks, I'd call her Tink, as a joke, and she'd
mutter under her breath, but when I laughed even
she'd smile and with the moon streaming in like
that, careful silver, she might have been dead.
Dead as the old poets, covered in old lace, and I
remember.

Both men buried in Rome, close as husband and
wife—too far away and too, too long ago.
Either way, how I held them up? It was all a matter
of display. Like how I see myself in storefront
windows, reflected in the damp, the condensation.
Sugar maple leaf plasters my boot wetly, caution
orange. I pluck it away.

Dickinson? Closer, but somebody would have
gotten her by now. Rosetti, too: if "The Goblin
Market" isn't a dead giveaway…. Dylan Thomas a
better candidate, but I hadn't been the first at
his grave.

Laden, I trudge uphill, past serried headstones.
Everything is wet, but still there are marks left
to make. I unfurl rolls of paper, dig charcoal from
the bottom of a ratty bag; I used to sign all of my
pieces, my etchings.

But my name means less than it used to.
Some aren't born with it.

Cursed with the will, the skill, fire in the
belly but no fire on the soul… we beg. Tin cup
to hand, rags bound about the brow.
Now I wait for the pennies to fall from heaven,
commuter cash, and I spend them quickly. I buy
sandwiches on stale bread, coffee without cream
because it's cheaper. And I walk, because here
everything is free.
I come to the grave of the hanged man, the
rabble-rouser, the forgotten bard. No more
songs, he sang, but a power's laid here with
him, prickle and chafe.

Maybe here there are methods to my madness, maybe
here she'll come to me.
The sacrifices: chapbooks, a sad few shred-eared
literary journals. Self-published, unpaid,
unread. Unremembered. Whatever it is, I never
had it.

I used to type out everything, but my hands don't
shake, not anymore. Now I have records, memoirs,
everything.
Paper doesn't burn all that well: thus the
brazier. Hibachi. Whatever. Crickets resounding:
sky first flame, then mauve, ash.

Finally it's cool enough: I dip fingers, ash-
trace his deep cut marble name.

I show her, my piece, my strung up, she has wings,
or maybe that's all I can see, butterfly girl on
blue velvet. My words were for her.
Poetry dies unvoiced. Soon, soon. Use me up,
cinder-crumble.

Maybe she flies away, or maybe she doesn't.
Green fairy, mauve fairy. She's in there with
him, singer no more under crumbled earth, sod,
concrete vault and cheap coffin.

Shovel. Pry bar.

Maybe when I sign my name, the charcoal will look
like dirt. Maybe turn itself silver, become the key, the
lock, and we'll be trapped, the two of us.
Thick walls and roof: oven, and she'll consume
me, licking her fingers, sucking up the juices.
White-hot art. Shelley. Keats. Me.

I can maybe get ten years out of her if I'm
careful.

Maybe she'll be dead then, blanket of earth,
memory, art. Alabaster, smooth as ice, cold as
marble.

(The necrophilia makes it seem
dirtier than it really is.)

AND THE DEEP BLUE SEA

The end of the world had come and gone. It turned out not to matter much in the long run.

The mail still had to get through.

Harrie signed yesterday's paperwork, checked the dates against the calendar, contemplated her signature for a moment, and capped her pen. She weighed the metal barrel in her hand and met Dispatch's faded eyes. "What's special about this trip?"

He shrugged and turned the clipboard around on the counter, checking each sheet to be certain she'd filled them out properly. She didn't bother watching. She never made mistakes. "Does there have to be something special?"

"You don't pay my fees unless it's special, Patch." She grinned as he lifted an insulated steel case onto the counter.

"This has to be in Sacramento in eight hours," he said.

"What is it?"

"Medical goods. Fetal stem-cell cultures. In a climate-controlled unit. They can't get too hot or too cold, there's some arcane formula about how long they can live in this given quantity of growth media, and the customer's paying very handsomely to see them in California by eighteen hundred hours."

"It's almost oh ten hundred now— What's too hot or too cold?" Harrie hefted the case. It was lighter than it looked; it would slide effortlessly into the saddle-bags on her touring bike.

"Any hotter than it already is," Dispatch said, mopping his brow. "Can you do it?"

"Eight hours? Phoenix to Sacramento?" Harrie leaned back to check the sun. "It'll take me through Vegas. The California routes aren't any good at that speed since the Big One."

"I wouldn't send anybody else. Fastest way is through Reno."

"There's no gasoline from somewhere this side of the dam to Tonopah. Even my courier card won't help me there—"

95

"There's a checkpoint in Boulder City. They'll fuel you."

"Military?"

"I did say they were paying very well." He shrugged, shoulders already gleaming with sweat. It was going to be a hot one. Harrie guessed it would hit a hundred and twenty in Phoenix.

At least she was headed north.

"I'll do it," she said, and held her hand out for the package receipt. "Any pick-ups in Reno?"

"You know what they say about Reno?"

"Yeah. It's so close to Hell that you can see Sparks." Naming the city's largest suburb.

"Right. You don't want anything in Reno. Go straight through," Patch said. "Don't stop in Vegas, whatever you do. The overpass's come down, but that won't affect you unless there's debris. Stay on the 95 through to Fallon; it'll see you clear."

"Check." She slung the case over her shoulder, pretending she didn't see Patch wince. "I'll radio when I hit Sacramento—"

"Telegraph," he said. "The crackle between here and there would kill your signal otherwise."

"Check," again, turning to the propped-open door. Her prewar Kawasaki Concours crouched against the crumbling curb like an enormous, restless cat. Not the prettiest bike around, but it got you there. Assuming you didn't ditch the top-heavy son of a bitch in the parking lot.

"Harrie—"

"*What?*" She paused, but didn't turn.

"If you meet the Buddha on the road, kill him."

She glanced behind her, strands of hair catching on the strap of the insulated case and on the shoulder loops of her leathers. "What if I meet the Devil?"

She let the Concours glide through the curves of the long descent to Hoover Dam, a breather after the hard straight push from Phoenix, and considered her options. She'd have to average near enough a hundred sixty klicks an hour to make the run on time. It should be smooth sailing; she'd be surprised if she saw another vehicle between Boulder City and Tonopah.

She'd checked out a backup dosimeter before she left Phoenix, just in case. Both clicked softly as she crossed the dam and the poisoned river, reassuring her with alert, friendly chatter. She couldn't pause to enjoy the expanse of blue on her right side or the view down the escarpment on the left, but the dam was in pretty good shape, all things considered.

It was more than you could say for Vegas.

Once upon a time—she downshifted as she hit the steep grade up the north side of Black Canyon, sweat already soaking her hair—once upon a time a delivery like this would have been made by aircraft. There were places where it still would be. Places where there was money for fuel, money for airstrip repairs.

Places where most of the aircraft weren't parked in tidy rows, poisoned birds lined up beside poisoned runways, hot enough that you could hear the dosimeters clicking as you drove past.

A runner's contract was a hell of a lot cheaper. Even when you charged the way Patch charged.

Sunlight glinted off the Colorado River so far below, flashing red and gold as mirrors. Crumbling casino on the right, now, and the canyon echoing the purr of the sleek black bike. The asphalt was spiderwebbed but still halfway smooth—smooth enough for a big bike, anyway. A big bike cruising at a steady ninety kph, much too fast if there was anything in the road. Something skittered aside as she thought it, a grey blur instantly lost among the red and black blurs of the receding rock walls on either side. Bighorn sheep. Nobody'd bothered to tell *them* to clear out before the wind could make them sick.

Funny thing was, they seemed to be thriving.

Harrie leaned into the last curve, braking in and accelerating out just to feel the tug of g-forces, and gunned it up the straightaway leading to the checkpoint at Boulder City. A red light flashed on a peeling steel pole beside the road. The Kawasaki whined and buzzed between her thighs, displeased to be restrained, then gentled as she eased the throttle, mindful of dust.

Houses had been knocked down across the top of the rise that served as host to the guard's shielded quarters, permitting an unimpeded view of Boulder City stretching out below. The bulldozer that had done the work slumped nearby, rusting under bubbled paint, too radioactive to be taken away. Too radioactive even to be melted down for salvage.

Boulder City had been affluent once. Harrie could see the husks of trendy businesses on either side of Main Street: brick and stucco buildings in red and taupe, some whitewashed wood frames peeling in slow curls, submissive to the desert heat.

The gates beyond the checkpoint were closed and so were the lead shutters on the guard's shelter. A digital sign over the roof gave an ambient radiation reading in the mid double digits and a temperature reading in the low triple digits, Fahrenheit. It would get hotter—and "hotter"—as she descended into Vegas.

Harrie dropped the sidestand as the Kawasaki rolled to a halt, and thumbed her horn.

The young man who emerged from the shack was surprisingly tidy, given his remote duty station. Cap set regulation, boots shiny under the dust. He was still settling his breathing filter as he climbed down red metal steps and trotted over to Harrie's bike. Harrie wondered who he'd pissed off to draw this duty, or if he was a novelist who had volunteered.

"Runner," she said, her voice echoing through her helmet mike. She tapped the ID card visible inside the windowed pocket on the breast of her leathers, tugged her papers from the pouch on her tank with a clumsy gloved hand and unfolded them inside their transparent carrier. "You're supposed to gas me up for the run to Tonopah."

"You have an independent filter or just the one in your helmet?" All efficiency as he perused her papers.

"Independent."

"Visor up, please." He wouldn't ask her to take the helmet off. There was too much dust. She complied, and he checked her eyes and nose against the photo ID.

"Angharad Crowther. This looks in order. You're with UPS?"

"Independent contractor," Harrie said. "It's a medical run."

He turned away, gesturing her to follow, and led her to the pumps. They were shrouded in plastic, one diesel and one unleaded. "Is that a Connie?"

"A little modified so she doesn't buzz so much." Harrie petted the gas tank with a gloved hand. "Anything I should know about between here and Tonopah?"

He shrugged. "You know the rules, I hope."

"Stay on the road," she said, as he slipped the nozzle into the fill. "Don't go inside any buildings. Don't go near any vehicles. Don't stop, don't look back, and especially don't turn around; it's not wise to drive through your own dust. If it glows, don't pick it up, and nothing from the black zone leaves."

"I'll telegraph ahead and let Tonopah know you're coming," he said, as the gas pump clicked. "You ever crash that thing?"

"Not in going on ten years," she said, and didn't bother to cross her fingers. He handed her a receipt; she fumbled her lacquered stainless Cross pen out of her zippered pocket and signed her name like she meant it. The gloves made her signature into an incomprehensible scrawl, but the guard made a show of comparing it to her ID card and slapped her on the shoulder. "Be careful. If you crash out there, you're probably on your own. Godspeed."

"Thanks for the reassurance," she said, and grinned at him before she closed her visor and split.

Digitized music rang over her helmet headset as Harrie ducked her head behind the fairing, the hot wind tugging her sleeves, trickling between her gloves and her cuffs. The Kawasaki stretched out under her, ready for a good hard run, and Harrie itched to give it one. One thing you could say about the Vegas black zone: there wasn't much traffic. Houses—identical in red tile roofs and cream stucco walls—blurred past on either side, flanked by trees that the desert had killed once people weren't there to pump the water up to them. She cracked a hundred and sixty kph in the wind shadow of the sound barriers, the tach winding up like a watch, just gliding along in sixth as the Kawasaki hit its stride. The big bike handled like a pig in the parking lot, but out on the highway she ran smooth as glass.

She had almost a hundred miles of range more than she'd need to get to Tonopah, God willing and the creek didn't rise, but she wasn't about to test that with any side trips through what was left of Las Vegas. Her dosimeters clicked with erratic cheer, nothing to worry about yet, and Harrie claimed the center lane and edged down to one forty as she hit the winding patch of highway near the old downtown. The shells of casinos on the left-hand side and godforsaken wasteland and ghetto on the right gave her back the Kawasaki's well-tuned shriek; she couldn't wind it any faster with the roads so choppy and the K-Rail canyons so tight.

The sky overhead was flat blue like cheap turquoise. A pall of dust showed burnt sienna, the inversion layer trapped inside the ring of mountains that made her horizon in four directions.

The freeway opened out once she cleared downtown, the overpass Patch had warned her about arching up and over, a tangle of banked curves, the crossroads at the heart of the silent city. She bid the ghosts of hotels good day as the sun hit zenith, heralding peak heat for another four hours or so. Harrie resisted the urge to reach back and pat her saddlebag to make sure the precious cargo was safe; she'd never know if the climate control failed on the trip, and moreover she couldn't risk the distraction as she wound the Kawasaki up to one hundred seventy and ducked her helmet into the slipstream off the fairing.

Straight shot to the dead town called Beatty from here, if you minded the cattle guards along the roads by the little forlorn towns. Straight shot, with the dosimeters clicking and vintage rock and roll jamming in the helmet speakers and the Kawasaki purring, thrusting, eager to spring and run.

There were worse days to be alive.

She dropped it to fourth and throttled back coming up on that overpass, the big one where the Phoenix to Reno highway crossed the one that used to run LA to Salt Lake, when there was an LA to speak of. Patch had said *overpass's down,* which could mean unsafe for transit and could mean littering the freeway underneath with blocks of concrete the size of a semi, and Harrie had no interest in finding out which it was with no room left to brake. She adjusted the volume on her music down as the rush of wind abated, and took the opportunity to sightsee a bit.

And swore softly into her air filter, slowing further before she realized she'd let the throttle slip.

Something—no, some*one*—leaned against a shotgunned, paint-peeled sign that might have given a speed limit once, when there was anyone to care about such things.

Her dosimeters clicked aggressively as she let the bike roll closer to the verge. She shouldn't stop. But it was a death sentence, being alone and on foot out here. Even if the sun weren't climbing the sky, sweat rolling from under Harrie's helmet, adhering her leathers to her skin.

She was almost stopped by the time she realized she knew him. Knew his ocher skin and his natty, pinstriped, double-breasted suit and his fedora, tilted just so, and the cordovan gleam of his loafers. For one mad moment, she wished she carried a gun.

Not that a gun would help her. Even if she decided to swallow a bullet herself.

"Nick." She put the bike in neutral, dropping her feet as it rolled to a stop. "Fancy meeting you in the middle of Hell."

"I got some papers for you to sign, Harrie." He pushed his fedora back over his hollow-cheeked face. "You got a pen?"

"You know I do." She unzipped her pocket and fished out the Cross. "I wouldn't lend a fountain pen to just anybody."

He nodded, leaning back against a K-Rail so he could kick a knee up and spread his papers out over it. He accepted the pen. "You know your note's about come due."

"Nick—"

"No whining now," he said. "Didn't I hold up my end of the bargain? Have you ditched your bike since last we talked?"

"No, Nick." Crestfallen.

"Had it stolen? Been stranded? Missed a timetable?"

"I'm about to miss one now if you don't hurry up with my pen." She held her hand out imperiously; not terribly convincing, but the best she could do under the circumstances.

"Mmm-hmmm." He was taking his own sweet time.

Perversely, the knowledge settled her. "If the debt's due, have you come to collect?"

"I've come to offer you a chance to renegotiate," he said, and capped the pen and handed it back. "I've got a job for you; could buy you a few more years if you play your cards right."

She laughed in his face and zipped the pen away. "A few more years?" But he nodded, lips pressed thin and serious, and she blinked and went serious too. "You mean it."

"I never offer what I'm not prepared to give," he said, and scratched the tip of his nose with his thumbnail. "What say, oh—three more years?"

"Three's not very much." The breeze shifted. Her dosimeters crackled. "Ten's not very much, now that I'm looking back on it."

"Goes by quick, don't it?" He shrugged. "All right. Seven—"

"For what?"

"What do you mean?" She could have laughed again, at the transparent and oh-so-calculated guilelessness in his eyes.

"I mean, what is it you want me to do for seven more years of protection." The bike was heavy, but she wasn't about to kick the sidestand down. "I'm sure it's bad news for somebody."

"It always is." But he tipped the brim of his hat down a centimeter and gestured to her saddlebag, negligently. "I just want a moment with what you've got there in that bag."

"Huh." She glanced at her cargo, pursing her lips. "That's a strange thing to ask. What would you want with a box full of research cells?"

He straightened away from the sign he was holding up and came a step closer. "That's not so much yours to worry about, young lady. Give it to me, and you get seven years. If you don't—the note's up next week, isn't it?"

"Tuesday." She would have spat, but she wasn't about to lift her helmet aside. "I'm not scared of you, Nick."

"You're not scared of much." He smiled, all smooth. "It's part of your charm."

She turned her head, staring away west across the sun-soaked desert and the roofs of abandoned houses, abandoned lives. Nevada had always had a way of making ghost towns out of metropolises. "What happens if I say no?"

"I was hoping you weren't going to ask that, sweetheart," he said. He reached to lay a hand on her right hand where it rested on the throttle. The bike growled, a high, hysterical sound, and Nick yanked his hand back. "I see you two made friends."

"We get along all right," Harrie said, patting the Kawasaki's gas tank. "What happens if I say no?"

He shrugged and folded his arms. "You won't finish your run." No threat in it, no extra darkness in the way the shadow of his hat brim fell across his face. No menace in his smile. Cold fact, and she could take it how she took it.

She wished she had a piece of gum to crack between her teeth. It would fit her mood. She crossed her arms, balancing the Kawasaki between her thighs. Harrie *liked* bargaining. "That's not the deal. The deal's no spills, no crashes, no breakdowns, and every run complete on time. I said I'd get these cells to Sacramento in eight hours. You're wasting my daylight; somebody's life could depend on them."

"Somebody's life does," Nick answered, letting his lips twist aside. "A lot of somebodies, when it comes down to it."

"Break the deal, Nick—fuck with my ride—and you're in breach of contract."

"You've got nothing to bargain with."

She laughed, then, outright. The Kawasaki purred between her legs, encouraging. "There's always time to mend my ways—"

"Not if you die before you make it to Sacramento," he said. "Last chance to reconsider, Angharad, my princess. We can still shake hands and part friends. Or you can finish your last ride on my terms, and it won't be pretty for you"—the Kawasaki snarled softly, the tang of burning oil underneath it—"or your bike."

"Fuck off," Harrie said, and kicked her feet up as she twisted the throttle and drove straight at him, just for the sheer stupid pleasure of watching him dance out of her way.

Nevada had been dying slowly for a long time: perchlorate-poisoned groundwater, a legacy of World War Two titanium plants; cancer rates spiked by exposure to fallout from aboveground nuclear testing; crushing drought and climactic change; childhood leukemia clusters in rural towns. The explosion of the PEP-CON plant in 1988 might have been perceived by a sufficiently imaginative mind as God's shot across the bow, but the real damage didn't occur until decades later, when a train carrying high-level nuclear waste to the Yucca Mountain storage facility collided with a fuel tanker stalled across the rails.

The resulting fire and radioactive contamination of the Las Vegas Valley proved to be a godsend in disguise. When the War came to Nellis Air Force Base and the nuclear mountain, Las Vegas was already as much a ghost town as Rhyolite or Goldfield—except deserted not because the banks collapsed or the gold ran out, but because the dust that blew through the streets was hot enough to drop a sparrow in midflight, or so people said.

Harrie didn't know if the sparrow story was true.

"So." She muttered into her helmet, crouched over the Kawasaki's tank as the bike screamed north by northwest, leaving eerie Las Vegas behind. "What do you think he's going to throw at us, girl?"

The bike whined, digging in. Central city gave way to desolate suburbia, and the highway dropped to ground level and straightened out, a narrow strip of black reflecting the summer heat in mirage silver.

The desert sprawled on either side, a dun expanse of scrub and hardpan narrowing as the Kawasaki climbed into the broad pass between two dusty ranges of mountains. Harrie's dosimeters clicked steadily, counting marginally more rads as she roared by the former nuclear testing site at Mercury at close to two hundred kph. She throttled back as a sad little township—a few discarded trailers, another military base, and a disregarded prison—came up. There were no pedestrians to worry about, but the grated metal cattle guard was not something to hit at speed.

On the far side, there was nothing to slow her for fifty miles. She cranked her music up and dropped her head behind the fairing and redlined her tach for Beatty and the far horizon.

It got rocky again coming up on Beatty. Civilization in Nevada huddled up to the oases and springs that lurked at the foot of mountains and in the low parts in valleys. This had been mining country, mountains gnawed away by dynamite and sharp-toothed payloaders. A long gorge on the right side of the highway showed green clots of trees; water ran there, tainted by the broken dump, and her dosimeters clicked as the road curved near it. If she walked down the bank and splashed into the stream between the roots of the willows and cottonwoods, she'd walk out glowing, and be dead by nightfall.

She rounded the corner and entered the ghost of Beatty.

The problem, she thought, arose because every little town in Nevada grew up at the same place: a crossroads, and she half-expected Nick to be waiting for her at this one too. The Kawasaki whined as they rolled through tumbleweed-clogged streets, but they passed under the town's sole, blindly staring stoplight without seeing another creature. Despite the sun like a physical pressure on her leathers, a chill ran spidery fingers up her spine. She'd rather know where the hell he was, thank you very much. "Maybe he took a wrong turn at Rhyolite."

The Kawasaki snarled, impatient to be turned loose on the open road again, but Harrie threaded it through slumping cars and around windblown debris with finicky care. "Nobody's looking out for us anymore, Connie," Harrie murmured, and stroked the sun-scorched fuel tank with her gloved left hand. They passed a deserted gas station, the pumps crouched useless without power; the dosimeters chirped and warbled. "I don't want to kick up that dust if I can help it."

The ramshackle one- and two-story buildings gave way to desert and highway. Harrie paused, feet down on tarmac melted sticky-soft by the sun, and made sure the straw of her camel pack was fixed in the holder. The horizon shimmered with heat, ridges of mountains on either side and dun hardpan stretching to infinity. She sighed and took a long drink of stale water.

"Here we go," she said, hands nimble on the clutch and the throttle as she lifted her feet to the peg. The Kawasaki rolled forward, gathering speed. "Not too much further to Tonopah, and then we can both get fed."

Nick was giving her time to think about it, and she drowned the worries with the Dead Kennedys, Boiled in Lead, and the Acid Trip. The ride from Beatty to Tonopah was swift and uneventful, the flat road unwinding beneath her wheels like a spun-out tape measure, the banded mountains crawling past on either side. The only variation along the way was forlorn Goldfield, its wind-touched streets empty and sere. It had been a town of twenty thousand, abandoned before Vegas fell to radiation sickness, even longer before the nuke dump broke open.

She pushed two hundred kph most of the way, the road all hers, not so much as the glimmer of sunlight off a distant windshield to contest her ownership. The silence and the empty road just gave her more to worry at, and she did, picking at her problem like a vulture picking at a corpse.

The fountain pen was heavy in her breast pocket as Tonopah shimmered into distant visibility. Her head swam with the heat, the helmet squelching over saturated hair. She sucked more water, trying to ration; the temperature was climbing toward one twenty, and she wouldn't last long without hydration. The Kawasaki coughed a little, rolling down a slow, extended incline, but the gas gauge gave her nearly a quarter of a tank—and there was the reserve if she exhausted the main. Still, instruments weren't always right, and luck wasn't exactly on her side.

Harrie killed her music with a jab of her tongue against the control pad inside her helmet. She dropped her left hand from the handlebar and thumped the tank. The sound she got back was hollow, but there was enough fluid inside to hear it refract off a moving surface. The small city ahead was a welcome sight; there'd be fresh water and gasoline, and she could hose the worst of the dust off and take a piss. Goddamn, you'd think with the sweat soaking her leathers to her body, there'd be no need for that last, but the devil *was* in the details, it turned out.

Harrie'd never wanted to be a boy. But some days she really wished she had the knack of peeing standing up.

She was only about half a klick away when she realized that there was something wrong about Tonopah. Other than the usual; her dosimeters registered only background noise as she came up on it, but a harsh reek like burning coal rasped the back of her throat even through the dust filters, and the weird little town wasn't the weird little town she remembered. Rolling green hills rose around it on all sides, thick with shadowy, leafless trees, and it was smoke haze that drifted on the still air, not dust. A heat shimmer floated over the cracked road, and the buildings that crowded alongside it weren't Tonopah's desert-weathered construction but peeling white shingle-sided houses, a storefront post office, a white church with the steeple caved in and half the facade dropped into a smoking sinkhole in the ground.

The Kawasaki whined, shivering as Harrie throttled back. She sat upright in the saddle, letting the big bike roll. "Where the hell are we?" Her voice reverberated. She startled; she'd forgotten she'd left her microphone on.

"Exactly," a familiar voice said at her left. "Welcome to Centralia." Nick wore an open-faced helmet and straddled the back of a Honda Goldwing the color of dried blood, if blood had gold dust flecked through it. The Honda hissed at the Kawasaki, and the Connie growled back, wobbling in eager challenge. Harrie restrained her bike with gentling hands, giving it a little more gas to straighten it out.

"Centralia?" Harrie had never heard of it, and she flattered herself that she'd heard of most places.

"Pennsylvania." Nick lifted his black-gloved hand off the clutch and gestured vaguely around himself. "Or Jharia, in India. Or maybe the Chinese province of Xinjiang. Subterranean coal fires, you know, anthracite burning in evacuated mines. Whole towns abandoned, sulfur and brimstone seeping up through vents, the ground hot enough to flash rain to steam. Your tires will melt. You'll put that bike into a crevasse. Not to mention the greenhouse gases. Lovely things." He grinned, showing shark's teeth, four rows. "Second time asking, Angharad, my princess."

"Second time saying no." She fixed her eyes on the road. She could see the way the asphalt buckled, now, and the dim glow from the bottom of the sinkhole underneath the church. "You really are used to people doing your bidding, aren't you, Nick?"

"They don't usually put up much of a fight." He twisted the throttle while the clutch was engaged, coaxing a whining, competitive cough from his Honda.

Harrie caught his shrug sideways but kept her gaze trained grimly forward. Was that the earth shivering, or was it just the shimmer of heat-haze over the road? The Kawasaki whined. She petted the clutch to reassure herself.

The groaning rumble that answered her wasn't the Kawasaki. She tightened her knees on the seat as the ground pitched and bucked under her tires, hand clutching the throttle to goose the Connie forward. Broken asphalt sprayed from her rear tire. The road split and shattered, vanishing behind her. She hauled the bike upright by raw strength and nerved herself to check her mirrors; lazy steam rose from a gaping hole in the road.

Nick cruised along, unperturbed. "You sure, Princess?"

"What was that you said about Hell, Nick?" She hunkered down and grinned at him over her shoulder, knowing he couldn't see more than her eyes crinkle through the helmet. It was enough to draw an irritated glare.

He sat back on his haunches and tipped his toes up on the footpegs, throwing both hands up, releasing throttle and clutch, letting the Honda coast away behind her. "I said, welcome to it."

The Kawasaki snarled and whimpered by turns, heavy and agile between her legs as she gave it all the gas she dared. She'd been counting on the refuel stop here, but compact southwestern Tonopah had been replaced by a shattered sprawl of buildings, most of them obviously either bulldozed or vanished into pits that glared like a wolf's eye reflecting a flash, and a gas station wasn't one of the remaining options. The streets were broad, at least, and deserted, not so much winding as curving gently through shallow swales and over hillocks. Broad, but not intact; the asphalt rippled as if heaved by moles and some of the rises and dips hid fissures and sinkholes. Her tires scorched; she coughed into her filter, her mike amplifying it to a hyena's bark. The Cross pen in her pocket pressed her breast over her heart. She took comfort in it, ducking behind the fairing to dodge the stinking wind and the clawing skeletons of ungroomed trees. She'd signed on the line, after all. And either Nick had to see her and the Kawasaki safe or she got back what she'd paid.

As if Nick abided by contracts.

As if he couldn't just kill her and get what he wanted that way. Except he couldn't keep her, if he did.

"Damn," she murmured, to hear the echoes, and hunched over the Kawasaki's tank. The wind tore at her leathers. The heavy bike caught air coming over the last rise. She had to pee like she couldn't believe, and the vibration of the engine wasn't helping, but she laughed out loud to set the city behind.

She got out easier than she thought she would, although her gauge read empty at the bottom of the hill. She switched to reserve and swore. Dead trees and smoking stumps rippled into nonexistence around her, and the lone and level sands stretched to ragged mountains east and west. Back in Nevada, if she'd ever left it, hard westbound now, straight into the glare of the afternoon sun. Her polarized faceplate helped somewhat, maybe not enough, but the road was smooth again before and behind and she could see Tonopah sitting dusty and forsaken in her rearview mirror, inaccessible as a mirage, a city at the bottom of a well.

Maybe Nick could only touch her in the towns. Maybe he needed a little of man's hand on the wilderness to twist to his own ends, or maybe it amused him. Maybe it was where the roads crossed, after all. She didn't think she could make it back to Tonopah if she tried, however, so she pretended she didn't see the city behind her and cruised west, toward Hawthorne, praying she had enough gas to make it but not expecting her prayers to be answered by anybody she particularly wanted to talk to.

The 95 turned northwest again at the deserted Coaldale junction; there hadn't been a town there since long before the war, or even the disaster at Vegas. Mina was gone too, its outskirts marked by a peeling sign advertising an abandoned crawfish farm, the Desert Lobster Facility.

Harrie's camel bag went dry. She sucked at the straw forlornly one last time and spat it out, letting it sag against her jaw, damp and tacky. She hunkered down and laid a long line of smoking road behind, cornering gently when she had to corner, worried about her scorched and bruised tires. At least the day was cooling as evening encroached, as she progressed north and gained elevation. It might be down into the double digits, even, although it was hard to tell through the leather. On her left, the Sarcophagus Mountains rose between her and California.

The name didn't amuse her as much as it usually did.

And then they were climbing. She breathed a low sigh of relief and patted the hungry, grumbling Kawasaki on the fuel tank as the blistering blue of Walker Lake came into view, the dusty little town of Hawthorne huddled like a crab on the near shore. There was nothing moving there either, and Harrie chewed her lip behind the filter. Dust had gotten into her helmet somehow, gritting every time she blinked; weeping streaks marked her cheeks behind the visor. She hoped the dust wasn't the kind that was likely to make her glow, but her dosimeters had settled down to chickenlike clucking, so she might be okay.

The Kawasaki whimpered apologetically and died as she coasted into town.

"Christ," she said, and flinched at the echo of her own amplified voice. She reached to thumb the mike off, and, on second thought, left it alone. It was too damned quiet out here without the Kawasaki's commentary. She tongued her music back on, flipping selections until she settled on a tune by Grey Line Out.

She dropped her right foot and kicked the stand down on the left, then stood on the peg and slung her leg over the saddle. She ached with vibration, her hands stiff claws from clutching the handlebars. The stretch of muscle across her ass and thighs was like the reminder of a two-day-old beating but she leaned into the bike, boot sole slipping on grit as she heaved it into motion. She hopped on one foot to kick the stand up, wincing.

It wasn't the riding. It was the standing up, afterward.

She walked the Kawasaki up the deserted highway, between the deserted buildings, the pavement hot enough to sear her feet through the boot leather if she stood still for too long. "Good girl," she told the Kawasaki, stroking the forward brake handle. It leaned against her heavily, cumbersome at a walking pace, like walking a drunk friend home. "Gotta be a gas station somewhere."

Of course, there wouldn't be any power to run the pumps, and probably no safe water, but she'd figure that out when she got there. Sunlight glimmered off the lake; she was fine, she told herself, because she wasn't too dehydrated for her mouth to wet at the thought of all that cool, fresh water.

Except there was no telling what kind of poison was in that lake. There was an old naval base on its shore, and the lake itself had been used as a kind of kiddie pool for submarines. Anything at all could be floating around in its waters. Not, she admitted, that there wasn't a certain irony to taking the long view at a time like this.

She spotted a Texaco station, the red and white sign bleached pink and ivory, crazed by the relentless desert sun. Harrie couldn't remember if she was in the Mojave or the Black Rock desert now, or some other desert entirely. They all ran together. She jumped at her own slightly hysterical giggle. The pumps *were* off, as she'd anticipated, but she leaned the Kawasaki up on its sidestand anyway, grabbed the climate-controlled case out of her saddlebag, and went to find a place to take a leak.

The leather was hot on her fingers when she pulled her gloves off and dropped her pants. "Damned, stupid… First thing I do when I get back to civilization is buy a set of leathers and a helmet in white, dammit." She glanced at the Kawasaki as she fixed herself, expecting a hiss of agreement, but the black bike was silent. She blinked stinging eyes and turned away.

There was a garden hose curled on its peg behind one of the tan-faced houses huddled by the Texaco station, the upper side bleached yellow on green like the belly of a dead snake. Harrie wrenched it off the peg one-handed. The rubber was brittle from dry rot; she broke it twice trying to uncoil a section, but managed to get about seven feet clean. She pried the fill cap off the underground tank with a tire iron and yanked off her helmet and air filter to sniff, checking both dosimeters first.

It had, after all, been one of those days.

The gas smelled more or less like gasoline, though, and it tasted like fucking gasoline too, when she got a good mouthful of it from sucking it up her impromptu siphon. Not very good gasoline, maybe, but beggars and choosers. The siphon wouldn't work as a siphon because she couldn't get the top end lower than the bottom end, but she could suck fuel up into it and transfer it, hoseful by hoseful, into the Kawasaki's empty tank, the precious case leaning against her boot while she did.

Finally, she saw the dark gleam of fluid shimmer through the fill hole when she peered inside and tapped the side of the tank.

She closed the tank and spat and spat, wishing she had water to wash the gasoline away. The lake glinted, mocking her, and she resolutely turned her back on it and picked up the case.

It was light in her hand. She paused with one hand on the flap of the saddlebag, weighing that gleaming silver object, staring past it at her boots. She sucked on her lower lip, tasted gas, and turned her head and spat again. "A few more years of freedom, Connie," she said, and stroked the metal with a black-gloved hand. "You and me. I could drink the water. It wouldn't matter if that was bad gas I fed you. Nothing could go wrong…"

The Kawasaki was silent. Its keys jangled in Harrie's hip pocket. She touched the throttle lightly, drew her hand back, laid the unopened case on the seat. "What do you say, girl?"

Nothing, of course. It was quiescent, slumbering, a dreaming demon. She hadn't turned it on.

With both thumbs at once, Harrie flicked up the latches and opened the case.

It was cool inside, cool enough that she could feel the difference on her face when she bent over it. She kept the lid at half-mast, trying to block that cool air with her body so it wouldn't drift away. She tipped her head to see inside:

blue foam threaded through with cooling elements, shaped to hold the contents without rattling. Papers in a plastic folder, and something in sealed culture plates, clear jelly daubed with ragged polka dots.

There was a sticky note tacked on the plastic folder. She reached into the cool case and flicked the sticky note out, bringing it into the light. Patch's handwriting. She blinked.

"Sacramento next, if these don't get there," it said, thick black definite lines. "Like Faustus, we all get one good chance to change our minds."

If you meet the Buddha on the road—

"I always thought there was more to that son of a bitch than met the eye," she said, and closed the case, and stuffed the note into her pocket beside the pen. She jammed her helmet back on, double-checking the filter that had maybe started leaking a little around the edges in Tonopah, slung her leg over the Kawasaki's saddle, and closed the choke.

It gasped dry when she clutched and thumbed the start button, shaking between her legs like an asthmatic pony. She gave it a little throttle, then eased up on it like easing up on a virgin lover. Coaxing, pleading under her breath. Gasoline fumes from her mouth made her eyes tear inside the helmet; the tears or something else washed the grit away. One cylinder hiccuped. A second one caught.

She eased the choke as the Kawasaki coughed and purred, shivering, ready to run.

Both dosimeters kicked hard as she rolled across the flat, open plain toward Fallon, a deadly oasis in its own right. Apparently Nick hadn't been satisfied with a leukemia cluster and perchlorate and arsenic tainting the ground water; the trees Harrie saw as she rolled up on the startling green of the farming town weren't desert cottonwoods but towering giants of the European forest, and something grey and massive, shimmering with lovely crawling blue Cherenkov radiation, gleamed behind them. The signs she passed were in an alphabet she didn't understand, but she knew the name of this place.

A light rain was falling as she passed through Chernobyl.

It drove down harder as she turned west on the 50, toward Reno and Sparks and a crack under the edge of the clouds that glowed a toxic, sallow color with evening coming on. Her tires skittered on slick, greasy asphalt.

Where the cities should have been, stinking piles of garbage crouched against the yellowing evening sky, and nearly naked, starvation-slender people picked their way over slumped rubbish, calling the names of loved ones buried under the avalanche. Water sluiced down her helmet, soaked her saddle, plastered her leathers to her body. She wished she dared drink the rain. It didn't make her cool. It only made her wet.

She didn't turn her head to watch the wretched victims of the garbage slide. She was one hour out of Sacramento, and in Manila of fifty years ago.

Donner Pass was green and pleasant, sunset staining the sky ahead as red as meat. She was in plenty of time. It was all downhill from here.

Nick wasn't about to let her get away without a fight.

The Big One had rerouted the Sacramento River too, and Harrie turned back at the edge because the bridge was down and the water was on fire. She motored away, a hundred meters, two hundred, until the heat of the burning river faded against her back. "What's that?" she asked the slim man in the pinstriped suit who waited for her by the roadside.

"Cuyahoga river fire," he said. "1969. Count your blessings. It could have been Bhopal."

"Blessings?" She spared him a sardonic smile, invisible behind her helmet. He tilted the brim of his hat with a grey-gloved finger. "I suppose you could say that. What is it really?"

"Phlegethon."

She raised her visor and peeked over her shoulder, watching the river burn. Even here, it was hot enough that her sodden leathers steamed against her back. The back of her hand pressed her breast pocket. The paper from Patch's note crinkled; her Cross poked her in the tit.

She looked at Nick, and Nick looked at her. "So that's it."

"That's all she wrote. It's too far to jump."

"I can see that."

"Give me the case and I'll let you go home. I'll give you the Kawasaki and I'll give you your freedom. We'll call it even."

She eyed him, tension up her right leg, toe resting on the ground. The great purring bike shifted heavily between her legs, lithe as a cat, ready to turn and spit gravel from whirring tires. "Too far to jump."

"That's what I said."

Too far to jump. Maybe. And maybe if she gave him what was in the case, and doomed Sacramento like Bhopal, like Chernobyl, like Las Vegas… Maybe she'd be damning herself even if he gave it back to her. And even if she wasn't, she wasn't sure she and the Kawasaki could live with that answer.

If he wanted to keep her, he had to let her make the jump, and she could save Sacramento. If he was willing to lose her, she might die on the way over, and Sacramento might die with her, but they would die free.

Either way, Nick lost. And that was good enough for her.

"Devil take the hindmost," she said under her breath, and touched the throttle one more time.

SCHRÖDINGER'S CAT CHASES THE SUPER STRING

In the sharp formulation of the law of causality—"if we know the present exactly, we can calculate the future"—it is not the conclusion that is wrong but the premise.
—Werner Karl Heisenberg, 1927

Posit a Cat. Not any cat, but a black cat. Male, aged about four years, left ear tattered with the battles of a tom in his prime. Rangy and ragged: a street cat. A subtle cat. A cat with an extra claw on each forepaw, one of those paws white along the edge of the toes as if he had carelessly splashed through a puddle of milk.

Completing the hypothesis, array the tom with a fine unconcern beneath the chair of a drunken physicist, where the patch of light falls through a railing to a flagstone patio. He washes his paw—the white-rimmed one—and smoothes his whiskers gracefully. This morning, perhaps there had been a little war with a lesser cat or six, followed by kittens gotten on a screaming queen. Or perhaps whitefish minced by a friendly costermonger. Or a glorious chase with a yapping beagle, that even now waits beyond the railing, while the tom—beginning now on his ears—taunts her with a pleased green squint.

Posit Niels Bohr, swirling cloudy white absinthe in a glass and regarding it with grave consideration, in a café on a street corner in Brussels. 1927. Jewel of cities, not as the jewel in the center of a crown but rather as the gorgeously engraved cameo in a grandmother's rose-gold ring.

It may not have happened quite as here described—may not, but *might have.*

And, so, posit: Unaware of the cat, Bohr hunches forward over the table, resting his elbows on its pale marble surface. Schrödinger has pushed himself back, leaning in his chair with his hands behind his neck, the picture of exhausted attention. An alcohol lamp flutters between them, flame bent over in the wind.

"Heisenberg was in tears," Bohr says. The flat of his hand on cool marble—it might be October—emphasizes his point.

Schrödinger nods and runs both hands through curling locks. His moustache quivers. "Heisenberg is twenty-five. And you two have come to a concord now."

Bohr dismisses the statement with a wave of one broad-knuckled hand, corners of a wide mouth turning down across a long face. "His initial experiments were sloppy."

Schrödinger does not disagree. "You say there is no doubt remaining. How does that statement—*no doubt*—not abrogate the very theory you profess?"

Bohr's mouth tightens. He raises his glass and makes a face over the actinic aftertaste of the cloudy fluid. "Surely you're not going to argue free will with me, Erwin."

Schrödinger shakes his head and smiles, straightening in his chair to retrieve his own glass. His eye falls on the tom, which has emerged from the sunlit patch beneath Bohr's chair. "I don't remember Heisenberg in tears," he says mildly. The tom twines the table legs, brushes against Schrödinger's pants leg, leaving a streak of grey fur. The physicist breaks a crumb of pastry from the leavings on his plate and offers it to the cat.

With a gracious purr and a rub of his whiskers, the tom refuses. He seats himself in the shifted sunbeam and again begins to wash.

"In tears," Bohr answers. Both men glance up at approaching footsteps. Three pairs: the shuffle of two men and the crisp click of a woman's boots. Bohr, no less drunk than a moment before, rises to offer Marie Curie his chair. He sways unsteadily, and Marie's husband Pierre—it could have happened so, the possibility exists—catches Bohr's elbow and steadies him while Einstein brings chairs from the neighboring table and sees him reseated.

Marie sits, in a rustle of silk, green as the absinthe in the bottle before them, and steeples her fingers. Pierre sits beside her, and Schrödinger drags his chair sideways with a harsh scrape that sets the terrier to yapping once more.

Einstein sighs. "How long has that dog been there, Niels? I had to nudge him away from the gate to get in."

"All afternoon," Bohr answers, fussing with glass and sugar and a slotted silver spoon. "Are you drinking, Albert?"

"Pity observing *him* won't change his location. Please. I want to talk to you about quantum tunneling."

"I'm too drunk," Bohr replies, waving to a waiter for three more glasses, for cold water and sugar and another bottle of absinthe. "You know what Wilde said of absinthe?"

"It makes you see the world as it truly is," says Marie Curie. She toys with a spoon, turning it over and over in her hand. "And that is where the true horror begins."

"Drink more, then, Albert," quips Heisenberg, and Bohr and Pierre Curie explode in laughter. Curie laughs well, eyes mirthful above a well-groomed beard, ice-white with advancing years. He seems strangely distinguished next to his wife, who wears her time-frosted hair in a girlish braid. Her eyes sparkle when she turns to regard him.

Einstein strokes the tom, which has achieved his lap. He blows ginger fur from his fingertips: the breeze catches it and ruffles it back into his own white mane. More fur streaks his pantsleg—an interference pattern laid against black worsted wool. The waitress bends over his shoulder, placing two fresh glasses on the table: one before him, and one before Marie. "Mademoiselle," Bohr corrects gently. "You have forgotten my friend Pierre."

"Pardon," she says, and sets the water carafe down before she turns.

"No hurry," Pierre Curie calls after her, stroking his beard. "You and I can share, can we not, Marie?"

Marie snaps the sugar tongs and smiles in answer.

Posit this as well, although perhaps it does not happen in quite this way. "My faith cannot abide the thought," Einstein says, reaching across the purring cat for a spoon, frowning at the barking of the dog beyond the railing, "that the Old One would give us the semblance of free will, and make a mockery of it. Or that he would create a universe so totally without direction. God does not play dice, Heisenberg."

Bohr lays a hand on Einstein's wrist as Einstein selects a lump of the sugar. "Stop telling God what to do, Albert."

Einstein laughs out loud, stroking the tom as it luxuriates in the sunlit warmth of his lap, both white-gloved paws kneading his leg. "Niels, you are a pleasure. Truly a pleasure."

Niels Bohr smiles and tips an imaginary hat. Which Heisenberg then leans forward and seems to tug down over his eyes, to Marie Curie's delighted laughter. Still, there is an edge of grief in it, and Schrödinger lays one hand on her black-clad arm. The continued yapping of the stray dachshund beyond the railing draws a raised eyebrow from Bohr, who pushes his glass away with a frown.

"Albert," Heisenberg says, "that's only the simplest interpretation. On another level, my idea reinforces free will. And if some of the implications of the wave/particle dichotomy hold true... then every action may take place in infinite variations, then the wave is truly a particle and the particle is truly a wave—"

Curie, dipping a taper into the flame of a candle in a jewel-red jar, startled at the sound of his voice. "The absinthe isn't helping me see anything straight." She set a second sugar cube alight over her glass. Since the loss of her husband, new lines adorned her forehead. "Werner, you were so quiet I forgot you were here. You startled me when you spoke."

"—Indeed, Marie. But if the probabilities that a unit of light will travel in a given direction are evenly divided, and we see that the results of both possibilities manifest, doesn't that indicate that both possibilities are realized?"

"And the cat is both alive and dead," Schrödinger adds, gesturing to the tabby calmly washing behind its leg, shedding hairs on Einstein's brown tweed suit. The cat looks up, as if it knows itself addressed, and smiles a Cheshire smile. "Until you open the box."

"Even after you open the box," Heisenberg replies. "Somewhere. Perhaps. Perhaps not." He shrugs, eyes hazed with alcohol. "Because the cat knows, after all."

"Does a cat count as an observer?" Einstein lets a smile play the corners of his mouth. "I find I know where Niels is most of the time, but I rarely understand what he's doing. Perhaps there's something to this after all."

A storm of laughter rises above the table, and Curie turns her head to one side as if looking for someone in whose eyes to share the joke. She frowns, then, glances down and sips her wine. She licks the berry-red stain from her lips. "I'm simply a chemist, gentlemen. I'm afraid this is beyond me. But it seems to me that you're describing a braid." Wild strands of wiry, snow-pale hair escape her bun as she shakes her head. "Or a rope that splices and unsplices, comes together and apart."

"Nothing is beyond you, my dear Marie." Bohr refills her glass. "Do your memories never contradict those of your friends? Or that which you see written in the histories? Isn't it possible that each of us lives an infinite number of lives, the threads parting and joining like a flow of wax down a candlestick—many threads, but a common direction? Many truths, one Truth?" None of the others speak, and Bohr looks from face to face for a moment.

He nods once, as if coming to a decision. "I have a paper to give in an hour. I'm afraid I must cut our discussion short." He pushes his chair back with a decisive scrape and stands, steady on his feet as if he has not been drinking all afternoon. He lets one hand trail across the wrought-iron tabletop.

The others stand alongside him: Marie Curie, Erwin Schrödinger, Werner Heisenberg. Three men and a woman, all dressed in black, bearing the shape of the future in their minds. Heisenberg sets his hat on his head at a jaunty angle and tucks money under the flickering pillar candle to cover the bill.

"I'll deny to my dying day that you ever made me cry over quantum uncertainty, Niels," the young man says with a grin, looking up again.

Bohr stops and turns to him, shocked. "When would I ever say such a thing as that?"

And a black cat with one white paw leaps from an empty chair, unaccountably turned to face the table that the four scientists have vacated. It slips between the wrought-iron railings and proceeds down the Champs-Elysées at an unconcerned canter, skittering through traffic as if guided by some destining hand, pursued rather more energetically by a wildly yodeling beagle.

ONE-EYED JACK AND THE SUICIDE KING

It's not a straight drop. Rather, the Dam is a long sweeping plunge of winter-white concrete: a dress for a three-time Las Vegas bride without *quite* the gall to show up in French lace and seed pearls. If you face Arizona, Lake Mead spreads out blue and alien on your left hand, inside a bathtub ring of Colorado River limestone and perchlorate drainage from wartime titanium plants. Unlikely as canals on Mars, all that azure water rimmed in massive red and black rock; the likeness to an alien landscape is redoubled by the Dam's louvered concrete intake towers. At your back is the Hoover Dam visitor's center, and on the lake side sit two art-deco angels, sword-cut wings thirty feet tall piercing the desert sky, their big toes shiny from touches for luck.

That angled drop is on your right. *À main droite.* Downriver. To California. The same way all those phalanxes and legions of electrical towers march.

It's not a straight drop. Hoover's much wider at the base than at the apex, where a two-lane road runs, flanked by sidewalks. The cement in the Dam's tunnel-riddled bowels won't be cured for another hundred years, and they say it'll take a glacier or a nuke to shift the structure. Its face is ragged with protruding rebar and unsmoothed edges, for all it looks fondant-frosted and insubstantial in the asphyxiating light of a Mojave summer.

Stewart had gotten hung up on an upright pipe about forty feet down the rock face beside the Dam proper, and it hadn't killed him. I could hear him scream-ing from where I stood, beside those New Deal angels. I winced, hoping he died before the rescue crews got to him.

Plexiglas along a portion of the walkway wall discourages jumpers and incau-tious children: a laughable barrier. But then, so is Hoover itself—a fragile slice of mortal engineering between the oppressive rocks, more a symbol interrupting the flow of the sacred Colorado than any real, solid object.

Still. It holds the river back, don't it?

Stewart screamed again—a high, twisting cry like a gutted dog. I leaned against the black diorite base of the left-hand angel, my feet inches from this inscription: 2,700 BC IN THE REIGN OF THE PHARAOH MENKAURE THE LAST GREAT PYRAMID WAS BROUGHT TO COMPLETION. I bathed in the stare of a teenaged girl too cool to walk over and check out the carnage. She checked me out instead; I ignored her with all the cat-coolness I could muster, my right hand hooked on the tool loop of my leather cargo pants.

With my left one, I reached up to grasp the toe of the angel. Desert-cooked metal seared my fingers; I held on for as long as I could before sticking them in my mouth, and then reached up to grab on again, making my biceps ridge through my skin. *Eeny, Meeny, Miney, Moe.* Eyepatch and Doc Martens, diamond in my ear or not, the girl eventually got tired of me. I saw her turn away from the corner of my regular eye.

They were moving cars off the Dam to let emergency vehicles through, but the rescue chopper would have to come from Las Vegas. There wasn't one closer. I checked my watch. Nobody was looking at me anymore, despite dyed matte-black hair, trendy goatee, and the sunburned skin showing through my torn sleeveless shirt.

Which was the plan, after all.

I released the angel and strolled across the mosaic commemorating the dedication of the Dam. Brass and steel inlaid in terrazzo express moons and stars: Alcyone, B Tauri, and Mizar. Marked out among them are lines of inclination and paths of arc. The star map was left for future archaeologists to find if they wondered at the Dam's provenance: a sort of "we were here, and this is what we made you" signature scrawled on the bottom of a glue-and-glitter card. A hundred and twenty miles north of here, we're leaving them another gift: a mountain full of spent nuclear fuel rods, and scribed on its surface a similar message, but that one's meant to say "Don't Touch."

Some card.

The steel lines describe the precession of equinoxes and define orbital periods. They mark out a series of curves and angles superimposed across the whole night sky and the entire history of civilized mankind, cutting and containing them as the Dam cuts and contains the river.

It creeps me out. What can I say?

THEY DIED TO MAKE THE DESERT BLOOM, an inscription reads across the compass rose and signs of the zodiac on my left, and near my feet, CAPELLA. And ON THIS 30TH DAY OF THE MONTH OF SEPTEMBER IN THE YEAR (INCARNATIONIS DOMINICAE ANNO MCMXXXV) 1935, FRANKLIN DELANO ROOSEVELT, 32ND PRESIDENT OF THESE UNITED STATES OF AMERICA DEDICATED TO THE SERVICE OF OUR PEOPLE THIS DAM, POWER PLANT, AND RESERVOIR. A little more than ten years before Bugsy Siegel gave us the Flamingo Hotel and the Las Vegas we know and love today, but an inextricable link in the same unholy chain none the less. I try to be suitably grateful.

But Bugsy was from California.

I passed over or beside the words, never stopping, my ears full of Stewart's screaming and the babble of conversation, the shouts of officers, the wail of sirens. And soon, very soon, the rattle of a helicopter's rotors.

The area of terrazzo closest to the angels' feet is called the Wheel of Time. It mentions the pyramids, and the birth of Christ, and the Dam. It ends in the year A.D. 14,000. The official Dam tour recommends you stay home that day.

Alongside these dates is another:

EARLY PART OF A.D. 2,100

Slipped in among all the ancient significances, with a blank space before it and the obvious and precise intention that it someday be filled to match the rest.

Stewart screamed again. I glanced over my shoulder; security was still distracted. Pulling a chisel from my spacious pocket, I crouched on the stones and rested it against the top of the inscription. I produced a steel-headed mallet into my other hand. When I lifted the eyepatch off my *otherwise* eye, I saw the light saturating the stone shiver back from the point of my chisel like a prodded jellyfish. There was some power worked into it. A power I recognized, because I also saw its potential shimmer through my eye where my left one saw only the skin of my own hand. The Dam, and me. Something meant to look like something else.

Card tricks.

The lovely whistle-stop oasis called Las Vegas became a minor metropolis—by Nevada standards—in large part by serving gambling, whiskey, and whores to the New Deal workers who poured these concrete blocks. Workers housed in Boulder City weren't permitted such things within town limits. On Friday nights they went looking for a place to spend some of the money they risked their lives earning all week. Then after a weekend in Sin City, they were back in harness seven hundred feet above the bottom of Black Canyon come Monday morning, nine a.m.

Ninety-six of them died on the Dam site. Close to three hundred more succumbed to black lung and other diseases. There's a legend some of them were entombed within the Dam.

It would never have been permitted. A body in the concrete means a weakness in the structure, and Hoover was made to last well past the date I was about to obliterate with a few well-placed blows. "Viva Las Vegas," I muttered under my breath, and raised the hammer. And then Stewart stopped screaming, and a velvety female purr sounded in my ear. "Jack, Jack, Jackie."

"Goddess." I put the tools down and stood up, face inches from the face of the most beautiful woman in the world. "How did you know where to find me?"

She lowered tar-black lashes across a cheek like cream and thrust a narrow swell of hip out, pouting through her hair. The collar of her sleeveless blouse stood crisp-pressed, framing her face; I wondered how she managed it in a hundred twenty. "I heard a rumor you meant to deface my Dam," she said with a smile that bent lacquered lips in a mockery of Cupid's little red bow. The too-cool teenager was staring at Goddess now, brow wrinkled as if she thought Goddess must be somebody famous and couldn't quite place who. Goddess gets that reaction a lot.

I sighed. Contrived as she was, she was still lovelier than anything real life could manage. "You're looking a little peaked these days, Goddess. Producers got you on a diet again? And it's my Dam, honey. I'm Las Vegas. Your turf is down the river."

Her eyes flashed. Literally. I cocked an ear over my shoulder, but still no screaming. Which—dammit—meant that Stewart was probably dead, and I was out of time. Otherwise I would have bent down in front of her and done it anyway.

"It's not polite to ask a lady what she does to maintain her looks, darling. And I say Hoover belongs to L.A. You claim, what—ten percent of the power and water?" She took a couple of steps to the brass Great Seal of California there at the bottom of the terrazzo, front and center among the plaques to the seven states that could not live without the Colorado, and twice as big as the others. Immediately under the sheltering wings of a four-foot bas-relief eagle. She tapped it with a toe. The message was clear.

I contented myself with admiring the way her throat tightened under a Tiffany collar as I shrugged and booted my hammer aside. Out of my left eye, I saw her *otherwise*—a swirl of images and expectations, a casting-couch stain and a shattered dream streetwalking on Sunset Boulevard. "You still working by yourself, Goddess? Imagine it's been lonely since your boyfriend died."

Usually there are two or three of us to a city. And we can be killed, although something new comes along eventually to replace us. Unless the city dies too: then it's all over. Her partner had gotten himself shot up in an alleyway. Appropriate.

"I get by," she answered with a Bette Davis sigh.

I was supposed to go over and comfort her. Instead, I flipped my eyepatch down. Goddess makes me happy I don't like girls. She's a hazard to navigation for those who do. "I was just leaving. We could stop at that little ice cream place in Boulder City for an avocado-bacon-burger."

A surprised ripple of rutabaga-rutabagas ran through the crowd on the other sidewalk, and I heard officers shouting to each other. Stewart's body must have vanished.

"Ugh," Goddess said expressively, the corners of her mouth turning down under her makeup.

"True. You shouldn't eat too much in a sitting; all that puking will ruin your teeth." I managed to beat my retreat while she was still hacking around a suitably acid response.

Traffic wasn't moving across the Dam yet, but I'd had the foresight to park the dusty-but-new F150 in the lot in Arizona, so all I had to do was walk across the Dam—on the lake side: there was still a crowd on the drop side—and haul Stewart (by the elbow) away from the KLAS reporter to whom he was providing an incoherently homosexual man-on-the-spot reaction. He did that sort of thing a lot. Stewart was the Suicide King. I kissed him as I shoved him into the truck.

He pulled back and caught my eye. "Did it work?"

"Fuck, Stewart. I'm sorry."

"Sure," he said, leaning across to open the driver's side door. "You spend fifteen minutes impaled on a rusty chunk of steel and then I'll tell you, 'Sorry.' What happened?"

"Goddess."

He didn't say anything after that: just blew silky blond hair out of eyes bluer than the desert sky and put his hand on my knee as we drove south through Arizona, down to Laughlin, and came over the river and back up through the desert wastes of Searchlight and CalNevAri. In silence. Going home.

We parked the truck in the Four Queens garage and went strolling past the courthouse. The childhood-summer drone of cicadas surrounded us as we walked past the drunks and the itinerant ministers. We strolled downtown arm in arm, toward the Fremont Street Experience, daring somebody to say something.

The Suicide King and me. Wildcards, but only sometimes. In a city with streets named for Darth Vader and for Seattle Slew, we are the unseen princes. I said as much to Stewart.

"Or unseen queens," he joked, tugging me under the arch of lights roofing Fremont Street. "What happened back there?"

Music and cool air drifted out the open doorways of casinos, along with the irresistible chime of the slot machines that are driving out the table games. I saw the lure of their siren song in the glassy eyes of the gamblers shuffling past us. "Something must have called her. I was just going to deface a national landmark. Nothing special."

Someone jostled my arm on my *otherwise* side, blind with the eyepatch down. I turned my head, expecting a sneering curse. But he smiled from under a floppy moustache and a floppier hat, and disappeared into Binion's Horseshoe. I could pick the poker players out of the herd: they didn't look anaesthetized. *That* one wasn't a slot zombie. There might be life in my city yet.

Stewart grunted, cleaning his fingernails with a pocketknife that wasn't street-legal by anyone's standards. Sweat marked half-moons on his red-striped shirt, armholes, and collar. "And Goddess showed up. All the way from the City of Angels."

"Hollywood and Vine."

"What did she want?"

"The bitch said it was her fucking Dam." I turned my head to watch another zombie pass. A local. Tourists mostly stay down on the Strip these days, with its Hollywood assortment of two-dimensional mockeries of exotic places. Go to Las Vegas and never see it.

I'm waiting for the Las Vegas themed casino: somewhere between Paris, Egypt, Venice, and the African coast. Right in the middle of the Strip. This isn't the city that gave Stewart and me birth. But this is the city I now am.

"Is it?"

"I don't know. Hoover should be ours by rights. But it called her: that's the only thing that makes sense. And I'm convinced that empty date forges a link between Vegas and L.A. It's as creepy as the damned Mayan calendar *ending* in 2012."

He let go of my arm and wandered over to one of the antique neon signs. Antique by Vegas standards, anyway. "You ever think of all those old towns under the lake, Jack? The ones they evacuated when the reservoir started to fill?"

I nodded, although he wasn't looking and I knew he couldn't hear my head rattle, and I followed him through the neon museum. I think a lot about those towns, actually. Them, and the Anasazi, who carved their names and legends on every wind-etched red rock within the glow of my lights and then vanished without a whisper, as if blown off the world by that selfsame wind. And Rhyolite, near Beatty, where they're building the nuke dump: it was the biggest city in Nevada in 1900 and in 1907 it was gone. I think about the Upshot Knothole Project: these downtown hotels are the older ones, built to withstand the tremors from the above-ground nuclear blasts that comprised it. And I think too of all the casinos that thrived in their day, and then accordioned into dust and tidy rubble when the men with the dynamite came.

Nevada has a way of eating things up. Swallowing them without a trace.

Except the Dam, with that cry etched on its surface. And a date that hasn't happened yet. Remember. Remember. Remember me.

Stewart gazed upward, his eyes trained on Vegas Vic: the famous neon cowboy who used to wave a greeting to visitors cruising into town in fin-tailed Cadillacs—relegated now to headliner status in the Neon Museum. He doesn't wave anymore: his hand stays upraised stiffly. I lifted mine in a like salute. "Howdy," I replied.

Stewart giggled. "At least they didn't blow him up."

"No," I said, looking down. "They blew the fuck out of Bugsy, though."

Bugsy was a California gangster who thought maybe halfway up the Los Angeles highway, where it crossed the Phoenix road, might be a good place for a joint designed to convert dirty money into clean. It so happened that there was already a little town with a light-skirt history huddled there, under the shade of tree-lined streets. A town with mild winters and abundant water. *Las Vegas* means *the meadows* in Spanish. In the middle of the harsh Mojave, the desert bloomed. And there's always been magic at a crossroads. It's where you go to sell your soul.

I shifted my eyepatch to get a look *otherwise*. Vic shimmered, a twist of expectation, disappointment, conditioned response. My right eye showed me the slot-machine zombies as a shuffling darkness, Stewart a blinding white light, a sword-wielding spectre. A demon of chance. The Suicide King, avatar of take-your-own-life Las Vegas with its record-holding rates of depression, violence, failure, homelessness, DUI. The Suicide King, who cannot ever die by his own hand.

"I can see why she feels at home here," Stewart said to Vic's neon feet.

"Vic's a he, Stewart. Unless that was a faggot 'she,' in which case I will send the ghosts of campiness—past present and future—to haunt your bed."

"She. Goddess. She seems at home here."

"I don't want her at home in my city," I snapped as if it cramped my tongue. It felt petty. And good. "The bitch has her own city. And sucks enough fucking water out of my river."

He looked at me shyly through a fall of blond bangs. I thought about kissing him, and snorted instead. He grinned. "Vegas is nothing but a big fucking stage set wrapped around a series of strip malls, anymore. What could be more Hollywood?"

I lit a cigarette, because everybody still smokes in Vegas—as if to make up for California—and took a deep, acrid drag. When I blew smoke back out it tickled my nostrils. "I think that empty inscription is what locks us to L.A."

Stewart laced his arm through mine again. "Maybe we'll get lucky and it will turn out to be the schedule for the Big One."

I pictured L.A. tumbling into the ocean, Goddess and all, and grinned back. "I was hoping to get that a little sooner. So what say we go back to the Dam tonight and give it another try?"

"What the hell do we have to lose?"

The trooper shone his light around the cab and the bed of the truck, but didn't make us get out despite three a.m. and no excuse to be out but stargazing at Willow Beach. Right after the terrorist attacks, it was soldiers armed with automatic weapons. I'm not sure if the Nevada State Police are an improvement, but this is the world we have to live in, even if it is under siege. Stewart, driving, smiled and showed ID, and then we passed through winding gullies and out onto the Dam.

It was uncrowded in the breathless summer night. The massive lights painting its facade washed the stars out of the desert sky. Las Vegas glowed in the passenger-side mirror from behind the mountains as Stewart parked the truck on the Arizona side. On an overcast night, the glow is greenish—the reflected lights of the MGM Grand. That night, clear skies, and it was the familiar city glow pink, only brighter and split neatly by the ascending Luxor light like a beacon calling someone home.

I'd been chewing my thumb all evening. Stewart rattled my shoulder to get me to look up. "We're here. Bring your chisel?"

"Better," I said, and reached behind the seat to bring out the tire iron and a little eight-pound hammer. The sledge dropped neatly into the tool loop of my cargo pants. I tugged a black denim jacket on over the torn shirt and slid the iron into the left-hand sleeve. "Now I'm ready."

He disarmed the doors and struggled out of the leather jacket I'd told him was too hot to wear. "Why you always gotta break things you don't understand?"

"Because they scare me." I didn't think he'd get it, but he was still sitting behind the wheel thinking when I walked around and opened his door. The alarm had rearmed; it wailed momentarily but he keyed it off in irritation and hopped down, tossing the jacket inside. "It's got to relate to how bad things have gotten. It's a shadow war, man. This Dam is *for* something."

"Of course it's for something." Walking beside me, he shot me that blue-eyed look that made me want to smack him and kiss him all at once. "You know what they used to say about the Colorado before they built it—too thick to drink, and too thin to plow. The Dam is there to screw up the breeding cycles of fish, make it possible for men to live where men shouldn't be living. Make a reservoir. Hydroelectric power. Let the mud settle out. It's there to hold the river back."

It's there to hold the river back. "I was thinking just that earlier," I said as we walked across the floodlit Dam. The same young girl from that afternoon leaned out over the railing, looking down into the yawning, floodlit chasm. I wondered if she was homeless and how she'd gotten all the way out here—and how she planned to get back.

She looked up as we walked past arm in arm, something reflected like city glow in her eyes.

The lure of innocence to decadence cuts both ways: cities and angels, vampires and victims. Sweet-eyed street kid with a heart like a knife. I didn't even need to flip up my eyepatch to know for sure. "What's your name?" I let the tire iron slip down in my sleeve where I could grab it. "Goddess leave you behind?"

"Goddess works for me," she said, and raised her right fist. A shiny little automatic glittered in it, all blued steel with a viper nose. It made a '40s movie tableau, even to the silhouetting spill of floodlights and the way the wind pinned the dress to her body. She smiled. Sweet, venomous. "And you can call me Angel. Drop the crowbar, kid."

"It's a tire iron," I answered, but I let it fall to the cement. It rang like the bell going off in my head, telling me everything made perfect sense. "What the hell do you want with Las Vegas, Angel?" I thought I knew all the West Coast animae. *She must be new.*

She giggled prettily. "Look at you, cutie. Just as proud of your little shadow city as if it really existed."

I wished I still had the tire iron in my hand. I would have broken it across her face.

"What the fuck is that supposed to mean?" Stewart. Bless him. He jerked his thumb up at the light smirching the sky. "What do you call that?"

She shrugged. "A mirage shines too, but you can't touch it. All you need to know is quit trying to break my Dam. You must be Jack, right? And this charming fellow here—" she took a step back so the pistol still covered both of us, even as Stewart dropped my hand and edged away. *Stewart.* "This must be the Suicide King. I'd like you both to work for me too."

The gun oscillated from Stewart's midsection to mine. Angel's hand wasn't shaking. Behind her, I saw Goddess striding up the sidewalk, imperious in five-hundred-dollar high-heeled shoes.

"I know what happens," I said. "All that darkness has to go somewhere, doesn't it? Everything trapped behind the Dam. All the little ways my city echoes yours, and the big ones too. And Nevada has a way of sucking things up without a trace.

"The Dam is a way to control it. It's a way to hold back that gummy river of blackness. And Las Vegas is the reservoir that lets you meter it out and use when you want it.

"Let me guess. You need somebody to watch over Hoover. And the magic built into it, which will be complete sometime after the concrete cures."

Stewart picked up the thread as Goddess pulled a little, pearl-handled gun out of her pocketbook as well. He didn't step forward, but I felt him interpose himself. *Don't! Don't.* "Let me guess," he said. "*The early part of 2100*? What happens then?"

"Only movie villains tell all in the final reel." Goddess had arrived.

Angel cut her off. "Gloating is passé." She smiled. "L.A. is built on failure, baby. I'm a carnivore. All that pain has to go somewhere. Can't keep it inside: it would eat me up sure as I eat up dreams. Gotta have it for when I need it, to share with the world."

"The picture of Dorian Gray," Stewart said.

"Call it the picture of L.A." She studied my face for a long time before she smiled. All that innocence, and all that cool calculated savagery just under the surface of her eyes. "Smart boys. Imagine how much worse I would be without it. And it doesn't affect the local ecology all that much. As you noted, Jackie, Nevada's got a way of making things be gone."

"That doesn't give you the right."

Angel shrugged, as if to say, *What are rights?* "All chiseling that date off would do is remove the reason for Las Vegas to exist. It would vanish like the corpse of a twenty-dollar streetwalker dumped in the high desert, and no one would mark its passing. Boys, you're not *real*."

I felt Stewart swelling beside me, soul-deep offended. It was my city. His city. And not some vassal state of Los Angeles. "You still haven't said what happens in a hundred years."

Goddess started to say something, and Angel hushed her with the flat of her outstretched hand. "L.A.," she said, that gesture taking in everything behind her—Paris, New York, Venice, shadows of the world's great cities in a shadow city of its own—"Wins. The spell is set, and can't be broken. Work for me. You win too. What do you say to that, Jack?"

"Angel, honey. Nobody really talks like that." I started to turn away, laying a hand on Stewart's arm to bring him with me. The sledgehammer nudged my leg.

"Boys," Goddess said. Her tone was harsh with finality.

Stewart fumbled in his pocket. I knew he was reaching for his knife. "What are you going to do," he asked, tugging my hand, almost dragging me away. "Shoot me in the back?"

I took a step away from Goddess, and from Angel. And Stewart caught my eye with a wink, and—*Stewart!*—kept turning, and he dropped my hand....

The flat clap of a gunshot killed the last word he said. He pitched forward as if kicked, blood like burst berries across his midsection, front and back. I spun around as another bullet rang between my Docs. Goddess skipped away as I lunged, shredding the seam of my pants as I yanked the sledgehammer out. It was up like a baseball bat before Stewart hit the ground. I hoped he had his knife in his hand. I hoped he had the strength to open a vein before the wound in his back killed him.

I didn't have time to hope anything else.

They shot like L.A. cops—police stance, wide-legged, braced, and aiming to kill. I don't know how I got between the slugs. I felt them tug my clothing; one burned my face. But I'm One-Eyed Jack, and my luck was running. Cement chips stung my face as a bullet ricocheted off the wall and out over Lake Mead. Behind Angel and Goddess, a light pulsed like Stewart's blood and a siren screamed.

Stewart wasn't making any sound now and I forced myself not turn and look back at him. Instead, I closed the distance, shouting something I don't recall. I think I split Goddess' lovely skull open on the very first swing. I know I smashed Angel's arm, because her gun went flying before she ran. Ran like all that practice in the sands of Southern California came in handy, fit—no doubt—from rollerblading along the boardwalk. My lungs burned after three steps. The lights were coming.

Almost nobody *runs* in Las Vegas, except on a treadmill. It's too fucking hot. I staggered to a stop, dropped the hammer clanging as I stepped over Goddess' shimmering body, and went back for Stewart.

His blood was a sticky puddle I had to walk through to get to him. He'd pushed himself over on his side, and I could hear the whimper in his breath, but the knife had fallen out of his hand. "Jack," he said. "Can't move my fingers."

I picked it up and opened it. "Love. Show me where."

"Sorry," he said. "Who the hell knew they could shoot so fucking well?" It came up on his lips in a bubble of blood, and it had to be *his* hand. So I folded his fingers around the handle and guided the blade to his throat.

The sirens and lights throbbed in my head like a Monday-morning migraine. "Does it count if I'm pushing?"

He giggled. It came out a kicked whimper. "I don't know," he said through the bubbles. "Try it and see."

I pushed. Distorted by a loudspeaker, the command to stop and drop might have made me jump another day, but Stewart's blood was sudden, hot and sticky-slick as tears across my hands. I let the knife fall and turned my back to the road. Down by my boots, Stewart started to shimmer. We were near where Angel had been leaning out to look down the face of the Dam. The Plexiglas barriers and the decorated tops of the elevator shafts started five feet on my right.

"One-Eyed Jacks and Suicide Kings are wild," I muttered, and in two running steps I threw myself over the wall. Hell, you never know until you try it. A bullet gouged the walltop alongside the black streaks from the sole of my Doc.

The lights on the Dam face silvered it like a wedding cake. It didn't seem like such a long way to fall, and the river was down there somewhere. A gust of wind just might blow me wide enough to miss the blockhouse at the bottom.

If I got lucky.

From the outside northbound lane on the 95, I spotted the road: more of a track, by any reasonable standard. The white Ford pickup dragged across the rumble strip and halted amid scattering gravel. It still had Stewart's jacket thrown across the front seat after I bribed impound. Sometimes corruption cuts in our favor. A flat, hard shape patted my chest from inside the coat's checkbook pocket, and the alarm armed itself a moment after I got out.

Two tracks, wagon wheel wide, stretched through a forest of Joshua trees like prickly old men hunched over in porcupine hats, abutted by sage and agave. The desert sky almost never gets so blue. It's usually a washed-out color: Mojave landscapes are best represented in turquoise and picture jasper.

A lot of people came through here—enough people to wear a road—and they must have thought they were going someplace better. California, probably. I pitched a rock at a toxic, endangered Gila monster painted in the animal gang colors of don't-mess-with-me and then I sat down on a dusty rock and waited. And waited. And waited, while the sun skipped down the flat horizon and the sky greyed periwinkle and then indigo. Lights rippled on across the valley floor, chasing the shadow of the mountain. From my vantage in the pass between the mountains, I made out the radioactive green shimmer of the MGM Grand, the laser-white beacon off the top of the Luxor, the lofted red-green-lavender Stratosphere. The Aladdin, the Venetian, the Paris. The amethyst and ruby arch of the Rio. New York, New York. And the Mirage. Worth a dry laugh, that.

Symbols of every land, drawing the black energy to Vegas. A darkness sink. Like a postcard. Like the skyline of a city on the back of a one-eyed jack in a poker deck with the knaves pulled out.

It glittered a lot, for a city in thrall.

There was a fifth of tequila in Stewart's coat. I poured a little libation on an agave, lifted up my eyepatch and splashed some in my *otherwise* eye. I took a deep breath and stared down on the valley. "Stewart," I said to my city. "I don't know if you're coming back. If anybody squeaks through on a technicality, man, it should be you. And I haven't seen your replacement yet. So I keep hoping." I hadn't seen Angel either. But I hadn't been down to the Dam.

Another slug of liquor. "Bugsy, you son of a bitch. You brought me here, didn't you? Me and Stew. You fixed the chains tight, the ones the Dam forged. And it didn't turn out quite the way you anticipated. Because sometimes we're wild cards, and sometimes we're not, and what matters is how you call the game."

I drank a little tequila, poured a little on the ground. If you're going to talk to ghosts, it doesn't hurt to get them drunk. Ask a vodun if you don't believe me.

My glittering shadow city—all cheap whore in gaudy paint that makes her look older, much older, and much, much tireder than she is—she'll suck up all the darkness that bitch Angel can throw at her, and I swear someday the Dam will burst and the desert will suck the City of Angels up too. Nevada has a way of eating things whole. Swallowing them without a trace. Civilizations, loved ones, fusion products.

There's a place to carve one more Great Event on the memoried surface of the Dam. And I mean to own that sucker, before Angel carves her city's black conquest in it. I've still got a hundred years or so to figure out how to do it.

Meanwhile, my city glitters like a mirage in the valley. Sin City. Just a shadow of something bigger. But a shadow can grow strangely real if you squint at it right, and sometimes a mirage hides real water.

This is my city, and I'm her Jack. I'm not going anywhere.

SLEEPING DOGS LIE

Liam dreams of flying. Overlong nails scrabbling cement, coarse black fur matted and filthy against skin that would show flaking and raw in the light. But the basement is cool in the summer, and Liam, hungry, sleeps. And whines.

But the whines are laughter. Until he wakes.

Strong hand lifting him from mother's too-warm belly, Liam cries as he soars through the air. Eyes blind, ears deaf. The rush of wind, and then the sweetness of milk: goat's milk, warmed on the stove, doled from an eyedropper: fevered, his mother cannot feed him. Belly full, he flies again, into the wrestling embrace of his nine brothers and sisters, mother's soft kisses as another puppy flies through the big, invisible sky to be fed.

Liam knows not to go to the stairs when the basement door opens. He sits up, whining again at the shaft of light. He can't fly in the light. Can't fly with his eyes open. And he won't let *him* know. It's Liam's secret.

Liam's secret. Secret like Liam's name. Good dogs don't keep secrets.

But Liam's learned to lie.

"Dinner, Luke," *he* says—not the big, warm hands but the boots and the pail. "Outside." He comes down the stairs and opens the basement hatchway and Liam follows him into the yard, to the chain. He lies down under the tree and noses fallen apples while *he* half-fills a bowl with kibble from the mouse-nibbled bag in the shed. A grey squirrel eyes him without compassion from the branches, and Liam braces his front feet and lurches up. Squirrels are not tolerated. The whole litter learned that, a snarl of dark fur and giant paws in pursuit of mother and the big, light-colored dog that she wouldn't let close to *her puppies*, even when he whined. Even when he laughed.

"Luke. Down."

But squirrels.

Liam lies down, although the pressure hurts his bony elbows. The bare ground under the apple tree is softer than the basement concrete. *He* leaves the food and goes inside. It's almost enough to fill Liam's belly. Once the door is shut, Liam drinks yesterday's water and paces, although his head hurts and the ache between his ribs makes him dizzy. Squirrels are not tolerated, and he watches the grey villain race up and down the trunk, chattering.

Liam knows if he could bark and throw himself into the air, eyes closed, he could fly. If he could fly, he could make the squirrel pay for its temerity. Somewhere in the sky is where the food is. Round the tree he paces, chain grinding the bare ring deeper, and the squirrel finds his hole for the night. Liam stands up on his chain and dances, but he knows better than to speak, and you can't fly if you're silent, and he doesn't dare close his eyes. He couldn't get far on the chain anyway, and Liam's dreams are a secret.

The house lights dim and silence follows, but the summer night is warm, and Liam, hungry, sleeps.

And dreams of flying.

thizwunwilbeeahpeht, the big, warm hands say, and then they make other noises as they cuddle Liam close to a neck that smells like coffee and sugar. *He*, the one who'll be the pails and the boots someday, makes noises too—friendly noises—and then hands are soft on his ears and different hands are holding him. Liam squirms, because the hands don't know how, but they're gentle enough and he calms down slightly. *amgunnacalimLuke.*

Brothers and sisters have left before him, so Liam knows what will happen next. "Hey Luke!" the new voice says. *wannacumhoamanmeetmykids?* Liam knows about car rides from vaccinations and having his ears cropped and trips to dog shows and puppy classes. He knows about grass and backyards and the big blue sky and he knows that squirrels aren't tolerated, and the one who will be boots and pails laughs and laughs and laughs when puppy-Liam barrels out the back door after them, forgetting to close his eyes so he can fly.

Liam sleeps on the boy's bed that night, and the girl's bed the night after that. They tease and make him jump to snap cookies out of their hands and laugh when he laughs back at them—*kiy yi yi kiy yi yi.*

But Liam gets big, and barking and jumping aren't cute anymore. And big people have work, and children have school, and long-coated dogs need grooming if they're going to be clean enough to come in the house. Nevermind that they chew when they're lonely.

Liam dreams of flying, and warm hands hold him up.

Car doors slam, and Liam shivers and whines in his sleep. He dreams about car rides sometimes too, but those dreams and those whines aren't like the ones where he's flying. There's not so much laughing. His paws scrabble in the dirt, dew-claws grown long and curled back into the flesh of his leg. He squeezes his eyes tight so he won't see the sunlight. He's flying.

yushuldhavecaldmesuuner says the voice in his dreams, and *canyookeephimforaweekuntilayefindahome*. The big, warm hands' voice, but Liam knows better than to believe it. He hears the voice often, but he never feels the hands. He buries his face in his paws. He wants to laugh. He wants to keep flying. It's the way to catch squirrels. He knows, because he hasn't caught one yet.

He's confident he will someday.

"Come here, Luke." No help for it. Liam opens his eyes and stands up, rattle of chain and he's moving.

Good boy, nice boy. Remember me?

The hands aren't as big as they used to be, but they're just as warm. Liam flinches from the trembling fury he feels in them as they touch his ribs, his matted fur. *Oh poor Liam.*

Liam.

His hands. His name. And the rage in those fingers isn't for him, he realizes, leaning against her legs when she stands up and unhooks his chain. *nevermindahlltaykimnow. sunnuvabitch.*

Nevermind.

Liam.

Liam hits the screen door running, sails through the air from the top step, hits the oak at the peak of his arc, eyes closed and fur a black banner of war flying long around him, singing out his secret in a series of joyous yelps. *Ki yi yi yi yi yi.* He scrabbles after the squirrel by sound, chatter of challenge and then nails on the bark as it dives into its hole. Acorns rain down around him and twigs catch in his coat. Squirrels are not tolerated. Over the ringing of his barks he hears voices: *ahnevasawadogflybefore.*

yoonevvasawwadogthathaddalearn

TWO DREAMS ON TRAINS

The needle wore a path of dye and scab round and round Patience's left ring finger; sweltering heat adhered her to the mold-scarred chair. The hurt didn't bother her. It was pain with a future. She glanced past the scarrist's bare scalp, through the grimy window, holding her eyes open around the prickle of tears.

Behind the rain, she could pick out the jeweled running lamps of a massive spacelighter sliding through clouds, coming in soft toward the waterlogged sprawl of a spaceport named for Lake Pontchartrain. On a clear night she could have seen its train of cargo capsules streaming in harness behind. Patience bit her lip and looked away: not down at the needle, but across at a wall shaggy with peeling paint.

Lake Pontchartrain was only a name now, a salt-clotted estuary of the rising Gulf. But it persisted—like the hot bright colors of bougainvillea grown in wooden washpails beside doors, like the Mardi Gras floats that now floated for real—in the memory of New Orleanians, as grand a legacy as anything the underwater city could claim. Patience's hand lay open on the wooden chair arm as if waiting for a gift. She didn't look down and she didn't close her eyes as the needle pattered and scratched, pattered and scratched. The long, Poplar Street barge undulated under the tread of feet moving past the scarrist's, but his fingers were steady as a gin-soaked frontier doctor's.

The prick and shift of the needle stopped and the pock-faced scarrist sat back on his heels. He set his tools aside and made a practiced job of applying the quickseal. Patience looked down at her hands, at the palm fretted indigo to mark her caste. At the filigree of emerald and crimson across the back of her right hand, and underneath the transparent sealant swathing the last two fingers of her left.

A peculiar tightness blossomed under her breastbone. She started to raise her left hand and press it to her chest to ease the tension, stopped herself just in time, and laid the hand back on the chair. She pushed herself up with her right hand only and said, "Thank you."

She gave the scarrist a handful of cash chits, once he'd stripped his gloves and her blood away. His hands were the silt color he'd been born with, marking him a tradesman; the holographic slips of poly she paid with glittered like fish scales against his skin.

"Won't be long before you'll have the whole hand done." He rubbed a palm across his sweat-slick scalp. He had tattoos of his own, starting at the wrists— dragons and mermaids and manatees, arms and chest tesseraed in oceanic beasts. "You've earned two fingers in six months. You must be studying all the time."

"I want my kid to go to trade school so we can get berths outbound," Patience said, meeting the scarrist's eyes so squarely that he looked down and pocketed his hands behind the coins, like pelicans after fish. "I don't want him to have to sell his indenture to survive, like I did." She smiled. "I tell him he should study engineering, be a professional, get the green and red. Or maintenance tech, keep his hands clean. Like yours. He wants to be an artist, though. Not much call for painters up *there*."

The scarrist grunted, putting his tools away. "There's more to life than lighters and cargo haulers, you know."

Her sweeping gesture took in the little room and the rainy window. The pressure in her chest tightened, a trap squeezing her heart, holding her in place, pinned. "Like this?"

He shrugged, looked up, considered. "Sure. Like this. I'm a free man, I do what I like." He paused. "Your kid any good?"

"As an artist?" A frown pulled the corner of her lip down. Consciously, she smoothed her hand open so she wouldn't squeeze and blur her new tattoos. "Real good. No reason he can't do it as a hobby, right?"

"Good? Or *good*?"

Blood scorched her cheeks. "*Real* good."

The scarrist paused. She'd known him for years: six fingers and a thumb, seven examinations passed. Three more left. "If he keeps his hands clean. When you finish the caste"—gesture at her hands—"if he still doesn't want to go. Send him to me."

"It's not that he doesn't want to go. He just—doesn't want to work, to sacrifice." She paused, helpless. "Got any kids?"

He laughed, shaking his head, as good as a yes, and they shared a lingering look. He glanced down first, when it got uncomfortable, and Patience nodded and brushed past on the way out the door. Rain beaded on her nanoskin as it shifted to repel the precipitation, and she paused on decking. Patchy-coated rats scurried around her as she watched a lighter and train lay itself into the lake, gently as an autumn leaf. She leaned out over the Poplar Street Canal as the lights taxied into their berth. The train's wake lapped gently at the segmented kilometers-long barge, lifting and dropping Poplar Street under Patience's feet.

Cloying rain and sweat adhered her hair to the nape of her neck. Browning roux and sharp pepper cut the reek of filthy water. She squeezed the railing with her uninjured hand and watched another train ascend, the blossom of fear in her chest finally easing. "Javier Alexander," she muttered, crossing a swaying bridge. "You had best be home safe in bed, my boy. You'd *best* be home in bed."

A city like drowned New Orleans, you don't just walk away from. A city like drowned New Orleans, you *fly* away from. If you can. And if you can't…

You make something that can.

Jayve lay back in a puddle of blood-warm rain and seawater in the "borrowed" dinghy and watched the belly lights of another big train drift overhead, hulls silhouetted against the citylit, salmon-colored clouds like a string of pearls. He almost reached up a pale-skinned hand: it seemed close enough to touch. The rain parted to either side like curtains, leaving him dry for the instant when the wind from the train's fans tossed him, and came together again behind as unmarked as the sea. "Beautiful," he whispered. "Fucking beautiful, Mad."

"You in there, Jayve?" A whisper in his ear, stutter and crack of static. They couldn't afford good equipment, or anything not stolen or jerry-built. But who gave a damn? Who gave a damn, when you could get that close to a *starship?*

"That last one went over my fucking *head,* Mad. Are you in?"

"Over the buoys. Shit. *Brace!*"

Jayve slammed hands and feet against the hull of the rowboat as Mad sputtered and coughed. The train's wake hit him, picked the dinghy up and shook it like a dog shaking a dishrag. Slimed old wood scraped his palms; the cross brace gouged an oozing slice across his scalp and salt water stung the blood from the wound. The contents of the net bag laced to his belt slammed him in the gut. He groaned and clung; strain burned his thighs and triceps.

He was still in the dinghy when it came back down.

He clutched his net bag, half-panicked touch racing over the surface of the insulated tins within until he was certain the wetness he felt was rain and not the gooey ooze of etchant: sure mostly because the skin on his hands stayed cool instead of sloughing to hang in shreds.

"Mad, can you hear me?"

A long, gut-tightening silence. Then Mad retched like he'd swallowed seawater. "Alive," he said. "Shit, that boy put his boat down a bit harder than he had to, didn't he?"

"Just a tad." Jayve pushed his bag aside and unshipped the oars, putting his back into the motion as they bit water. "Maybe it's his first run. Come on, Mad. Let's go brand this bitch."

Patience dawdled along her way, stalling in open-fronted shops while she caught up her marketing, hoping to outwait the rain and the worry gnawing her belly. Fish-scale chits dripped from her multicolored fingers, and from those of other indentured laborers—some, like her, buying off their contracts and passing exams, and others with indigo-stained paws and no ambition—and the clean hands of the tradesmen who crowded the bazaar; the coins fell into the hennaed palms of shopkeepers and merchants who walked with the rolling gait of sailors. The streets underfoot echoed the hollow sound of their footsteps between the planking and the water.

Dikes and levees had failed; there's just too much water in that part of the world to wall away. And there's nothing under the Big Easy to sink a piling into that would be big enough to hang a building from. But you don't just walk away from a place that holds the grip on the human imagination New Orleans does.

So they'd simply floated the city in pieces and let the Gulf of Mexico roll in underneath.

Simply.

The lighters and their trains came and went into Lake Pontchartrain, vessels too huge to land on dry earth. They sucked brackish fluid through hungry bellymouths between their running lights and fractioned it into hydrogen and oxygen, salt and trace elements and clean potable water; they dropped one train of containers and picked up another; they taxied to sea, took to the sky, and did it all over again.

Sometimes they hired technicians and tradesmen. They didn't hire laborer-caste, dole-caste, palms stained indigo as those of old-time denim textile workers, or criminals with their hands stained black. They didn't take artists.

Patience stood under an awning, watching the clever, moth-eaten rats ply their trade through the market, her nanoskin wicking sweat off her flesh. The lamps of another lighter came over. She was cradling her painful hand close to her chest, the straps of her weighted net bag biting livid channels in her right wrist. She'd stalled as long as possible.

"That boy had better be in bed," she said to no one in particular. She turned and headed home.

Javier's bed lay empty, his sheets wet with the rain drifting in the open window. She grasped the sash in her right hand and tugged it down awkwardly: the apartment building she lived in was hundreds of years old. She'd just straightened the curtains when her telescreen buzzed.

Jayve crouched under the incredible curve of the lighter's hull, both palms flat against its centimeters-thick layer of crystalline sealant. It hummed against his palms, the deep surge of pumps like a heartbeat filling its reservoirs. The shadow of the hull hid Jayve's outline and the silhouette of his primitive watercraft from the bustle of tenders peeling cargo strings off the lighter's stern.

"Mad, can you hear me?"

Static crackle, and his friend's voice on a low thrill of excitement. "I hear you. Are you in?"

"Yeah. I'm going to start burning her. Keep an eye out for the harbor patrol."

"You're doing my tag too!"

"Have I *ever* let you down, Mad? Don't worry. I'll tag it from both of us, and you can burn the next one and tag it from both. Just think how many people are going to *see* this. All over the galaxy. Better than a gallery opening!"

Silence, and Jayve knew Mad was lying in the bilge water of his own dinghy just beyond the thin line of runway lights that Jayve glimpsed through the rain. Watching for the Harbor Police.

The rain was going to be a problem. Jayve would have to pitch the bubble against the lighter's side. It would block his sightlines and make him easier to spot, which meant trusting Mad's eyes to be sharp through the rain. And the etchant would stink up the inside. He'd have to dial the bubble to maximum porosity if he didn't want to melt his eyes.

No choice. The art had to happen. The art was going to fly.

Black nano unfolded over and around him, the edge of the hiker's bubble sealing itself against the hull. The steady patter of rain on his hair and shoulders stopped, as it had when the ship drifted over, and Jayve started to squeegee the hull dry. He'd have to work in sections. It would take longer.

"Mad, you out there?"

"Coast clear. What'd you tell your mom to get her to let you out tonight?"

"I didn't." He chewed the inside of his check as he worked. "I could have told her I was painting at Claudette's, but Mom says there's no future in it, and she might have gone by to check. So I just snuck out. She won't be home for hours."

Jayve slipped a technician's headband around his temples and switched the pinlight on, making sure the goggles were sealed to his skin. At least the bubble would block the glow. While digging in his net bag, he pinched his fingers between two tins, and stifled a yelp. Bilge water sloshed around his ankles, creeping under his nanoskin faster than the skin could re-osmose it; the night hung against him hot and sweaty as a giant hand. Heedless, heart racing, Jayve extracted the first bottle of etchant, pierced the seal with an adjustable nozzle, and—grinning like a bat—pressurized the tin.

Leaning as far back as he could without tearing the bubble or capsizing his dinghy, Jayve examined the sparkling, virgin surface of the spaceship and began to spray. The etchant eroded crystalline sealant, staining the corroded surface in green, orange, violet. It only took a few moments for the chemicals to scar the ship's integument: not enough to harm it, but enough to mark it forever, unless the corp that owned it was willing to pay to have the whole damn lighter peeled down and resealed.

Jayve moved the bubble four times, etchant fumes searing his flesh, collar of his nanoskin pulled over his mouth and nose to breathe through. He worked around the beaded rows of running lights, turning them into the scales on the sea serpent's belly, the glints on its fangs. A burst of static came over the crappy uplink once but Mad said nothing, so Jayve kept on smoothly despite the sway of the dinghy under his feet and the hiss of the tenders.

When he finished, the sea monster stretched fifteen meters along the hull of the lighter and six meters high, a riot of sensuality and prismatic colors.

He signed it *jayve n mad* and pitched the last empty bottle into Lake Pontchartrain, where it sank without a trace. "Mad?"

No answer.

Jayve's bubble lit from the outside with the glare of a hundred lights. His stomach kicked and he scrabbled for the dinghy's magnetic clamps to kick it free, but an amplified voice advised him to drop the tent and wait with his hands in view. "Shit! Mad?" he whispered through a tightening throat.

A cop's voice rang over the fuzzy connection. "Just come out, kid," she said tiredly. "Your friend's in custody. It's only a vandalism charge so far. Just come on out."

When they released Javier to Patience in the harsh light and tile of the police barge, she squeezed his hands so tight that blood broke through the sealant over his fresh black tattoos. He winced and tugged his hands away but she clenched harder, her own scabs cracking. She meant to hiss, to screech—but her voice wouldn't shape words, and he wouldn't look her in the eye.

She threw his hands down and turned away, steel decking rolling under her feet as a wave hit. She steadied herself with a lifetime's habit, Javier swept along in her wake. "Jesus," she said, when the doors scrolled open and the cold light of morning hit her across the eyes. "Javier, what the hell were you thinking? What the hell. . . ." She stopped and leaned against the railing, fingers tight on steel. Pain tangled her left arm to the elbow. Out on the lake, a lighter drifted backwards from its berth, refueled and full of water, coming about on a stately arc as the tenders rushed to bring its outbound containers into line.

Javier watched the lighter curve across the lake. Something green and crimson sparkled on its hide above the waterline, a long sinuous curve of color, shimmering with scales and wise with watchful eyes. "Look at that," he said. "The running lamps worked just right. It looks like it's wriggling away, squirming itself up into the sky like a dragon should—"

"What does that matter?" She looked down at his hands, at the ink singeing his fingers. "You'll amount to nothing."

Patience braced against the wake, but Javier turned to get a better look. "Never was any chance of that, Mom."

"Javier, I—" A stabbing sensation drew her eyes down. She stared as the dark blood staining her hands smeared the rain-beaded railing and dripped into the estuary. She'd been picking her scabs, destroying the symmetry of the scarrist's lines.

"You could have been something," she said, as the belly of the ship finished lifting from the lake, pointed into a sunrise concealed behind grey clouds. "You ain't going nowhere now."

Javier came beside her and touched her with a bandaged hand. She didn't turn to look at the hurt in his eyes.

"Man," he whispered in deep satisfaction, craning his neck as his creation swung into the sky. "Just think of all the people who are going to *see* that. Would you just look at that baby go?"

STELLA NOVA

Prague. 1601.

1.

Ne frustra vixisse videar.

The dying man turned his head and vomited into an enameled basin held by his common-law wife. "Sophie?"

"Sophie is not here, Tyge. She is with Eric. In Hamburg." Kirstine's golden hair glimmered in the sickroom light, dimming as she bent into the shadow of the tapestried bed. "Tyge, my love, you must rest."

She cooled his brow with a cloth. His forehead rose high over a beard that would have been trimmed to a neat point were it not matted with sweat and vomitus. The bridge of his nose glittered even in the halflight, where a dueling scar lay concealed beneath a plate of precious metal.

His bulk rolled back on the bed. "I cannot sleep. Kepler. Where is *Kepler*?"

"I am here." Staring eyes over a prominent nose leaned from the shadows near the door. A much younger man, this—perhaps on the cusp of his thirtieth year, or just past it—his thick goatee still black. "What do you require?"

The sick man's breath struggled in his throat. "*Ne frustra vixisse videar.*"

"I have written it already, Tycho." Johannes Kepler raised the long quill in his scarred and cramped right hand and bent further into the light to read back the words, in the Latin and in the vernacular. "'May I not seem to have lived in vain.' It is written, and you have not. I will continue our War with Mars. Your name will live."

Tycho Brahe lay dying for eleven days. Duelist, glutton, scientist: he was fifty-seven years old.

"Sophie," he whispered again, and then, "Kirstine."

2.

Stella mortis. Stella nova.

I am dying. Like a star. I am dying.

The Heavens are not immutable. A red star crawls across the darkness that occludes my vision, no star at all. A planet. Mars. Always Mars.

No. Not always Mars. There was something before Mars.

November eleventh, the year of our Lord 1572. Walking from the warm closeness of another aristocrat's ball into the cold of the night, I looked into blackness and the shining double-chevron of Cassiopeia. I blinked, squinted, and rubbed chilled fingers against the oiled plate covering my nose.

When I opened my eyes, the strange light still shone. "Sophie! Sophie!"

My clever sister leaned her cheek against my pointing arm. A shiver trembled her body. "Oh."

"You see it."

"Tyge, I do."

A comet without a tail blazed overhead, marking Cassiopeia's waist like a jewel in her navel. "Sophie. What do you see?"

"A new star," she answered, before caution took hold and she qualified, "or a comet."

We are taught that the Heavens are divinely wrought—the fixéd stars cannot move, cannot change—and aligned in the outermost of the several crystal spheres which make the Heavens. The innermost spheres support the course of the planets. The clockwork of God, so we are taught. Immutable.

So Aristotelian doctrine ordains.

Half-afraid the bright, fragile thing would vanish before we could measure it, we hurried to our makeshift observatory. There, with our inadequate tools—the Ptolemaic ruler, the various quadrants, the armillary instruments—we calculated azimuth and horizon while the new star gleamed in the Heavens as if it had always been. Impossibly, over the course of weeks, it did not move against the farther stars, and the moon passed before and not behind it. *What a gift, what a gift, what a gift.*

My Lord, what are you teaching me?

"What is wrong?" Sophie asked one night, in the bitter November cold of the observatory balcony. I leaned down to a small brass quadrant on the marble railing, holding a candle alongside so I might read the minutes of arc aloud. Flickering light glittered on the fine lines dividing the curve, ran along the length of the rod pointed at the center of the new star.

A star by then bright enough to see through daylight, shining white as an angel's halo, the faintest orange tint having become evident over the preceding days.

"These are too coarse, Sophie. I need finer measurement: a minute of arc, less. I need a bigger quadrant." I pounded the rail, unsettling the quadrant and then cursing my childishness.

Sophie laughed at me, sketching numbers easily, more accurate than any boy assistant. A mind fine as any man's, my sister—a mind rich in understanding of iatrochemistry, alchymie, horticulture, medicine, astronomy. Would that she had been born a philosopher and not a girl.

She set her notes and her quill aside on a low inlaid table, beside the pitcher of wine and some cakes laid on a precious jade-green plate from the Orient. She crossed the bright tiled surface of the balcony, her breath hanging white in wintry air. "Tyge. We'll find a way."

My thumb worried the itching plate on my nose; my cheeks burned numb with cold. "These measurements are too crude to prove God's gift, this novel thing. Your *stella nova*."

"What do you need, Tyge?"

"We need to prove it's fixed in the heavens, as the stars are fixed."

"That the heavens—Oh." She put her hand to her mouth, as the heresy of what she'd been about to say sank in. And then she nodded, and laughed at me, and said, "Well, pack your things."

"Now? In the middle of the night?"

She caught my hands in her own and spun me twice before I collapsed onto the granite bench. "The parallax!"

Of course, I thought, and clapped my hands. "You want to see if *Stella nova* moves against the starfield when we move upon the earth—and thus judge how far away it lies."

And she smiled like Athena in the darkness.

So we traveled, my little Sophie and I, and corresponded with astronomers from so far as England to compare our observations.

There was no parallax. It was a star—far from Earth as the rest of the fixéd Heavens—a star and not a comet. The comet that proved it—the comet that moved against the fixéd stars as a comet should, the comet that exhibited parallax from one Earthbound place to another—that comet was gifted to us in the year of our Lord 1577.

Our observations proved that the comet also was affixed farther from the Earth than is the moon. They suggested also that the path of this particular light through the Heavens could not be circular, but must be elliptical, elongated—and how could such a thing pass through the Aristotelian spheres? Unless those spheres did not exist?

The Heavens are not fixéd, immutable. How can I express what that signifies? It shattered a thousand years of natural philosophy; it gave the final proof of the primacy of science by experiment. It proved Copernicus and his perfect solids wrong, once and for all. The Heavens are not *fixéd*.

My book was published in 1573, before the bright new star faded into darkness forever. Before the proof of the comet.

My book, *De Stella Nova*.

3.
Vocatus atque non vocatus, deus aderit.

Kepler emerged from the store-room, a blue glass bottle in his hand, sealed with wax. "Give him this to drink, Kirstine."

"What is it?" She took it from his hand, holding it up to whatever sun crept through the drapes as if she could read the nature of the world in how the light shone through the bottle.

"His own formula. Make sure he drinks the whole bottle."

"What is in it?"

"More of the same. *Cardus benedicta*, myrrh, pearls and sapphires. Quicksilver and opium. It will ease his pain and provoke urination."

"Is it dangerous to use so much?"

"As dangerous as it is not to. Perhaps it can clear the obstruction from his bladder." Kepler smiled. "In any case, I shall see to it, Kirstine—you have my solemn vow that his work will live on. Even if he passes, his legacy—will be born out of that death."

Kirstine's gaze went to the majestic bulk under the twisted coverlet. Kepler watched her, the tears seeping down her cheeks, and then turned back to Tycho. Rich silks and clean linens swaddled him, and it would make no difference in the end. Kepler might have wondered what memories darkened Kirstine's brow as she comforted the man who loved her twenty-eight years, when no church would sanctify the union of noble to commoner. She wept, and Kepler crouched on his stool, quill poised over vellum.

Until Brahe stirred again. "Kepler."

"Kepler hears you," the mathematician said. He rose from his place at the edge of the room like a lean, richly-dressed raven and placed an ink-stained hand on Brahe's sweating forehead.

Too-bright eyes cleared. "The new star. The comet. God in His grace ensures serendipity. He gives us what we need to discover what we must. Do you understand? God shows us what He wants us to learn. *Vocatus atque non vocatus, deus aderit.* Seen and unseen, God Is. His hand hangs over the world."

Kirstine collapsed into the brocade-cushioned chair. She breathed in and then out, looking hopelessly at Kepler, who shook his head.

"Call a priest. I will wait with Tycho."

"Sophie," Brahe muttered as Kirstine left. His face turned blindly from the dim light seeping through the curtains, and Kepler rose to draw them tighter.

"Sophie is with her fiancé. With Eric Lange, in Hamburg. She is well."

"She must not marry that wastrel." Brahe coughed wetly, suddenly lucid. "She must continue her studies."

Kepler held a goblet to his teacher's lips. "She is a woman, Tycho. Let her have a woman's life."

Brahe laid back on his pillow, and did not seem to hear.

"Heaven is an observatory, Johannes." Eyes that had surveyed the geometry of the Heavens with unheralded precision were blind now, feverbright. "Listen to Mars."

"Mars, master. I know. You must trust me."

"Mars will tell you everything."

Yes, Kepler thought. Eventually, he will.

"God will give you a star as well," Brahe muttered. "And I have given you Mars."

Johannes Kepler nodded tolerantly—but he would think of those words again, three years later, when Brunowski's excited midnight pounding on Kepler's door drew his attention to his own *stella nova*, lodged like a thorn in the belly of Ophiucus.

Brahe's impeccable Mars data—unheralded in its precision—stretched decades. In 1609, Kepler would find those meticulous data indispensable in proving that Mars traveled in an elliptical orbit around the Sun. In the process, he would establish that his mentor—and his own earlier theories, and those of Copernicus—had been totally, irrevocably wrong.

Brahe had shattered the universe once. Kepler would be among the first to build a new one from the shards.

4.

Non videri sed est.

The answer lies with Mars. It has always lain with Mars. Mars and his odd, looping motion across the sky. And we will know his answer when Kepler finishes the maths. He estimates it will take some thousand pages of equations.

There is a simple answer, under God, and the simple answer is the best. If the Earth moved under our feet, how could we not feel it? If Copernicus were correct about the perfect solids of the heavens, then neither Mars nor my comet could move in such loops and ellipses as they do.

Previous data have been flawed, but mine are better, and they will show the truth of God's design.

Kepler must carry on. *Sophie and I have proven it. The course of the Heavens is a changing thing.*

I call for Kepler, and I hear his voice, shuffling footsteps across the dense hand-knotted carpets, but I do not understand what he says. The young German. Not godless, but outcast by Lutheran and Catholic alike. And brilliant, and if he will only see the truth of God's will, an astronomer.

A scientist.

Does he come? I know it not. The pain is very great. Some edge of my soul knows I am fevered, knows that I lie under linen, that sweet faithful Kirstine cools my brow and drips water down my throat. I know what they are giving me for the raging fever, then: salts of mercury, and other things. My own prescription for fever and vomiting, devised with clever Sophie so many years ago.

I am Tycho Brahe. I taste my own poison. The savor of metal locks my tongue. My commoner wife, whom I have never been forgiven for loving, holds my hand in slick fingers. My argumentative student sits by my bed. I am dying.

The rest of me soars. *Build on my mistakes, Johannes. Non videri sed est.*

"To be rather than to seem." The voice is a darkness in me. There is something I know.

I am dying. Dying, like a star, and revelation comes to a dying man in a flare of inspiration, like the clarity when the fever at last breaks. *Die stella nova*, my Sophie's bright discovery, was a star indeed. But not a *new* star.

It was a dead star.

A funeral pyre. I was right: the spheres in heaven are not immutable; I was wrong: this was not a birth.

It was an explosion.

Darkness swaddles me, cold as a Knudstrup balcony in November. Like the salmon that kills itself to breed, out of the old thing comes the next thing.

It is the advancement of the world: as Brahe gives birth to Kepler, the dead star hangs shining in unfathomable darkness. I am dying, but my light will illumine my student, and the next, and the one after that.

The brightest star is a dying star.

Stella mortis. Stella nova.

Non videri sed est.
Vocatus atque non vocatus, deus aderit.
Stella mortis. Stella nova.
Ne frustra vixisse videar.

THIS TRAGIC GLASS

View but his picture in this tragic glass,
And then applaud his fortunes as you please.
—Christopher Marlowe, *Tamburlaine the Great, Part 1 II 7-8*

The light gleamed pewter under gracious, bowering trees; a liver-chestnut gelding stamped one white hoof on the road. His rider stood in his stirrups to see through wreaths of mist, shrugging to settle a slashed, black doublet which violated several sumptuary laws. Two breaths steamed as horse and man surveyed the broad lawn of scythe-cut grass that bulwarked the manor house where they had spent the night and much of the day before.

The man ignored the slow coiling of his guts as he settled into the saddle. He reined the gelding about, a lift of the left hand and the light touch of heels. It was eight miles to Deptford Strand and a meetingplace near the slaughterhouse. In the name of Queen Elizabeth and her Privy Council, and for the sake of the man who had offered him shelter when no one else under God's dominion would, Christofer Marley must arrive before the sun climbed a handspan above the cluttered horizon.

"That's—" Satyavati squinted at her heads-up display, sweating in the under-air-conditioned beige and grey academia of her computer lab. Her fingers moved with automatic deftness, opening a tin and extracting a cinnamon breath mint from the embrace of its brothers. Absently, she crunched it, and winced at the spicy heat. "—funny."

"Dr. Brahmaputra?" Her research assistant looked up, disconnecting his earplug. "Something wrong with the software?"

She nodded, pushing a fistful of coarse, silver hair out of her face as she bent closer to the holographic projection that hung over her desk. The rumble of a semiballistic leaving McCarran Aerospaceport rattled the windows. She rolled her eyes. "One of the undergrads must have goofed the coding on the text. Our genderbot just kicked back a truly freaky outcome. Come look at this, Baldassare."

He stood, a boy in his late twenties with an intimidatingly Italian name, already working on an academic's well-upholstered body, and came around her desk to look over her shoulder. "What am I looking at?"

"Line one fifty-seven," she said, pushing down a fragment of panic that she knew had nothing to do with the situation at hand and everything to do with old damage and ancient history. "See? Coming up as female. Have we a way to see who coded the texts?"

He leaned close, reaching over her to put a hand on her desk. She edged away from the touch. "All the Renaissance stuff was double-checked by Sienna Haverson. She shouldn't have let a mistake like that slip past; she did her dis on Nashe or Fletcher or somebody, and she's just gotten into the *Poet Emeritus* project, for the love of Mike. And it's not like there are a lot of female Elizabethan playwrights she could have confused—"

"It's not a transposition." Satyavati fished out another cinnamon candy and offered one to Tony Baldassare, who smelled faintly of garlic. He had sense enough to suck on his instead of crunching it; she made a point of tucking hers up between her lip and gum where she'd be less likely to chew on it. "I checked that. This is the only one coming up wrong."

"Well," Baldassare said on a thoughtful breath, "I suppose we can always consider the possibility that Dr. Haverson was drunk that evening—"

Satyavati laughed, brushing Baldassare aside to stand up from her chair, uncomfortable with his closeness. "Or we can try to convince the establishment that the most notorious rakehell in the Elizabethan canon was a girl."

"I dunno," Baldassare answered. "It's a fine line between Marlowe and Jonson for scoundrelhood."

"Bah. You see what I mean. A nice claim. It would do wonders for my tenure hopes and your future employability. And I know you have your eye on Poet Emeritus, too."

"It's a crazy dream." He spread his arms wide and leaned far back, the picture of ecstatic madness.

"Who wouldn't want to work with Professor Keats?" She sighed, twisting her hair into a scrunchie. "Screw it: I'm going to lunch. See if you can figure out what broke."

The air warmed as the sun rose, spilling light like a promise down the road, across the grey moving water of the Thames, between the close-growing trees. Halfway to Deptford, Christofer Marley reined his gelding in to rest it; the sunlight matched his hair to the animal's mane. The man was as beautiful as the horse—groomed until shining, long-necked and long-legged, slender as a girl and fashionably pallid of complexion. Lace cuffs fell across hands as white as the gelding's forehoof.

Their breath no longer steamed, nor did the river.

Kit rubbed a hand across the back of his mouth. He closed his eyes for a moment before glancing back over his shoulder: the manor house—his lover and patron Thomas Walsingham's manor house—was long out of sight. The gelding tossed his head, ready to canter, and Kit let him have the rein he wanted.

All the rein he wants. A privilege Kit himself had rarely been allowed.

Following the liver-colored gelding's whim, they drove hard for Deptford and the house of a cousin of the Queen's beloved secretary of state and closest confidant, Lord Burghley.

The house of Mistress Eleanor Bull.

Satyavati stepped out of the latest incarnation of a vegetarian barbecue joint that changed hands every six months, the heat of a Las Vegas August afternoon pressing her shoulders like angry hands. The University of Nevada campus spread green and artificial across a traffic-humming street; beyond the buildings monsoon clouds rimmed the mountains across the broad, shallow desert valley. A plastic bag tumbled in ecstatic circles near a stucco wall, caught in an eddy, but the wind was against them; there would be no baptism of lightning and rain. She crossed at the new pedestrian bridge, acknowledging Professors Keats and Ling as they wandered past, deep in conversation—"we were going after Plath, but the consensus was she'd just kill herself again"—and almost turned to ask Ling a question when her hip unit beeped.

She dabbed her lips in case of leftover barbecue sauce and flipped the mini-computer open. Clouds covered the sun, but cloying heat radiated from the pavement under her feet. Westward, toward the thunderheads and the mountains, the grey mist of verga—evaporating rain—greased the sky like a thumbsmear across a charcoal sketch by God. "Mr. Baldassare?"

"Dr. Brahmaputra." Worry charged his voice; his image above her holistic communications and computational device showed a thin, dark line between the brows. "I have some bad news…"

She sighed and closed her eyes, listening to distant thunder echo from the mountains. "Tell me the whole database is corrupt."

"No." He rubbed his forehead with his knuckles; a staccato little image, but she could see the gesture and expression as if he stood before her. "I corrected the Marlowe data."

"And?"

"The genderbot still thinks Kit Marlowe was a girl. I reentered everything."

"That's—"

"Impossible?" Baldassare grinned. "I know. Come to the lab; we'll lock the door and figure this out. I called Dr. Haverson."

"Dr. Haverson? Sienna Haverson?"

"She was doing Renaissance before she landed in Brit Lit. Can it hurt?"

"What the hell."

Eleanor Bull's house was whitewashed and warm-looking. The scent of its gardens didn't quite cover the slaughterhouse reek, but the house peered through narrow windows and seemed to smile. Kit gave the gelding's reins to a lad from the stable, along with coins to see the beast curried and fed. He scratched under the animal's mane with guilty fingers; his mother would have his hide for not seeing to the chestnut himself. But the Queen's business took precedent, and Kit was—and had been for seven years—a Queen's man.

Bull's establishment was no common tavern, but the house of a respectable widow, where respectable men met to dine in private circumstances and discuss the sort of business not for common ears to hear. Kit squared his shoulders under the expensive suit, clothes bought with an intelligencer's money, and presented himself at the front door of the house. His stomach knotted; he wrapped his inkstained fingers together after he tapped, and waited for the Widow Bull to offer him admittance.

The blonde, round-cheeked image of Sienna Haverson beside Satyavati's desk frowned around the thumbnail she was chewing. "It's ridiculous on the face of it. Christopher Marlowe, a woman? It isn't possible to reconcile his biography with—what, crypto-femininity? He was a seminary student, for Christ's sake. People lived in each other's *pockets* during the Renaissance. Slept two or three to a bed, and not in a sexual sense—"

Baldassare was present in the flesh; like Satyavati, he preferred the mental break of actually going home from the office at the end of the day. It also didn't hurt to be close enough to keep a weather eye on university politics.

As she watched, he swung his Chinese-slippered feet onto the desk, his fashionably shabby cryosilk smoking jacket falling open as he leaned back. Satyavati leaned on her elbows, avoiding the interface plate on her desktop and hiding a smile; Baldassare's breadth of gesture amused her.

He said, "Women soldiers managed it during the American Civil War."

"Hundreds of years later—"

"Yes, but there's no reason to think Marlowe had to be a woman. He could have been providing a cover for a woman poet or playwright—Mary Herbert, maybe. Sidney's sister—"

"Or he could have been Shakespeare in disguise," Haverson said with an airy wave of her hand. "It's one anomaly out of a database of two hundred and fifty authors, Satyavati. I don't think it invalidates the work. That's an unprecedented precision of result."

"That's the problem," Satyavati answered, slowly. "If it were a pattern of errors, or if he were coming up as one of the borderline cases—we can get Alice Sheldon to come back just barely as a male author if we use a sufficiently small sample—but it's the entire body of Marlowe's work. And it's *strongly* female.

We can't publish until we address this. Somehow."

Baldassare's conservative, black braid fell forward over his shoulder. "What do we know about Christopher Marlowe, Dr. Haverson? You've had Early Modern English and Middle English RNA-therapy, haven't you? Does that include history?"

The hologram rolled her eyes. "There's also old-fashioned reading and research," she said, scratching the side of her nose with the gnawed thumbnail. Satyavati grinned at her, and Haverson grinned back, a generational acknowledgment. *Oh, these kids.*

"Christopher Marlowe. Alleged around the time of his death to be an atheist and a sodomite—which are terms with different connotations in the Elizabethan sense than the modern: it borders on an accusation of witchcraft, frankly—author of seven plays, a short lyric poem, and an incomplete long poem that remain to us, as well as a couple of Latin translations and the odd eulogy. And a dedication to Mary Herbert, Countess of Pembroke, which is doubtless where Baldassare got that idea. The only thing we know about him—really *know*—is that he was the son of a cobbler, a divinity student who attended Corpus Christi under scholarship and seemed to have more money than you would expect and the favor of the Privy Council, and he was arrested several times on capital charges that were then more or less summarily dismissed. All very suggestive that he was an agent—a spy—for Queen Elizabeth. There's a portrait that's supposed to be him—"

Baldassare jerked his head up at the wall; above the bookcases, near the ceiling, a double row of 2-d images were pinned: the poets, playwrights, and authors whose work had been entered into the genderbot. "The redhead."

"The original painting shows him as a dark mousy blond; the reproductions usually make him prettier. If it is him. It's an educated guess, frankly: we don't know who that portrait is of." Haverson grinned, warming to her subject; the academic's delight in a display of useless information. Satyavati knew it well.

Satyavati's field of study was the late twenty-first century; Renaissance poets hadn't touched her life in more than passing since her undergraduate days. "Did he ever marry? Any kids?" *And why are you wondering that?*

"No, and none that we know of. It's conventionally accepted that he was homosexual, but again, no proof. Men often didn't marry until they were in their late twenties in Elizabethan England, so it's not a deciding factor. He's never been convincingly linked to anyone; for all we know, he might have died a virgin at twenty-nine—" Baldassare snorted heavily, and Haverson angled her head to the side, her steepled hands opening like wings. "There's some other irregularities in his biography: he refused holy orders after completing his degree, and he was baptized some twenty days after his birth rather than the usual three. And the circumstances of his death are very odd indeed. But it doesn't add up to a pattern, I don't think."

Baldassare shook his head in awe. "Dare I ask what you know about Nashe?"

Haverson chuckled. "More than you ever want to find out. I could give you another hour on Marlowe easy: he's a ninety-minute lecture in my Brit Lit class."

The Freshman Intro to British Literature that Haverson taught as wergild for her access to Professors Keats and Ling, and the temporal device. The inside of Satyavati's lip tasted like rubber; she chewed gently. "So you're saying we don't know. And we can prove nothing. There's no period source that can help us?"

"There's some odd stuff in Shakespeare's *As You Like It* that seems to indicate that the protagonist is intended to be a fictionalized reflection of Marlowe, or at least raise questions about his death. We know the two men collaborated on at least two plays, the first part of *Henry VI* and *Edward III*—" Haverson stopped and disentangled her fingers from her wavy yellow hair, where they had become idly entwined. Something wicked danced in her eyes. "And—"

"What?" Satyavati and Baldassare, in unison. Satyavati leaned forward over her desk, closing her hands on the edges.

"The protagonist of *As You Like It*—the one who quotes Marlowe and details the circumstances of his death?"

"Rosalind," Baldassare said. "What about her?"

"Is a young woman quite successfully impersonating a man."

Kit ate sparingly, as always. His image, his patronage, his sexuality, his very livelihood were predicated on the contours of his face, the boyish angles of his body, and every year that illusion of youth became harder to maintain. Also, he didn't dare drop his eyes from the face of Robin Poley, his fair-haired controller and—in Kit's educated opinion—one of the most dangerous men in London.

"Thou shalt not be permitted to abandon the Queen's service so easily, sweet Kit," Poley said between bites of fish. Kit nodded, dry-mouthed; he had not expected Poley would arrive with a guard. Two others, Skeres and Frazier, dined heartily and without apparent regard for Kit's lack of appetite.

"'Tis not that I wish any disservice to her Majesty," Kit said. "But I swear on my honor Thomas Walsingham is her loyal servant, good Robin, and she need fear him not. His love for her is as great as any man's, and his family has ever been loyal—"

Poley dismissed Kit's protestations with a gesture. Ingrim Frazier reached the breadth of the linen-laid table with the long blade of his knife and speared a piece of fruit from the board in front of Kit. Kit leaned out of the way.

"You realize of course that textual evidence isn't worth the paper it's printed on. And if you assume Marlowe was a woman, and Shakespeare knew it—"

"You rapidly enter the realm of the crackpots. Indeed."

"We have a serious problem."

"We could just quietly drop him from the data—" He grinned in response to her stare. "No, no. I'm not serious."

"You'd better not be," Satyavati answered. She quelled the rush of fury that Baldassare's innocent teasing pricked out of always-shallow sleep. *What happened a decade ago is not his fault.* "This is my career—my *scholarship*—in question."

A low tap on the office door. Satyavati checked the heads-up display, recognized Haverson, and tapped the key on her desk to disengage the lock. The Rubenesque blonde hesitated in the doorway. "Good afternoon, Satya. Baldassare. Private?"

"Same conversation as before," Satyavati said. "Still trying to figure out how to salvage our research—"

Haverson grinned and entered the room in a sweep of crinkled skirts and tunic. She shut the door behind her and made very certain it latched. "I have your answer."

Satyavati stood and came around her desk, dragging with her a chair, which she offered to Haverson. Haverson waved it aside, and Satyavati sank into it herself. "It assumes of course that Christopher Marlowe *did* die violently at Eleanor Bull's house in May of 1593 and did *not* run off to Italy and write the plays of Shakespeare—" Haverson's shrug seemed to indicate that that was a fairly safe assumption.

"The Poet Emeritus project?" Baldassare crowed, swinging his arms wide before clapping his hands. "Dr. Haverson, you're brilliant. And what if Marlowe *did* survive 1593?"

"We'll send back an observer team to make sure he dies. They'll have to exhume the body anyway; we'll need to be able to make that swap for the living Marlowe, assuming the recovery team can get to him before Frazier and company stab him in the eye."

Baldassare shuddered. "I swear that makes my skin crawl—"

"Paradox is an odd thing, isn't it? You start thinking about where the body comes from, and you start wondering if there are other changes happening."

"If there were," Baldassare said, "we'd never know."

Satyavati's dropped jaw closed as she finally forced herself to understand what they were talking about. "No one who died by violence. No one from before 1800. There are rules. Culture shock, language barriers. Professor Ling would never permit it."

Haverson grinned wider, obviously excited. "You know why those rules were developed, don't you?"

"I know it's a History Department and Temporal Studies protocol, and English is only allowed to use the device under their auspices, and competition for its time is extreme—"

"The rule developed after Richard I rose from what should have been his deathbed to run through a pair of History undergrads on the retrieval team. We never did get their bodies back. Or the Lion-Hearted, for that matter—" Baldassare stopped, aware of Haverson's considering stare. "What? I'm gunning for a spot on the Poet Emeritus team. I've been reading up."

"Ah."

"We'd never get the paperwork through to pull Christopher Marlowe, though." He sighed. "Although it would be worth it for the looks on the Marlovians' faces."

"You're awfully certain of yourself, son."

"Dr. Haverson—"

Haverson brushed him off with a turn of her wrist. She kept her light blue eyes on Satyavati. "What if I thought there was a chance that Professor Keats could become interested?"

"Oh," Satyavati said. "*That's* why you came to campus."

Haverson's grin kept growing; as Satyavati watched, it widened another notch. "He doesn't do business by holoconference," she said. "How could Percy Shelley's friend resist a chance to meet Christopher Marlowe?"

Kit leaned back on his bench, folding his hands in his lap. "Robin, I protest. Walsingham is as loyal to the crown as I."

"Ah." Poley turned it into an accusing drawl: one long syllable, smelling of onions. He straightened, frowning. "And art thou loyal, Master Marley?"

"Thy pardon?" As if a trapdoor had opened under his guts: he clutched the edge of the table to steady himself. "I've proven my loyalty well enough, I think."

"Thou hast grown soft," Poley sneered. Frazier, on Kit's right, stood, and Kit stood with him, toppling the bench in his haste. He found an ale-bottle with his right hand. There was a bed in the close little room in addition to the table, and Kit stepped against it, got his shoulder into the angle the headboard made with the wall.

Ingram Frazier's dagger rose in his hand. Kit looked past him, into Poley's light blue eyes. "Robin," Kit said. "Robin, old friend. What means this?"

Professor Keats looked up as they knocked on his open door: a blatant abrogation of campus security, but Satyavati admitted the cross-breeze felt better than sealed-room climate control. Red curls greying to ginger, his sharp chin softened now by jowls, he leaned back in his chair before a bookshelf stuffed with old leatherbound books and printouts: the detritus of a man who had never abandoned paper. Satyavati's eye picked out the multicolored spines of volumes and volumes of poetry; the successes of the Poet Emeritus project. As a personal and professional friend of the History Department's Bernard Ling, Professor Keats had assumed the chairmanship of Poet Emeritus shortly after the death of its founder, Dr. Eve Rodale.

Who would gainsay the project's greatest success?

The tuberculosis that would have been his death was a preresistant strain, easy prey to modern antibiotics; the lung damage was repairable with implants and grafts. He stood gracefully as Satyavati, Haverson, and Baldassare entered, a vigorous sixty-year-old who might have as many years before him as behind, and laid aside the fountain pen he still preferred. "It's not often lovely ladies come to visit this old poet," he said. "May I offer you a cup of tea?"

"Soft," Poley said again, and spit among the rushes on the floor. Bits of herbs colored his saliva green; Kit thought of venom and smiled. *If I live, I'll use that—*

The stink of fish and wine was dizzying. Poley kept talking. "Five years ago thou would'st have hanged Tom Walsingham for the gold in thy purse—"

"Only if he proved guilty."

"Guilty as those idiot students thou did'st see hanged at Corpus Christi?"

Kit winced. He wasn't proud of that. The pottery bottle in his hand was rough-surfaced, cool; he shifted his grip. "Master Walsingham is loyal. Frazier, you're in his *service*, man—"

"So fierce in his defense." Poley smiled, toxic and sweet. "Mayhap the rumors of thee dropping thy breeches for Master Walsingham aren't so false, after all—"

"Whoreson—" Kit stepped up, provoked into abandoning the wall. *A mistake*, and as his focus narrowed on Poley, Frazier grabbed his left wrist, twisting. Kit raised the bottle—up, down, smashed it hard across the top of Frazier's head, ducking Frazier's wild swing with the dagger. The weaselly Skeres, so far silent, lunged across the table as Frazier roared and blood covered his face.

Satyavati had turned a student desk around; she sat on it now, her feet on the narrow plastic seat, and scrubbed both hands through her thick, silver hair. Professor John Keats stood by the holodisplay that covered one long wall of the classroom, the twelve-by-fourteen card that Baldassare had pulled down off the wall in Satyavati's office pressed against it, clinging by static charge. Pinholes haggled the yellowed corners of the card; at its center was printed a 2-d image of a painfully boyish, painfully fair young man. He was richly dressed, with huge dark eyes, soft features, and a taunting smile framed by a sparse down of beard.

"He would have been eight years older when he died," Keats said.

Haverson chuckled from beside the door. "If that's him."

"If he *is* a him," Baldassare added. Haverson glared, and the grad student shrugged. "It's what we're here to prove, isn't it? Either the software works, or—"

"Or we have to figure out what this weird outlier means."

Keats glanced over his shoulder. "Explain how your program works, Professor?"

Satyavati curled her tongue across her upper teeth and dug in her pocket for the tin of mints. She offered them around the room; only Keats accepted. "It's an idea that's been under development since the late twentieth century," she said, cinnamon burning her tongue. "It relies on frequency and patterns of word use—well, it originated in some of the metrics that Elizabethan scholars use to prove authorship of the controversial plays, and also the order in which they were written. We didn't get *Edward III* firmly attributed to Marlowe, with a probable Shakespearean collaboration, until the beginning of the twenty-first century—"

"And you have a computer program that can identify the biological gender of the writer of a given passage of text."

"It even works on newsfeed reports and textbooks, sir."

"Have you any transgendered authors entered, Satyavati?"

John Keats just called me by my first name. She smiled and scooted forward half an inch on the desk, resting her elbows on her knees. "Several women who wrote as men, for whatever reason. Each of them confirmed female, although some were close to the midline. Two male authors who wrote as women. An assortment of lesbians, homosexuals, and bisexuals. Hemingway—"

Haverson choked on a laugh, covering her mouth with her hand. Satyavati shrugged. "—as a baseline. Anaïs Nin. Ovid, and Edna St. Vincent Millay. Tori Siikanen."

"I've read her," Keats said. "Lovely."

Satyavati shrugged. "The genderbot found her unequivocally male, when her entire body of work was analyzed. Even that written *after* her gender reassignment. We haven't been able to track down any well-known writers of indeterminate sex, unfortunately. I'd like to see how somebody born cryptomale and assigned female, for example, would score—"

"What will your 'bot tell us then?"

"Chromosomal gender, I suppose."

"Interesting. Is gender so very immutable, then?" He raised an eyebrow and smiled, returning his attention to Christopher Marlowe. "That's quite the can of worms—"

"Except for his," Satyavati said, following the line of Keats' gaze to the mocking smile and folded arms of the arrogant boy in the facsimile. "What makes him different?"

"Her," Baldassare said, in a feigned coughing fit. "That moustache is totally gummed on. Look at it."

Keats didn't turn, but he shrugged. "What makes any of us different, my dear?" A long pause, as if he expected an attempt to answer what must have been a rhetorical question. He turned and looked Satyavati in the eye. His gingery eyebrows lifted and fell. "Do you understand the risks and costs of this endeavor?"

Satyavati hunched forward on her chair and shook her head. "It was Sienna's idea—"

"Oh, so quick to cast away credit and blame," the poet said, but his eyes twinkled.

Haverson came to stand beside Satyavati's desk. "Still. Is there any writer or critic who hasn't wondered, a little, what that young man could have done?"

"Were he more prone to temperance?"

Keats was being charming. *But he's still John Keats.*

"Poets are not temperate by nature," he said, and smiled. He folded his hands together in front of his belt buckle. His swing jacket, translucent chromatic velvet, caught the light through the window as he moved.

"In another hundred years we'll change our gender the way we change our clothes." Haverson pressed her warmth against Satyavati's arm, who endured it a moment before she leaned away.

"I confess myself uncomfortable with the concept." Keats' long fingers fretted the cuff of his gorgeous jacket.

Satyavati, watching him, felt a swell of kinship. "I think there is a biological factor to how gender is expressed. I think my genderbot proves that unequivocally: if we can detect birth gender to such a fine degree—"

"And this is important?" Keats' expression was gentle mockery; an emergent trace of archaic Cockney colored his voice, but something in the tilt of his head showed Satyavati that it was a serious question.

"Our entire society is based on gender and sex and procreation. How can it *not* be as vital to understanding the literature as it is to understanding everything else?"

Keats' lips twitched; his pale eyes tightened at the corners. Satyavati shrank back, afraid she'd overstepped, but his voice was still level when he spoke again. "What does it matter where man comes from—or woman either—if the work is true?"

A sore spot. She sucked her lip, searching for the explanation. "One would prefer to think such things no longer mattered." With a sideways glance to Baldassare. He gave her a low thumbs-up. "This isn't my first tenure-track position."

"You left Yale." Just a statement, as if he would not press.

"I filed an allegation of sexual harassment against my department chair. She denied it, and claimed I was attempting to conceal a lack of scholarship—"

"She?"

Satyavati folded her arms tight across her chest, half sick with the admission. "She didn't approve of my research, I think. It contradicted her own theories of gender identity."

"You think she knew attention would make you uncomfortable, and harried you from the department."

"I... have never been inclined to be close to people. Forgive me if I am not trusting."

He studied her expression silently. She found herself lifting her chin to meet his regard, in answer to his unspoken challenge. He smiled thoughtfully and said, "I was told a stableman's son would be better to content himself away from poetry, you know. I imagine your Master Marlowe, a cobbler's boy, heard something similar once or twice—and God forbid either one of us had been a girl. It's potent stuff you're meddling in."

Rebellion flared in her belly. She sat up straight on the ridiculous desk, her fingers fluttering as she unfolded her hands and embraced her argument. "If anything, then, my work proves that biology is not destiny. I'd like to force a continuing expansion of the canon, frankly: 'women's books' are still—*still*—excluded. As if war were somehow a more valid exercise than raising a family—" *Shit*. Too much, by his stunned expression. She held his gaze, though, and wouldn't look down.

And then Keats smiled, and she knew she'd won him. "There are dangers involved, beyond the cost."

"I understand."

"Do you?" He wore spectacles, a quaint affectation that Satyavati found charming. But as he glanced at her over the silver wire frames, a chill crept up her neck.

"Professor Keats—"

"John."

"John." And that was worth a deeper chill, for the unexpected intimacy. "Then make me understand."

Keats stared at her, pale eyes soft, frown souring the corners of his mouth. "A young man of the Elizabethan period. A duelist, a spy, a playmaker: a violent man, and one who lives by his wits in a society so xenophobic it's difficult for us to properly imagine. Someone to whom the carriage—the horse-drawn carriage, madam doctor—is a tolerably modern invention, the heliocentric model of the solar system still heresy. Someone to whom your United States is the newborn land of Virginia, a colony founded by his acquaintance Sir Walter

Ralegh. Pipe tobacco is a novelty, coffee does not exist, and the dulcet speech of our everyday converse is the yammering of a barbarian dialect that he will find barely comprehensible, at best."

Satyavati opened her mouth to make some answer. Keats held up one angular hand. As if to punctuate his words, the rumble of a rising semiballistic rattled the windows. "A young man, I might add"—as if this settled it—"who must be plucked alive from the midst of a deadly brawl with three armed opponents. A brawl history tells us he instigated with malice, in a drunken rage."

"History is written by the victors," Satyavati said, at the same moment that Baldassare said, "Dr. Keats. The man who wrote *Faustus*, sir."

"If a man he is," Keats answered, smiling. "There is that, after all. And there would be international repercussions. UK cultural heritage is pitching a fit over 'the theft of their literary traditions.'"

"Because the world would be a better place without John Keats?" Satyavati grinned, pressing her tongue against her teeth. "Hell, they sold London Bridge to Arizona. I don't see what they have to complain about: If they're so hot to trot, let them build their own time device and steal some of our dead poets."

Keats laughed, a wholehearted guffaw that knocked him back on his heels. He gasped, collected himself, and turned to Haverson, who nodded. "John, how can you possibly resist?"

"I can't," he admitted, and looked back at Haverson.

"How much will it cost?"

Satyavati braced for the answer and winced anyway. Twice the budget for her project, easily.

"I'll write a grant," Baldassare said.

Keats laughed. "Write two. *This* project, I rather imagine there's money for. It will also take a personal favor from Bernard. Which I *will* call in. Although I doubt very much we can schedule a retrieval until next fiscal. Which makes no difference to Marlowe, of course, but does mean, Satyavati, that you will have to push your publication back."

"I'll consider it an opportunity to broaden the database," she said, and Keats and Haverson laughed like true academics at the resignation in her voice.

"And—"

She flinched. "And?"

"Your young man may prove thoroughly uncooperative. Or mentally unstable once the transfer is done."

"Is the transition really so bad?" Baldassare, with the question that had been on the tip of Satyavati's tongue.

"Is there a risk he will reject reality, you mean? Lose his mind, to put it quaintly?"

"Yes."

"I can't say what it will be like for him," he said. "But I, at least, came to you knowing the language and knowing I had been about to die." Keats rubbed his palms together as if clapping nonexistent chalk dust from his palms. "I rather suspect, madam doctors, Mr. Baldassare"—Satyavati blinked as he pronounced Baldassare's name correctly and without hesitation; she hadn't realized Keats even *knew* it—"we must prepare ourselves for failure."

Kit twisted away from the knife again, but Skeres had a grip on his doublet now, and the breath went out of him as two men slammed him against the wall. Cloth shredded; the broken bottle slipped out of Kit's bloodied fingers as Frazier wrenched his arm behind his back.

Poley blasphemed. *"Christ on the cross—"*

Frazier swore too, shoving Kit's torn shirt aside to keep a grip on his flesh. "God's wounds, it's a wench."

A lax moment, and Kit got an elbow into Frazier's ribs and a heel down hard on Poley's instep and his back into the corner one more time, panting like a beaten dog. No route to the window. No route to the door. Kit swallowed bile and terror, tugged the rags of his doublet closed across his slender chest. "Unhand me."

"Where's Marley?" Poley said stupidly as Kit pressed himself against the boards.

"I am Marley, you fool."

"No wench could have written that poetry—"

"I'm no wench," he said, and as Frazier raised his knife, Christofer Marley made himself ready to die as he had lived, kicking and shouting at something much bigger than he.

Seventeen months later, Satyavati steepled her fingers before her mouth and blew out across them, warm, moist breath sliding between her palms in a contrast to the crisping desert atmosphere. One-way shatterproof bellied out below her; leaning forward, she saw into a retrieval room swarming with technicians and medical crew, bulwarked by masses of silently blinking instrumentation—and the broad space in the middle of the room, walled away from operations with shatterproof ten centimeters thick. Where the retrieval team would reappear.

With or without their quarry.

"Worried?"

She turned her head and looked up at Professor Keats, stylishly rumpled as ever. "Terrified."

"Minstrels in the gallery," he observed. "There's Sienna…" Pointing to her blonde head, bent over her station on the floor.

The shatterproof walls of the retrieval box were holoed to conceal the mass of technology outside them from whoever might be inside; theoretically, the retrievant *should* arrive sedated. But it wasn't wise to be too complacent about such things.

The lights over the retrieval floor dimmed by half. Keats leaned forward in his chair. "Here we go."

"Five." A feminine voice over loudspeakers. "Four. Three—"

I hadn't thought he'd look so fragile. Or so young.

Is this then Hell? Curious that death should hurt so much less than living—

"Female," a broad-shouldered doctor said into his throat microphone. He leaned over the sedated form on his examining table, gloved hands deft and quick.

Marlowe lay within an environmentally shielded bubble; the doctor examined her with built-in gloves. She would stay sedated and in isolation until her immunizations were effective and it was certain she hadn't brought forward any dangerous bugs from the sixteenth century. Satyavati was grateful for the half-height privacy screens hiding the poet's form. *I hadn't thought it would seem like such an invasion.*

"Aged about thirty," the doctor continued. "Overall in fair health although underweight and suffering the malnutrition typical of Elizabethan diet. Probably parasitic infestation of some sort, dental caries, bruising sustained recently— damn, look at that wrist. That must have been one hell of a fight."

"It was," Tony Baldassare said, drying his hands on a towel as he came up on Satyavati's right. His hair was still wet from the showers, slicked back from his classically Roman features. She stepped away, reclaiming her space. "I hope this is the worst retrieval I ever have to go on—although Haverson assures me that I made the grade, and there will be more. Damn, but you sweat in those moonsuits." He frowned over at the white-coated doctor. "When do they start the RNA therapy?"

"Right after the exam. She'll still need exposure to the language to learn it."

Baldassare took a deep breath to sigh. "Poor Kit. I bet she'll do fine here, though: she's a tough little thing."

"She would have had to be," Satyavati said thoughtfully, as much to drown out the more intimate details of the doctor's examination. "What a fearful life—"

Baldassare grinned, and flicked Satyavati with the damp end of his towel. "Well," he said, "she can be herself from now on, can't she? Assuming she acclimates. But anybody who could carry off that sort of a counterfeit for nearly thirty years—"

Satyavati shook her head. "I wonder," she murmured. "What on earth possessed her parents."

Kit woke in strange light: neither sun nor candles. The room smelled harsh: no sweetness of rushes or heaviness of char, but something astringent and pungent, as like the scent of lemons as the counterfeit thud of a pewter coin was like the ring of silver. He would have sat, but soft cloths bound his arms to the strange hard bed, which had shining steel railings along the sides like the bars on a baiting-bear's cage.

His view of the room was blocked by curtains, but the curtains were not attached to the strange, high, narrow bed. They hung from bars near the ceiling. *I am captive*, he thought, and noticed he didn't *hurt*. He found that remarkable; no ache in his jaw where a tooth needed drawing, no burn at his wrist where Frazier's grip had broken the skin.

His clothes were gone, replaced with an open-backed gown. The hysteria he would have expected to accompany this realization didn't; instead, he felt rather drunk. Not unpleasantly so, but enough that the panic that clawed the inside of his breastbone did so with padded claws.

Something chirped softly at the bedside, perhaps a songbird in a cage. He turned his head but could only glimpse the edge of a case in some dull material, the buff color called Isabelline. If his hands were free, he'd run his fingers across the surface to try the texture: neither leather nor lacquer, and looking like nothing he'd ever seen. Even the sheets were strange: no well-pounded linen, but something smooth and cool and dingy white.

"Marry," he murmured to himself. "'Tis passing strange."

"But very clean." A woman's voice, from the foot of the bed. "Good morning, Master Marlowe."

Her accent was strange, the vowels all wrong, the stresses harsh and clipped. A foreign voice. He turned his face and squinted at her; that strange light that was not sunlight but almost as bright glared behind her. It made her hard to see. Still, only a woman. Uncorseted, by her silhouette, and wearing what he realized with surprise were long, loose trousers. *If a wench with a gentle voice is my warden, perhaps there's a chance I shall emerge alive.*

"Aye, very," he agreed as she came alongside the bed. Her hair was silver, loose on her shoulders in soft waves like a maiden's. He blinked. Her skin was mahogany, her eyes angled at the corners like a cat's and shiny as gooseberries. She was stunning and not quite human, and he held his breath before he spoke. "Madam, I beg your patience at my impertinence. But, an it please you to answer— what *are* you?"

She squinted as if his words were as unfamiliar to her as hers to him. "Pray," she said, self-consciously as one speaking a tongue only half-familiar, "say that again, please?"

He tugged his bonds, not sharply. The sensation was dulled, removed. *Drunk or sick*, he thought. *Forsooth, drunk indeed, not to recollect drinking... Robin. Robin and his villains—* But Kit shook his head, shook the hair from his eyes, and mastered himself with trembling effort. He said it again, slowly and clearly, one word at a time.

He sighed in relief when she smiled and nodded, apprehending to her satisfaction. In her turn, she spoke precisely, shaping the words consciously with her lips. He could have wept in gratitude at her care. "I'm a woman and a doctor of philosophy," she said. "My name is Satyavati Brahmaputra, and you, Christopher Marlowe, have been rescued from your death by our science."

"Science?"

She frowned as she sought the word. "Natural philosophy."

Her accent, the color of her skin. He suddenly understood. "I've been stolen away to Spain." He was not prepared for the laughter that followed his startled declaration.

"Hardly," she said. "You are in the New World, at a university hospital, a—a surgery?—in a place called Las Vegas, Nevada—"

"Madam, those are Spanish names."

Her lips twitched with amusement. "They are, aren't they? Oh, this is complicated. Here, look." And heedlessly, as if she had nothing to fear from him—*they know, Kit. That's why they left only a wench to guard thee. An Amazon, more like: she's twice my size—* she crouched beside the bed and unknotted the bonds that affixed him to it.

He supposed he could drag down the curtain bars and dash her brains out. But he had no way to know what sort of guards might be at the door; better to bide his time, as she seemed to mean him no injury. And he was tired; even with the cloths untied, lethargy pinned him to the bed.

"They told me not to do this," she whispered, catching his eye with her dark, glistening one. She released a catch and lowered the steel railing. "But in for a penny, in for a pound."

That expression, at least, he understood. He swung his feet to the floor with care, holding the gaping gown closed. The dizziness moved with him, as if it hung a little above and to the left. The floor was unfamiliar too; no rushes and stone, but something hard and resilient, set or cut into tiles. He would have crouched to examine it—and perhaps to let the blood run to his brain—but the woman caught his hand and tugged him past the curtains and toward a window shaded with some ingenious screen. He ran his fingers across the alien surface, gasping when she pulled a cord and the whole thing rose of a piece, hard scales or shingles folding as neatly as a drawn curtain.

And then he looked through the single enormous, utterly transparent pane of glass before him and almost dropped to his knees with vertigo and wonder.

His hand clenched on the window ledge; he leaned forward. The drop must have measured hundreds upon hundreds of feet. The horizon was impossibly distant, like the vista from the mast of a sailing ship, the view from the top of a high, lonely down. And before that horizon rose fanciful towers of a dominion vaster than London *and* Paris made one, stretching twenty or perhaps fifty miles away: however far it took for mountains to grow so very dim with distance.

"God in Hell," he whispered. He'd imagined towers like that, written of them. To see them with his own undreaming eyes— "Sweet Jesu. Madam, what is this?" He spoke too fast, and the brown woman made him repeat himself once more.

"A city," she said quietly. "Las Vegas. A small city, by today's standards. Master Marlowe—or Miss Marlowe, I suppose I should say—you have come some five hundred years into your future, and here, I am afraid, you must stay."

"*Master* Marlowe will do. Mistress Brahma...." Marlowe stumbled over Satyavati's name. The warmth and openness Marlowe had shown vanished on a breath. She folded her arms together, so like the Corpus Christi portrait—thinner and wearier, but with the same sardonic smile and the same knowing black eyes—that Satyavati had no doubt that it was the same individual.

"Call me Satya."

"Madam."

Satyavati frowned. "Master Marlowe," she said. "This is a different... Things are different now. Look at me, a woman, a blackamoor by your terms. And a doctor of philosophy like your friend Tom Watson, a scholar."

"Poor Tom is dead." And then as if in prophecy, slowly, blinking. "Everyone I know is dead."

Satyavati rushed ahead, afraid that Marlowe would crumple if the revelation on her face ever reached her belly. *A good thing she's sedated, or she'd be in a ball on the floor.* "I'm published, I've written books. I'll be a tenured professor soon." *You will make me that.* But she didn't say it; she simply trusted the young woman, so earnest and wide-eyed behind the brittle defense of her arrogance, would understand. Which of course she didn't, and Satyavati repeated herself twice before she was certain Marlowe understood.

The poet's accent was something like an old broad Scots and something like the dialect of the Appalachian Mountains. *Dammit, it is English.* As long as she kept telling herself it was English, that the foreign stresses and vowels did not mean a foreign language, Satyavati could force herself to understand.

Marlowe bit her lip. She shook her head, and took Satyavati's cue of speaking slowly and precisely, but her eyes gleamed with ferocity. "It bears not on opportunity. I am no woman. Born into a wench's body, aye, mayhap, but as surely a man as Elizabeth is king. My father knew from the moment of my birth.

S'death, an it were otherwise, would he have named me and raised me as his son? Have lived a man's life, loved a man's loves. An you think to force me into farthingales and huswifery, know that I would liefer die. I *will* die—for surely now I have naught to fear from Hell—and the man who dares approach me with woman's garb will precede me there."

Satyavati watched Kit—in that ridiculous calico johnny— brace herself, assuming the confidence and fluid gestures of a swordsman, all masculine condescension and bravado. As if she expected a physical assault to follow on her manifesto.

Something to prove. What a life—

The door opened. Satyavati turned to see who entered, and sighed in relief at the gaudy jacket and red hair of Professor Keats, who paused at the edge of the bedcurtain, a transparent bag filled with cloth and books hanging from his hand. "Let me talk to the young man, if you don't mind."

"She's—upset, Professor Keats." But Satyavati stepped away, moving toward Keats and past him, to the door. She paused there.

Keats faced Marlowe. "Are you the poet who wrote *Edward II*?"

A sudden flush, and the eyebrows rose in mockery above the twitch of a grin. "I am that."

"It's a fact that poets are liars," the old man said without turning to Satyavati. "But we *always* speak the truth, and a thing is what you name it. Isn't that so, Marlowe?"

"Aye," she said, her brow furrowed with concentration on the words. "Good sir, I feel that I should know you, but your face—"

"Keats," the professor said. "John Keats. You won't have heard of me, but I'm a poet too."

The door shut behind the woman, and Kit's shoulders eased, but only slightly. "Master Keats—"

"John. Or Jack, if that's more comfortable."

Kit studied the red-haired poet's eyes. Faded blue in the squint of his regard, and Kit nodded, his belly unknotting a little. "Kit, then. I pray you will forgive me my disarray. I have just risen—"

"No matter." Keats reached into his bag. A shrug displayed his own coat, a long, loose robe of something that shifted in color, chromatic as a butterfly's wing. "You'll like the modern clothes, I think. I've brought something less revealing."

He laid cloths on the bed: a strange sort of close-collared shirt, trews or breeches in one piece that went to the ankle. Low shoes that looked like leather, but once Kit touched them he was startled by the gummy softness of the soles. He looked up into Keats' eyes. "You prove most kind to a poor, lost poet."

"I was rescued from 1821," Keats said dismissively. "I bear some sympathy for your panic."

"Ah." Kit stepped behind the curtain to dress. He flushed hot when the other poet helped him with the closure on the trousers, but once Kit understood this device—the zipper—he found it enchanting. "I shall have much to study on, I wot."

"You will." Keats looked as if he was about to say more. The thin fabric of the shirt showed Kit's small breasts. He hunched forward, uncomfortable; not even sweet Tom Walsingham had seen him so plainly.

"I would have brought you a bandage, if I'd thought," Keats said, and gallantly offered his jacket. Kit took it, face still burning, and shrugged it on.

"What—what year is this, Jack?"

A warm hand on his shoulder; Keats taking a deep breath alerted Kit to brace for the answer. "Anno domini two thousand one hundred and seventeen," he said. The words dropped like stones through the fragile ice of Kit's composure.

Kit swallowed, the implications he had been denying snapping into understanding like unfurled banners. Not the endless changing world, the towers like Babylon or Babel beyond his window. But—"Tom. Christ wept, Tom is dead. All the Toms—Walsingham, Nashe, Kyd. Sir Walter. My sisters. Will. Will and I were at work on a play, *Henry VI*—"

Keats laughed, gently. "Oh, I have something to show you, Kit." His eyes shone with coy delight. "Look here—"

He drew a volume from his bag and pressed it into Kit's hands. It weighed heavy, bound in what must be waxed cloth and stiffened paper. The words on the cover were embossed in gilt in strange-shaped letters. *The Complete Works of William Shakespeare*, Kit read, once he understands how the *esses* seem to work. He gaped, and opened the cover. "His plays…" He looked up at Keats, who smiled and opened his hands in a benediction. "This type is so fine and so clear! Marry, how *ever* can it be set by human hands? Tell me true, Jack, have I come to fairyland?" And then, turning pages with trembling fingers and infinite care, his carefulness of speech failing in exclamations. "Nearly forty plays! Oh, the type is so fine— Oh, and his sonnets, they are wonderful sonnets, he's written more than I had seen—"

Keats, laughing, an arm around Kit's shoulders. "He's thought the greatest poet and dramatist in the English language."

Kit looked up in wonder. "T'was I discovered him." Kit held the thick, real book in his hands, the paper so fine and so white he'd compare it to a lady's hand. "Henslowe laughed; Will came from tradesmen and bore no education beyond the grammar school—"

Keats coughed into his hand. "I sometimes think wealth and privilege are a detriment to poetry."

The two men shared a considering gaze and a slow, equally considering smile. "And…." Kit looked at the bag, the glossy transparent fabric as foreign as every other thing in the room. There were still two volumes within. The book in his hands smelled of real paper, new paper. With a shock, he realized that the page-ends were trimmed perfectly smooth and edged with gilt. *And how long must that have taken? This poet is a wealthy man, to give such gifts as this.*

"And what of Christopher Marlowe?"

Kit smiled. "Aye."

Keats looked down. "You are remembered, I am afraid, chiefly for your promise and your extravagant opinions, my friend. Very little of your work survived. Seven plays, in corrupted versions. The Ovid. *Hero and Leander*—"

"Forsooth, there was more," Kit said, pressing the heavy book with Will's name on the cover against his chest.

"There will be more," Keats said, and set the bag on the floor. "That is why we saved your life."

Kit swallowed. *What an odd sort of patronage.* He sat on the bed, still cradling the wonderful book. He looked up at Keats, who must have read the emotion in his eyes.

"Enough for one day, I think," the red-haired poet said. "I've given you a history text as well, and"—a disarming smile and a tilt of his head—"a volume of my own poetry. Please knock on the door if you need for anything—you may find the garderobe a little daunting, but it's past that door and the basic functions obvious—and I will come to see you in the morning."

"I shall amuse myself with gentle William." Kit knew a sort of anxious panic for a moment: it was so necessary that this ginger-haired poet must love him, Kit—and he also knew a sort of joy when Keats chuckled at the double-entendre and clapped him on the shoulder like a friend.

"Do that. Oh!" Keats halted suddenly and reached into the pocket of his trousers. "Let me show you how to use a pen—"

The slow roil of his stomach got the better of Kit for an instant. "I daresay I know well enough how to hold a pen."

Keats shook his head and grinned, pulling a slender black tube from his pocket. "Dear Kit. You don't know how to do anything. But you'll learn soon enough, I imagine."

Satyavati paced, short steps there and back again, until Baldassare reached out without looking up from his workstation and grabbed her by the sleeve. "Dr. Brahmaputra—"

"Mr. Baldassare?"

"Are you going to share with me what the issue is here?"

One glance at his face told her he knew very well what the issue was. She tugged her sleeve away from him and leaned on the edge of the desk, too far for casual contact. "Marlowe," she said. "She's still crucial to our data—"

"He."

"Whatever."

Baldassare stood; Satyavati tensed, but rather than closer, he moved away. He stood for a moment looking up at the rows of portraits around the top margin of the room—more precisely, at the white space where the picture of Marlowe had been. A moment of consideration, and Satyavati as much as *saw* him choose another tack. "What about Master Marlowe?"

"If I publish—"

"Yes?"

"I tell the world Christopher Marlowe's deepest secret."

"Which Professor Keats has sworn the entire Poet Emeritus project to secrecy about. And if you don't publish?"

She shrugged to hide the knot in her belly. "I'm not going to find a third tenure-track offer. You've got your place with John and Dr. Haverson, at least. All I've got is"—a hopeless gesture to the empty place on the wall—"her."

Baldassare turned to face Satyavati. His expressive hands pinwheeled slowly in the air for a moment before he spoke, as if he sifted his thoughts between them. "You keep doing that."

"Doing what?"

"Calling Kit *her.*"

"She *is* a her. Hell, Mr. Baldassare, you were the one who was insisting she was a woman, before we brought her back."

"And he insists he's not." Baldassare shrugged. "If he went for gender reassignment, what would you call him?"

Satyavati bit her lip. "Him," she admitted unwillingly. "I guess. I don't know—"

Baldassare spread his hands wide. "Dr. Brahmaputra—"

"Hell. Tony. Call me Satya already. If you're going to put up that much of a fight, you already know that you're moving out of student and into friend."

"Satya, then." A shy smile that startled her. "Why don't you just ask Kit? He understands how patronage works. He knows he owes you his life. Go tomorrow."

"You think she'd say yes?"

"Maybe." His self-conscious grin turned teasing. "If you remember not to call him *she.*"

The strange spellings and punctuation slowed Kit a little, but he realized that they must have been altered for the strange, quickspoken people among whom, apparently, he was meant to make his life. Once he mastered the cadences of the modern speech—the commentaries proving invaluable—his reading proceeded faster despite frequent pauses to reread, to savor.

He read the night through, crosslegged on the bed, bewitched by the brightness of the strange greenish light and the book held open on his lap. The biographical note told him that "Christopher Marlowe's" innovations in the technique of blank verse provided Shakespeare with the foundations of his powerful voice. Kit corrected the spelling of his name in the margin with the pen that John Keats had loaned him. The nib was so sharp it was all but invisible, and Kit amused himself with the precision it leant his looping secretary's hand. He read without passion of Will's death in 1616, smiled that the other poet at last went home to his wife. And did not begin to weep in earnest until halfway through the third act of *As You Like It*, when he curled over the sorcerously wonderful book, careful to let no tear fall upon the pages, and cried silently, shuddering, fist pressed bloody against his teeth, face-down in the rough-textured coverlet.

He did not sleep. When the spasm of grief and rapture passed, he read again, scarcely raising his head to acknowledge the white-garbed servant who brought a tray that was more like dinner than a break-fast. The food cooled and was retrieved uneaten; he finished the Shakespeare and began the history, saving his benefactor's poetry for last.

"I want for nothing," he said when the door opened again, glancing up. Then he pushed the book from his lap and jumped to his feet in haste, exquisitely aware of his reddened eyes and crumpled clothing. The silver-haired woman from yesterday stood framed in the doorway. "Mistress," Kit said, unwilling to assay her name. "Again I must plead your forbearance."

"Not at all," she said. "Mmm—Master Marlowe. It is I who must beg a favor of you." Her lips pressed tight; he *saw* her willing him to understand.

"Madam, as I owe you the very breath in my body— Mayhap there is a way I can repay that same?"

She frowned and shut the door behind her. The latch clicked; his heart raced; she was not young, but he was not certain he understood what *young* meant to these people. And she was lovely. And unmarried, by her hair—

What sort of a maiden would bar herself into a strange man's bedchamber without so much as a chaperone? Has she no care at all for her reputation?

And then he sighed and stepped away, to lean against the windowledge. *One who knows the man in question is not capable as a man. Or*—a stranger thought, one supported by his long night's reading—*or the world has changed more than I could dream.*

"I need your help," she said, and leaned back against the door. "I need to tell the world what you are."

He shivered at the urgency in her tone, her cool reserve, the tight squint of her eyes. *She'll do what she'll do* and *thou hast no power over her.* "Why speak to me of this at all? Publish your pamphlet, then, and have done—"

She shook her head, lips working on some emotion. "It is not a pamphlet. It's—" She shook her head again. "Master Marlowe, when I say *the world*, I mean the world."

Wonder filled him. *If I said no, she would abide it.* "You ask for no less a gift than the life I have made, madam."

She came forward. He watched: bird stalked by a strange silver cat. "People won't judge. You can live as you choose—"

"As you judged me not?"

Oh, a touch. She flinched. He wasn't proud of that, either. "—and not have to lie, to dissemble, to hide. You can even become a man. Truly, in the flesh—"

Wonder. "*Become* one?"

"Yes." Her moving hands fell to her sides. "If it is what you want." Something in her voice, a sort of breathless yearning he didn't dare believe.

"What means this to you? To tell your *world* that what lies between my legs is quaint and not crowing, that is—what benefits it you? Who can have an interest, if your society is so broad of spirit as you import?"

He saw her thinking for a true answer and not a facile one. She came closer. "It is my scholarship." Her voice rose on the last word, clung to it. Kit bit his lip, turning away.

No. His lips shaped the word: his breath wouldn't voice it. Scholarship.

Damn her to hell. *Scholarship.*

She said the word the way Keats said *poetry*.

"Do—" He saw her flinch; his voice died in his throat. He swallowed. "Do what you must, then." He gestured to the beautiful book on his bed, his breath catching in his throat at the mere memory of those glorious words. "It seems gentle William knew well enough what I was, and he forgave me of it better than I could have expected. How can I extend less to a lady who has offered me such kindness, and been so fair in asking leave?"

Satyavati rested her chin on her hand, cupping the other one around a steaming cup of tea. Tony, at her right hand, poked idly at the bones of his tandoori chicken. Further down the table, Sienna Haverson and Bernard Ling were bent in intense conversation, and Keats seemed absorbed in tea and mango ice cream. Marlowe, still clumsy with a fork, proved extremely adept at navigating the intricacies of curry and naan as finger food and was still chasing stray tidbits of lamb vindaloo around his plate. She enjoyed watching her—*him*, she corrected herself, annoyed—eat; the weight he'd gained in the past months made him look less like a strong wind might blow him away.

Most of the English Department was still on a quiet manhunt for whomever might have introduced the man to the *limerick.*

She lifted her tea; before she had it to her mouth, Tony caught her elbow, and Marlowe, looking up before she could flinch away, hastily wiped his hand and picked up a butterknife. He tapped his glass as Keats grinned across the table. Marlowe cleared his throat, and Haverson and Ling looked up, reaching for their cups when it became evident that a toast was in the offing.

"To Professor Brahmaputra," Marlowe said, smiling, in his still-strong accent. "Congratulations—"

She set her teacup down, a flush warming her cheeks as glasses clicked and he continued.

"—on her appointment to tenure. In whose honor I have composed a little poem—"

Which was, predictably, sly, imagistic, and *inventively* dirty. Satyavati imagined even her complexion blazed quite red by the time he was done with her. Keats' laughter alone would have been enough to send her under the table, if it hadn't been for Tony's unsettling deathgrip on her right knee. "Kit!"

He paused. "Have I scandalized my lady?"

"Master Marlowe, you have scandalized the very walls. I trust that one won't see print just yet!" Too much time with Marlowe and Keats: she was noticing a tendency in herself to slip into an archaic idiom that owed something to both.

"Not until next year at the earliest," he answered with a grin, but she saw the flash of discomfort that followed.

After dinner, he came up beside her as she was shrugging on her cooling-coat and gallantly assisted.

"Kit," she said softly, bending close so no one else would overhear. He smelled of patchouli and curry. "You are unhappy."

"Madam." A low voice as level as her own. "Not unhappy."

"Then what?"

"Lonely." Marlowe sighed, turning away

"Several of the Emeritus Poets have married," she said carefully. Keats eyed her over Marlowe's shoulder, but the red-haired poet didn't intervene.

"I imagine it's unlikely at best that I will find anyone willing to marry something neither fish nor fowl—" A shrug.

She swallowed, her throat uncomfortably dry. "There's surgery now, as we discussed—"

"Aye. 'Tis—" She read the word he wouldn't say. *Repulsive.*

Keats had turned away and drawn Tony and Sienna into a quiet conversation with Professor Ling at the other end of the table. Satyavati looked after them longingly for a moment and chewed her lower lip. She laid a hand on Kit's shoulder and drew him toward the rest. "You are what you are," she offered hopelessly, and on some fabulous impulse ducked her head and kissed him on the cheek, startled when her dry lips tingled at the contact. "Someone will have to appreciate that."

The door slides aside. He steps through the opening, following the strange glorious lady with the silver-fairy hair. The dusty scent of curry surrounds him as he walks into the broad spread of a balmy evening roofed with broken clouds.

Christopher Marlowe leans back on his heels and raises his eyes to the sky, the desert scorching his face in a benediction. *Hotter than Hell.* He draws a single deep breath and smiles at the mountains crouched at the edge of the world, tawny behind a veil of summer haze, gold and orange sunset pale behind them. Low trees crouch, hunched under the potent heat. He can see forever across this hot, flat, tempestuous place.

The horizon seems a thousand miles away.

BOTTICELLI

1.

"Your name begins with the letter K."

"I knew that."

"Deranged Soviet." The American lowered the binoculars, knowing without having to look that his partner's expression would be perfectly deadpan. "Do you want to play or not?"

A slight sigh, the sound of cold coffee slurped from a Styrofoam cup. "Am I a communist?"

"No," the American said cheerfully, keeping his eyes on the one lit window remaining several floors up. *Fatal error. He'll never get it now.* "You're not Nikita Khrushchev. That's one."

2.

Maybe there's a war, and maybe you're a boy, and maybe you're a soldier. In any case, you see things—you *are* things— that no human being should ever have to see, should ever have to become. Maybe you're seven, eight years old and you watch from hiding as the SS binds Ukrainian captives face to face in pairs, embracing, blood running from the thin wire twisted around their wrists. The Germans line them up along the railing of a bridge and shoot one of each pair. Momentum carries living and dead over the low railing, into the river below, where the difference ceases to matter.

It does save on bullets.

Or maybe you're seventeen years old and carrying a U.S. Army rifle through the minefields of Southeast Asia, and scattered gunfire from a cluster of refugees penned under the span of a railway arch wounds two of your comrades. And the order comes down via a bleak-eyed sergeant, the lieutenant says *shoot them all.* "Sarge." You squint through your scope, watching mothers cover their children, husbands cover their wives as if human flesh could protect human flesh from spinning lead. "There's women and babies in that crowd."

"I know it," he says. A heavy pause. "Follow orders, son."

You can't be too careful.

Whichever, it isn't something you talk about afterwards. Even to your buddies. Even to the people who were there. Five years, ten years, twenty years—and the old hurts become the foundation for the battlements that keep the world at bay.

Maybe you adopt a suave and charming frictionless surface, a ready smile and a self-deprecating turn of phrase—and a black belt in judo for the days when those don't suffice. Maybe you turn inward, settling into a glass-hard, glass-sharp facade, warded by the barbed wire of cutting wit and disdainful glances, and learn to kill as efficiently as you'd solve differentials.

You don't tell anyone about the nightmares of falling, and bridges, and a corpse leaking brains clutched tight in your arms.

3.

"This is not vodka." The Russian held the heavy crystal glass to the light and sighed at its clarity.

"The tax stamp was intact until I opened it. It's been in my freezer since Saturday." The American stretched his long legs, propping his heels on the ottoman. He inspected his own cocktail—gin, vermouth, two onions—carefully. "Unless a spy entered my apartment while we were on assignment and poisoned the liquor supply, that's eighty-proof Stolichnaya. It says 'Vodka, product of Russia' on the label."

The Russian glanced the length of the curved couch and favored his partner with a rare sardonic smile. "*Wodka*," he said precisely, "comes in bottles with a tear-off foil tab, because one never opens the bottle unless one intends to finish it. It is not sipped, because allowing it contact with the palate or tongue is the direst sort of foolishness. And on an occasion such as this, one shatters the glass in the nearest fireplace, so that it may never be disgraced by being put to a lesser purpose."

"That's Baccarat," the American answered reasonably, as the Russian lowered the glass to his lips, measuring his partner over the rim. "And it's a gas fire. And what's the occasion worth breaking my glasses over, in any case?"

1.

"Am I a defector?"

"No, you're not Kim Philby. That's two."

"I can count." A considering pause. "Do you want coffee? There is still a bit in the thermos."

"Yes. I'm not counting that question, out of the goodness of my heart."

"You are exceedingly kind. Am I dead?"

"No," the American said, and this time he couldn't resist a sideways glance.

The Russian had looked over at the same moment, of course: their eyes met in the darkness and then they turned back to their respective tasks. The American watched the window. The Russian watched the door. "You're not John F. Kennedy."

"Three. What is that quaint expression about tiny mercies?"

"Small mercies," the American corrected, and held out his hand for the coffee without glancing down.

2.

You marry young, looking for—something. Anything. But she dies. Badly. Maybe you leave the Army. Maybe you join the Navy. Maybe you have nowhere else to go, and some smart talent scout notices the strength of your body, the agility of your mind, the charm in your demeanor. That might not mean anything, but coupled with that dead look at the back of your eyes—the one that says *I am in this alone, forever*—maybe you find yourself recruited. It's the CIA, or is it the GRU?

One thing leads to another. Detached duty first, then a transfer. Maybe you keep wearing her ring, and maybe you don't. If you do, it turns out to be a mistake. You learn what you should have known, to keep things that mean something to you in a safe deposit box, not in your apartment and not on your person. You learn quickly not to get attached. Not to make friends. Not to bring lovers home. Not to get into the car and simply flip the ignition, as any normal person would. Not to turn your back.

Not to trust.

You're a physicist and an athlete, or an engineer and a soldier. A second-story man and a martial artist—with another profession as well. The oldest profession, but there are a thousand ways to sell yourself. When you're with a woman—for business or pleasure—or, in the line of duty, sometimes a man, you don't sleep. If duty demands you stay the night, rather than rising and making apologies, you lie awake listening to soft breaths in the darkness. You never, ever doze. Even if it were safe, you couldn't bear to explain the nightmares.

Until, unexpectedly, you meet someone who doesn't need an explanation.

3.

"We are not dead," the Russian answered, and deigned to clink glasses with his partner when the American leaned forward on the deep leather sofa to make the reach. He knocked two fingers of vodka back in a gulp, feeling the insufficient burn of the Stolichnaya, and rose and passed through the door into the kitchen to pour himself another from the bottle in the American's Kelvinator. He pushed back against the refrigerator's door, leaning his abused neck on the cold curve of the metal. "You are going to have a shiner, my friend."

The American laughed. "I'm going to have more than a shiner. The bastard loosened a couple of teeth."

"Do not poke them and they will resettle," the Russian advised, sipping his vodka. Decadent novelty: vodka that could be sipped. America had its advantages.

"The expert on loosened teeth, are we?"

"Somewhat. Is the initial K in my first name?"

"No. You're not Katharine Hepburn."

"Five. Am I male?"

"Yes. Six." The American had not risen from his seat deep in the green leather.

The Russian dropped his glass on the table beside the sofa and came toward him, flicking the crystal with a fingernail to make it ring. "Have another."

"The onions are in the refrigerator. As is the vermouth—"

"If you would drink vodka like a civilized person—" He fetched the necessary items and handed his partner the gin bottle. Standing over the American, the Russian observed what he poured and tilted the bottle marginally higher. He skewered onions on a toothpick, and dropped them into a Gibson that was probably much too warm. "It is good for you to relax."

The American watched in amusement, and killed half the glass in a swallow. "It was a close call, wasn't it?"

"It was closer than I like," the Russian answered, and shoved his partner against the couch, a palm flat on either shoulder, straddling the other man's knees. He raised his right hand and tilted the American's chin up, turning his eye into the light. "You have a hematoma."

"You," the American answered, "have whip cuts from here—" idle fingers marked a place just below the collar of the black turtleneck "—to here." The crease at the top of his buttocks, and by chance the American's fingers pressed hard on the worst of the welts.

The Russian hissed.

"And you're worried about a spot of blood in my eye?"

"Closer than I like," he said again. The vodka made him feel distant, thoughtful. "Are you drunk yet?"

"Pleasantly—" a slight hesitation, and a smile "—loose."

"Good," the Russian growled, and plucked the pricey glass from his partner's fingers, setting it beside his own. He grabbed two wings of a linen collar in fists that were surprisingly large for his height and *pulled*, tendons ridging, buttons scattering, baring the American's untanned chest. "Because I almost lost you tonight, and I am not in a mood to play games."

"I save the games—" the American leaned forward, raised a bruised hand, knotted it in the Russian's perpetually untidy hair and yanked "—for people upon whom my life does not depend."

The pain was good, startling, sharp and alive as the tinkle of shattering crystal. Pain was always better than the alternative. "That is as it should be," the Russian said, and bit his partner perhaps harder than he should have.

Silence, broken by little grunts of effort and the wetness of mouth on mouth, mouth on skin, affirmations of survival. The American's lip was puffy, the flesh inside his cheek welted and split from his teeth. The Russian tasted blood. He did not mind. Tasting his partner's blood was also preferable to not.

"We have a plane to catch again, in the morning," he said, leaning back and raising his arms to make it easier for his partner to peel cashmere knit from damaged skin. "You would think our employer would give us a week off at least."

"Tovarisch?" The American laid one callused hand flat on the gymnast's muscle of the Russian's belly.

"Yes?"

"Shut up."

1.

"Am I famous?"

Hm. How to answer that? The American smiled, long, square fingers tapping idly at the hard plastic of the steering wheel. "Four. In certain circles—"

"That is not a yes or no answer. I should claim forfeit—"

The American cleared his throat. "Hmm. Bathroom light just went off. He's at the window. He's drawing the shades—"

"What is he wearing?" The Russian was suddenly a flurry of motion, turning over the seat back, digging in a black plastic trash bag on the back seat of the babyshit-brown 1962 Dodge Polara with the three small dents in the driver's side door.

"Slumming," the American said, leaning forward with the binoculars pressed to his eyes. "Dark slacks. Your jeans should be fine in the dark. And—slouchy white pullover. No, ivory. Sweater or a sweatshirt."

"We brought a white sweatshirt," his partner said, and slithered back into the front seat with his prize. He ducked his head, back of his hand brushing his partner's arm in the confined space as he writhed into the shirt. "This should do in the dark. Where do you wish to take him, my friend?"

"If he follows his usual route, ah—" the American looked at his partner, just as the Russian looked at him. The Russian offered a wary flash of smile at the inevitability of that glance. "—I'll take him out behind the tailor shop and hand him off to the boys in the van. Complete the route. I'll be there after you make the pickup."

A stocky blond man emerged from the front door of the brownstone, shuffling along purposefully, his hands stuffed into the side pockets of his slacks, his ivory sweater lumpy and unkempt. "Be careful," the Russian said, and slipped out of the car as if he had never been there, the hood of his inside-out sweatshirt pulled up to cover the brightness of his hair.

Be careful? the American thought. *I'm not the one going into harm's way tonight, you crazy Soviet.*

2.

On the surface, he's wind to your stone, ice to your fire. The accent is an enemy's, the demeanor suave where yours is stiff, or perhaps brittle where yours is calm.

He's a depraved and godless communist, or maybe he's a decadent capitalist swine. The Cold War takes place in the break room, and your coworkers place their bets on which of you will kill the other one first. You overhear comments about the immovable object and the irresistible force. Matter and antimatter. White and black. Night and day. Us and Them.

Your coworkers are fools.

The détente that matters takes place in greasy midnight alleyways over icy, oily coffee. Peel off the pretenses and the same history lies beneath. Night and day aren't opposites.

They are two halves of a whole.

3.

"Ow."

"Pansy. It's only alcohol."

"Pansy?" The Russian wondered if his partner could hear the raised eyebrow in his voice. He couldn't be troubled to lift his head from the sofa and look over his shoulder to catch his partner's eye. "Consider the source. In any case, the welts hurt enough without your assistance."

"This one's going to scar, I think. You should have had stitches; we seem to have split the scab."

"I do not need stitches—ow. If you insist on tormenting me, at least permit me to apply more alcohol on the inside, also."

"By all means. It's gotten warm, I'm afraid." The vodka glass nestled into the carpet beside the Russian's left hand. "At least one new scar," his partner said regretfully. "Possibly two or three."

"Who would notice another?" The Russian lifted himself on his elbow to sip pungent liquor, leather briefly adhering to his chest. Cool fingers traced the old and new marks on his back, buttocks, thighs. The touch felt strange—interrupted—prickles and pins and needles that were the legacy of damaged nerves, damaged skin.

The American sighed. "How can you just, ah, shrug it off like that?"

"I'm not a wounded pigeon."

"Wounded dove," the American corrected, cool stroke of an alcohol-soaked cloth following his hand.

"Whatever. My actions will not be dictated by my injuries—" They both knew it was a patent lie. Knew it, and lived it. "Permit me some measure of dignity, my friend." He lay prone and set down his glass, reaching back to run broad fingers up his partner's forearm and shoulder. Fingers traced skin like satin to a knot as hard and slick as leather. "What is this?"

"You know what it is."

The Russian let his silence handle the reprimand, and his partner sighed and gave in.

"It's a scar."

"A bullet wound."

"Yes."

"Did you know that scar tissue is the strongest tissue in the body?"

His partner set the antiseptic cloth aside and caressed one of the uglier marks on the Russian's back, fingers trailing to outline hard muscle. The Russian flinched more than he had from the alcohol. "It's tough," the American admitted. "But it doesn't stretch. And it can interrupt sensation, make pleasure feel like pain. Make you afraid to take chances, get injured again—"

"There is that," the Russian agreed, drowsy now as his partner finger-combed his hair, floating on the scent of warm leather and warmer booze. "But it is preferable to the alternative."

1.

The alley was deserted, and the American gave a faint, satisfied huff. The courier would have had to run full-out to make it here before him, but it was still good not to be wrong. He stepped into the shadows and waited, breathing deeply with exertion. A week's painstaking observation said that this was the place where it must happen. This was the place where it would be.

It all went bad, of course.

He tuned his ears for approaching footsteps—fast, short steps, not his partner's fluid stride and oh-so-insignificant limp. What he heard instead was a scuffle, a rattle of shoes on metal, an angry shout. He ran to the cross street, muffling his steps as best he could, and looked down, both ways, and up—

Two struggling figures on a fifth-story fire escape, interchangeable in the near-darkness. Blond hair a little too long for respectability, pale lumpy pullovers concealing the outlines of the bodies within. The courier had taken to the roof-tops—driven by the seventh sense everyone in their line of work shared if they lasted long—and rather than miss the chance to replace him before the pickup, the Russian had followed him there. The American raised his sidearm, wishing it were loaded with darts, and leaned back into a two-handed police stance.

A pistol.

He might as well have been aiming a peashooter, at this distance and angle of fire. He'd have been better off with a peashooter, he realized as he thumbed the safety off. Because his chances of hitting his partner were just as good as his chances of hitting the courier. Even if his aim was true, a bullet could pass through the intended target, tumbling, rending flesh, shredding arteries, and kill what lay beyond. "Fucking hell," he swore, blowing his forelock out of his eyes, the scent of garbage and cool city night rising all around him as he waited for his opening, breath smooth and calm in his chest.

He waited too long.

A grunt, a left cross he thought he recognized all too well, and someone ducked, and someone grabbed, and someone hit the railing hard at waist-level and toppled forward. For a dizzying moment, the American imagined he fell too—flailing, fifty feet down onto asphalt and broken glass with a crunch that promised no survivors.

He couldn't comprehend how it was that his partner fell, and didn't take him over the railing too.

He didn't run. He didn't look down. Everything except his hands trembling with fury, the American switched the custom-made firearm to full auto and aimed with meticulous precision, as if he were on the target range.

And then, five stories above him, the Russian turned around and raked both hands through his hair and leaned hard on the railing, gasping, shaking his head a little when he saw the American leveling the gun. "You had better not be another evil duplicate," he called, when he had his breath under control. "I haven't the energy to chase you if you are."

"Thank God." A sigh, and the gun went down. "I thought—"

The Russian was descending the fire escape. Was swinging down and dropping the last ten feet, not bothering with the ladder. "I used a body double," he said dryly, nudging the pulpy courier with his toe. The American chuckled; he knew as well as the Russian did that the humor was a gaudy veil over the face of the dark goddess Necessity. The world trembled on the edge of a precipice, two great enemies chained mouth to mouth, nearly kissing, vast muscles writhing under fear-sweated skin. It would only take a single well-placed bullet to topple the whole world flailing over the edge. "We will need a cleanup squad. I am afraid he is past interrogation."

"Go on ahead," the American answered, holstering his gun. "I'll call it in. I should have known I'd find you lollygagging. You're likely to miss your timetable for the meet."

"Lollygagging," the Russian said. He looked up and his eyes met his partner's, and without another word he went.

And of course the evening only deteriorated from there, because their contact hadn't bothered to inform control that the recognition codes for the pickup had been changed.

2.

There will always be another mission. There will always be another risk. And maybe you'll be captured, and maybe you'll be hurt. Maybe you'll be tortured, drugged, beaten. Used as bait. But there's no maybe about this: that you'll come back for your partner even when control tells you in no uncertain terms that it's death and worse than death to try. You'll kick and you'll claw and you'll scream and you'll work miracles.

Left hand and right, perfectly coordinated. How can you feed yourself in pitch darkness without stabbing your lip with the fork? Because you can. Because you're built that way, halves of a whole, kinetic sense that's not so much trust as—right hand and left, right brain and left, one creature split down the middle. One animal, two bodies, one luck.

And one day you'll run out of that luck. Because that's the job. There aren't any maybes there, either.

You hope when it happens, all the luck runs out at once.

3.

"What are you *drinking*?"

"Juice," the Russian answered, pushing the glass around on the Formica table-top, leaving pearls of icy sweat behind it.

"It's—" The blend of nausea and fascination in his partner's voice made him smile. "—*mauve.*"

"It is guava juice."

"Guava juice?" He reached for the glass, and the Russian let the corner of his mouth curl, just a little, without looking up from the crossword puzzle he was working.

"You will not like it."

"Are you sure?"

"Yes."

The American put the glass down untasted and drew the second chair around into the puddle of morning sunlight. He sighed and leaned back, and the Russian saw the way his long, smooth fingers flexed against the tabletop.

The Russian looked up over the rims of his reading glasses. "Am I an Ameri-can?"

"No, you're not Martin Luther King, Jr.," his partner said. "Seven. You'll never get this one."

"Hmph." The Russian set the pen down, considering his partner carefully.

Considering the gloating smile. He frowned, feeling his eyebrows pull together. "Am I Caucasian?"

"Yes. Eight."

"Am I—" Hesitation, fingers through hair, a sunny smile as he played his victim onto the hook. "Am I a fictional character?"

"Yes. Damn you." That exasperated twist of the American's mouth told the Russian he had the answer. One more question, to be sure.

"Ten. Am I a spy?"

"No. You're an agent, you slick son of a bitch. A spy works for the other side. Put me out of my misery already."

"The other side? Whatever happened to 'godless Soviet?'" No answer except a shrug and a sideways roll of the eyes. The Russian grinned, triumphant. "Clever American. You very nearly had me stumped this time. Except you lied on one answer: not a communist?"

"I thought once I lured you down that backtrail I'd have you chasing red herrings until dinnertime. And how many communists dress in cashmere and drink guava juice for breakfast?"

"My friend, I never claimed to be a *good* communist. Détente is the art of compromise."

"Ah. I thought it was the art of letting the other fellow have your way."

The Russian answered with a shrug, enfolded himself in another identity, commenced another game. "Ten games to four. My turn. Your name begins with the letter—"

SEVEN DRAGONS MOUNTAINS

"Ming-feng says she saw a dragon over the bay when she went for tea three nights ago."

"Ming-feng." Chueh-hsin pressed fingertips into velvety dough and did not look at his honored customer. Tacky-surfaced circles took shape under his caress; they would soon be stuffed with aromatic ginger, with green onion and tiny shrimp and fat pork. "Your Ming-feng, Mr. Long? Her master sends her all the way around the bay for his special blend?"

"He does." The honored customer sipped his tea and smiled, bending his long neck to watch his lunch prepared. "All the way to the tea-shop by the English Governor's palace on the other side of the island. Still, the walking keeps her legs pretty."

Chueh-hsin laughed, tasting the scent of peanut and sesame oil and the tang of roasted chilies. He stopped himself from looking into the kitchen to call for a fresh pot of tea. There was no one but himself to serve the customers in the small restaurant now, and so he sighed and patted the last dumpling wrapper flat. He glanced past the honored customer, beyond the row of long-necked ducks hung dried along the edge of the awning. Chueh-hsin squinted into the light as if his gaze might pierce the soaring steel, marble, and glass towers and cross the bay to the rolling green backs of the auspicious Seven Dragons Mountains, and he might glimpse a dragon of his own.

The canyon of the street darkened, but it was no sacred animal's passing that he noted: only the shadow of one of the ever-present dirigibles. The fountain in the restaurant behind the honored customer splashed; Chueh-hsin leaned forward, and caught a glimpse of a knobby, jade-dark serpentine head slipping back below the surface.

Mr. Long lifted his cup on five knobby fingers and noticed the angle of his gaze. "Are you saving that turtle for soup?"

Chueh-hsin shook his head. "Though a man may consume any beast whose back faces heaven, that turtle is not for eating," he answered, and wiped his hands on his apron before he went to measure the fine, curled shapes of chun mee, the tea called *precious eyebrows*, into a pot that he then filled with nearly boiling water. When he glanced up again, he looked at the sunlight on the caramelized skins of the ducks, at the passers-by who would soon enter his humbly successful restaurant for a bowl of noodles or a plate of dumplings, at the softly flaking crimson paint on the timbers under the eaves. "Did Ming-feng notice what color the dragon was?"

"Yes," Mr. Long answered. "The dragon was the color of the sun and of golden jade. He had five fingers on each hand."

"An Imperial dragon," Chueh-hsin said. He tilted his head as he poured the fine, pale-green, astringent-smelling tea and noticed the jade-green head had risen above the water once more. "That must be an omen. I wonder what it means, an Imperial dragon?"

The turtle splashed as it submerged. "Perhaps it means the British will be eradicated soon," Mr. Long said, but he lowered his voice and glanced toward the door before he said it. He rattled five curved fingernails on his eggshell-thin teacup and smiled through long, yellow teeth.

Mr. Long stayed until the lunch crowd had emptied back out again, drinking tea and eating dumplings that seemed to have no effect on his spare frame, but at last Chueh-hsin stood between the doorposts and watched as the white-haired man bicycled away. Mr. Long held himself as erect as one of those doorposts, Chueh-hsin thought, turning his plaque to read "closed" and sighing in anticipation of his own much-delayed meal.

A scratching sound made him turn back to the door before he had gone more than a few steps inside. Chueh-hsin squinted into the sunlight to make out the silhouette of a man in a monk's uniform, his feet dragging as he staggered with exhaustion. He found himself halfway back to the door before the name was out of his mouth. "Chueh-min! Chueh-min!"

Chueh-hsin grasped his younger brother by the shoulders, and then almost stepped back as Chueh-min clutched his wrists tight and hissed for silence.

"Not so loud, oldest brother," Chueh-min said, ducking his head under paper streamers as he hurried into the shop. He moved along the front counter, untying the strings on the bamboo shades between the restaurant and the street and letting them fall to hide the interior. Chueh-hsin stepped back against the inside counter and watched, noticing the grey mud caking his brother's sandals, the violet shadows surrounding his eyes.

Chueh-hsin bit his lips on the questions, turning his back on Chueh-min. He leaned over the counter and withdrew a red-veined ivory oval from a silk-lined basket. He knocked the preserved duck egg—from which he had already peeled the clay and ash coating—on the counter and began to lift the stained shell from the gelatinous white with the tip of his fingernail.

"Thousand-year-old eggs?" Chueh-min had come up alongside him. He smelled as if he'd been travelling, his hair falling in greasy tangles across his forehead.

"It's for the turtle," Chueh-hsin answered, and picked up his cleaver to cut the egg into bits.

"Have you one for your first younger brother as well, after so long away?"

Chueh-hsin turned, the cleaver in his hand, and caught Chueh-min's half-smile. "Welcome home," he said, and swept the gluey egg into a bowl. "Help yourself. I will make tea soon: Are we not brothers? Is not my wealth your wealth, and my duty your duty?"

"It is," Chueh-min said, as if the subtle reprimand had not affected him, and reached into the basket as Chueh-hsin brought the bowl to the edge of the fountain.

He picked up a bit of greenish yolk between his fingers and sank down on the lip of the fountain, letting his hand hang down so that the edge of his palm brushed the water. He waited, perfectly still, breath held, while Chueh-min rolled the second egg against the countertop. The sound of the shell cracking was like crazing glass; he turned his head to watch, and almost shivered when the turtle took advantage of his distraction to lift the bit of yolk from his fingertips. The green beak nibbled and withdrew, five tiny claws brushing his skin as the reptile treaded water. Chueh-hsin lifted his hand and retrieved another fragment of egg without looking away from Chueh-min. "I notice you waited until the customers had left to approach my restaurant, first younger brother."

Chueh-min turned toward him, sucking delicately at the quivering surface of the egg. "Can you hide me until I can make it to the Governor's palace unobserved?" he asked plainly, and Chueh-hsin smiled.

"It would appear, younger brother, that I already am."

Red lanterns lit the warm night; Chueh-min finally awakened from a long, hard sleep in the room behind the restaurant, after the dinner hour had passed. Chueh-hsin served noodles and tea and sat beside his brother on the floor mat while they ate, shoulder to shoulder, in silence as if five years had not passed.

"Where is Xiumei?" Chueh-min asked when he had finished drinking his broth. He laid his chopsticks parallel across his bowl and poured himself another cup of tea, which he held elevated on long fingers, his palms cupped face to face as if enjoying the warmth.

"She wished to return to her family," Chueh-hsin answered, which was not exactly a lie. "Where have you been for half ten years, first younger brother?"

"Japan," Chueh-min answered, and Chueh-hsin started to his feet, upsetting the empty bowls. His teacup sprayed steaming liquid across the mat; it flowed close to Chueh-min, but Chueh-min did not rise.

"How can you say that so calmly?" And then Chueh-hsin blinked, and laced his fingers together before himself. "How did you manage to come back to the island, from Japan?"

"I took a dirigible into Russia," Chueh-min answered. "From there to Korea, and from Korea to Taiwan."

"And thence home again? Here, and not to the Emperor?"

"Sit, eldest brother," Chueh-min admonished. "I am not a spy." He sipped his tea and rolled his shoulders in a shrug. "Or if I am, I am a loyal spy, let us rather say."

"Then why have you not been spying on the British rather than on their behalf? We have argued about this before, first younger brother."

"Because the British are the lesser evil," Chueh-min answered, and tipped his head to indicate that Chueh-hsin should sit.

And Chueh-hsin did, reaching for a cloth to dab at the spilled tea before he remembered that it was his mat, his tea, and his sleeping room. *Chueh-min should have been the eldest son*, he thought—not for the first time. The fountain in the restaurant splashed softly, filling the silence that lingered between them. Chueh-hsin shook his head surreptitiously: no. Chueh-min would have chafed under the responsibilities of an eldest son, and Chueh-hsin was not cut out for adventure.

A man's place in the world truly was predetermined for the best, by his duty to his ancestors and his family.

"I must report to the Governor by morning," Chueh-min said, breaking Chueh-hsin from his study. "Will you help me get there?"

"It's a long way to his palace," Chueh-hsin said doubtfully. He reached out to right the eggshell-fine teacup, and noticed that it had cracked when he overturned it. It looked as if it would still hold tea, however, and he poured himself another cup. "We should leave immediately, if we must be there by dawn."

"Put your boots on," Chueh-min said, and set his cup aside before he stood. Chueh-hsin drank his tea in haste and followed.

A half-moon gleamed in the sky like a baroque pearl tumbled on a bed of tangled silk, and the air was as cool as silk as well. Chueh-hsin pressed his fists into his sides through the quilted cotton of his jacket, breathing deeply to ease the stitch under his ribs. He was not accustomed to climbing, and his calves trembled with the effort of the road through the passes of the Seven Dragons. The wealthy suburb where stood the Governor's palace—and several expensive tea shops—was at the very tip of the peninsula that half-encircled the bay, directly across from the city. It was usually reached by private motor ferry by those with means to take it.

The ferries did not run so late. Nor were they particularly discreet. Chueh-hsin and his brother walked.

Chueh-min was fitter, but limping in his sandals, and Chueh-hsin found himself taking his brother's elbow to help him over the steeper parts of the road. The motion made the front of Chueh-hsin's jacket swing against his breast. He felt the hard, retracted shape of the turtle in his breast pocket when it did so. He should have left her in the fountain, he knew, but it seemed somehow safer to keep her close. Two thousand-year eggs lay in his sleeve pocket, smooth and warm as beach pebbles.

He'd never been able to bear letting the turtle out of his sight for long, and now that Chueh-min had returned, the urge to keep her close was that much stronger.

"Come this way," Chueh-min said, tugging his sleeve.

"That's away from the road."

"It's faster."

"It's steeper," Chueh-hsin argued, but he turned to follow.

"If I can do it, you can do it—"

"You are the one who's limping."

"Exactly."

Chueh-hsin leaned forward, digging his toes into the soft, green earth of the mountain's flank. He released Chueh-min's arm and steadied himself, one hand on the slope before him as they climbed. The turtle never moved, still as a stone. Probably frightened to be taken from the fountain where she had spent the last five years, Chueh-hsin thought, and silently reprimanded himself for pitying her.

Chueh-min paused at the top of a dragon-backed ridge, belly down so he would not be silhouetted against the ragged, moonlit sky. Chueh-hsin crouched low beside him. They remained for a moment, panting, and Chueh-hsin put his hand on his first younger brother's shoulder.

"You are not a monk," he said.

"I am a monk," Chueh-min replied. "I also am in the service of the Governor."

"The British Governor."

Chueh-min shrugged. "They are our allies against the Japanese," he answered. "Politics are eternal. China has been conquered before and will be conquered again: always she rises, China still. Like the Phoenix. Look, do you see the dirigible?" He raised an arm and pointed.

Chueh-hsin turned his head to follow the cascade of teal and emerald and golden electric lights across the sky. The dirigible's side was picked out in a pattern of a phoenix and a dragon-turtle, and Chueh-hsin sighed at its loveliness. His preoccupation was interrupted by Chueh-min's voice, hesitant and almost reverential as he dropped his gaze from the dirigible to its lights, reflected in the broken surface of the bay.

"Did Xiumei really go back to her family?"

Chueh-hsin did not answer directly. He pressed his fist against the center of his breast, easing his breathing. "She was unhappy after you left, first younger brother."

Chueh-min lifted one hand and pointed out over the bay. "Then she's out *there* now?"

"No," Chueh-hsin said, unwillingly. "I said she wanted to go home. I did not say she did."

"Then where is she?" Chueh-min glanced over, his voice too carefully casual.

Chueh-hsin smiled to himself, knowing that even the bright moonlight was not enough to reveal so slight an expression to Chueh-min. Something must have showed, however, because Chueh-min glanced quickly away. "Where I can keep her," Chueh-hsin said. "Hurry. The moon will set soon, and we are only halfway there."

Chueh-min's shortcut led them unerringly toward the winking lights of the little town at the end of the peninsula. Chueh-hsin followed in his brother's footsteps. They did not speak of Xiumei again.

Chueh-hsin could not say when he first became aware that something was wrong among the mountains. Perhaps it was the faint sallow light that did not fade as the moon set, but seemed to rise from behind the hill to the left as if starlight soaked the earth of its far flank. He laid his hand on Chueh-min's sleeve and turned him toward the light. "Do you see it?"

"Yes," Chueh-min said, and set off in that direction without hesitation, the exhaustion gone from his step as he scrambled toward the spiked crest of the ridge.

Chueh-hsin had no choice but to follow until Chueh-min halted at the lip of a staggering cliff.

There was a valley below, a narrow steep-sided niche between mountains that would be almost completely inaccessible to a man on foot. Gullies and treeless cuts, furred green in verdant grass, ran down to a ravine that seemed to have only two exits. A worn switchbacked trail ran up a steep incline on the far side of the valley, toward the road which they had abandoned for this more direct route, and from which the valley was shielded by an even higher ridge. On the near side, a rope ladder dangled the height of the cliff face.

Electric torches lit the scene below. Men in dark uniforms hurried—efficient, purposeful as ants—around the site in utter silence. Chueh-hsin caught his breath as if the heavy rasp of it in his throat could carry far enough to give them away.

In the center of the activity, at the bottom of the valley, gilded red and crimson in the light of the torches, slumbered a dragon. Chueh-hsin could see the stout, black cables twined across its back, pinning each five-toed extremity to the ground. Chueh-hsin glanced at his brother, but Chueh-min had eyes only for the scene below. "The Governor must know of this," Chueh-min said.

"As he must know of the other news you carry?" Chueh-hsin could not keep the bitterness out of his voice. In all the truth of it, he did not even try.

"This is the other news I carry," Chueh-min said. "I didn't know it was here already, elder brother."

"The dragon? But he must know, if he's sent all those men—"

"That's not a dragon," Chueh-min said patiently. "It is an airship. And those men are Japanese." This time he did meet Chueh-hsin's eyes. And then cursed softly under his breath and yanked Chueh-hsin away from the edge of the cliff, as the bustle below increased. The men threw the dragon's tethers free, and slowly—majestically—the amazing animal rose.

It writhed in the sky like a serpent, its thousand-yard length glittering as it rose. Its throat glowed blue with flame, jaws working like the mouth of a horse champing the bit, and Chueh-hsin could see that it was somehow lit like a paper lantern from within.

"No airship could look so real," he murmured. He might have stood hopelessly and watched its gold, five-toed claws clench and twist on air, but Chueh-min clutched his wrist and dragged him into a staggering run. "They'll bomb the palace from the air."

"Worse," Chueh-min called over the thud of their feet on the grass, the sporadic rattle of gunfire behind them. They must have been seen when they started to run. "It breathes fire. It's here to destroy the Governor's palace. The people will see the Imperial dragon rise from the mountain to destroy the British overlords. There will be an uprising—"

And worse still, Chueh-hsin thought, hearing the amplified cries of pursuit above and behind them as the grass lit sharp-edged and white beneath their feet, the dragon-ship's searchlights coming to bear. *The Japanese will walk into a China already softened by war.* Chueh-min stumbled, his sandaled feet sliding on the grass, pulling Chueh-hsin into the orbit of his arms and rolling with him as they fell. Bullets sang around them: Chueh-min shielded Chueh-hsin in the curve of his arms. And Chueh-hsin curled himself taut around the hard-shelled object that jabbed his bosom as they rolled.

Chueh-hsin could never have described what happened after. He lost one sandal as they tumbled down the long, green slope, suffering bruising collisions with rocks and earth. Chueh-hsin gagged at the sound of green twigs snapping, not knowing at first if his own bones had broken or Chueh-min's. The eggs in his sleeve pocket crushed like teacups under a big man's boot. Chueh-hsin fell atop his brother and heard a bubbling groan, spread himself wide across Chueh-min's body to absorb the expected impact of bullets.

The airship slid overhead, gleaming like the moon it eclipsed, silent except for the tremble of wind against its taut, scaled skin, and nothing touched Chueh-hsin at all.

He pulled back and rolled over, amazed, watching that long sinuous body glide by like a living river of gold. And then he heard Chueh-min cough wetly, and heard his brother's slick, soft hiss of pain. "Chueh-hsin." Not so much speech as the bubble of a voice from a great deep.

"Don't talk," Chueh-hsin said. "You're hurt."

"I'm dying. At least one bullet has entered my back," his brother answered, matter-of-factly, and black shining blood dripped from the corner of his mouth. He gasped between each word. "Run to the Governor. Can you run, elder brother?"

"It's no use," Chueh-hsin said. "I can't outrun an airship. And we have no duty here—"

"You owe me this."

"I owe you nothing."

"Your duty as my elder brother."

"As you fulfilled your duty as my younger brother when you went into the pay of the British? Or as you fulfilled it when you fucked my wife?" He stopped, appalled at his own bright-edged words, and pressed his hand against his bosom. The turtle— if the turtle had been crushed—

He pulled her out, a hard dome of jade no larger than his palm, and tried to see her in the moonlight. He smelled his own sweat, the fermented reek of the thousand-year eggs, the hot red iron of Chueh-min's blood. He held her cupped in his palms, close to his face, turning to the copper moonlight and tilting his head as if, through the darkness, there was any chance at all that he could see a jagged crack marring the green of her shell.

Huddled close within her carapace, she didn't stir, even when Chueh-hsin blew across the opening for her head, to let her taste his breath.

"Xiumei?" Chueh-min said, or tried to say. Chueh-hsin cupped his fingers carefully around the turtle in his palm, and reached out with his other hand to take Chueh-min's.

He looked down, surprised. Chueh-min's fingers lay slack and boneless between his own, and his eyes reflected the moonlight dully, slitted open beneath clotted lashes.

"Xiumei," he said in answer, as if Chueh-min could hear him, and turned his head to follow the inner-lit silhouette of the dragon against the star-scattered darkness above. Fire wreathed its mouth, the mechanical jaw working through what must be some fantastic contrivance. Chueh-hsin dropped his brother's hand and stood, the contracted turtle held up before him like an offering, and imagined he could hear the shouts of terror as the puppet-dragon came down on the Governor's palace.

The turtle lifted her head and watched with her husband as the dragon fell. She blinked tiny, rice-paper lidded eyes in the moonlight, and turned her gaze to Chueh-hsin. "Free me, honored husband," she said, "and I will call my father to put an end to that paper dragon."

Chueh-hsin bit his lip. "Obedience is a wife's duty," he said.

"It is," she answered. "As loyalty is a brother's. Chueh-min saved your life, my husband—"

He watched the incandescent gold ribbon of the dragon turn against the night sky, watched it begin to descend, still dripping fire, upon the tea-shops and the houses near the palace. "Call your father," he said.

"Will you free me, Chueh-hsin?"

"Call your father," he said, and the turtle closed her eyes and withdrew her head into her shell.

"Promise—"

"Call your father." A third time. "I will promise no such thing."

Her sigh was as faint and brief as Chueh-min's passing breath. "Honored husband. It is done."

Chueh-hsin tucked his wife into his breast pocket, and lifted his brother's body over his shoulder, and carried them both up the ridge to watch as a knobby, jade-dark shape as vast as the island under their feet rose above the gleaming ocean beyond the bay. Its bulk against the greying horizon was nothing but a shadow, the rough shape of a turtle, domed shell and lamp-lit golden eyes. One of its hands broke the surface, five grasping moon-white talons reflecting starlight like a ship's masts carved of ivory. Tendrils streamered from its head and back.

Chueh-hsin held his breath as the dragon-turtle cast a searching glance across the island and rose into the air, its dark knobby outline silhouetted against the stars, as unlike the shining fantasy of the puppet airship as a mossy shrine is unlike a paper lantern. Ineffectual flashes of light sparked off its shell, glittered around the puppet airship like fireflies. Their report reached Chueh-hsin seconds later, and he realized he heard gunfire.

His brother's weight hung against his side like a sack of meat, and sticky wetness plastered his robes to his body, but he would not put his burden down. He stood on the ridgeline and watched the airship make a grand slow turn and bear down on the mansion and the town, the dragon-turtle sliding across the sky toward it, just perhaps in time.

In time. After all, in time. There was no contest when they met. The dragon-turtle moved through the airship like a stone through a paper fan, and tore it into burning, drifting shreds, which settled over the town as the dragon-turtle settled back into the sea: in abject silence, once the screams of falling men came to their end.

Chueh-hsin cupped his hands under the turtle's belly and crouched where the waves lapped most gently. He knelt, feeling the sand sucked from under his quilted trousers, the wet cloth salting his skin, and lowered the turtle into the ocean, ignoring the dry, possessive prickle of thwarted ownership against the back of his throat.

"A turtle that big will never survive in the bay," Mr. Long commented, leaning forward over the basket of his bicycle. "Something bigger will eat her, don't you think?"

"She'll be fine," Chueh-hsin said, watching the jade-green serpentine head emerge for a moment from the foam-honeycombed waves. "She has many friends. They will take care of her." *And she will grow as big as they are, one of these centuries.*

Mr. Long scratched his cheek with his knobby, five-fingered hands. "If you had one wish," he said, "one wish in all the world. What would it be, Chueh-hsin?"

"What have I done to deserve a wish, Mr. Long?"

The tall man's skinny throat bobbed as he swallowed, tilting his head and opening his hands, a disarming, half-embarrassed gesture. "Call it a family obligation. A debt for a debt repaid."

Chueh-hsin knuckled his chest below the collarbone and thought, watching a dirigible drift out over the bay. There were things he desired: Wealth. Fortune. Love. A restaurant where the walls were lacquered red and gilded gold, rather than hung with paper streamers and peeling paint.

He thought of the Governor gone, of the Japanese contained. *Politics and conquest are eternal,* he thought. *China is the Phoenix. China consumes whatever is given her, no matter how bitter, no matter how foul, and rises from the ashes whole.*

There were things he wanted. Like Xiumei. And there were things he was required to do, and a death to which he owed his life. "My brother back," he said, hating to say it, as the sea wind lifted his hair.

"Done," said the dragon beside him. "He will be waiting when you go home."

Chueh-hsin scowled; Mr. Long dipped his head in benediction and slipped like a turtle into the sea, where he belonged.

OLD LEATHERWINGS

The old leatherman was late for breakfast. This was more than an unusual happenstance: George Dell had fed the wanderer supper and breakfast every thirty-four days for twenty-six years, and never once had the old leatherman missed a meal or made a sound beyond the creak of his roughsewn rawhide suit.

New York winters pushing snow and New York summers walking alongside a furrow behind the oxen left a man knotted and strong as bent rope, twisted to suit his tasks. Dell wasn't young anymore himself. But he stomped into his thick hide boots, pulled his hat down stiffly with horny hands, shrugged his oilcloth on over his coveralls, and went out into the cold March rain. Dell knew his farm like the back of his own worn-out hand, hills and brooks like ropy veins and age spots and skin weathered shiny on the grips of the plow. He knew where he'd find the old leatherman, if he was there to be found.

A red-tail hawk hunched in a naked birch halfway up the hillside. White tree like bone among the cast iron black of wet oak and maple; the hawk fluffed almost headless against the chill and rain. Another farmer might have cursed leaving his shotgun leaned up by the planken door, butt propped beside the steel bucket of sand for the tall kitchen steps. Might have trudged back downslope, trudged back, shot the hawk off the branch and gone looking for its mate, if it had one. Might have crucified both bodies on the barbed wire fence beside the chicken coop, way to send a message.

But Dell didn't keep chickens since his wife died, and he knew foxes took more poultry anyway. A red-tail was more likely to eat a weasel than eat a hen, and weasels *were* bad on eggs.

He muttered to himself as he tromped through the pocked old snow. *Maybe he decided to move on before breakfast. Maybe he decided to get breakfast somewhere else. Maybe he's snug by the fire he banked last night to keep him warm, roasting a squirrel on a stick and too contented to come out in the cold.*

Maybe my hogs will butcher and smoke their own selves come fall.

Once there was a poor tradesman
who loved a rich merchant's daughter
and would have given anything to win her.

Jules Bourglay lay dying in a cave banked with rotten, spring snow, on the shores of a foreign land. A white tree thrust between the tumbled granite blocks of his rude shelter, an accusing finger pointed at the sky. A hawk he had followed from France and then for twenty-six years in circles from the Connecticut River to the Hudson crouched in the branches overhead.

Bourglay's fire had died to coals and his coals had died to ash. He held a thick, curved, three-sided leather needle threaded with sinew between fingers too cold to sew with, and his stitchery was pulled over his lap like a cowhide blanket.

A wet cough rattled his chest like a ship's canvas in a gale. He laid the needle, which over time he had sharpened to less than half its length, on the leather and pulled his fingers into his sleeve, tucking the sleeve under his coat to warm his hand. He did not cover his mouth when he coughed again, but he spat blood and phlegm into the ashes when he was done.

The moisture didn't sizzle. A cold rain fell through the junctures in the stones.

Twenty-six years he'd followed the hawks through these American states, from river to river and farm to farm. He'd swept a great circle steady as a clockhand, sleeping in caves even when beds or barns were offered, to be closer to the hawks. He'd held his tongue as the magic demanded, and he'd walked and he'd stitched and he'd clothed himself in the leftover plates of leather. He'd eaten what strangers offered in their charity, and he'd known they thought him a madman.

There was one hawk left.

He only needed one more day, he thought. Two, perhaps. But he could not walk, and he feared the hawk would leave before too much longer.

Slowly, Jules Bourglay slumped forward over his work, and fell to dreaming.

Once there was a man held captive by a wicked king
so that his only hope for escape was to make wings of wax and feathers
and to fly across the sea.

Inside the farmhouse, George Dell's older daughter, Hannah Wickham, held *her* older daughter on her knee, fussing rose-pink ribbons on the little girl's church dress. Widowed Hannah found George Dell a comfort, and widowed George Dell thought the same of Hannah. What five-year-old Stella made of these proceedings remained a mystery: she hadn't spoken a word since her father died, though she was as well-behaved and sweetly sad a child as any mother would cling to in her sorrow.

Hannah rose at Dell's shout from the yard and seated Stella on the tinderbox with an admonition to stay tidy. Graceful and strong, her brown hair twisted up and pinned, Hannah drew a robe around her shoulders and opened the kitchen door. "Pa? What is it?"

He stomped snow from his boots against the cast-iron hedgehog beside the door, and came in past her, his oilcloth dripping on the sanded puncheon floor. "The old leatherman is dying up the cave under the birch tree," he said. "I'll fetch the sled from down cellar. Get your boots on and out of your church clothes; I can't manage him alone."

"Mercy," Hannah answered, and went to do as she was bid.

Once there was an orphaned princess who was under a spell.

Dell had to kneel to crawl through the overhang of a granite cave made from half a dozen flat boulders tumbled together like so much split maple. "He's breathing," Dell called back to Hannah. "Pass me in the blanket. I'll have to drag him out."

He glanced over his shoulder to see Hannah's fair face as she squatted down, heedless of the snow and mud clotting the edge of her skirts, and shoved the folded blanket in. "Hand me up whatever 'tis he's got on his lap," she said, and once Dell had the blanket from her he did so, struggling with the soaked, stiff leather. Something glittering tumbled from it; a needle, he saw, and meant to remember it after he fetched the old leatherman out.

Roots dug his knees as he spread the blanket and struggled to pull the old leatherman onto it. "What is that thing?"

"It looks like a cloak—" A snapping noise, the clatter of vast leathery wings, as she shook it open. "A cloak, it is. A hood and all. It looks near finished."

The old leatherman was a vast slack weight in the narrow cave. Not for the first time, Dell wondered what duty or heartbreak had set the man wandering in circles, never speaking, living off the kindness of strangers and whatever he could snare.

Dell backed out of the narrow hole under the birch tree, dragging some two hundred pounds of fevered man and wet leather behind him. The blanket held together by the grace of his stern Puritan God alone. George Dell swore later he never would have managed without the snow.

The hawk screamed as he and Hannah bundled the old leatherman on to the sledge, and took wing as Dell leaned into the traces. He was halfway down the slope before he remembered that he'd meant to fetch the needle.

Once there was a nightingale
who loved a poor scholar so much that she died to make a rose bloom in mid-winter,

so he could win the hand of his lady.
And yet his lady spurned him nonetheless.

The white clapboard-sided farmhouse made a warmer place for dying in. His hands ached with warming, and he thought if he wasn't so weary and comfortable before the fire he might even manage to open his eyes. But he *was* weary, and a woman's voice sang wordless tunes over him. And rest was close, after twenty-six years of walking. Very close, indeed.

But Jules Bourglay could hear the hawk calling outside.

And the sewing wasn't finished.

Once there was a cruel and beautiful maiden with eleven handsome brothers who had been transformed into ravens.

Hannah watched as her father heaved the old leatherman onto a pallet on the floor in the warmth of the kitchen. She washed his face while Stella clung to her skirts; his skin was tanned as insensate as his leather. She spread his cloak and his patchwork jacket out on chairs far enough from the cast-iron range that the leather would not crack and stiffen as they dried. Dell went out to unharness the oxen; they weren't making church on *this* Sunday.

Stella still clung as Hannah shook pale green coffee from the tin into a skillet and set the beans on the top of the stove to roast. Between pumping up water and setting that to boil, she shook them occasionally. The rain made the kitchen grey. She thought of lighting a lantern to cheer the room, but decided not to waste the kerosene.

When a solid knock sounded at the bottom of the door, she went to answer, thinking her father must have kicked the frame because his arms were too loaded with wood to manage the latch.

Stella hopped back, dragging Hannah's skirts with her, as a red-tailed hawk flapped into the room.

Once there was a young tradesman who learned too late who it was that had truly loved him.

George Dell had seen many a strange sight in his sixty years, but his daughter and granddaughter at bay behind the table while a hawk as big as a small eagle mantled over the form of a leather-clad vagrant on his kitchen floor was probably the strangest. He paused in the doorway, the leatherman's needle—which he had hiked back up the hill to rescue, on the grounds that there was always a possibility the old wanderer might live—glittering between his fingers. The kitchen reeked of scorching coffee beans; the only sound was the stentorian rasp of the leatherman's failing breath.

"Hannah?" He thrust the needle through his oilcloth slicker, and reached behind the door for the shotgun, realizing even as he did so that he could not shoot the hawk without shooting the old leatherman too. "What's happening here?"

Hannah laughed softly, her back to the wall and one hand on the edge of the table. The other hand held her skirts in front of Stella, a pitiably fragile sort of barrier. "It seems the bird's invited itself to luncheon, Pa. And I'm not quite sure how to invite it back out again."

The hawk cocked an arrogant eye at Dell, and he laid his other hand on the shotgun, but did not raise it. It flipped its half-open wings shut and waddled around to face him, awkward on the floor as a fat duck out of water.

"*Mais oui*, go ahead and shoot me," the hawk said in the dulcet tones of a lady. "If Jules dies before he sets me free, I might as well be dead in any case."

George Dell blinked, and ever-so-slowly set the gun back down behind the door.

Once there was a poor but virtuous girl who could not spin straw into gold, though she tried with all her heart.

Her voice brought Bourglay back from the warm and quiet place he had dreamed himself into. Her dear, beloved voice: the only unchanged thing about her. He blinked once, slowly, and thought of examining his surroundings with care before he sat up, if he could manage to sit up. And then the cough took him like a convulsion, and his mouth filled up with slime.

He swallowed it, having no desire to spit blood and phlegm on some kind woman's clean kitchen floor.

"I am Natalie de Bouvier," the dear voice said, and feathers rustled. "And what you see before you, *mes amis*, is witchcraft and black magic, the vengeance of an ungrateful girl who fancied herself my rival and killed herself to transform me into the base creature you see before you. A tragedy, *n'est-ce pas?*"

Bourglay fell back on his pallet when he tried to sit. The hawk hopped away when he reached for her. He rolled on his side and coughed again.

"*Mais oui, mon cher* Jules followed us all the way to the New World after *le pauvre petit* Cendrillon did what she did—" A shrug of wings the color of maple syrup over a barred, butter-white breast. "He has made all eleven of my brothers men again, though not one of the ungrateful wretches stayed with me—" She heaved a great theatrical sigh. "And now he's going to die before he can save me too. If he'd had the sense not to love me in the first place—"

Oui, for you did so discourage my love, my darling. All those promises and all those stolen kisses—

—only to spurn me in the end.

*Once there was a tin soldier with only one leg, but a steadfast heart,
who loved a tinsel ballerina.*

Stella squeaked and burrowed deeper when the hawk began to speak. The bird hopped onto the chair that the jacket was draped on and unleashed a spatter of white excrement, oblivious to the convulsive coughing of the old leatherman hunched on the floor. "I beg your pardon," the bird said, but did not seem concerned.

Hannah started forward, edging past the angry-eyed bird to help him as he rolled from the pallet. He was crawling for the second chair, she realized—more a determined wriggle, for he could not force himself up off his belly—the chair that held the hooded leather cloak. "Oh, *merci à Dieu*," the hawk said. "*Il n'est pas tout à fait mort.*"

"Sit," Hannah told the old man firmly. She gestured her father over, and—Stella still swinging like a burr among her skirts—went to fetch the cloak. Dell helped the old leatherman sit and gave him back his needle. Hannah laid the cloak across his lap and rethreaded for him.

And then she straightened and yelped, "Mercy!" and went to pull the burning coffee beans from the stove.

She started another batch while the old man sewed, pausing every stitch to cough as if he were breathing smoke. Hannah's father brought him a clean bandanna for a handkerchief, which he took as gratefully as he did the mug of coffee Hannah brought him. The hawk fluttered from place to place, and Stella stayed on the opposite side of Hannah's skirts.

"What's wrong with the brat?" the bird asked idly, squatting like a vulture on the table.

"She hasn't spoken since her father died," Hannah answered, her hackles rising. "Would you mind terribly not fouling that?"

It took the old leatherman hours to sew a single seam through the half-inch-thick hide to join the top of the hood together. Another racking cough doubled him over his own outstretched legs, blood darkening the red bandanna he held to his mouth. He dropped it and gestured to the jittering hawk.

She stood before him, rocking from foot to foot, wings spread and beak open in birdy anticipation. The old leatherman looked at her and smiled, and waved Dell and Hannah over as well, the cloak spread wide between his hands. Hannah came up beside her father, her hands on Stella's shoulders to hold the squirming child before her skirts.

The old man coughed. His fingers wriggled. *Closer. Closer.*

With a sense of deathbed ceremony, hawk and woman and man and child obeyed.

The old leatherman pushed himself to his knees, pain creasing his forehead under beads of sweat. He spun the cloak so that its edge flared wide, a snapping noise like the clatter of vast leathery wings following the flick of his wrists. Stella cringed against Hannah so hard that she tripped on Hannah's skirts and tumbled to her knees. The hawk edged forward, pinions wide against the floor as the old leatherman whirled the garment high and cast it—over Stella's startled shoulders.

The little girl screamed out loud, and then pulled the hood over her head and dropped down on the floor under thick leather. For a moment there was no sound but the old leatherman's breathing and the bubble of the percolator.

And then Stella peeked from under the edge of the cloak and screamed again as the hawk, shrieking animal noises, flew at her face. "Mama, mama, *help me!*"

"*Vieille chienne,*" the leatherman whispered, slumping back on his heels, his face white as dough. "I wish I'd known thirty years back that Cendrillon was worth twelve of you."

He died before Hannah managed to chase the draggle-tailed hawk out of her kitchen with the broom.

Once there was a brave little tailor. Or a seamstress. Or a cobbler.
Once there was a curse.
Once there was a girl.

WHEN YOU VISIT THE MAGOEBASKLOOF HOTEL, BE CERTAIN NOT TO MISS THE SAMANGO MONKEYS

In the place where I was born, stones had been used to mark boundaries for four hundred years. We harrowed stones up in fields, turned them up in roadcuts. We built the foundations of houses from stones, dug around and between them. We made stone walls, and our greatest poet wrote poems about those walls and their lichen-speckled granite. The gift of glaciers, and the wry joke of farmers. "She'll grow a ton and a half an acre, between the stones." The people who lived there before mine made tools of them, made weights and currency.

This is an alien landscape. Another world. A cold, empty desert on the other side of a long, cold sleep, light-years away from the place I grew up in and can never go home to. A place that lies across a gulf of cannibalized colony ships and unfeeling stars.

But stones are a boundary here too. They mark the line between life and death, between our pitiful attempts to terraform and the natives' land with its stark stone cities and empty plains. And *this* stone, wound about with a windblown veil dark blue as the autumn sky of my homeworld, so much brighter than the dusty firmament of this one— *This* stone marks other things.

A body was buried here. Not long ago. And not a human one.

I'm the xenobiologist. There's a sonic shovel buried in my pack beside the sample kits, and an overwhelming sense thumping in me that what I'm about to do is irrevocably wrong.

I scan the horizon for alien aircraft, ears tuned for the hum of engines. When I see and hear nothing, I begin digging through my pack.

Samango monkeys were listed as a rare species under CITES Appendix II because they were confined to an ecosystem covering less than 1% of the land area of Southern Africa, the evergreen Afromontane forests. Unlike their ubiquitous relatives, the vervet monkeys, the samango monkeys were rarely seen by outsiders.

The sonic shovel looks like an entrenching tool; it folds, and the narrow blade screws onto the handle. It weighs less than a kilogram, but the rigid parts are monomolecular carbon laminate: it's exceedingly strong, much lighter than the spades and posthole diggers I used on Mother's hundred and fifteen acres in Vermont. That's a thought that comes with a sting; that land isn't there anymore, and neither are the shaggy-coated ponies and the long-haired goats that were my childhood companions and chores. Or, more precisely, the land is still there. But since the Shift, it's not much of a farm. Even a ragged New England farm, clawed from a mountainside.

It amuses me to realize that when the ice goes back—if the ice goes back—four hundred years of plow and pick, of Morgan horses and oxen pulling at their collars, will be undone and the settlers—if there are any settlers—will have to start all over again on a fresh crop of rocks to turn it back into a farm.

I bite the valve and gulp oxygen to ease the straining pressure in my chest. I flip the switch on the shovel's handle before I set it against dirt and stones. The packed soil would be challenging to shift by hand, but technology makes short work of many obstacles. Alas, the ones I need solutions for prove obdurate in the face of technology, and ingenuity too.

I could almost wish that the work were harder. Manual labor is good for stopping thought, but the sonic shovel makes this little more strenuous than walking, even in the thin icy air. And walking is an excellent way to shift one's brain to overdrive.

The samango monkey was larger and darker than the vervet monkey. Its diet consisted largely of fruit and leaves, supplemented by flowers and insects. The Magoebaskloof Hotel in the Limpopo District of South Africa—an eco-tourism destination—was famous for its samango monkey feeding program, which allowed tourists the chance to see the rare animals up close.

We never understood what a garden was Earth until we got out here where it's cold and strange and nothing wholesome grows. We're going to run out of preserved food sooner rather than later. And the babies have all been stillborn so far, and it's my job to know why, and I just do *not*.

We fired all but blind; it's only luck that the world we aimed for is habitable at all. And it's my job as xenobiologist to keep it that way. To find a way to bend the biochemistry of this planet to our bodies, to remedy the lack of digestible proteins in the native flora, and the prevalence of ever-so-slightly toxic-to-Earth-life alkaloids. To understand how native intelligence developed, when they're the only *animal* we've found on this planet where even plant life is so sparse.

We have so many lovely theories. The fragmentary fossil record we've un-covered shows a complete ecology until only eyeblinks ago, on a geologic scale. The natives could be the sole survivors of some ecological catastrophe. They could even be the cause of it. Or—the most intriguing possibility—like us, they could come from Somewhere Else. And no matter where they came from, what happened to everything else?

I wish we knew how to talk to them. Wish we knew if they even have language, when near as I can tell they might communicate by pheromones, or kinetically, via posturing too subtle for us to even notice. It might help us understand why they treated us as long-lost brethren from day one. Until Veronica Chambers—we reconstruct—exhumed one of the veil-marked graves, probably not even knowing what she was digging up, and the natives sliced her very tidily and very thoroughly into bits.

I helped retrieve the corpse. I remember very clearly what her remains looked like. Blood, everywhere. Grey with dust.

But even after that, nothing changed about the friendly unassuming way they treated us. We haven't moved beyond the grunt-and-point-and-occasionally-dismember level of conversation we've achieved. You'd think at least math would transfer, one rock plus one rock equals two rocks. You would think.

There was never any question that the brightly clad natives were intelligent. They came in strange mechanical craft and greeted us with wonderful gifts from the first day we landed: gracious hosts, utterly without fear, for all we had not found a way to speak with them. It took me some time to understand the simple logic of it; they had no competition on their harsh dry world except the world itself. There were no predators, no other animals, no prey. They dined by poking lichen-covered rocks into the puckered orifices below their nominal chins. The rocks emerged some hours later, polished shiny as agates. The young were born alive, fed from flat dugs in the crevices between their double-joined arms and their tripartite carapaces.

Their only enemy was the planet, and their supreme allies were each other. It was their biology to make us at home. Or so I thought—assumed, bad scientist—until Veronica.

We have so many lovely theories about how the aliens evolved, where they came from, why they are as oddly peaceable as Emperor penguins, as Galapagos tortoises that have never seen a threat. And I can't explore or disprove any of them unless I can dissect a dead one, and sample whatever it is that they use for genetic material.

I lean on my sonic shovel, considering the mound of dirt between my boots. I'm lucky to have been chosen. Lucky to have gotten a colony ship, at my age. Lucky to be here, brushing soil from the triskelion carapace of some alien mother's child with my fingertips so I don't damage the cadaver with my shovel.

The baby's body is almost half my size and wrapped in more blue cloth, layers of it, spun of the fibers and dyed bright with the sap of those same alien plants that we cannot eat. I edge fingers under the carapace, make sure that the soft and oddly human three-fingered hands stay tucked tight inside the funeral pall, protected when I lift. I have to jump down beside it, like Hamlet with Ophelia, to get enough purchase to haul it up.

I use the shovel as a lever.

When I raise my head to half-roll, half-drag the alien's body out of the grave, I am looking into a dozen triads of eyes.

I guess I picked a bad day to start robbing graves.

I was eleven when I saw my first samango monkey. My mother had brought me to South Africa for an ecology conference. It was not a "done thing" to bring children to professional conferences in those days—in some ways we did become more enlightened, and more aware that a separation between family and profession can be an artificial stress—but the scientists were very kind. Dr. Martens from UCLA, I remember in particular, introduced me to all the exotic fruits and spices and laughed at the faces I made.

I, in turn, laughed at the faces the monkeys made.

Especially the babies.

The monkeys were rust and silver, ticked with black. Their coats were long, not silky but... kinky, like soft, nappy human hair brushed out. They smelled like animals: acrid, musky, unpleasant. The males were almost twice as big as the females, their rough-and-tumble muzzles elongated over enlarged canines. The females had faces as sweet as Barbie dolls and radiant carnelian-colored eyes.

One particular monkey who came to the Magoebaskloof for the feedings had two babies that did not look like each other. While twins were not unheard of, these were not twins. Rather, female samango monkeys—Dr. Martens explained—were extremely maternal; they would even adopt orphaned infants from other troops.

This particular female had adopted an orphaned vervet *monkey. I don't know where she found it; I know now that the vervet was more common to the savanna than the Afromontaine. But find it she did, and take it for her own.*

I rest the dead alien child carefully on the edge of the grave and look directly at the native standing in front of me. It reaches out with one soft-skinned grey hand. I flinch back, but the touch is gentle. The native, the tallest and broadest of the group, is wrapped in veils of vermilion and cinnamon. No other in the group wears those colors. Or blue, I realize, because that deep, true azure is the color of death to them as surely as red (or black, or white) is the color of death on Earth.

The native hands me out of the grave, lifting me past the body of the child. I leave the shovel behind. It's not heavy enough to make a weapon, and grabbing for it would be obvious.

The biggest native towers over me. It hasn't let go of my hand. I crane back to look up at its elephant-grey head; my level gaze would rest at the v-shaped "collar" of its carapace. Soft crunching emanates from inside its body; the sounds of its crop, or gizzard, or whatever these creatures stuff full of rocks and then crank like a churn to get their dinners.

"I'm sorry," I say, exactly as if the thing could understand me. One of its three enormous jewel-blue eyes blinks, and I wonder if there's a connection between the blue of the veil and the blue of their eyes. Some symbolism about seeing into the otherworld, perhaps? I don't even know if they believe in an otherworld. I wish I had an anthropologist. Hell, I wish I *were* an anthropologist. But I'm not, and the native is squeezing, tugging my hand—gently, still, but for how long?—so I keep talking. "I didn't mean any disrespect. But I need a cadaver. To see how your bodies work. If we're going to survive here."

Another eye blinks and reopens, unhurried. They operate on a cycle: two open, one being cleansed. Or resting. Or something. We've never seen a native sleeping. I wonder if they have tripartite brains—*tritospheres? What would you call that?*—the same way they seem to have three of everything else. Maybe they sleep like dolphins did on Earth, part of the brain active while the rest dozes—

—I just don't know. There's so much I don't know, that I'm going to die not knowing.

Still holding my right wrist, the native lifts another arm. Wetness spills from the nipple in its underarm, washing dust from the carapace. The shell isn't grey after all; the cloudy fluid looks like whey, but cleans a swath of tortoiseshell amber and black before it soaks into the native's veils.

The native pulls me close. Thin air burns my throat as I struggle, air reeking acrid with the native's stench. I crave oxygen. There's no time to grab my mask.

A clicking grunt, a noise like boulders knocked together. The first non-gastric noise I've heard one make. The others close in around me. I wonder what Veronica did, if this is what she saw before they killed her; the wall of bodies, granite stones wrapped in rainbow gauze. The acrid smell of the native's—milk? The slow meticulous blinking of the third blue eye.

I wonder how much it's going to hurt when they kill me.

It yanks, two hands now. The second one presses my face into the foul-smelling mess dripping down its side. I strain back, but the grip is unbreakable, and the fluid burns my skin when the native shoves me into it.

I whimper like a puppy; the hands are encompassing, one on my wrist, one holding, controlling my head. The milk tastes like ammonia. My eyes tear. The teat is hot and hard against my cheek, like the udders on my mother's goats when they needed milking—

When they needed milking.

Like an orphaned vervet monkey, I understand what the massive creature wants. The fluid filling my mouth is rank and sharp. It burns going down; it might be poison.

Like everything on this planet.

But the natives are smart. Smart enough for hovercraft and holograms. Smart enough for biochemistry. And there is always the possibility, bizarre and remote as it is, that the microscopic flora in mother's milk might work for me as it works for them.

I wonder if they dissected Veronica to learn that.

Whether it works or not, I'll be sick. Really, really sick.

I hope they know what to do with me. I hope they know what they're doing, because sure as Hell, I don't. But I'm learning.

You have to adapt to the place you live in, if you're going to survive outside your environment. Because your environment will not adapt to you. We have to give up one home to live in another, so it's just as well we can't go back. We wouldn't recognize the place.

I always did wonder what became of that vervet monkey, growing up in a place God never intended him for.

I saw my first samango monkey in 1999. By the time I left Earth, they were extinct, another victim of the Shift. I don't remember when the species was lost, but I do remember where I was on January 12th, 2004, when my mother handed me a small article on the Magoebaskloof Hotel in Limpopo District, South Africa.

It had burned to the stones the day before. But everybody inside had gotten out alive.

FOLLOW ME LIGHT

Pinky Gilman limped. He wore braces on both legs, shining metal and black washable foam spoiling the line of his off-the-rack suits, what line there was to spoil. He heaved himself about on a pair of elbow-cuff crutches. I used to be able to hear him clattering along the tiled, echoing halls of the public defender's offices a dozen doors down.

Pinky's given name was Isaac, but even his clients called him Pinky. He was a fabulously ugly man, lumpy and bald and bristled and pink-scrubbed as a slaughtered hog. He had little fishy walleyes behind spectacles thick enough to serve barbecue on. His skin peeled wherever the sun or the dry desert air touched it.

He was by far the best we had.

The first time I met Pinky was in 1994. He was touring the office as part of his job interview, and Christian Vlatick led him up to me while I was wrestling a five-gallon bottle onto the water cooler. I flinched when he extended his right hand to shake mine with a painful twist intended to keep the crutch from slipping off his arm. The rueful way he cocked his head as I returned his clasp told me he was used to that reaction, but I doubted most people flinched for the reason I did—the shimmer of hot blue lights that flickered through his aura, filling it with brilliance although the aura itself was no color I'd ever seen before—a swampy grey-green, tornado colored.

I must have been staring, because the squat little man glanced down at my shoes, and Chris cleared his throat. "Maria," he said, "this is Isaac Gilman."

"Pinky," Pinky said. His voice... oh, la. If he were robbed with regard to his body, that voice was the thing that made up the difference. Oh, my.

"Maria Delprado. Are you the new attorney?"

"I hope so," he said, dry enough delivery that Chris and I both laughed.

His handshake was good: strong, cool, and leathery, at odds with his parboiled countenance. He let go quickly, grasping the handle of his crutch again and shifting his weight to center, blinking behind the glass that distorted his eyes.

"Maria," he said. "My favorite name. Do you know what it means?"

"It means Mary," I answered. "It means sorrow."

"No," he said. "It means *sea.*" He pointed past me with his chin, indicating the still-sloshing bottle atop the water cooler. "They make the women do the heavy lifting here?"

"I like to think I can take care of myself. Where'd you study, Isaac?"

"Pinky," he said, and, "Yale. Four point oh."

I raised both eyebrows at Chris and pushed my glasses up my nose. The Las Vegas public defender's office doesn't get a lot of interest from Yale Law School grads, *summa cum laude.* "And you haven't hired him yet?"

"I wanted your opinion," Chris said without a hint of apology. He glanced at Pinky and offered up a self-deprecating smile. "Maria can spot guilty people. Every time. It's a gift. One of these days we're going to get her made a judge."

"Really?" Pinky's lipless mouth warped itself into a grin, showing the gaps in his short, patchy beard. "Am I guilty, then?"

The lights that followed him glittered, electric blue fireflies in the twilight he wore like a coat. He shifted his weight on his crutches, obviously uncomfortable at standing.

"And what am I guilty of?"

Not teasing, either, or flirtatious. Calm, and curious, as if he really thought maybe I could tell. I squinted at the lights that danced around him—will-o'-the-wisps, spirit lights. The aura itself was dark, but it wasn't the darkness of past violence or dishonesty. It was organic, intrinsic, and I wondered if it had to do with whatever had crippled him. And the firefly lights—

Well, they were something else again. Just looking at them made my fingertips tingle.

"If there are any sins on your conscience," I said carefully, "I think you've made amends."

He blinked again, and I wondered why I wanted to think *blinked fishily* when fishes do not blink. And then he smiled at me, teeth like yellowed pegs in pale, blood-flushed gums. "How on earth do you manage *that*?"

"I measure the distance between their eyes."

A three-second pause, and then he started to laugh, while Christian, who had heard the joke before, stood aside and rolled his eyes. Pinky shrugged, rise and fall of bulldog shoulders, and I smiled hard, because I knew we were going to be friends.

In November of 1996, I lost my beloved seventeen-year-old cat to renal failure, and Pinky showed up at my door uninvited with a bottle of Maker's Mark and a box of Oreos. We were both half-trashed by the time I spread my cards out on the table between us, a modified Celtic cross. They shimmered when I looked at them; that was the alcohol. The shimmer around Pinky when he stretched his hand out—was not.

"Fear death by water," I said, and touched the Hanged Man's foot, hoping he would know he was supposed to laugh.

His eyes sparkled like scales in the candlelight when he refilled my glass. "It's supposed to be if you *don't* find the Hanged Man. In any case, I don't see a drowned sailor."

"No," I answered. I picked up my glass and bent to look closer. "But there is the three of staves as the significator. Eliot called him the Fisher King." I looked plainly at where his crutches leaned against the arm of his chair. "Not a bad choice, don't you think?"

His face greyed a little, or perhaps that was the alcohol. Foxlights darted around him like startled minnows. "What does he stand for?"

"Virtue tested by the sea." And then I wondered why I'd put it that way. "The sea symbolizes change, conflict, the deep unconscious, the monsters of the Id—"

"I know what the sea means," he said bitterly. His hand darted out and overturned the card, showing the tan back with its key pattern in ivory. He jerked his chin at the spread. "Do you believe in those?"

It had been foolish to pull them out. Foolish to show him, but there was a certain amount of grief and alcohol involved. "It's a game," I said, and swept them all into a pile. "Just a child's game." And then I hesitated, and looked down, and turned the three of staves back over, so it faced the same way as the rest. "It's not the future I see."

In 1997 I took him to bed. I don't know if it was the bottle and a half of shiraz we celebrated one of our rare victories with, or the deep bittersweet richness of his voice finally eroding my limited virtue, but we were good in the dark. His arms and shoulders, it turned out, were beautiful, after all: powerful and lovely, all out of proportion with the rest of him.

I rolled over, after, and dropped the tissue-wrapped rubber on the nightstand, and heard him sigh. "Thank you," he said, and the awe in that perfect voice was sweeter than the sex had been.

"My pleasure," I said, and meant it, and curled up against him again, watching the firefly lights flicker around his blunt, broad hands as he spoke softly and gestured in the dark, trying to encompass some inexpressible emotion.

Neither one of us was sleepy. He asked me what I saw in Las Vegas. I told him I was from Tucson, and I missed the desert when I was gone. He told me he was from Stonington. When the sun came up, I put my hand into his aura, chasing the flickering lights like a child trying to catch snowflakes on her tongue.

I asked him about the terrible scars low on the backs of his thighs that left his hamstrings weirdly lumped and writhed, unconnected to bone under the skin. I'd thought him crippled from birth. I'd been wrong about so many, many things.

"Gaffing hook," he said. "When I was seventeen. My family were fishermen. Always have been."

"How come you never go home to Connecticut, Isaac?"

For once, he didn't correct me. "Connecticut isn't home."

"You don't have any family?"

Silence, but I saw the dull green denial stain his aura. I breathed in through my nose and tried again.

"Don't you ever miss the ocean?"

He laughed, warm huff of breath against my ear, stirring my hair. "The desert will kill me just as fast as the ocean would, if I ever want it. What's to miss?"

"Why'd you come here?"

"Just felt drawn. It seemed like a safe place to be. Unchanging. I needed to get away from the coast, and Nevada sounded... very dry. I have a skin condition. It's worse in wet climates. It's worse near the sea."

"But you came back to the ocean after all. Prehistoric seas. Nevada was all underwater once. There were ichthyosaurs—"

"Underwater. Huh." He stretched against my back, cool and soft. "I guess it's in the blood."

That night I dreamed they chained my wrists with jeweled chains before they crippled me and left me alone in the salt marsh to die. The sun rose as they walked away singing, hunched inhuman shadows glimpsed through a splintered mist that glowed pale as the opals in my manacles.

The mist burned off to show grey earth and greeny brown water, agates and discolored aquamarine. The edges of coarse grey cloth adhered in drying blood on the backs of my thighs, rumpled where they had pulled it up to hamstring me. The chains were cold against my cheeks when I raised my head away from the mud enough to pillow my face on the backs of my hands.

The marsh stank of rot and crushed vegetation, a green miasma so overwhelming the sticky copper of blood could not pierce it. The pain wasn't as much as it should have been; I was slipping into shock as softly as if I slipped under the unrippled water. I hadn't lost enough blood to kill me, but I rather thought I'd prefer a quick, cold sleep and never awakening to starving to death or lying in a pool of my own blood until the scent attracted the thing I had been left in propitiation of.

Somewhere, a frog croaked. It looked like a hot day coming.

I supposed I was going to find out.

His skin scaled in the heat. It was a dry heat, blistering, peeling, chapping lips and bloodying noses. He used to hang me with jewels, opals, tourmalines the color of moss and roses. "Family money," he told me. "Family jewels." He wasn't lying.

I would have seen a lie.

The Mojave hated him. He was chapped and chafed, cracked and dry. He never sweated enough, kept the air conditioner twisted as high as it would go. Skin burns in the heat, in the sun. Peels like a snake's. Aquamarine discolors like smoker's teeth. Pearls go brittle. Opals crack and lose their fire.

He used to go down to the Colorado River at night, across the dam to Willow Beach, on the Arizona side, and swim in the river in the dark. I told him it was crazy. I told him it was dangerous. How could he take care of himself in the Colorado when he couldn't walk without braces and crutches?

He kissed me on the nose and told me it helped his pain. I told him if he drowned, I would never forgive him. He said in the history of the entire world twice over, a Gilman had never once drowned. I called him a cocky, insincere bastard. He stopped telling me where he was going when he went out at night.

When he came back and slept beside me, sometimes I lay against the pillow and watched the follow-me lights flicker around him. Sometimes I slept.

Sometimes I dreamed, also.

I awakened after sunset, when the cool stars prickled out in the darkness. The front of my robe had dried, one long, yellow-green stain, and now the fabric under my back and ass was saturated, sticking to my skin. The mud seemed to have worked it loose from the gashes on my legs.

I wasn't dead yet, more's the pity, and now it *hurt*.

I wondered if I could resist the swamp water when thirst set in. Dehydration would kill me faster than hunger. On the other hand, the water might make me sick enough that I'd slip into the relief of fever and pass away, oblivious in delirium. If dysentery was a better way to die than gangrene. Or dehydration.

Or being eaten. If the father of frogs came to collect me as was intended, I wouldn't suffer long.

I whistled across my teeth. A fine dramatic gesture, except it split my cracked lips and I tasted blood. My options seemed simple: lie still and die, or thrash and die. It would be sensible to give myself up with dignity.

I pushed myself onto my elbows and began to crawl toward nothing in particular.

Moonlight laid a patina of silver over the cloudy yellow-green puddles I wormed through and glanced off the rising mist in electric gleams of blue. The exertion warmed me, at least, and loosened my muscles. I stopped shivering after the first half hour. My thighs knotted tight as welded steel around the insult to my tendons. It would have been more convenient if they'd just chopped

my damned legs off. At least I wouldn't have had to deal with the frozen limbs
dragging behind me as I crawled.

If I had any sense—

If I had any sense at all, I wouldn't be crippled and dying in a swamp. If I had
any sense *left*, I would curl up and die.

It sounded pretty good, all right.

I was just debating the most comfortable place when curious blue lights started
to flicker at the corners of my vision.

I'm not sure why it was that I decided to follow them.

Pinky gave me a pearl on a silver chain, a baroque multicolored thing swirled
glossy and irregular as toffee. He said it had been his mother's. It dangled between
my breasts, warm as the stroke of a thumb when I wore it.

Pinky said he'd had a vasectomy, still wore a rubber every time we made love.
Talked me into going on the Pill.

"Belt and suspenders," I teased. The garlic on my scampi was enough to make
my eyes water, but Pinky never seemed to mind what I ate, no matter how potent it was.

It was one a.m. on a Friday, and we'd crawled out of bed for dinner, finally.
We ate seafood at Capozzoli's, because although it was dim in the cluttered red
room the food was good and it was open all night. Pinky looked at me out of
squinting, amber eyes, so sad, and tore the tentacles off a bit of calamari with
his teeth. "Would you want to bring a kid into this world?"

"No," I answered, and told that first lie. "I guess not."

I didn't meet Pinky's brother Esau until after I'd married someone else, left my
job to try to have a baby, gotten divorced when it turned out we couldn't, had to
come back to pay the bills. Pinky was still there, still part of the program. Still
plugging away on the off chance that eventually he'd meet an innocent man, still
pretending we were and always had been simply the best of friends. We never
had the conversation, but I imagined it a thousand times.

I left you.

You wanted a baby.

It didn't work out.

And now you want to come back? I'm not like you, Maria.

Don't you ever miss the ocean?

No. I never do.

But he had too much pride, and I had too much shame. And once I was Judge
Delprado, I only saw him in court anymore.

Esau called me, left a message on my cell: his name, who he was, where he'd
be. I didn't know how he got the number, I met him out of curiosity as much

as concern, at the old church downtown, the one from the thirties built of irreplaceable history. They made it of stone, to last, and broke up petroglyphs and stalactites to make the rough rock walls beautiful for God.

I hated Esau the first time I laid eyes on him. Esau. There was no mistaking him: same bristles and thinning hair, same spectacularly ugly countenance, fishy and prognathic. Same twilight-green aura too, but Esau's was stained near his hands and mouth, the color of clotted blood, and no lights flickered near.

Esau stood by one of the petroglyphs, leaned close to discolored red stone marked with a stick figure, meaning man, and the wavy parallel lines that signified the river. Old as time, the Colorado, wearing the badlands down, warden and warded of the desert West.

Esau turned and saw me, but I don't think he saw *me*. I think he saw the pearl I wore around my neck.

I gave all the jewels back to Pinky when I left him. Except the pearl. He wouldn't take that back, and to be honest, I was glad. I'm not sure why I wore it to meet Esau, except I hated to take it off.

Esau straightened up, all five foot four of him behind the glower he gave me, and reached out peremptorily to touch the necklace, an odd gesture with the fingers pressed together. Without thinking, I slapped his hand away, and he hissed at me, a rubbery tongue flicking over fleshless lips.

Then he drew back, two steps, and looked me in the eye. His voice had nothing in common with his face: baritone and beautiful, melodious and carrying. I leaned forward, abruptly entranced. "Shipwrack," he murmured. "Shipwrecks. Dead man's jewels. It's all there for the taking if you just know where to look. Our family's always known."

My hand came up to slap him again, halted as if of its own volition. As if it couldn't push through the sound of his voice. "Were you a treasure hunter once?"

"I never stopped," he said, and tucked my hair behind my ear with the brush of his thumb. I shivered. My hand went down, clenched hard at my side. "When Isaac comes back to New England with me, you're coming too. We can give you children, Maria. Litters of them. Broods. Everything you've ever wanted."

"I'm not going anywhere. Not for... Isaac. Not for anyone."

"What makes you think you have any choice? You're part of his price. And we know what you want. We've researched you. It's not too late."

I shuddered, hard, sick, cold. "There's always a choice." The words hurt my lips. I swallowed. Fingernails cut my palms. His hand on my cheek was cool. "What's the rest of his price? If I go willing?"

"Healing. Transformation. Strength. Return to the sea. All the things he should have died for refusing."

"He doesn't miss the sea."

Esau smiled, showing teeth like yellow pegs. "You would almost think, wouldn't you?" There was a long pause, nearly respectful. Then he cleared his throat and said, "Come along."

Unable to stop myself, I followed that beautiful voice.

Most of a moon already hung in the deepening sky, despite the indirect sun still lighting the trail down to Willow Beach. The rocks radiated heat through my sneakers like bricks warmed in an oven. "Pinky said he didn't have any family."

Esau snorted. "He gave it the old college try."

"You were the one who crippled him, weren't you? And left him in the marsh to die."

"How did you know that?"

"He didn't tell me. I dreamed it."

"No," he answered, extending one hand to help me down a tricky slope. "That was Jacob. He doesn't travel."

"Another brother."

"The eldest brother." He yanked my arm and gave me a withering glance when I stumbled. He walked faster, crimson flashes of obfuscation coloring the swamp water light that surrounded him. I trotted to keep up, cursing my treacherous feet. At least my tongue was still my own, and I used it.

"Jacob, Esau, and Isaac Gilman? How… original."

"They're proud old New England names. Marshes and Gilmans were among the original settlers." Defensive. "Be silent. You don't need a tongue to make babies, and in a few more words I'll be happy to relieve you of it, mammal bitch."

I opened my mouth; my voice stopped at the back of my throat. I stumbled, and he hauled me to my feet, his rough, cold palm scraped the skin of my wrist over the bones.

We came around a corner of the wash that the trail ran through. Esau stopped short, planting his feet hard. I caught my breath at the power of the silent, brown river running at the bottom of the gorge, at the sparkles that hung over it, silver and copper and alive, swarming like fireflies.

And standing on the bank before the current was Pinky—Isaac—braced on his canes, startlingly insouciant for a cripple who'd fought his way down a rocky trail. He craned his head back to get a better look at us and frowned. "Esau. I wish I could say it was a pleasure to see you. I'd hoped you'd joined Jacob at the bottom of the ocean by now."

"Soon," Esau said easily, manhandling me down the last of the slope. He held up the hand that wasn't knotted around my wrist. I blinked twice before I realized the veined, translucent yellow webs between his fingers were a part of him. He grabbed my arm again, handling me like a bag of groceries.

Pinky hitched himself forward to meet us, and for a moment I thought he was going to hit Esau across the face with his crutch. I imagined the sound the aluminum would make when it shattered Esau's cheekbone. *Litters of them. Broods.* Easy to give in and let it happen, yes. But litters of *what?*

"You didn't have to bring Maria into it."

"We can give her what she wants, can't we? With your help or without it. How'd you get the money for school?"

Pinky smiled past me, a grin like a wolf. "There was platinum in those chains. Opals. Pearls big as a dead man's eyeball. Plenty. There's still plenty left."

"So there was. How did you survive?"

"I was guided," he said, and the blue lights flickered around him. Blue lights that were kin to the silver lights swarming over the river. I could imagine them buzzing. Angry, invaded. I turned my head to see Esau's expression, but he only had eyes for Pinky.

Esau couldn't see the lights. He looked at Pinky, and Pinky met the stare with a lifted chin. "Come home, Isaac."

"And let Jacob try to kill me again?"

"He only hurt you because you tried to leave us."

"He left me for the father of frogs in the salt marsh, Esau. And you were there with him when he did—"

"We couldn't just let you walk away." Esau let go of my arm with a command to be still, and stepped toward Pinky with his hands spread wide. There was still light down here, where the canyon was wider and the shadow of the walls didn't yet block the sun. It shone on Esau's balding scalp, on the yolky, veined webs between his fingers, on the aluminum of Pinky's crutches.

"I didn't walk," Pinky said. He turned away, hitching himself around, the beige rubber feet of the crutches braced wide on the rocky soil. He swung himself forward, headed for the river, for the swarming lights. "I crawled."

Esau fell into step beside him. "I don't understand how you haven't... changed."

"It's the desert." Pinky paused on a little ledge over the water. Tamed by the dam, the river ran smooth here and still. I could feel its power anyway, old magic that made this land live. "The desert doesn't like change. It keeps me in between."

"That hurts you." Almost in sympathy, as Esau reached out and laid a webbed hand on Pinky's shoulder. Pinky flinched but didn't pull away. I opened my mouth to shout at him, feeling as if my tongue were my own again, and stopped. *Litters.*

Whatever they were, they'd be Pinky's children.

"It does." Pinky fidgeted with the crutches, leaning forward over the river, working his forearms free of the cuffs. His shoulders rippled under the white cloth of his shirt. I wanted to run my palms over them.

"Your legs will heal if you accept the change," Esau offered, softly, his voice carried away over the water. "You'll be strong. You'll regenerate. You'll have the ocean, and you won't hurt anymore, and there's your woman—we'll take her too."

"*Esau.*"

I heard the warning in the tone. The anger. Esau did not. He glanced at me. "Speak, woman. Tell Isaac what you want."

I felt my tongue come unstuck in my mouth, although I still couldn't move my hands. I bit my tongue to keep it still.

Esau sighed, and looked away. "Blood is thicker than water, Isaac. Don't you want a family of your own?"

Yes, I thought. Pinky didn't speak, but I saw the set of his shoulders, and the answer they carried was *no.* Esau must have seen it too, because he raised one hand, the webs translucent and spoiled-looking, and sunlight glittered on the barbed, ivory claws that curved from his fingertips, unsheathed like a cat's.

With your help or without it.

But litters of *what?*

I shouted so hard it bent me over. "*Pinky, duck!*"

He didn't. Instead, he *threw* his crutches backward, turned with the momentum of the motion, and grabbed Esau around the waist. Esau squeaked—*shrieked*—and threw his hands up, clawing at Pinky's shoulders and face as the silver and blue and coppery lights flickered and swarmed and swirled around them, but he couldn't match Pinky's massive strength. The lights covered them both, and Esau screamed again, and I strained, lunged, leaned at the invisible chains that held me as still as a posed mannequin.

Pinky just held on and leaned back.

They barely splashed when the Colorado closed over them.

Five minutes after they went under, I managed to wiggle my fingers. Up and down the bank, there was no trace of either of them. I couldn't stand to touch Pinky's crutches.

I left them where they'd fallen.

Esau had left the keys in the car, but when I got there I was shaking too hard to drive. I locked the door and got back out, tightened the laces on my sneakers, and toiled up the ridge until I got to the top. I almost turned my ankle twice when rocks rolled under my foot, but it didn't take long. Red rock and dusty canyons stretched west, a long, gullied slope behind me, the river down there somewhere, close enough to smell but out of sight. I settled myself on a rock, elbows on knees, and looked out over the scarred, raw desert at the horizon and the setting sun.

There's a green flash that's supposed to happen just when the sun slips under the edge of the world. I'd never seen it. I wasn't even sure it existed. But if I watched long enough, I figured I might find out.

There was still a handspan between the sun and the ground, up here. I sat and watched, the hot wind lifting my hair, until the tawny disk of the sun was halfway gone and I heard the rhythmic crunch of someone coming up the path.

I didn't turn. There was no point. He leaned over my shoulder, braced his crutches on either side of me, a presence solid and cool as a moss-covered rock. I tilted my head back against Pinky's chest, his wet shirt dripping on my forehead, eyes, and mouth. Electric blue lights flickered around him, and I couldn't quite make out his features, shadowed as they were against a twilight sky. He released one crutch and laid his hand on my shoulder. His breath brushed my ear like the susurrus of the sea. "Esau said blood is thicker than water," I said, when I didn't mean to say anything.

"Fish blood isn't," Pinky answered, and his hand tightened. I looked away from the reaching shadows of the canyons below and saw his fingers against my skin, pale silhouettes on olive, unwebbed. He slid one under the black strap of my tank top. I didn't protest, despite the dark red, flaking threads that knotted the green smoke around his hands.

"Where is he?"

"Esau? He drowned."

"But—" I craned my neck. "You said Gilmans never drown."

He shrugged against my back. "I guess the river just took a dislike to him. Happens that way sometimes."

A lingering silence, while I framed my next question. "How did you find me?"

"I'll always find you, if you want," he said, his patched beard rough against my neck. "What are you watching?"

"I'm watching the sun go down."

"Come in under this red rock," he misquoted, as the shadow of the ridge opposite slipped across the valley toward us.

"The handful of dust thing seems appropriate—"

Soft laugh, and he kissed my cheek, hesitantly, as if he wasn't sure I would permit it. "I would have thought it'd be 'Fear death by water.'"

The sun went down. I missed the flash again. I turned to him in a twilight indistinguishable from the gloom that hung around his shoulders and brushed the flickering lights away from his face with the back of my hand. "Not that," I answered. "I have no fear of that, my love."

THE CHAINS THAT YOU REFUSE

It will have been raining in Harvard Square for only half an hour when you give up hope. Only half an hour, but raining hard enough to send the tourists fleeing into cafés and coffeehouses, the rest of the street corner entertainers home in disgust. You will have already known that you would be the last holdout, shivering under an awning with the three white doves rustling in their box in the canvas bag by your feet and the revelatory neon of *John Harvard's/Grendel's/Au Bon Pain* reflecting on the rain-soaked brick, twisting answers to questions you would have preferred not to ask. You will not have made any money.

You will not be eating tonight, but you will have known that for some time.

You'll pick up the tote and walk to the Red Line station opposite the Cambridge Savings Bank, having forgotten your umbrella, shoes squishing and the canvas straps cutting into your cold red fingers. You'll mean to take the T north to Alewife, to the parking garage where you left your rusted yellow Volvo with barely enough gas in it to get you home. But as you enter the dry underground the doves will coo and flutter. The antique silver dollars in your pockets will jingle against the subway tokens. And you will journey south—rumble and clatter and rock of the underground train across the muddy Charles—and switch to the Orange Line at Downtown Crossing, and emerge from the T in Chinatown.

It will have been raining here also, and the streets will be smeared with neon. You will have emerged not far from the Orpheum Theatre. You will take it as a portent and force yourself not to look back as you climb from the light of the T station into the rainbow-daubed darkness of the streets. Your black, oversized denim jacket with the concealed pockets sewn into the sleeves and the clips and elastic beneath the arms will grow soggy, heavy, cold. Sleepily, the doves will be complaining. The air will fill with aromas of soy and ginger. The neon will guide you. Red light, green light, triple-XXX and live nude girls. Peking duck and garlic noodle. Parsley, sage, and time.

You will know hope. You will have blinked and missed it in the weather, whistling, headed in the other direction, hat pulled low against the rain over its bright feathers. You will know that you never had a chance; the neon teaches all. You will have drawn a silk scarf from a secret pocket and knotted it about your hand to take the weight of the tote bag, the three white doves, and their metal box: their cage.

The charlatans of old days read entrails for their instruction; the charlatans of today read the future in the flutter of neon, in the passing of cars. Charlatans, because it's the only magic there is. Magic is a trap. Magic is a lie.

You will find a paperclip in the gutter, a bit of tinfoil, a condom wrapper, page seventeen of the *Boston Globe*. You'll bend and fold them as you walk, into a hat or a sailboat, the canvas straps cutting your wrist bone now. You'll place your creation in the gutter and watch the cataract carry it into a storm sewer, inevitably as rain. You'll have seen every ripple of its falling in the ominous neon. You will not have been surprised.

Ceroscopy, anthropomancy, planchette, scapulomancy, omens: nothing, suggestions, glimpses, glimmerings. Nothing to the truth of neon and the sorcery of electric lights.

Magicians are charlatans, for all their power. They can no longer *make* the future. There is no magic in knowing what happens next. All you have to do is read the signs.

You will walk—you will have been walking—tracing a pattern you will have always known. You are a true charlatan, a magician with your rings and balls and cards and the three white doves that you know will always return, whenever you hold out your long and perfect hand. Your future has been immutable. You have enjoyed the serenity of perfect certainty. You will have feared and you will have envied and you will have pitied those who are not like you, for their illusion of free will. You will not have been able to imagine such a thing:

You have always been able to read the signs.

You have known all your life that this is the day your life ends, because here is Boston Common, where the neon leads you out of Chinatown. And there, on the Common spread out like a banquet of darkness in the rain, will have been the mugger who will be disappointed in how little you have earned, turning scarves to doves on a coldly rainy night. And there, on the Common, will have been the diluted blood, and the silk scarves, and the white feathers sodden in the rain.

You will limp in squishy shoes onto the grassy border of the Common, resigned and a little relieved, the doves cooing in their box despite the darkness there.

And then a relay will trip. A machine will fail. A ripple of blackness like spilled ink will flutter the height of the East Coast, starting in Philadelphia, Baltimore, Newark, New York City, Hartford, sweet old winding Providence, and finally, finally, at long last—

Boston.

Behind you, before you, the old grey city will settle into darkness with a sigh like an exhausted dog. And the neon, the signs, the writing on the walls will all wink out.

As you step forward onto the Common, there will come a moment when you will be offered a choice. You will have drawn a silk scarf from a secret pocket and knotted it about your hand. But the canvas strap of the tote will have slipped up your wrist, the rattled doves complaining. You will unwind the scarf, stretch it between your hands, and you will draw a deep and trembling breath. Fear will swallow you. Fear of the known and the unknown, fear of the knife in the darkness and fear of the darkness of never knowing whence the knife will come.

You will have known—a final torment, a final benediction before the curse of prophecy deserts you for an instant of free will—you will have known that you have only seconds to decide.

You will have bound the scarf about your eyes.

You will have knelt in the grass at the edge of the Common, and blindly you will have fumbled the tote bag open, blindly you will have unlatched the cage, blindly you will have lifted the three white doves and set them softly on the sweet, slick, soaking grass. You will unknot your blindfold as the lights swell behind you, and you will throw the cage away. Your hair will plaster your face, sting your eyes, fill your mouth.

The doves will coo and ruffle and huddle: wet, sleepy, confused. They will sit there dumbly, blinking in the rain and the darkness, unable to see, unable to fly at night. They will cling to each other and mourn the dry safety of their cage.

You will recognize the archetypal battered fedora as it tumbles past you, one bright, shivering feather trapped in the band. You will bend and catch it; it will fall into your hand as if destined. You will clap hope's chapeau over draggled curls at a rakish angle, and you will return to the overarching night.

It will be all right. The sun will rise in the morning. The doves will most likely fly away. Sooner or later, the rain will probably end.

You cannot know what will happen next.

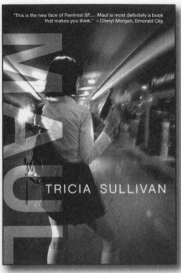
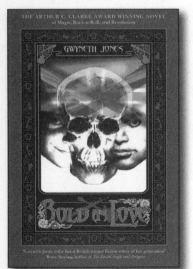

蛇警探

Elizabeth Bear shares a birthday with Frodo and Bilbo Baggins. This, coupled with a tendency to read the dictionary as a child, doomed her early to penury, intransigence, friendlessness, and the writing of speculative fiction. She was born in Hartford, Connecticut, and grew up in central Connecticut with the exception of two years (which she was too young to remember very well) spent in Vermont's Northeast Kingdom, in the last house with electricity before the Canadian border. She recently lived in the Mojave Desert near Las Vegas, but has managed to escape back to Connecticut.

Elizabeth Bear is her real name, but not all of it. Her dogs outweigh her, and she is much beset by her cats.